D1063225

Tales Of Nevaeh
Volume I

Born To Magic

DAVID WIND

This is a work of fiction. The names, characters, places and events are fictitious. Any similarity to real persons, living or dead, places or incidents are coincidental and not intended by the author.

SBN-10: 0990003523
ISBN-13: 978-0-9900035-2-6

Copyright © 2015 by David Wind. All rights reserved, including the right to reproduce, distribute, or transmit in any form or by any means. For information regarding subsidiary rights, please contact David Wind at: http://www.davidwind.com

Edited by Terese Ramin
Cover design by Adrijus G. of Rockingbookcovers.com
First Edition February 2015

◇◇◇

Other novels written by David Wind are listed at the end of this book.

◇◇◇

This book is dedicated to

Sawyer Micah

A special person who holds the future in his hands
&
In memory of two very special women of power who had faith in me:
Katherine Duffy (1953-2009)
Andre Norton (1912-2005)

'It is not in the stars to hold our destiny but in ourselves'
—William Shakespeare

'Change is the law of life. And those who look only to the past or present are certain to miss the future'
—John F. Kennedy

ACKNOWLEDGMENTS

I would like to thank everyone who has helped me on this journey into the future.

To Bonnie Wind for all her support and love, to my fabulous Beta readers who gave me the feedback necessary to make this story special — Terry Vanlandingham, Sandra Kitt, C.B. Pratt, Vivienne Mathews, Christian Bunyan, Makiela Vasquez, Amanda Rabinowitz Tibbets, Brenda Hiatt, Kyra Betheil, Joe Manber, and a special Beta thank you to Effrosyni Moschoudi for her invaluable insights.

To Lou Aronica for his advice, to Terese Ramin, my editor, and to Adrijus G, the force behind the cover art and design.

.

CHAPTER 1
Nevaeh: the Fifth Millennium
5267

DESPITE THE HEAT of the summer sun, the deep forest was cool. From a distance, the crackle of a branch stepped upon by a large animal drifted to her. The breeze rustling through the tree leaves cooled the sweat beading young Areenna's brows. She was on the last day of the traditional cleansing period before her fourteenth birthday. She had spent the time wandering the forests, adjusting to the changes within her body and her mind—changes that had begun weeks before with her first flow of blood, and had increased a hundredfold in the past days.

Her mother had explained—not for the first time—how the final five days leading to her return home would be among the most important days of her life. During these days, she would find her aoutem, her object of guidance. For some it was a bird, for others an animal. Her mother's aoutem was a gorlon, a four-legged huntress of incredible strength. "Remember," Her mother had said in parting, "be vigilant, always, for you do not choose an aoutem, it chooses you."

There would also be changes in her body, her mother had warned. In their maternal line, it would most likely be a darkening of her skin from its almond shade to a deeper pale brown hue. Conversely, her

3

mother had added, there could also be a lightening of her dark blonde hair.

In the branches high above her, she sensed something watching. Looking up, she spotted an unusually large treygone guarding its nest. The silver feathered male bird, lethal to any animal unfortunate enough to weigh less than its own twenty pounds, stood guard over two hatchlings.

Areenna sensed the treygone knew she posed no threat, yet it watched her closely.

Areenna smiled at it and started forward. The lands she was upon belonged to her family. Few people came to this area, which bordered the outlands of the Blue Desert, a place where hideaways and outcasts lived. The people who inhabited the desert were not those one wanted to meet—thieves, murderers, runaways and other criminals were the mainstay of the Blue Desert's population—yet her father had made a truce with them years before. It was a strange truce, but one which still held.

Before Areenna could take her second step, a shock tore through her head. She stumbled and fell to her knees. She clutched at her head, fighting off the lance of pain that burned into her. A scream built in her throat, but died, unable to pass her lips while she stared helplessly at the giant treygone falling from its high perch to the forest floor.

A bolt had pierced its body and driven into one of the two hatchlings. *How is this possible?* Hunting was not permitted on this portion of the lands. *Not a hunter...a poacher.*

From above and behind came a scream unlike any she had ever heard. She looked up at the sapphire sky from where the sound had come. Between two tall trees, a magnificent cinnamon and black female treygone appeared, its triangular head pointed at a spot twenty paces from where Areenna knelt. It was the mate of the treygone just killed, the mother of the hatchlings, and the hunter of the family, and its rage tore through her mind like a brand.

Turning in the direction the bird arrowed, she spotted the poacher sitting in the joint of two large branches, his crossbow already set with a new bolt. He was looking up at the charging treygone, its wingspan nearly blocking the sun. In that instant, Areenna acted without thought.

Raising her hands toward the hunter, she allowed her pain at the male's death to create a storm within her. An explosion of heat spread through her and her hand glowed white. As she was about free the weapon her mother had trained her to use, a command within her mind stopped her.

The sensation lasted but an instant, yet it was time enough for the hunter to release his bolt, and for the bird to strike the hunter. A second blast of pain tore through Areenna's heart and head when the two met. The hunter shrieked as the bird hit him and buried its talons into the unarmored flesh of his face. Locked together, they fell the thirty feet to the ground.

They lay still at the base of the tree. Areenna saw from the angle of the poacher's neck that it had been broken in the fall. The treygone's breast had been pierced by the bolt. Its gasps for breath were forced.

Areenna fought to rid her mind of the pain she knew was coming from the huge bird. She staggered over to them and scooped the treygone to her. Despite its weight, she held it gently, looking to see if there was a way to remove the bolt and save its life.

While she struggled to find a way to save it, the treygone looked at her. Its eyes, black circles buried within cinnamon feathers, stared up at her. Again, something tugged inside her mind, and she knew it was the treygone.

She was not surprised by this, even though it had never happened to her before. For years, she had listened to the stories of people who had become paired with treygones. Then she remembered her mother's parting words to be watchful when she had started this *becoming* walk.

Sadness for the treygone weighed heavily on her. The bird had prevented her from using her powers to stop the hunter from shooting it, but she knew why. Treygones mated for life. When one mate died, the other found a means to follow its mate. Today was no different.

But the hatchling...what about the baby?

The answer came as a gentle tug in her mind, not the forceful scream of moments before. She shook her head, trying to understand how this was happening when the bird's chest gave a final rise and fall, its large head falling backward.

Areenna walked to a small clearing where she scooped out a grave and placed the mother within. She returned for the male and the hatchling, brought them to the open grave, and laid them next to the female. She filled the grave with loose earth and used a star shaped stone she'd uncovered in her digging to mark the grave. When she finished, she climbed the tree to the nest.

Carefully scooping up the remaining hatchling, she cradled it to her chest and returned to the ground. She held the cinnamon, black and silver hatchling against her for warmth and started homeward, leaving the poacher to his reward…dinner for the scavengers.

Why was this happening on the day before her fourteenth birthday? Areenna wondered while she hummed a soothing melody to the hatchling.

◇◇◇

5271

"There is no choice." Cupping the sides of his head, the High King of Nevaeh held himself as if trying to ease a headache of astonishing proportions.

"There is always a choice." The High Queens's voice was as soothing as was the hand stroking his back. While smaller than most men of Nevaeh, the King was broad across the chest and shoulders, narrow at the hips with powerful legs and arms. Yet none would have pictured him a king for his size combined with the delivery of his words served to make him appear slow-witted. He, however, was far from slow-witted. He considered every word he spoke carefully before allowing it to pass his lips.

His special combination of strength and intelligence had allowed him to defeat the sorceresses controlled and led by the Masters of the Circle of Afzal—the leaders of the shadowy empire across the sea. These witches had held Nevaeh in virtual slavery, using the fighting between the ten dominions to keep their Dark Masters' strength high— for they fed not upon earthly food, but by keeping the rulers of Nevaeh at each other's throats, living and growing in the power created by the dark energies born from the fighting.

By defeating the Afzaleem, he became the first person to unite the dominions of Nevaeh under a single rule while at the same time denying the Circle their Nevaen puppets.

The king lifted his head to look into the gray eyes of his mate.

"There is no choice," he repeated. "We must keep the trust and willingness of all rulers to allow themselves and their families to be led rather than forced."

"There are still those who resist what we do to help them," she said.

"No, it is because those few have no faith in me," he whispered. While his words were simple, they were true.

"Perhaps...Yet I know there will be one who comes to your aid, when the time is right," she whispered. "I have foreseen it in my dreams, My Lord. You have changed much since you became high king and you ask the people to do the same. And remember, what follows this change is what you seek to guide, not the change itself. The rest will take more time than you and I have, which is why you must wait for the right person."

"How long is the wait? We both know the situation grows dire. The lords of the ten will start feuding again as the remnants of the Circle try to rise. The Afzaleem are all but dead. But we know the Circle will find new vassals to fill with darkness...if they have not done so already. Soon there will begin fighting. The people will be easily swayed should the dark power find a way to regain a foothold...and such can only happen when dominion fights dominion. They almost won, and they will try again—they will never stop. How long must the wait be?" he repeated, not seeking an answer but putting forth the question to the very air itself. "Days? Weeks? Years?"

In from the window floated the voice of their sixteen year old son, Mikaal, as he trained for combat in the courtyard below. "This person will come. It will not be...overly long, my husband, my...Lord. It will happen—perhaps not in the way you think it should, but it will come about the way it must."

CHAPTER 2

5273

"AREENNA."

When her father entered the chamber, Areenna smiled while at the same time noticing how tired he appeared. So much had happened in so short a time it had aged him prematurely. Though only in his forty-fifth year, his hair, which had been jet black, was now pure silver and contrasted sharply with his dark skin. His eyes and face had barely changed in the eighteen years since her birth, except perhaps for the increased paths of lines radiating from his eyes, yet the pain trapped behind those forest green eyes was so powerful she could feel it.

"Father?"

"A messenger from Tolemac has arrived." He went to the large window to look out at the lands spread before him. He turned back. "The High King has called for a council."

Areenna was puzzled by her father's concern. "This is not unusual. Why are you troubled?"

His features were thoughtful. "There have been rumors of fighting between the dominions."

"This can't be." Her eyes darted over his face, trying to read what had not been spoken.

"Hence the King's call for council."

"How long will you be gone?" Since her mother's death, two years before, Areenna had acted as queen in her father's absence.

"No, Areenna, it is time. You come as well."

"Father..."

He stopped her with a single look. "You are eighteen. Old enough to counsel me in state matters, as your mother would do had she lived."

She shook her head. "I'm not ready."

"What your mother taught you in the two years since you returned from the school would take anyone else a decade to learn. We leave in the morning. Going to Tolemac will give us an opportunity to put the rumors to rest and to learn for ourselves what is happening."

His eyes softened. He placed his hands on her shoulders. "See to the packing and make certain everything is arranged for our departure tomorrow. Oh, the messenger will be joining us for the evening meal."

The formal eating hall was filled with sound. Four musicians played string instruments at the far end of the dining hall. Today, the oval table was set for three, although it could accommodate many more. Areenna's father, King Nosaj II sat at the head of the table, his chair slightly elevated. Areenna sat on her father's right, signifying she was the right hand of the King—the King's highest advisor.

To the King's left sat Duke Yermon of Llawnroc, messenger of the high king. The duke was the twin brother of Olrac, King of Llawnroc— Yermon was the younger twin, born two minutes behind Olrac. Areenna had met him and his daughter when her father had delivered her to the School of the Lords, upon her eleventh birthday.

The King of Llawnroc was childless and so the King's niece, Nylle, daughter of Duke Yermon, would be the successor to Llawnroc's throne.

"You have grown into an enchanting woman, Princess," the duke said.

"Thank you, Duke Yermon. And your daughter, Nylle, how does she fare?"

Glowing with pride he said, "She is well, Princess Areenna. She is betrothed to the King's second son, Theron of Lokinhold."

"That will be a good match, Duke Yermon. They were good friends at the school. From what I remember, Theron will make a good Father Guardian for Llawnroc and a good mate for Nylle."

"It is our greatest hope," he said. Although he smiled, his eyes reflected something else.

"You are troubled," Areenna's father said. He motioned to Areenna and himself. "Can I...can we be of help?"

"You are as kind and as perceptive as ever, Highness," the duke said, careful to use the proper title. The title of My Lord was used only toward two kings, the High King, and the King of a person's 'dom'. The other kings were either Highness, or Sire. "But fear not, all is well."

"Is there a reason for the high king's call to council? There have been rumors of raids upon the northern kingdoms," King Nosaj asked.

"I have heard the same. I have no answer for the high king's convening of the council."

"Unusual," Nosaj said thoughtfully.

"These are unusual times," the duke admitted.

A few hours later Areenna stood on the parapet of the north tower, three stories above her bedroom. Stars filled the sky and the air was quiet. Her eyes were closed, yet she was able to see everything—the trees below, the animals foraging within them, and those few people who were still awake. She saw two lovers fall into each other's arms beneath a sprawling old gazebow tree outside the castle's south wall and wondered if such would ever happen to her.

She also thought about the duke's daughter and wondered if she, too, would be so lucky as to find a noble son of the ten-dominions to become her husband and, when she became the Queen, Father-Guardian to the future heir of Freemorn. Or even if she'd find any man to be her mate? Sadly, yet without rancor, and barely past her eighteenth birthday, Areenna knew well that the sons of the kings and brother-regents of the other domains wanted women they could mold to reign as Queen over their own lands. None of them would serve beneath a Queen who already ruled her own lands, even though it was only to a small degree. And Freemorn's men of title could not court her because she was their princess, the future mother of their next king, and as such was inviolate by law and untouchable to them.

No, it would be her lot to be a maiden queen without a king. The line of succession would fall to one of her cousins.

Her thoughts and the sights of the night were cut short as a giant treygone landed on the balustrade surrounding the parapet. Its long talons grasped the masonry while the giant bird arched its neck, rotating its triangular head left and right before thrusting its curved beak toward Areenna. The folds of its six foot wingspread appeared more like fabric than feathers; her long body and elongated, tightly feathered tail were what artists of millennia past had envisioned as dragons.

The treygone's job was done for the day. She had flown high and wide in order for Areenna to see the land through her eyes and know all was well.

Reaching out, Areenna stroked the female's head, cooing softly. "Gaalrie," she said to her aoutem, "how will you fare in Tolemac?"

In response, Gaalrie arched further and spread her wings to their full six foot width before she leapt from the edge of the wall and soared upward into the night to hunt and play. The giant bird sent a parting thought—a feeling to Areenna—it was one of calmness and strength.

Morning came swiftly for Areenna, who had woken long before dawn to finalize the preparations for their departure to Tolemac. A half hour after sun-up she was seated with her father and the duke at breakfast. The servants moved quickly about them, following her orders to waste no time.

"Will you be going to Tolemac with us?" Areenna asked the duke.

Duke Yermon glanced at her father and then at her. "If I could... My brother sent me a message asking me to sit his throne while he attends the council." He paused to sip the heated spice water, and then smiled off-handedly. "In another year my daughter and her husband will handle such chores."

Areenna studied him silently. In the space of a breath, a familiar feeling swelled within her. Unable to stop, she reached out to touch the top of the duke's hand with three fingertips. There was a sudden rush of colors across her eyes from palest yellow to the inky darkness of a black mud bog that sucked her mind toward it. She flinched, snatched her hand away, and said, "I…you must allow Nylle to sit the throne in Llawnroc." A dark blood-red flash replaced the inky bog and she returned her fingers to the back of his hand so the pieces of the vision would finish playing out.

When it finally came, her gasp was loud and uncontrolled. It took her another minute before she could speak. Her voice was tight, almost choking. "You have to be at court. Your daughter must stand in your place. If you are not there…I fear…I am afraid of what might happen."

She pulled her fingers from his skin as if they'd been burned. "My apologies, Sir, I—"

"No, Areenna, no apologies," the duke said quickly. "What might happen to whom? What saw you?"

She looked first at her father, who nodded. To the duke she said, "I cannot be sure, but there is something dark, something foreboding at Court. Your brother is in grave danger, which is all I know. I…the seeing, it is not yet strong within me," she explained.

"But stronger than any other woman your age." Her father looked at Areenna with great concern, and then turned to the duke. "I would suggest you listen to my daughter, Sir."

Duke Yermon glanced from the King to Areenna. "I fully intend to, Highness, I felt something at her touch as well. I will return to Llawnroc first and meet you at Tolemac as swiftly as possible."

"Do not fail in this," Areenna said, her voice carried the disturbance of her vision.

Duke Yermon left shortly after breakfast. Llawnroc was a full day's ride Southwest from Freemorn and another day and a half to Tolemac.

Nosaj, Areenna, and ten of the King's most trustworthy guards left the castle two hours after the duke. Normally, the journey to Tolemac would be done in a day and two-thirds, with one night of encampment. This time they left at midmorning. There would be no encampment on this journey, in order for them to arrive the following morning. Sleep would come only to those who had learned to sleep astride their mounts.

Her father was a few paces ahead of her, sitting straight and emanating strength from every pore. His deep brown kraal stood almost seventeen hands, its flanks powerfully muscled, its legs thick and strong. Larger and longer than its un-mutated equine ancestor, the kraal's body was broad, its coat short and dense. The kraal's flaring triangular shaped head was high and proud, and its powerful gait smoothly consumed the distance.

Her gray and black spotted kraal, a hand smaller than her father's, moved swiftly. His wide silvery gray mane spiked upward as he sped gracefully along. Above her and the muscular kraal she had named Hero flew Gaalrie. With Gaalrie's sharp sight, Areenna saw the road ahead with full clarity. Gaalrie would give timely warning of any danger along their route.

She urged Hero to her father's side. They rode silently for several minutes until he asked, "Are you ready to tell me what you saw on Duke Yermon?"

"Yes Father. It took me a while to fully understand."

Her father waited silently. "When it happened, a sheet of red…of blood washed across my sight. I felt danger to the duke's brother. I have been working the vision, as mother taught me, and was finally able to open the blood curtain."

She took a breath. "What I saw was a knife flying toward Llawnroc's king. He had been unprotected. The killer was someone seated at the council. I feel certain of it, but I did not see a face, nor could I sense who it was. I am sorry, Father."

"Never!" her father growled. "Never apologize for something like that. What you saw was a gift given to you. You get only what is given freely by those who watch. You must never apologize for them or for yourself."

While Areenna had at first stiffened at her father's tone, the words themselves served to ease her tense muscles. "Yes, Father, I shall remember."

"My Lord," Enaid called.

Turning to his wife, the High King of Nevaeh raised his eyebrows.

"All but two have arrived. They are quartered and being fed. Freemorn and Lokinhold will be here in the morning."

"Thank you," he said.

She took his hand and gently squeezed it. "You must go and greet them."

"In a moment," he whispered.

"What troubles you?"

"The past," he said, seeing not the woman standing before him, but the world he had come from, and knowing every aspect of his previous life was gone…except for memories.

The Journal of Solomon Roth, 5253 AD

This will be my last entry in this journal. In a few hours I depart this flying coffin and go back to the planet of my birth, a trip started three thousand years ago. We began with 200 people...now there is only me.

It has been 2 years, 5 months and 12 days of consciousness since I boarded the shuttle at Earthport in 2136 A.D. 2 plus years of life rationed out over 3,000 years of stasis. My ship has voyaged through the universe for 3,117 years, following a huge elliptical orbit. I have been awakened 9 different times for my service rotations as had all the surviving crew members. Each time I was revived, there were less and less travelers. I spent as much time as possible, trying to find out what had killed them, but could not find an answer before I returned to the blackness of stasis.

My last awakening started routinely. It ended with the knowledge I would never return to stasis. I was the last—all the others were dead. Some by the malfunction of equipment, but most died mysteriously, at least at the time it was a mystery until I finally solved it, much too late.

A dormant mutated virus had been brought aboard by one of the colonists. When the colonist's stasis pod had malfunctioned, the live virus entered the ship's stasis circulation units. Of the 200 people on the ship, over three quarters died from the virus. The others died due to various equipment failures. I alone proved immune.

Those who started the war had finally succeeded in destroying their enemy...and themselves, by killing every inhabitant of the earth.

For the 5 months after my last awakening, I was insane— a skeletal lunatic, ranting and raving, crying for no reason and every reason. I know now how long my insanity lasted, but during those five months, I knew nothing. I don't even know how I remembered to eat and drink.

Then the day came when the ship's proximity alarms went off.

What I saw in the ship's scopes should have been the last straw of whatever doubtful shreds of sanity I had left; but instead, what lay before me triggered a return to reality.

200,000 miles ahead, was the small blue green dot of Earth. I stared at it for hours, not moving, barely breathing and, as my insanity fled, my training resurfaced. My ship had been in an elliptical orbit through the solar system for three thousand years. It had finally returning home. I took control of the ship, despite thinking there was no point in having remained alive.

The original mission was to save the human race. Sadly, I knew I would not be the new version of Adam, for there was no Eve—the women were long dead—unless you counted the embryos in stasis. But I doubt they will survive when they are removed from stasis.

I put the ship into high orbit 19 hours after the

first warning sounded. Once the orbit was established, and even though I knew my world was dead, I sent out a dozen automated bot probes.

I don't know why I bothered. Perhaps it was because, just before we had left Earth, I learned the scientists had created a strain of bacteria that, somehow, absorbed radiation. In reality, it had sounded like a Hail Mary pass that was nothing more than a basketful of hope.

The all but invisible bots—mini drones—spent 26 hours covering the entire planet, axis by axis. When the bots returned, I spent weeks watching every second of the videos they'd recorded. Against every eventuality the scientists had been able to theorize, I discovered the unbelievable truth — the earth had not been destroyed by the radiation of the nuclear holocaust. In fact, the bacteria the scientists had released at the time my voyage, had not just succeeded, but surpassed all imagination. But the radiation had done its deed, leaving mutations of every sort in its wake.

America was filed with life and such life as I could never have imagined. Yet, the inhabitants were seemingly backwards—appearing more like the people who had lived during Earth's medieval period. They wore armor of leather and metal, fought with sword and knife and bow. They lived in castle-like keeps with towns spread out about each keep. Science appeared to have been forgotten: a happenstance I think is for the best, seeing how science had murdered my earth.

I spent the next weeks reviewing the visual records, and then I cried for the billions who had died 3,000 years ago. Perhaps these people who had survived would do better.

Then I, Captain Solomon Roth, the last survivor of my race, and of all the races of the peoples of the earth, did the only thing possible, maybe even the wisest thing I've ever done. Nothing. Rather, I waited, studied and most importantly, learned.

I took the next 7 months to learn about the world below. I sent probes out daily until every inch of the planet was charted, I learned the language and the customs of the people inhabiting what was left of the North American continent. The language had changed, it was English, but strange. Words were different, yet had a similar sound. Some of the names of things were the same, others were strange, almost like contractions or misspellings or, even weirder, seemed to have evolved from some form of dyslexia.

What I saw in the remnants of Europe, Asia and Eastern Europe terrified me like nothing before. That part of the world held the widespread desolate ruins of nuclear war. What remained was populated by horribly misshapen beings—mindless masses being ruled by hidden beings that did not appear in any of the probe recordings. These beings, this darkly threatening force, I was instinctively certain, were the remnants of the Unified Circle of the Middle East—the very ones who had destroyed my world, who had killed everyone I knew and loved.

South America was barren of life, both human and animal and separated from North America by a swirling ocean of what had once been the lands of Central America and Mexico: the giant rainforests of the equator were gone. Canada and Alaska were ice infested oceans and tar fields.

The land masses of North America's had incredibly changed. The nuclear attacks that had destroyed so much of the world had not destroyed North America. I found proof of attacks, but the reports from the bots showed me only a few small hits and two massive strikes on the remaining lands: the finger-like island of Manhattan was there, but only the rubble of the once mighty center of American and world commerce remained. Central Park was a giant fused crater. The damage from the explosion had radiated outward in a huge circle of destruction and left almost nothing standing.

A strange red haze floated over Manhattan, like a dome of quarantine set upon the island. Boston was gone, and where the west coast and the western state had once been was only ocean. The great lands of North America had lost at least 40% of its mass.

From that time on, I studied North America. Although the land mass itself had changed, everyone spoke the same strange English language. There were dialects, true, but only slight differences between the ten dominions, which I learned from the bots, made up this new world.

I studied what I could of their sciences, which seemed to be more spiritual than physical— metaphysical. My belief of this comes from studying the women whom I discovered were the scientists or...sorcerers. Actually, I think I'm more inclined to view their science as parapsychology because of what

I've seen on the probes' recordings. They call it magic. The women are—I don't know how to describe it— amazing is the first word that comes to mind, but parapsychology doesn't have the right feel. Their science is a form of paranormal abilities, but more than I have ever considered possible.

After learning this, I had no choice but to study the ecology. It shouldn't have, but it took me a while to understand what happened to my world. The animals and the foods were not the same as when I left, but the principles of evolution controlling the world are the same. One of the wonders of the mutations produced by the radiation is a strain of moss that glows in darkness and is used everywhere to illuminate the interiors of living structures.

The animals fascinate me the most—the people have tamed large four legged horse-like beasts called kraals. Kraals are perhaps twenty percent larger than a horse, with thick strong legs and triangular shaped heads, which looked like a cross between a horse's and viper's head, only much larger. Faster than any horse I ever rode or watched, they carry riders with ease. There are gorlons, large mutated dogs, somewhere between a Mastiff and a Great Dane but fiercer. And like dogs, they are everywhere people are. There are also smaller dog-like creatures called coors.

There so many parallels in every form of life; large cat-like animals called rantors hunt the mountains and the forests with king-like majesty of lions while snakes—which are now called snucks—and fish and birds of all varieties flourish. The birds caught my imagination as much as the horse-like kraals. The largest of the birds are called treygones. They are larger than an eagle used to be, but anyone with any sort of imagination could draw a parallel to miniature dragons. Their heads are oval and triangular at the same time; the double folds of their wings, long bodies and elongated tails are similar to what earthly artists had, for thousands of years, envisioned as dragons. The biggest difference between treygones and dragons is treygones have feathers, not scales.

Because the probes were nearly invisible and could receive audio from within a quarter mile of wherever they flew or hovered, I got a full working study of the evolved version of the strange English they spoke. Within weeks I had the computers programmed to give me the full meaning and syntax.

Mankind had mutated and evolved— there were

no longer lines between the distinct races of my time. The people of Nevaeh were an ethnic mixture of multiple races. Yet, they were not what had once been considered bi-racial, the people of this new earth were a homogeneous race—their features a mixture of every race I had ever known. The color of their skin had nothing to do with the color or shape of their eyes, mouths, or the color or elasticity of their hair. The men, as a race, were larger and stronger than me, and while the women were somewhat larger than from my time, their strength lay in their paranormal abilities.

After spending a month studying the reports from every probe, I set up a strict training routine. I exercised after breakfast, from mid-morning until lunch break, I learned not just the language, but the inflections and accents. After lunch it was sword practice (I made a sword in the machine shop to work with) and after practice, I studied the people, their society and its political hierarchy.

I learned that what appeared medieval was far from it. A king ruled his dominion with the aid of his queen in a partnership of equals. Both had their strengths and each needed the other's support to rule properly. The people in a domain had the right to stay within that domain or leave for a new domain should they feel the need to change fealty. Loyalty was given, not taken by strength. The rulers knew this and by and large treated their people with respect.

Yet, there was a strange discord among the 10 dominions. They fought in skirmishes and larger battles. But no matter how close my probes came, these drones could not find the most important information I needed, why these dominions fought each other so fiercely but experienced no change with their individual borders at the end of a battle. Something about this strange situation told me I had to know why this happens if I am to survive on this new earth.

When I finally reached the point of being ready to return home, I put together everything I thought necessary to begin my new life. I knew this meant I could take nothing of what caused my earth to fail— especially weapons! I created two swords made of Trilimion, a metal found on the surface of Saturn's moon, Titan. It was the hardest and strongest metal mankind had ever discovered, with ten times the strength of titanium, and was used primarily for satellites and the hull of the star cruiser that had brought me here.

I made two knives of the same metal and used the ship's computers to replicate the armor worn by the planet's inhabitants—primarily armor for the upper torso, biceps and thighs. This too was made of Trilimion. I built a second set of armor as back-up should I need it.

I spent a week going through the ship to decide what to bring with me. In the end, I knew I could bring only a little of what the world had once been.

Technology would not only be unnecessary, it would be foolish as the inhabitants had not found any need for technology. It wasn't an easy decision, but in the end, I came to the only conclusion I could—the racial memory of what happened 3 millenniums before had prevented the growth of technology as a means of preservation of the species.

I questioned myself if I should I bring books from the long dead version of what my world had once been. What reason would anyone have to learn about a world which destroyed itself because its people needed to control every aspect of their planet from its weather to its energy filled core to its religious beliefs, while ignoring anything that might stop them from living their lives selfishly, denying themselves nothing and doing their best to use up every last natural resource of their world?

There wasn't much reason. Finally, I decided to bring only those things I needed to stay alive until I could adapt and blend. With my mind made up, I loaded water and the weapons I'd made along with thirty pounds of raw Trilimion. There were other things as well, but those would never be seen by anyone now living on Nevaeh.

Two months ago I began a series of inoculations to assure my biological survival and acclimation. These meds were created by the medical computer designed for that purpose 3,000 years ago, in preparation for the people of the ship to populate a new world—a joke to end all jokes for the new world was the old world....

Now that I find myself at the control console for the last time, having reprogrammed the ship's main computer, part of me is saddened. But another part of me, the part that says you were twenty four years old when you left Earth and now it's time to live, is jumping with anticipation. I have, perhaps, two hours of time before I take the life boat to my new home.

I can only wonder what my life will be like once I set foot on the land of my birth.

CHAPTER 3

THE FORTIFICATIONS OF the circular outer walls of Tolemac stood tall against the backdrop of a cloudless blue sky. The walls reflected the already bright sun, which had climbed but a short way into the morning sky. They had ridden through the night, eating a late meal at the side of the road and then breaking fast in the morning with dried fruit and nuts while riding. Their only other stops were for personal toilet.

Passing through the guarded gateway of the outer walls, Areenna and King Nosaj led their men toward the second gateway, forty yards distant. Once past the second wall, they headed to the main keep.

Tolemac's castle keep was the heart of the High King's realm and like no other in Nevaeh. Instead of rising straight up, the walls curved outward like prongs on a crown. And those walls, although built of rock, showed no masonry lines where the carved stones were joined; rather, they were covered with a smooth finish created by Roth himself.

The walls rose thirty un-scalable feet into the air. Many had tried to climb the walls at Roth's invitation, but no man had been able to collect the sizeable reward offered to the first person who accomplished the feat. From the highest parapets flew Roth's personal banner—a circle of eleven black bordered red stars embroidered upon blue and white strips.

"We are the last," Areenna said, pointing to the banners flying on Tolemac's southwest parapet. Even as they looked, the banner of Freemorn was being hoisted.

"Still, we made good time," Nosaj acknowledged. Ahead of them, within the second ring, the townspeople went about their business as if it were just another morning and the rulers of Nevaeh's ten domains were not there.

From above, Gaalrie touched her mind. She saw what Gaalrie saw, Queen Enaid standing in the courtyard, her large white gorlon at her side as always, waiting patiently for her father and herself. The queen wore a loose dress of white trimmed violet that flowed smoothly in the breeze of the high walkway.

When Queen Enaid looked up at Gaalrie, she raised her hand in greeting and Gaalrie dipped downward in a slow spiral of acknowledgement. As the bird did so, Areenna studied the high queen she hadn't seen in almost a half year. A tall woman with burnished mocha skin, Enaid had fire polished black hair that sparkled under the morning sun.

While the high queen was the same age as her father, she appeared not more than five years older than Areenna herself. As High Queen, Enaid was respected throughout the dominions for her wisdom and guidance. It was said, as a sorceress, Enaid had no equal in Nevaeh—it was a truth Areenna knew well.

Areenna had met the high queen many times in her life, and was a cousin three times removed, but in the two years since her mother's death, Enaid had become her mentor. The high queen had visited many times to help with her studies of the women's art. Those visits had been both wonderful and sad, for Enaid had taken on the responsibility of Areenna's mother, helping her to understand not only the powers she had been born with, but continuing the special training her mother had given her during the last months of her life—a training which was not supposed to be taught for several more years.

No one knew of this, as Enaid had sworn Areenna to secrecy. Politically, it was not in Areenna's or her father's best interests to be so favored. Even her father could not know. When they met, it was always in the deep forest, near the Blue Desert, where she had found Gaalrie four years earlier.

When they entered Tolemac's huge courtyard, a dozen stable boys ran to take the reins of the exhausted kraals. Two men dressed in castle livery came out to bring King Nosaj's men to their quarters while Queen

Enaid came to greet Areenna and her father.

"May the sun continue to shine on Freemorn, Highness," she said, with a slight bow of her head to Nosaj.

In turn, Areenna's father bent slightly from the waist while taking the high queen's hand. "And may it brighten all of your days, My Lady. You know my daughter, Areenna," he added.

"Of course," Enaid smiled warmly. "You grow lovelier each time I see you, Princess."

"Thank you, E...Your Majesty," she said, correcting herself quickly. She glanced at her father who, thankfully, had not caught her slip.

"I am glad to see you have stepped into you duties, Areenna. It is good for you to be here with your father. He will need your counsel. Please, the others await you," she said, turning and motioning them to follow.

When they reached the meeting chamber in the main section of the castle, Enaid turned to Nosaj. "Please go in. With your permission, I would speak a moment with Areenna. It has been too long."

"Of course, My Lady," Nosaj replied.

When the door shut behind him, Enaid guided Areenna down a hallway and into a small nook where she turned and drew the younger woman into her arms. "It is good to see you, my dear."

"And you," Areenna replied. She had indeed missed Enaid these past few months as well as the lessons the Queen had given her during the past two years.

"I wish it were under better circumstances. Areenna, dark times are coming. It is why I have been unable to visit Freemorn, and why my husband called this meeting."

"Dark times?" The words sent a tremor through her, bringing up the vision she had uncovered when she'd touched Duke Yermon.

"The power of the dark circle is growing again. They have rested these past years since their downfall at my husband's hands, but they have been slowly gaining strength. The Northern kingdoms are beginning to fight amongst themselves. While it may appear to be simple border disputes, I sense it is much more than that. I will need your help."

"How can I possibly help? I have not your knowledge or your

strengths—"

"Oh, child, do you still not know how strong you truly are? You must not doubt yourself. Your mother was the most powerful sorceress I have ever known, second only to me. And you, child, no matter how you fight it, will shortly surpass everyone, including me. But we need not discuss such things now," she said, cutting off Areenna's protest.

"Listen well to what is said in the chamber. Listen well and advise well. Do not be caught in the games these kings play in their efforts to make their 'doms' stronger. Listen to your mind and to your heart. Promise me this."

Areenna closed her eyes for a moment. "You have my pledge, My Lady."

"Remember, Areenna, all I ask is for you to do what you know is right. Let your thoughts quest through the room, let your instincts guide you. Do you understand?"

Areenna searched the Queen's face before nodding.

Enaid smiled. "Come then, let us join the council as they are about to begin."

It was the first time Areenna had come to the chamber as a King Advisor. And it was the first time she had the clarity to understand the way the chamber had been set up and discerned it could have been done no other way.

Each king sat in a chair made of simple wood. Another chair was set on the right side of each king. These chairs were set slightly back and elevated, allowing whoever sat in them to speak directly into their king's ear without bending or stretching. The chamber was circular, with the twenty-two chairs spread in a semi-circle, radiating from the simple throne and advisor chair which was the fulcrum of the room.

Sitting in the advisor chair to the right of her father, Areenna surveyed the room. Enaid moved into her chair on the right side of the high king. The stewards closed the three sets of double doors and sealed the meeting chamber—only kings and advisors remained. The happenings inside the chamber would not be known until the Kings were ready to speak of it.

There was a tingling at the base of her neck. Slowly, without appearing to look at anyone in particular, Areenna gazed about the chamber. The feeling came from Queen Eetak of Fainhall. *Why,* she wondered. Closing her eyes, she concentrated. An instant later she found Fainhall's queen trying to read her. Areenna raised a block against the woman and the sensation died immediately. From the corner of her eye, she saw Eetak stiffen.

In the silence following the closing of the doors, the pale skinned high king of Nevaeh, Solomon Roth, rose. "I thank each of you for disrupting your lives to answer my call. I hope you know, I would not lightly ask such a thing of you." He paused and looked around the circle of faces.

"When I arrived at Brumwall, the ten 'doms' were at war. For untold years, your domains fought each other, and yet none of you ever moved beyond your own holdings. No matter how the fighting went, who won and who lost, everything stayed equal. And it remained equal for a purpose. Because it was the way *they* needed it. If any one of you became stronger than the others, the possibility existed that he would conquer the next and the next and so on. The end result would have been one king ruling the lands. It was a situation *they* could not allow. Without the dominions of Nevaeh fighting, their power would diminish and their grip over you would fail."

"Why do you think that for so long a time—a time stretching so far back not even your own histories had started to be recorded—you fought each other?"

When no one responded, Roth said, "It was what *they* wanted. *They* needed you to fight. The dark ones, and the Afzaleem, needed your warfare. *They* and their minions needed your hatred and your battles to feed themselves and their masters to continue living."

"How have they been living since we stopped fighting?" called King Retlaw of Morvene.

"They are strong yet. Not strong enough to battle us, but strong enough to survive. They live off the hatred and the fighting within the Blue Desert, in the tar fields of the north, the icy regions of the northwest, and in the southern swamplands as well. They also draw power from their masters across the sea. While it is not what they direly crave, it's enough to keep them going. Enough to let them plan…"

"I have had raiders attack us from the tar fields. It took no big effort to repel them. They are unorganized and untrained—there is nothing to fear," declared King Maslo of Northcrom, the kingdom closest to the arctic tar fields.

"So it would seem," Roth said after Enaid whispered in his ear. "You have had but one attack, yes?"

"Yes."

"How long ago did it happen?"

"Eight months," King Maslo replied.

Turning, King Roth pointed to Libon, King of Welkold. "And you, Highness," Roth said, "How many raids have you had to deal with?"

Libon's mother whispered to him, after which the young unmarried king stood. "There have been four raids since my father's passing. The first, a year ago, was easily stopped, as was the next. But the third one, five months ago cost us thirty guardsmen and seventeen infantry men before we pushed them back. The last, as you know, was three weeks ago."

Libon paused while he worked hard to maintain himself. His young voice held strong as he continued. "Three weeks ago they attacked again. This time they went after an outer province. By the time we reached them, the province had been decimated. Women had been taken and too many men killed. They were stronger this time, much stronger. We went after them, and caught them just before the wastelands of the Frozen Mountains. The fight lasted most of a day. When it ended, a third of my force was lost. We saved many of the women, but not all."

"Thank you, King Libon," Roth said before raking his eyes over the rest. "We face a problem without easy solution. There is another reason the dark ones are gaining strength. The reason is you," he snapped, glaring at each king in turn.

"Do you still not understand what we accomplished twenty years ago? Can you not see it was because the ten dominions agreed to be ruled by a High King that we were able to gain enough strength in unification to defeat them? When the dominions stopped warring among themselves, the energy we regained was too much for them. But they have found a way by using the runaways, criminals, and castoffs to begin rebuilding their power. By taking young, untrained women they gain even more power.

And you are fighting amongst yourselves again. Is that not right, Nomis? You have challenged Kalshold's rights to hunt the land between your two domains?"

"Those lands are mine!" Nomis shouted while shrugging his wife's restraining hand from his shoulder. His eyes were wide and wild.

"No! The unanimous treaty signed by all realms, the treaty you yourself signed, states the lands between kingdoms are not claimable by any kingdom. Whoever hunts there, hunts free, no matter to what dominion he gives fealty."

"They were my lands before you came, High King," Nomis, king of Fainhall, snapped with a disdainful sneering of the words 'High King'.

"Good," Roth said, his words almost an exhalation. "You speak your heart. Perhaps you should speak with your brain as well. Do you think you could survive if they come back again? You defeated them, killed two of the Afzaleem yourself. Do you believe they would allow you to live undisturbed or even to die quickly? You damned well know better! Yet you play into their hands because of your ego, your anger, and your greed. And make no mistake, they feed well from it!"

"How dare you!" Nomis began, his hand going to his sword.

Areenna saw Queen Enaid turn and favor her with a meaningful look. Before anyone could move, Areenna grasped her father's shoulder. "You must stop them," she hissed. "Now!"

Without hesitation, Nosaj rose quickly and strode to the center of the semicircle. "Who are you to challenge what all have decided? How dare you," Nosaj said, echoing Nomis' own words, "treat us this way? You agreed, as we all did, to accept the rule of a high king. Now you want to return to what we once were—savages fighting each other for no greater purpose than to be controlled by *them*—is that what you want?"

Silver hair swirling, Nosaj shook his head sharply. He took a deep breath and said, "The lands you speak of are nothing. You have no use for them other than for hunting and there is enough game in all our border lands to satisfy everyone."

"And if I do not feel the same?" Nomis challenged.

"Then you again become pawn to the Dark Ones. And as such, you must answer to each of us before you can challenge Roth. I do not believe, my old friend," Nosaj said in a gentler voice, "you truly want to do such a thing."

Nomis stared at Nosaj for several tense seconds before the anger in his eyes altered. He took in a staggered breath and, almost reluctantly, drew his hand from his sword's pommel.

"Thank you." Nosaj said.

Nomis shook his head, as if ridding himself of a vision, "I…" He turned to the Roth. "I do not know what came upon me."

Roth stood and joined Nomis and Nosaj, putting a hand on each man's shoulder. "I am blessed by having such strength within this council."

Unnoticed by the men, the women looked at each other, their faces reflecting a concern shared by all.

CHAPTER 4

"DID YOU SEE his face?" Roth asked through clenched teeth. "He was taken over."

"He was…almost, and more could be also as we hold these councils. We must be more attentive," Enaid said. "His anger invited such."

"Too many years of fighting, of death, and of vigilance has gotten us here. How much more will be necessary?"

Enaid turned to him, a vein on her forehead pulsed angrily. "You of all people.… How can you even ask how much more will be necessary? You know well how much more. Forever! For all time! We must always be alert—always be aware. We cannot allow the world to return to what it once was."

Roth withstood the assault of her ire. Then smiling, he crossed the distance between them and took her into his arms. She pulled back, but not too hard. "You are my anchor, Enaid. You are my sounding board. Who else could I ask that question of?"

When she did not respond, he said, "You know it was frustration speaking?"

Giving in, she said, "I know. I but remind you of our purpose."

"Reminders are what greet me when I open my eyes each morning; they are what I dream of when I close them each night. I need no reminders."

Twisting quickly, Enaid escaped his arms. "Then ask not the question if you do not want the answer." The smile ran from her lips as a frown creased her brow. "I am needed. Luncheon is almost ready. I will meet you in the hall."

With that she was gone. Laughing, Roth shook his head. *How much more, indeed?* The answer did not surprise him as he had found that particular answer years before. *As long as it takes.* He would not trade anything for the life he now lived. There was a deep purpose to his life now—a journey begun three thousand years before and one he welcomed eagerly every day, almost as eagerly as greeting Enaid upon awakening every morning. *How lucky I truly am.*

◇◇◇

"What happened this morning could have been more divisive than anyone might believe," Nosaj said to Areenna. "You acted wisely in sending me to stop them."

"It seemed to be what was necessary."

Her father laughed. "You are so young, yet so old. You would make your mother proud."

"I would rather she was here instead of me."

Nosaj placed his hands on her shoulders. "What we wish for and what we must live with are rarely the same. Nonetheless, you are everything best about your mother, and more, you are becoming a powerful woman in your own right. Go refresh yourself before the noon meal. I intend on changing out of these road-coated clothes before we eat."

Areenna left her father and went to her rooms, where she found three servants waiting and a bath already set.

Ten minutes later, as she lay in the warm waters, Queen Enaid entered the bathing chamber. "With your permission, Princess?" When Areenna nodded, Enaid motioned the servants out. She knelt at the edge of the large oval bathing tub set flush within the floor, its rim carved with intricate visions of animals.

"You acted swiftly today—"

Areenna shook her head. "No it was you. I was caught in the moment."

Enaid stroked Areenna's hair. "No child, it would have been only a second or two longer before you knew what actions were needed. All I did was to help make you aware sooner."

"It was only the beginning. Tomorrow something will happen to Llawnroc."

"You had a foreseeing?"

Areenna explained her vision, going over it in greater detail than she had with her father. When she finished, Enaid said, "You acted wisely by telling the duke he would be needed here. I will set a guard upon Llawnroc until the duke arrives. It is too bad we do not know who will attempt this."

She studied Areenna a moment longer. "This afternoon's council will allow the seconds to participate—from now on as well. Tonight you and your father will join us after the meal."

"With delight," Areenna responded even as she found herself wondering why the seconds would be permitted into the council. Seconds were those who were either next in line or guardians of the lineage. It was unusual.

"Not so unusual," Enaid said, catching Areenna off guard. "No, I did not read your mind," Enaid laughed. "I read your face."

Areenna nodded. Though she'd learned much over the years, how to read faces was something she had not yet learned.

As though she sensed the direction of the younger woman's thoughts, Enaid explained, "The reading of faces is not of our magic, it is something I will teach you, as Roth taught me. He calls it psychology. Having the seconds attend the council will be for safety as well. If someone is going after Llawnroc, then we must have enough eyes in the room to prevent it."

"I understand." Areenna paused before saying, "I felt Eetak trying to read me in the council just before Nomis spoke."

Enaid's brows furrowed. "He was caught in something dark. Their domain borders the outlands where the darkness is growing. We will have to watch them."

"She read nothing from me, of that I am certain."

"Good. We eat in a half hour. I will see you there," Enaid declared, and left Areenna to her own thoughts. Her father had no second, but almost everyone else did, including King Roth's son, Mikaal. Alone in the silence of the room, she found herself wondering about Mikaal. It had been a while since she had last seen him. She wondered if he was still the same laughing boy he had always been. Mikaal had never been one to take anything, especially life, too seriously.

The thought of Mikaal brought up a memory so clear it was as if time had reversed itself and she was twelve years old, standing in the Hall of the Tale at the School of the Kings....

Areenna sensed the nervousness of the second year students who sat together in the center of the hall as Master Thrumweld said, "Listen carefully for the tale I impart is of great importance."

He took a long and deep breath—the sound loud in the silent room. Areenna watched his eyes go from one student to the next and felt the power of his gaze when his eyes reached her. "Hear me well. This will be the only time I speak this tale. Remember what is said here, for it is your true history and one day your lives may depend on it."

Areenna counted five of her heartbeats when the old master again scanned the faces of the six students sitting before him. Once again, his eyes fell on her.

"Areenna of Freemorn," he said, "Stand."

Areenna stood, the pale reaches of her long hair fell to her waist in waves; her shoulders straight and she refused to let her face showed any trace of fear. "Yes, Master Thrumweld?"

"What do you know of the Old Ones, of those who came before?"

Areenna's brow creased across forehead. "I know they were strong. Their magic was powerful. They could build high towers and fill the desert with water when there was no water to find. They could control the sky, and even the stars themselves."

She fell silent and waited, the master's eyes still locked on hers. Seconds later, a boy at the end of the semi-circle squirmed nervously. Master Thrumwald looked away from Areenna and fixed the boy with a glare. The boy froze and she was once again beneath the master's gaze. "Yes, they could do all that. But what do you really know of them?"

"Only that they are our ancestors. What we are is because of them. The magic we possess comes from them. It is said they left our world to find a new one, and we are still in waiting for their return."

"Ah... and do you think they will return?"

Areenna hesitated, her brows knitted thoughtfully. While not a test, she sensed it was something no less important—and possibly even more so. She held his stare. "No, Master Thrumweld, I do not think they will return...because I do not believe they went to a new world to return from."

Stunned faces turned toward her. The others looked at her as if she'd lost her mind—some faces showed fear while others just looked sad for her.

"Do tell us why you feel this, Areenna."

She shook her head. Blonde hair flared outward like a whip around her face before settling on her shoulders. "I don't know, not for sure. I...I sense it."

When the old master smiled, she saw white teeth glow from behind red lips that had been hidden within thick whiskers. "Well, Areenna, everyone is allowed to believe however they feel. But believing in something, and acting on it are two different things.

"Who can tell me about magic?" he asked, motioning Areenna to sit back down.

She was all too conscious of how he ignored her raised hand and pointed to another.

"Trebor of Lokinhold, stand!" the master commanded, pulling Areenna abruptly from her thoughts. She turned back as a one of the young boys in her class flew to his feet. "Yes Master Thrumweld?"

"Tell me, Trebor...tell me about magic."

The brown-headed man-child, barely in his thirteenth year took a shaky breath. "Magic is all around us. Women can create spells and use them to do what is needed."

"That is how one *might* use magic," the teacher said dryly, "but, young Trebor, what exactly is magic and where does it come from?"

She watched the confusion settle on Trebor's face. He started to speak, stopped, then shook his head and tried again. "Magic is...magic. It came from our ancestors."

Master Thrumweld's voice was not unkind. "You are half-right. Magic is magic. To describe it is impossible since every woman's magic is their own. However, magic does not simply come from our ancestors, it comes from within!"

"But why then do we learn spells to use magic if it comes from within us?" a small blond woman-child interrupted.

The old master turned his eyes to her. "Yes, Akassia of Welkold, women learn to make formulas which become spells so women can use magic, but the formulas and spells do not create magic…they only allow you to use it."

"I don't understand," Akassia said.

"Neither do I," added Trebor.

"Who understands?" he asked, looking from face to face. When his lingered on Areenna for just a hundredth of a second longer than the others, she saw he knew she understood, but could not say so aloud. She had to live with the others in her group for the next two years and for her to say that what people call magic is but the witnessing of sciences they cannot comprehend would mark her as different from them.

Then, she became aware of something else—a sensation of being watched.

She turned toward the far wall, her eyes flicked over the older students. When her glance fell across one in particular, she knew it was he who had been watching her. There was an aura about him, floating near his skin. Not a shadow of darkness, but rather of something else, though she knew not what. Then, slowly, recognition surfaced. He was Mikaal, the son of the High King. *Why is he watching me?*

Mikaal spun to face his mother. "I have plans for the afternoon."

"What plans are those?" He could almost be a twin of his father, except he was taller, his eyes were the same gray as Enaid's, and his mouth was somewhere between Roth's and hers. But overall, he was tall, strong and much too handsome for his own good, or for the good of the women inside and outside of Tolemac.

"Plans," he responded in a softer voice.

"I am sorry Mikaal, today the council is more important."

"Of course it is, Mother," he said without sarcasm. "How was this morning's session?"

"There were a few bumps," she told him and explained what had happened.

When she finished, Mikaal said, "Then it is best we go fortify ourselves with food before, yes?"

Enaid laughed. "Yes, but not too much. I don't want you sleeping through this. Today and tomorrow will be important, Mikaal, possibly more important than any day before."

"I will not sleep," he promised with another broad smile.

Unlike most of the women present, Areenna wore leggings and a short tunic rather than a dress. Only two other women dressed the same. Areenna's tunic was pale green and cut to mask the fullness of her breasts, de-emphasizing her body in favor of her position as king's advisor. Her pale hair was pulled back and tied in a simple manner.

When she and her father entered the small hall, she reacted as she always had, with a slow indrawn breath. The small hall was a misnomer as the room was small in name only. The walls were triple the height of a man, and arched domelike, meeting a huge skylight in the center. While the walls and ceiling were plain and coated with a pale white wash, the artwork created upon them was spectacular. Greens and blues, yellows and reds mingled with earth tones of browns, beiges and tans to create murals of Nevaeh representing a millennium of history. Sunlight streamed through the large skylight in the center of the ceiling, which illuminated the chamber and brought the murals to life. There was no need for artificial light to see clearly in daytime.

She and her father were seated to Roth's left. There was an open chair between her and the high king. The meal started off smoothly with almost all in attendance. The talk was calm and completely off the subject of the earlier discussions. Within moments of the meal's start, Roth's son Mikaal appeared; for just an instant, Areenna thought she was seeing two high kings, before she realized it was Mikaal.

Surprisingly, he had grown taller since their last meeting. The change was unexpected because he was two years older than she, and should have stopped growing well before. But his height was the least of the changes. Areenna saw he had become broader as well, and she did not miss the powerful muscles rippling beneath his light shirt.

She felt a foot kick her shin and looked at her father. "What?"

"Staring at Mikaal is rude," he admonished in a whisper, but she saw his eyes sparkle.

Unable to control her blush, she picked up a napkin and coughed into it. "Please, Father," she whispered, but knew more eyes were on her. *Am I that obvious?* She looked around and saw there were only two sets of eyes focused on her—the gray eyes that belonged to Enaid and the matching gray of Mikaal's.

"Areenna." Mikaal smiled at her. "Finally a pleasure amongst the drags of duty." He sat in the chair next to her.

"Hello, Mikaal," Areenna replied. "And why does duty become a drag?"

He laughed. "Try not to sound like my mother."

Areenna smiled. "Try to act like a prince."

"Yes, Mother," he said with a wink.

Areenna laughed nonchalantly, yet there was something heavier beneath the laugh. A light afternoon wine was served along with the first course of a tallow fruit. She had been hungry earlier, but something ominous in the chamber stole away her hunger. As she nibbled politely at the fruit, she gazed around the long oval table. Spread out evenly were the ten kings, the high king, and the wives, mothers, daughters, and brothers or sisters who were the royal advisors. The seconds, for those who had such, sat to their king's left. Llawnroc and Freemorn were the only kingdoms with empty chairs to the left of their rulers and Llawnroc's chair would be filled by tonight.

To the other side of Roth and Enaid, was Enaid's father, King Ecaroh of Brumwall. His wife, Queen Enna sat on one side. Their son, Enaid's brother Prince Darb, sat in the seconds' chair.

"Where are you?" Mikaal asked Areenna, interrupting her thoughts with his deep voiced whisper.

She shook free of her inspection and favored him with a halting smile. "Admiring the way the hall was created. The paintings and the skylight always amaze me."

Mikaal looked around and shrugged. "I see nothing more than what has surrounded me all my life."

"Which means what…that you cannot see the beauty in your life?"

"It means he cannot see what is before him, only what is distant," Enaid said with a smile.

"Sad, is it not?" Areenna replied with a matching smile.

"So this is today's game, try to find the chink in Mikaal's armor?" he responded to both women.

"More like taking the blinders off your eyes," Areenna retorted without thinking. She paused, momentarily looking away from him. When she turned back to the young prince, she said, "Forgive me, my prince, I spoke out of turn."

Mikaal stared her for several seconds before a smile lifted the corners of his mouth. "Forgive you for speaking your mind? There are so many who are afraid to do more than agree with whatever I say."

"Because you are the heir," Areenna whispered as the servants cleared the first course.

"Which I care nothing about. Must I remind you it takes all ten dominions to accept a high king?"

"You will care, and no, I know it well," Areenna said and heard Enaid echo her words at the exact same time.

Mikaal threw his hands into the air. "Two of you and I am stuck in the middle. Can we stop discussing me and enjoy our meal?

"Of course," Areenna replied. She picked up the cup of wine. It tasted of berries and oak and delighted her senses while at the same time she warned herself to be careful not to drink too much.

When the food was served—roast chillen breasts and vegetables— the myriad conversations around the table became muted while everyone ate their fill.

From the corners of her eyes, Areenna watched Mikaal eat, drink, and talk with his mother between bites. She admired their closeness, which seemed more like friendship than a chat between mother and son.

"Look at Roth," her father said in a whisper that carried only as far as her ear.

The high king's face was etched with tension, his eyes darting around the room, and she knew Enaid had told him of her vision. Coupled with what had happened earlier, she was certain he was trying to pierce whatever dark curtain was drawing around them.

Areenna turned her attention to the plate before her. Eating slowly, she concentrated on the food, ignoring the conversations, and did as Enaid had asked—allowed her senses to range outward in the room.

She was not powerful enough to sense specific thoughts—very few women could—but she could sense emotions. The high queen had shown her how to build her strength for this over a year ago. Outwardly, Areenna kept her face stoic while she allowed her senses to roam freely.

A sensory sweep of the room, showed her nothing unusual until she discovered a blocked mind. She reached for her wine and looked around the room, trying to ferret out the person whose thoughts were shielded.

The emotions of the others in the room were clear and mostly calm and their faces reflected such. Beneath the calmness was a sense of anticipation. But when her eyes settled on Olrac, king of Llawnroc, she knew it was he who hid his thoughts from others.

Llawnroc was the southernmost domain of the ten realms, and was charged with the watch of the Eastern Ocean. Areenna wondered what Olrac was protecting to require so heavy a shield. Or was it a who, not what he protected?

His emotions are blocked as well. The words came not through her ears, but into her mind. Areenna paused with her wine cup suspended on its return journey to the table as she intuitively recognized the feel of Enaid behind the words.

She looked at the High Queen, who was staring directly at her. She blinked once, and formed a question with her thoughts. *You can talk this way? You can see into my thoughts?*

A trickle of laughter danced in her head. *No child, I cannot see into your head. But I can 'feel' your words—nothing more. When I feel them, I can respond. Concentrate and 'push' your thoughts. Now, what did you find?*

Olrac, she thought toward Enaid. *He is...blank.*

She watched the Queen's eyes track to Olrac and close. An instant later Enaid's eyes flew open and she turned to Areenna. *He is not Olrac!*

CHAPTER 5

ENAID SCANNED THE council room, her eyes stopping briefly on Olrac. Olrac was the ruler of the southernmost domain and the protector of the southern shores of the Eastern Sea—it had been called the Atlantic Ocean in the time from whence Roth had come, he had told her—it was the most vulnerable area of Nevaeh.

Was it possible? If Olrac had been replaced by a look-alike, then his kingdom would be open. There was but one person who might be able to see through the duplication—his brother, Yermon, Duke of Llawnroc: The connection within bloodlines was strong throughout Nevaeh and stronger yet with twin brothers.

Enaid was deeply concerned. Whispered tales from the old days, stories handed down from mothers to daughters for many centuries, told of how such duplication was possible for the depravity from across the sea.

With sudden clarity, Enaid understood Areenna's vision. Olrac's brother, Duke Yermon, would know *it* was an impostor. It was also an accepted fact Duke Yermon would sit Olrac's throne in the King's absence.

She found Areenna watching her and, with an imperceptible nod, directed a thought to her. *Now you know what the vision meant. The*

Llawnroc bloodline is strong and even stronger when the brothers are twins. Yermon will see through the deception.

What of my vision of the knife?

I do not know, Enaid responded.

She turned to Roth and leaned into his ear. "There is a great danger here. We must talk privately."

"We cannot. The council has started," he reminded her.

"Find a way. We must wait for Yermon to arrive before continuing the council."

Roth knew his wife would not ask this lightly. Standing, he raised his arms, his palms parallel to the floor and lowered them slowly to ask for silence. When his hands reached the table, the room was quiet.

"I ask the indulgence of the council. An urgent matter has arisen and it must be dealt with immediately."

He paused to take in the surprise registering on all the faces. "I understand this is an inconvenience, but a necessary one. We will begin again, tomorrow morning. Please avail yourselves of Tolemac's hospitality. We will see you all at the evening meal."

With his fading words, confusion rose among all the retinues. Roth stood and, with Enaid and Mikaal following, left the council chamber.

◇◇◇

While Roth spoke, Areenna heard Enaid's mind touch again. *When we leave, meet us in our chambers. Bring your father.*

"That was unexpected," Nosaj whispered to Areenna.

"But important," she replied, her voice so low it reached only her father's ear. "The high king and Enaid want us to meet them in their chamber."

He started to speak, stopped, and instead favored her with a penetrating look. "Then we should leave."

They stood and, with her father in the lead, were the first through the door after the high king. Only a few followed. The rest stayed in the council chamber, talking about what had just happened. Outside, Areenna took the lead and brought them to their chambers.

"We should wait a few more minutes. I don't think Enaid wants us to be seen."

48

Her father's brows knit together. "Enaid did not speak to you. How can you know this?"

She took a breath and, before answering, exhaled slowly. "She told me so…without words."

His eyes remained locked on hers. His arm rose, his fingers grazed her cheek before he dropped his arm to his side. "You are like your mother. She had the mind touch as well. How much more is there you haven't told me?"

Before she could respond, there was a knock on their door. Thankful for the interruption, Areenna opened it to find one of Enaid's maids waiting. "Please come with me."

The girl took them to the King's chambers, through an empty side hall passage and to a room where Enaid met them. "Thank you for coming, your Highness," Enaid said to Nosaj.

"Your majesty," Nosaj responded with a slight bow of his head.

"Can we dispense with the formalities, Nosaj? We are family."

Nosaj nodded to his wife's cousin. "What is happening, Enaid?"

"Come," she said, "Roth needs your advice."

Nosaj's eyebrows rose but he remained silent.

Enaid led them through a short maze of rooms and into Roth's private chamber. Two of the room's walls were lined with shelves holding books. A large map was centered on the third wall; each of the ten domains highlighted with varying shades of color. Beneath the map was an ornate, hand-carved desk of deep red wood. A matching chair with burgundy cushions was tucked into the desk. The forth wall was windowed, with a view of Tolemac's green rolling hills. The floor was covered with a woven rug, and centered in the room was a table of the same red wood as the desk. Six chairs surrounded the table and on the table were goblets and several pitchers. Sconces of illuminating night-moss were spaced evenly on the walls.

A moment after Enaid, Nosaj and Areenna entered the room, Roth and Mikaal joined them. Roth pulled Nosaj into a quick embrace. He released him but held him at arm's length. A full smile broke his lips. "It is good to see you again, my friend. It has been too long."

"It has, Sire," Nosaj responded with his own smile.

"No titles. In this room we are all equals."

"As you ask…Solomon."

49

The name sounded strange in her ears as Areenna studied the byplay between the two men. The name was indeed peculiar, and she found it intriguing. The high king was the only man she had ever known who had two names rather than a single name bounded to a domain. But why would the high king have a domain, since unlike she or her father, all of Nevaeh was his domain? It was said the high king had not been born of a kingly line but rather poor born. No one knew what domain he had been born to; they only knew his strength and intelligence surmounted any bloodline distinction.

"Let us sit so what is happening can be explained."

While they seated themselves, Enaid poured each two glasses: one of wine and one of water as Nevaen custom dictated. When his wife sat next to him, Roth lifted his wine goblet. "To friends, to family, and to a safe world."

They raised their glasses—in a tradition started by Roth—and sipped. "A very dangerous situation has arisen." He turned to Enaid and nodded.

Enaid looked at Areenna. "Areenna had a vision, two days past," she began, looking from Areenna to Roth and Mikaal. "In this vision she sensed a great danger to Olrac of Llawnroc, and advised, correctly, his brother Yermon to find a way to join Olrac here. Today, with Areenna's help, we discovered why."

Enaid paused, took a drink of water, and said, "King Olrac is not the person who attends this council."

"How is this possible? I have seen him with my own eyes not ten minutes ago!" Mikaal stated.

"The person you see is a duplicate, his visage is controlled by a powerful person, so powerful I could not see through the deception."

"Duplication is an old wives tale. Even if Olrac is a...ah...duplicate, how can you know this as a fact?" Nosaj questioned carefully.

"Areenna discovered the deception. Your daughter is much more powerful than your wife."

While all eyes were focused on her, Areenna looked only at her father. "I...I am able to sense people's minds," she admitted. "I didn't know how well until today, when Enaid pushed me to do so. Everyone in the room except for one was open to me. Olrac was completely blocked."

"Which might mean you just cannot read him," Mikaal cut in.

Turning to Mikaal, she reached out with her mind for an instant and felt a shock run through her. She inhaled sharply. "You don't believe that. You feel the same as I, don't you?"

Enaid and Roth turned to him, Enaid's eyes as wide as coins. "Mikaal?" she asked, her voice cracking.

Mikaal held her stare for several seconds before slowly nodding. He turned to Areenna. "How?"

"Until just now I didn't know. I…."

"Is this true?" Roth asked. "Can you sense things?"

Mikaal's brows furrowed. He looked from his father to his mother. "It started just after my thirteenth birthday. I…I didn't want anyone knowing."

Stunned, Enaid stared at her son. She shook her head slowly and turned to Areenna and Nosaj, and then back at Mikaal. "No one must ever know." Then she looked directly at the high king. "Solomon, it is because of you."

"How could you not sense this?" Roth asked his wife.

Enaid shook her head. "It never occurred to me to try. He is male."

"Is it a male sensitivity like Master Thrumweld?" Nosaj asked.

"No." Enaid stood and walked behind Mikaal's chair. She put one hand on Roth's shoulder, the other on Mikaal's, and looked at Roth. When he gave a slow nod, Enaid said, "What I am going to tell you is known by only six people. Three of those are in this room. The others are my father, mother, and brother. Should it become known, every effort of the black forces from across the sea—every dark and evil power they possess, every action they take, will be directed against Mikaal and Roth. I do mean every force they can muster, be it physical or dark sorcery. And they have become very, very strong again."

All eyes rested on Areenna and Nosaj, waiting. Nosaj was the first to nod. Areenna was unable to do so. Not because she was weighing her options; rather, because she was too stunned to think clearly even though she'd heard, saw and had taken in everything.

"Areenna," her father said gently.

Areenna blinked then nodded. "I am sorry, I…"

"It is fine, I understand," Enaid assured her. She stepped from behind Mikaal's chair to her own, but did not sit. Some of her long, raven hair fell across her face. Brushing the hair back absently, she said, "I had always wondered if something like this was possible. Deep inside, I knew it was, but I could never be certain. Our people, all of the people in Nevaeh, follow the same growth. Men have been granted the abilities of both internal and physical strength; women have mental abilities beyond the normal. My husband once explained the abilities the women of Nevaeh have is called paranormal. We have these abilities because of the Old Ones and of what is called radiation, and of what happened to our world thousands of years ago. A few men, like Master Thrumweld of The School, have sensitivity to a woman's power. Still, there has never been a man who has been gifted with a woman's paranormal abilities."

Enaid looked at her husband, a gentle smile shadowing her lips. "But there has not been a man like Solomon Roth in three thousand years."

Nosaj looked at Roth but remained silent as the high queen continued. "My husband is the last of the 'Old Ones'. The legends were true, and my husband has returned to our world."

Enaid watched shock spread across both Nosaj and Areenna's faces. She saw Areenna grasp her father's hand and squeeze it to anchor him in reality. She waited until they both visibly relaxed. Yet, she read well the deep wariness behind Nosaj's eyes and knew he, of all the rulers of Nevaeh's domains, would have the most open mind. It was why his wife had loved him. And Enaid's cousin had been a very wise woman.

"Nosaj?"

At his name, Areenna's father finally shook himself free of his surprise. "How is this even remotely possible without anyone knowing?"

"It was necessary. How would you react if Solomon walked into your throne room and declared himself to be an Old One?"

"I would believe him insane," Nosaj said honestly. "I would exile him to the Blue Desert."

"Of course you would. He would have been banished to the borderlands and labeled misfit and Nevaeh would still have ten realms battling each other's borders, being tricked like thoughtless animals into keeping everything as it has been for centuries—stagnant."

"Yes," Nosaj agreed.

"Exactly! And if you—or any king—had done so, Nevaeh would never have become united. In fact, the ten dominions would have grown weaker and weaker until the dark circle conquered us once and for all and turned us as mindless as the mutated minions they rule across the sea."

Nosaj looked down at the hand his daughter held. He raised it to his lips and kissed the soft skin before releasing it. He looked at Roth and said, "I still don't understand how this is possible. Your strength is equal to any man's. It is known the 'Old Ones' were not strong physically and they preferred to fight with machines they could control from great distances."

"You speak truly. I am not as strong as you."

"Then how could you have defeated us? You fought all of the Kings. You overpowered each of us."

Roth's eyes danced with humor. "Were you to challenge a huge acont tree with your sword, who would win? Would it be you or the tree?"

Nosaj's brows knitted together as he worked out the riddle. Then he too smiled. "The tree, of course. My sword might damage it, but I would tire long before I could cut it down."

"Exactly. It was not my physical strength, but the strength of my armor. The material of my armor is made of a special metal. In my time, the metal was used to build ships, and these ships had to withstand anything. This metal was used to build the ship that carried me into space—up toward the stars."

Nosaj looked puzzled. "I…"

"Nosaj, I will explain all when the time is right; today is not that time. Will you trust me until I can fully explain?"

Nosaj looked at Areenna and then back at Roth. "You have been my king for many years. We have bled together in battle. Why would I not trust you?"

"Thank you," Roth said simply. "Let me explain about the armor. The metal is strong enough to resist any sword blow. Inside the armor is padding, which absorbs the shock of a sword blow. When I fought, I was able to outwait my opponent. Tire him to the point where he could barely lift his sword. Was that not so when we fought eighteen years ago?"

Nosaj nodded again. "So it was endurance which defeated me. I always wondered why not a single drop of blood was ever spilled when you fought all of us."

"Why would I maim or kill those who are needed to protect and oversee our world?" Roth fell silent. He reached past his wife to grasp Mikaal's shoulder. "For now we must forget what we have discovered about Mikaal. No one must know, or his life could be forfeit. The people would think it black sorcery."

"Which I will never allow," Enaid declared. "How strong are you?" she asked her son.

"I don't know. The only time I can experiment is when I'm alone, which has been almost impossible, as you well know." His words were an explosion of frustration.

"Then we must find out, and soon. But before we do that, we need a plan of action to unmask this duplicate and find Olrac before it's too late." With that Enaid turned to Roth. What think you my liege?"

"We must send a messenger to Yermon to warn him."

Areenna drew in a breath. Her fingers curled into her palms. She looked from the high king to Enaid. "It must be me."

"No," Nosaj said quickly.

"Yes, Father. Yermon is coming because of what I told him. Would he believe or trust a messenger who tells him his brother is not his brother?"

"She is right," Roth said.

"I know," Nosaj said.

A moment later the sharp cry of a treygone came through the open windows of the chamber as Gaalrie came to rest on the outer sill. Areenna looked fondly at the giant bird and sent her a command to find Yermon.

An instant later the treygone was airborne. "I need to change into riding clothes."

"As do I," Mikaal stated, standing at the same time as Areenna. "It makes sense. People will think it strange for a king's daughter to go riding alone. The two of us going together will not raise suspicions."

Areenna nodded. "Mikaal is right."

"So be it," Roth said. "We will send a small guard detail." Before

Areenna could protest, Roth added. "They will go out ten minutes after you leave. It will not be connected. I am concerned about what you might find on the road. Go now."

CHAPTER 6

THEY RODE SLOWLY through the gates of Tolemac, as if going for nothing more than an afternoon ride. Prince Mikaal led the way, his large blue, almost black coated kraal prancing handsomely forward while Areenna's smaller mount glided effortlessly next to him.

Many a head turned to watch the pair ride from the city. More than one lady sighed at the prince's passing. The same could be said about the young men and Areenna, but before anyone could point a finger, the men averted their eyes. Such was the way of the land. Coveting royalty was not something done lightly.

But neither Areenna nor Mikaal were aware of the glances cast their way for they had a much heavier matter on their minds. Three hundred yards after the soldiers guarding the outer gates had saluted their prince, both Areenna and Mikaal urged their kraals forward.

"Have you their location?" Mikaal asked as soon as they turned the first bend and disappeared from the soldiers' view.

"Just. Duke Yermon is two miles north, but something…I'm not sure what, something is not right."

Mikaal started to speak, but she cut him off with a wave of her hand. Closing her eyes, Areenna concentrated on Gaalrie, pushing her thoughts toward the giant bird in an effort to clear their foggy communication—it was as if something dark and hidden and powerful was trying to block her.

What could cause such a thing?

Pushing her mind hard, she focused on Gaalrie and broke through the mental barrier. A moment later she was able to see through her treygone's eyes, and watched the duke and his men galloping toward Tolemac. They rode frantically and she felt the visceral fear her treygone sensed emanating from the riders. She knew there was little time left to save the duke when something dark and shimmering appeared behind the riders.

As if struck by lightning, Areenna understood what chased the duke. "We must move fast, now!" she shouted to Mikaal, pressing her heels hard into Hero's side while also sending the kraal a mental command.

Behind her, Mikaal reacted instantly. Leaning forward, he urged his mount on while at the same time futilely shouting, "What is it?"

When she did not respond, he pushed his kraal harder and came abreast of Areenna, "What?" he shouted. Then he saw how pale Areenna's face was. It seemed as if every drop of blood had been drained from her head.

"Yermon is in danger. Terrible danger."

"From what realm?"

"The Dark Ones!"

The Dark Ones. The words sent a chill along Mikaal's back. The Dark Ones had not been seen since his father and mother managed to banish the last of them behind the furthest borders of Nevaeh. "How can they be back?"

"Doubt me not. They are here now," she half shouted while through Gaalrie's crystal clear vision, she continued to watch the duke's mad ride toward them.

Mikaal's eyes widened when he caught both the words she had spoken, and the vision of Yermon she had somehow sent to his mind. There was something else as well, something dark and malevolent trying to edge into his thoughts. *No,* he corrected himself, *into Areenna's mind.*

In a state of shock, Mikaal fought for control over himself. Growing up, he had heard stories of mind melding, but he had never before been inside the mind of another and it had unnerved him.

He bent low over the powerful, long neck of his kraal. A glance at Areenna showed her eyes were fixed straight ahead and her mind was her own. He reached over his left shoulder and withdrew his sword from the leather scabbard strapped across his back. The feel of the leather wrapped steel grip helped to settle his mind.

When he drew the sword, Areenna wanted to tell him it would do no good, but she knew he'd sensed the darkness trying to push into her mind and his sword was his grounding force. So, rather than speak, she concentrated on the road ahead. Only minutes separated them from Yermon. She hoped they'd be in time. Then Gaalrie's cry cut into her consciousness.

The dark swirling thing—a wraith—was almost upon the duke. Gaalrie dove toward a dark misty mass barely a hairsbreadth behind the duke. The bird hit the dark shape and turned upward, but not before her huge claws rippled through the shifting effervescent mist surrounding the creature.

There was a loud horrendous screech, not from the Treygone, but from the dark mist itself. *Good!* Areenna sent the arrow-like thought toward Gaalrie with the command to come back to her.

Seconds later the giant bird circled her head and a few desperate heartbeats later, Duke Yermon and his men appeared at full gallop from around the bend in the road. Areenna drew her kraal to a sharp halt, its back legs digging into the ground in an effort to stop even as she jumped from the saddle and motioned the men past.

"Go!" she commanded, waving them by. "Do not stop!"

Mikaal followed suit, coming to a running halt beside Areenna, his sword at the ready, his breathing short and tight.

She gazed at him, knowing how futile his sword would be against the wraith's dark abilities. "How strong is your power?"

"I don't know," he admitted.

"Then do nothing. Stand behind me! If you feel me, join me. If you feel the darkness fight it with everything you possess!"

Before he could respond, a cold wind whipped across them, its chill penetrating bone deep in the space of a breath. A force such as Areenna had never known before hit her. She stumbled backward from the mental strike and fought for balance. The force hit her again, and knocked her to the ground.

Above her, Gaalrie screamed. Twisting quickly, Areenna rose to her feet, planted them solidly, and drew forth her powers.

"Now!" she shouted to Mikaal.

Mikaal stepped next to Areenna and, without understanding what was happening, and working on instinct alone, he let his mind free. He did nothing but open his mind rather than close it off. The instant he did, a force more powerful than anything he had experienced filled him.

"Yes," whispered Areenna. "Hold and brace yourself."

Instinct alone led him to whirl his sword and then, point down, slam it into the dirt road. The sword's tip bit deeply into the earth's crust. Right hand grasping the pommel, he reached out with his left hand and gripped Areenna's hand.

Shaken by the attack, Areenna accepted everything Mikaal opened to her. Using the strength flowing from him, she took command of the powers within her and settled her mind.

And then the dark shimmering mist was upon them; tentacles of fear wrapped cold coils around both of them. The icy fingers of darkness sought a hold, and failed. The mist coalesced into a large, ominous shape the color of burnt charcoal. It grew tall and wide and cast a black shadow upon them, filling the air with such vileness it made Areenna gag even as it morphed into the shape of a bird, ten times the size of Gaalrie.

Darkness crept into her mind, attacking her thoughts and sucking the very light from the day, causing the sun to disappear and the forest around them to fade into nothingness. She had never felt such vileness— never known the anguish attacking her mind and her body. As revulsion filled her, she screamed her defiance at the dark, malevolent, swirling beast.

She raised her left arm, holding her palm forward while her right hand grasped Mikaal's tightly, using his hand and his strength as her anchor. She took a deep breath and, feeling Mikaal's mind open even more fully to her, took command of his thoughts and combined them with hers to build a wall of solid power before them. Fire built in her belly. *Push*, she commanded the prince with a quick thought. *Follow what I do.*

She concentrated on strengthening the wall she had built, widening and thickening it as the wraith shrieked and fought to find a way through, its probing tentacles seeking any chink within the mental wall. *White* she said in her mind, *white to hold strong. White to keep free, white to protect.* She stopped thinking when she finished the old formula for protection. Fear leached into the edges of her mind, its power unlike any she had ever encountered.

Then a new sensation filled her as Mikaal's strength vibrated through her. Their minds became one in the battle against the dark power before them. Allowing this new strength to build, she solidified the wall and held it steady, cutting off the dark mist's forward movement.

While the evil behind the mist continued to writhe against the mental wall, she chased away the twists of fear and pushed with all her strength and, taking a half step forward, forced the dark apparition backward. Gaalrie gave vent to a ferocious cry as she circled tightly above.

The bird-shaped mist grew denser and forced itself against Areenna's defenses, its huge claws and beak tearing at the protective wall. A sudden flare of purples and reds exploded at the barrier and the dark, wraithlike mist backed off. The creature held still for several long seconds before beginning to churn like a tornado gone mad. Dirt and leaves, branches and stones rose within the whirling madness, spinning wildly until the swirling stopped abruptly. An instant later the rocks and branches flew at them. But Areenna's wall held against the torrent; the rain of rocks and branches hit the invisible wall and fell harmlessly to the ground.

Still, Areenna maintained the wall, refusing to let the wraith gain an inch. Then, like shifting sands, the dark mist solidified into a shadow of a man standing three heads above them. Burning red eyes glowed down at them and its arms spread wide as the creature grew even broader and taller.

Areenna clutched Mikaal's hand tighter. The wraith attacked her with a focus that tore at the corners of her mind. She held her space firmly and built further on the strength she and Mikaal had created and then used the training her mother had given her years before.

Concentrating on the head of the evil beast, she stared directly into its malicious red eyes and, working rapidly, combined thought and energy into a solid weapon within her mind in exactly the way her mother had taught her so many years before. The energy grew within and without her body, a powerful spinning of revolving white and gold streaks built larger and larger.

And only when she could barely stand against the evil force pushing at her did she raise her free hand, its palm aimed at the creature's face, dropped the mental shield protecting them and released the pure force of the weapon she had created. Never once did she forget the man standing next to her and the strength he added to her power.

The instant she released the power, Gaalrie screamed and launched herself at the creature. The power hit it a microsecond before Gaalrie's huge talons ripped at the spot where the red glaring eyes had been.

The thing screamed, writhing like a snuck with its poisonous head cut off. A blast of evil, dark and thick, radiated from it as its two tentacle-like arms whipped about until, suddenly, a huge white gorlon hurled itself at the creature.

My mother's aoutem, came Mikaal's crystal clear thought.

The dark mist disappeared and the attack was over.

Areenna exhaled slowly, released Mikaal's hand and then fell to the ground, her mind as dark as her consciousness.

Mikaal reached for her. As he did, his mind too went black and he crashed to the earth next to Areenna.

The soldiers sent to protect Prince Mikaal and Princess Areenna as well as Duke Yermon reached the duke moments after Yermon had passed the two. When they drew their mounts to a halt, the duke said, "They are fighting it now."

The commander bade half his detachment to surround and protect Yermon. Then he and the rest of his men raced off to help their prince.

They reached the unconscious forms of Mikaal and Areenna and dismounted quickly. When they tried to go to their aid, the gorlon and the treygone gave forth warning cries that stopped the men short. None of them wished to tangle with their queen's ninety pound gorlon or a treygone the size of Gaalrie.

Fortunately for the soldiers, within minutes of the standoff, both King Roth and Queen Enaid arrived at a gallop. Behind them rode another full platoon of soldiers and Duke Yermon and his men as Enaid had told them the danger was now past.

Enaid dismounted at a run and when she reached her unconscious son and her pupil, she knew what must be done. Although she yearned to go to Mikaal, she knelt first at Areenna's side and grasped the girl's head with both her hands. She closed her eyes and pushed into Areenna's mind, carefully and gently wandering the passages within until she found the mind-lock. Again, carefully and with a loving gentleness, she pushed the lock aside and withdrew.

Areenna's gasp was loud. She took in several gulping breaths. Then she exhaled slowly and opened her eyes. "Enaid," she whispered. "I—Mikaal?"

Hush child, Enaid cooed within her mind before she whispered into Areenna's ear, "Say nothing more, except to Yermon. We will talk later."

"Mikaal," Areenna repeated, still unable to sense his mind.

Enaid said in another low whisper only Areenna could hear, "He is waking now. I had to wake you first to release your mind lock."

Enaid shifted toward Mikaal. While the Queen tended her son, Areenna rose to her feet with Roth's aid. Looking into the high king's eyes, she tried to smile, but her lips would not move.

"I understand," Roth said.

Areenna nodded. "My lord." Her voice was low and cracked. She ran her tongue over her lips, doing her best to moisten them. Turning, she looked at the duke.

"Duke Yermon," she started toward him, walking as stiffly as though the battle just fought had been a physical one. "The danger is passed, but there is something you must know."

Dismounting from his kraal, the duke went to Areenna and bowed lightly. When he straightened, he said, "My thanks to you Princess, for your help."

Areenna shook her head. "You must brace yourself."

"Brace myself? What else could happen after that…thing?"

"It is about your brother. Mikaal and I…we were on our way to warn you." She hesitated a moment, trying to figure out how best to explain things. But there was no best way. "Your brother is not your brother."

The duke's features turned puzzled. His brows knitted together and the corners of his lips quirked down. "I don't understand."

"The person who is attending the council is not your brother. He is a...a duplicate."

"Impossible," Yermon said.

"If that is so," came Roth's powerful baritone, "what call you that thing which was chasing you? Was it not impossible, too? Was it not something out of legends, out of the dark power? Have you ever seen a wraith before? Can you imagine it to be anything other than a wraith of darkness?"

"Your Highness, I—"

"—exactly. Now be aware of what was said to you and act accordingly. You will be escorted to a safe place outside the walls of Tolemac until dinner time. Then you will join us. You will be the last to enter the dining chamber. No one will know you are in Tolemac until that moment. When you enter the chamber, keep your eyes upon your brother. Queen Enaid will stand watch over the chamber to protect you. And you will need protection, for the man there, if a man at all, will proclaim you to be a duplicate as well. It will be up to you to disprove this."

"And how will I be able to tell?" demanded the duke, still unable to believe what he had been told.

Areenna stepped forward. "My Duke," she said gently, laying a hand on his bared forearm. "I believe it will take naught but a glance at him for you to know his falseness. You must trust yourself, and trust me as you did the other day at Freemorn."

"My Lady," Yermon said, dipping his head slowly. "I trust you completely, but I find it hard to..."

"I understand. Trust me and trust yourself."

Duke Yermon nodded. "I do and I will." He turned to Roth and nodded. "My liege, what need have you of me?"

Roth went to Yermon and placed an arm over his shoulders. "Come, and I will explain."

When Roth led the duke away, Areenna turned back to Enaid and Mikaal. She found them talking quietly and went over to them. "Are you all right," she asked Mikaal.

He nodded slowly, but his eyes, searched her face. "You are

powerful. I never imagined something as powerful as what happened."

"Without your help, it would have the duke, me, and then the castle," Areenna said. The powers she had mustered when Mikaal had joined her mind were like nothing she had ever known or imagined. She started to say more, but Enaid stopped her with a sharp thought.

Accepting her queen's command, she reached for Mikaal's hand and smiled at him. "Thank you my Prince."

Mikaal gently squeezed her hand before releasing it. He nodded, not willing to trust himself to speak further.

A moment later, Gaalrie circled her mistress and slowly landed on her shoulders. Areenna accepted the weight of the giant bird. Then her aoutem entered her mind and she welcomed its soothing maternal energy. In less than a minute, the remnants of the darkness that had attacked her mind were gone and Gaalrie lifted from her shoulder to once again circle above her.

Areenna saw Mikaal was still feeling the effects of mental battle and knew that without an aoutem, it would take a while for those effects to disappear. She saw Enaid nod in agreement with her thought, but wondered if there was something she could do to help.

Taking tentative steps forward, she moved next to Mikaal. From the corner of her eyes, she saw Enaid and Roth go to Yermon. While they did, she closed the distance between herself and Mikaal, grasped his hands and held them tightly. She did nothing except look into his eyes and let her mind seek his, her thoughts as calming and smooth as was the grip in which she held his hands.

Mikaal's eyes closed. Seconds later he exhaled and Areenna knew he was again himself. "Your sword," she said, nodding to where it still stood in the road.

Turning, she went to Hero. The kraal held still while she mounted, and waited for Mikaal to mount as well. Together, they turned their kraals and started toward Tolemac.

Behind her, Enaid stared at their backs, a smile building within her. But the smile faded while she watched, knowing today's battle was but the beginning of a long and dangerous road her son and Areenna had embarked on—and her heart cried out for what she could not yet tell them and for what they must face.

CHAPTER 7

ROTH PACED THE chamber, his restless energy filled every square inch of space while Enaid sat calmly on a long bench with Areenna. Across from them, Mikaal and Nosaj talked quietly.

Roth made another tour of the chamber, pausing to look out the large window at the courtyard below. "Waiting until the evening meal might be a mistake. It gives Orlac time to learn we know of his subterfuge."

"Is it not more important to unmask him before the other rulers? Will that not be what makes the necessary impression?" Enaid responded gently.

"Yes, but dangerous should something go wrong. What make you of this...this imposter?"

Enaid shook her head. "I am not sure. No one in recent memory has ever seen a duplicate. All we have are the old tales."

Roth stopped pacing and looked at his wife. "What tales?"

"My mother passed on the tales in my fourteenth year when I returned from school as is custom. It is said that the dark circle has the magic to create duplicates from nothing—they can produce an exact double, grown in some sort of a vat."

Roth stared at his wife. In the twenty-four years he had been planet side...in all the time since he had returned to Earth, he had seen no evidence of the science he had left behind three millennia ago. Solomon Roth, the former science officer of a starship, exhaled slowly. "They are called clones. They are full human beings, grown from a single cell belonging to the original."

He paused to see their reactions. With the exception of Enaid, they showed varying stages of shock, surprise, and disbelief and he knew it was time for explanations.

With a sibilant exhalation, Roth sat next to his wife. "It was roughly three thousand years ago. In the calendar we used it was the year twenty-one thirty-six, and the world was wrapped in turmoil. Those whom you call the Dark Ones had increased its war with the rest of the world. They'd unleashed weapons of such power that a single explosion could kill hundreds of thousands of people at once, and they unleashed many of these weapons, killing hundreds of millions of people. The end of our world was approaching and I—with a hundred and ninety-nine other men and women, untouched by the radiation that was changing everyone—was sent to a starship, and charged with the saving of what was left of humanity. I alone survived the journey..."

An hour after Roth had begun his tale, he fell silent. Nosaj looked at Roth, and then at the others. "It is incomprehensible. I had no idea. So much death and hatred, for what?"

Roth pulled his strained features into a shadow of a smile. "What other reason could there be but power and control over others, the ability to force their views and beliefs on everyone else. It has always been so, since the beginning of time. They used what they called religion to make people believe in what they believed, and when there were enough believers, they set about making everyone else in the world a believer, too. But first, they had to conquer those who did not believe. They are the ones who created the world we now live in."

"So it seems," Nosaj agreed. "But at least I think I understand a little more—I need time to absorb it all. It is..."

"Hard, I know. But it is the truth nonetheless."

"The problem is," Areenna said, having a similarly hard time with everything she was hearing, "if someone is controlling this dupli…ah, clone, what will happen when it is unmasked?"

Wondering and amazed at how this barely eighteen year old woman-child was able to handle everything he had spoken of, Roth stared at Areenna for several seconds before turning to Enaid, "Your thoughts?"

"It will not be simple, but with Areenna's aid, we will be able to control it. Areenna and I will work out the method."

"Good enough. Mikaal, you are recovered from the fight with that thing?"

Mikaal looked at his father, a smile tugged at one corner of his mouth. "I am, father, and looking forward to more."

"Do not be so eager," Roth said. "What you found today was but a taste of their power. You have no idea how potent the dark ones can be. No idea! What used to be a world filled with people of all beliefs, of all races and colors is gone because of their need for control. We are the last…we are one people and the single remaining obstacle to them, and have been for many millennia. We are the only ones who can keep humanity alive."

He broke the stare with his son and turned to the others. "I suggest we rest before the meal. We will need all our strength. Nosaj, we will arrange the seating so you will sit next to Olrac. He looked at Enaid. "Talk with your mother. Have her, your father, and Darb stay with the others at all times. We need ears within the council."

Leaning against the balustrade of the highest ramparts of Tolemac, Areenna stared at the horizon. Her mind twisted and turned with the memory of the battle fought that afternoon. She'd had no idea what they would be facing when she and Mikaal had ridden through the gates, but when the fight ended, she had become aware of the vast power of her enemy.

What Roth had said about the dark circle and their powers was true, but after reviewing the battle for the twentieth time, she knew that not even Roth grasped the full depth of the power of the dark circle.

A chill ran through her. She shuddered and hugged herself. A moment later, Gaalrie landed on the balustrade and sidled over to her, talons clicking along the surface. The giant bird looked into her eyes, and then rested its head upon her shoulder. Calmness followed the bird's gesture and Areenna took a deep breath.

Ten minutes later, when the sun touched the horizon, Areenna sent Gaalrie to search the area around Tolemac before releasing her to hunt.

While Gaalrie swept the area from above, Areenna barely saw what the bird was seeing; rather, a picture of Mikaal floated before her mind's eye. Too handsome for his own good, she thought, but after having his mind open to her she knew his beauty affected him not at all.

When she'd touched his mind, she had immediately known he was different from any other man or boy. He possessed a mental strength far surpassing others. As far as she could tell, vanity held no sway—she now knew that his carefree attitude was but a façade to protect others from knowing he was different from them.

That she liked him, she could not deny, but how much she was hesitant to even consider. What she did know, was how well his power had complemented hers.

A tug in her mind pulled her from her thoughts. Gaalrie had finished her scouting and all was clear. *Thank you sister, go to the night,* Areenna whispered in her mind before leaving the parapet's walkway to return to her chamber and prepare for evening meal.

Downstairs, she found her bath was waiting and a single handmaid standing in readiness. She disrobed and stepped into the bath, sank into its warm waters and leaned back. She closed her eyes and exhaled gently.

Tossing aside the towel she used to dry herself, Enaid looked into the high mirror. What she saw both pleased and disturbed her. She was finally showing the signs of her age: there were silver strands threading through the deep raven of her hair; lines radiated outward from the corners of her eyes, but they were not too deep; and yet, the skin of her face and neck was more like a woman in her second decade than her fourth.

"It is time, My Lady," said her personal maid, as Enaid sat in a chair off to one side of the bath.

Enaid nodded. "Leave me for a few minutes," she commanded. When the chamber door shut, Enaid closed her eyes and settled back in the small chair. She cleared her mind of all thought and built a mind picture of Areenna.

Enaid knew Areenna was the one. Knew the young woman was the one Roth has been waiting for. *But do I tell him it will be this wonderful child, or do I wait for him to discover it for himself?*

She exhaled and settled her mind. She would wait to see what developed. *And Mikaal?* She knew that Mikaal was involved, completely and had been since the moment he was born twenty years before, yet she had to admit she had been blind to his powers. But now that she was aware of them, fear struck deeply into her. The danger to Mikaal was unimaginable. If anyone should learn of his abilities... She cast away the thought, but the fear stayed.

And Areenna? Enaid was proud that Areenna had not only handled the threatening darkness, but had been able to accept and deal with what she had learned today of Roth and Mikaal; yet, because of her own powers, Enaid knew only too well that Areenna faced so much more. And, to speak of it now would be unfair to Areenna at this point in time.

Musicians played softly in the background. The level of conversation was high, but with so many talking at the same time, most was unintelligible to those not part of the individual conversations.

The council had entered the chamber ten minutes earlier and everyone was present with the exception of Duke Yermon. Roth and his queen, Enaid, sat in their chairs: Mikaal as his father's second, his chair at the same level as his father's.

Roth surveyed the room, satisfied all were seated and in conversation. He looked toward Olrac, who was talking with King Nomis of Fainhall. Roth wondered how Nomis was so completely unaware that Olrac was not the man he had known for so many years.

Roth looked at his wife who nodded imperceptibly. He stood at her signal, knowing Enaid had summoned Yermon to the chamber. Roth stood and raised his wine goblet. "To my loyal Council," he said in a deep and strong voice, "with my thanks for answering my summons."

The council members, kings only, raised their glasses high and drank. An instant later a page entered, came over to Roth, and whispered in his ear. Roth nodded.

When the page left, he turned to Olrac with a smile. "Good news, your Highness, your brother is just arrived. Duke Yermon will be here in a moment."

From the expression on the face of the cloned version of Olrac, the thing was taken by surprise, but covered it quickly. Roth doubted any but those aware had seen anything.

Roth sat just as the doors opened and Duke Yermon entered the chamber. He was still dressed in his traveling clothing, as if he had just ridden in rather than having been outside the walls for hours. Yermon went directly to Roth and bowed.

"Welcome," Roth said. "It is good to see you, old friend."

"And you, Highness," Yermon responded, before going to his seat.

Roth watched him carefully as did Enaid, Mikaal, Nosaj and Areenna, all waiting to see if the clone would react. When he didn't, Yermon, as he had been coached by Enaid, went to his seat, smiled at his brother and sat in the chair of Advisor.

Timed to perfection, as Yermon sat, the serving doors opened and a stream of servers entered, carrying trays of steaming broth for the first course.

Observing as everything unfolded, Areenna caught a dark emotion escape the clone. Surprise, shaded with a touch of fear, shot from the man, its putrid texture akin to rotting meat.

She glanced at Enaid and saw her cousin's eyes widen. *Be ready,* came the command, but it was unnecessary as Areenna had already begun to build the powers within her. Her blood raced through her veins, yet her heart, instead of speeding faster, had slowed. Low in her belly, the heat of her power was released. Her senses went acute; she heard every sound in the room including the cricket in the far corner between each heartbeat. The power burning deep within her built stronger.

She watched Yermon and Olrac. The duke's timing had to be perfect or they could not protect him. Within her chest and abdomen there was a whirling—a sign of danger about to happen.

Gaalrie's mind melded with hers and she saw a dark creature flying high above Tolemac. *Protect*, she commanded her aoutem. She sensed Enaid commanding her gorlon to do the same if necessary.

Yermon stood, knocking his chair backwards and pointing at Olrac. "Olrac you are not! Who are you?" he demanded, his voice echoing through the chamber.

The room went silent. Every eye turned to the duke.

"Are you mad?" Olrac the clone challenged. "Have you lost your wits, Brother?"

"You are no brother to me! Where is my brother? What have you done with him?" he demanded, grasping the hilt of his dagger, but not yet drawing it.

"Madness," the clone shouted in a voice as loud as Yermon's. He turned to Roth. "My Lord, my brother has become mad. You must help me."

When Roth stood, a powerful, dark force shot downward at him. Instinctively, Areenna released the power she had built up and sent it swirling around the high king. At the same instant, she sensed Enaid fighting the darkness above. Outside the castle walls, Gaalrie attacked the dark bird-like wraith from above it.

The force Areenna resisted was powerful and filled with such darkness it threatened to make her sick. Yet she held herself strong and fought back the retched darkness attacking the high king, building her powers and herself to greater heights.

Then, as clear as if it were noon and she was watching the fight, she saw Gaalrie strike the creature in the center of its back. The dark bird-like thing screamed in rage, but did not stop trying to fight through Areenna's defense of Roth.

Protect Yermon! Enaid's thought hit her hard. She started to withdraw from Roth but stopped when Mikaal joined her and added his strength to hers as he had that afternoon, allowing her to protect Roth and, at the same time, Yermon, spreading her shielding powers around him like an invisible ball.

Above the keep, the dark creature turned and grabbed Gaalrie, its talons searching for a death grip. *Hold,* Enaid commanded the instant Areenna's powers faltered. Areenna solidified her defenses, watching helplessly as the huge dark bird's claws sank into her aoutem's flesh. Together the two giant birds battled, plummeting toward the ground at a speed she knew would kill Gaalrie.

Hold, Enaid repeated, and Areenna did. Her fear for her aoutem grew frantic until a burst of power, unlike anything she had ever experienced grew within her. Holding Roth and Yermon safe, she released the energy as she would have an arrow, and sent it directly at the creature.

Gaalrie broke free and stopped her fall. The dark creature hit the earth hard, but Areenna saw that—impossibly—the creature still lived. She pushed herself harder and used her power to pin the wraith to the ground. While Gaalrie circled above it, and as Areenna held the creature down, Enaid's gorlon launched itself in a huge leap and fell upon the dark beast, its large fangs and powerful claws ripping it to shreds.

At the same time the gorlon attacked the wraith, the clone pulled a dagger from its vestments and charged Yermon. Mikaal leaned forward, his arm drawn back. Before the clone could reach Yermon, he released the dagger he held.

Exactly as it had in Areenna's vision, the dagger flew true and landed in the clone's neck, severing its spine. Blood spewed everywhere—the clone crashed to the floor inches from the duke.

Pandemonium erupted. Roth stood and shouted above the noise until silence returned. "My Lords, be seated so I may explain."

The council members and their staff reseated themselves and Roth spoke. His voice was low, but could be clearly heard. The corners of his mouth were turned down. The distaste on his face easy to read.

"What you have just witnessed was the power of the dark ones. They have grown stronger, as you can see. That *thing,*" he said, pointing to the unmoving body of the clone, "was not King Olrac; rather, it was a duplicate of Olrac, made by the dark forces who want nothing less than to control everyone here and everyone who walks this earth. Do you now better understand what we spoke of this morning? Do you understand why the only way to remain strong and free is by standing together, without infighting and petty jealousies; by protecting not only our own lands, but the lands of our neighbors; and, finally, by honoring the treaties we have made with each other. If you fail in this, we are all doomed."

"Are we not already doomed?" King Namron of Aldimor demanded, pointing to the clone. "If they can do this, what cannot they do?"

Areenna saw Enaid begin to rise, and watched Roth put a gently restraining hand on her shoulder. "They cannot overpower us as long as we stand together and stay strong. Did you not see how we, not *they*, have ruled the day?"

"Only by the luck of his brother recognizing the imposter was not Olrac."

"Luck played no part in this: the imposter was recognized days ago. The duke was advised to come here instead of sitting his brother's throne for the purpose of unmasking this deception before the council. You all needed to see how strong the danger to us and to all of Nevaeh has become."

While this was going on, much was happening. The body of Olrac was removed and the floor cleaned even as Roth spoke. Yermon moved into the seat the clone had occupied and Areenna was regaining her strength from her second battle of the day.

"May I suggest we have our meal, spend the rest of the evening at peace, and resume the council in the morning, after we have had a night to rest and think on the events of this day?"

Roth turned to the musicians and commanded them with a nod. They began to play, and more food was brought into the chamber. It took a while, but the mood, although more somber, picked up and conversation began to grow.

And while the rulers talked amongst themselves, Areenna looked toward Enaid, who nodded a single time. *Well done, Areenna, well done.*

CHAPTER 8

HALF CURVED ALONG the edge of a cushion, Areenna was pressed into the corner of a large chair. Sleep had become impossible as the scene from the dining chamber kept repeating over and over.

Still tasting the sour revulsion of the clone's darkness, Areenna could not stop wondering just how darkly powerful was this force she seemed destined to fight. If such a thing as the wraith could be so powerful, what could be said of its masters? With that thought, she remembered Enaid's words: 'The wraith was controlled by a powerful woman; it could not act by itself'.

She rose and paced the bedchamber. *What about me? Why is this happening now?* Mixed with the fearful thoughts of the dark powers was an awareness of the incredible difference in her powers from the moment Mikaal had joined her mental battle.

While there had been a synergy between them earlier in the forest bordering Tolemac, what had happened in the dining hall defied description. Aided by Mikaal, her powers had grown inconceivably strong during the battle. But now, hours after he had withdrawn from her mind, she still held the changes within her and tasted new strengths as well.

She rose and went to the bed where her robe lay in disarray. Putting it on and moving quietly so as not to disturb the sleeping maid, Areenna left the bedchamber and descended to the empty circular garden in the center of the keep. The slant of the moon told her it was two hours before dawn. In a keep such as Tolemac she thought herself lucky to be alone.

Walking slowly around the gardens, she did her best to concentrate on what was happening within her. Intuition told her she must get used to this new power by learning what it was and what its limits were.

She would no longer take anything for granted—that was the lesson she had gained from her original vision with Duke Yermon. In the vision, when she had seen the dagger flying toward Olrac, she had assumed it meant Olrac was in danger. But reality proved far different. It was an important lesson, and one she must remember.

Stopping near the center of the garden, which was illuminated by the fading moon and the multitude of stars afloat in the cloudless sky, Areenna gazed at the fountain built in the exact center of the castle keep. The simply carved fountain was fed by a deep underwater spring and it was the force of the spring that pushed water to the top, where it spilled over the edges in a constant waterfall.

Staring at the cascading water, she found herself tracing the water back to its origination, though she had no idea how she did this. Her only awareness was of being drawn into the blue crystal liquid. Then she was moving—floating above the swiftly rushing current and moving through the underground passage.

She followed the fresh, cool water and, rising with it, she sped upward to the surface of Nevaeh, where it opened into a woodlands river for a thousand yards before dipping back into the earth. The water's path led her to mountains hundreds of miles away. When the churning and now raging river disappeared into the base of a large mountain, she was carried upward by the underground river to rise lava-like in a volcano shaft until she reached the snow covered peak and emerged into the moonlit night.

Bodiless yet fully aware of herself and everything around her, Areenna saw the edge of the world from the mountain top and the first bands of day beginning to chase the black sky away.

She floated calmly above the mountain, staring in the direction of Tolemac, and breathing in the feeling of wonder before her—until a hand fell on her shoulder.

The vision shattered, she gasped and spun, only to find herself face to face with Mikaal.

"Pardon, Princess, I meant not to startle you."

Areenna took a slow calming breath. "I was…. It is all right," she whispered.

"You were elsewhere," Mikaal said, concern obvious in his gold-flecked gray eyes.

"I was…in the mountains," she said and then let a low laugh slip from between her lips.

Mikaal smiled. "Was it a good trip?"

Areenna laughed. "A trip by mind only…but it was such a journey…" Her last words were barely audible.

"You were strong this evening. I have never seen such a thing before. What you did…"

"We, Mikaal. Without your willing help I could not—"

His brows knit. "You have no idea do you?"

"Idea?"

"I did not push myself to you, I…I wouldn't know how. It was you. You brought me into your mind."

"That's not possible," she whispered.

His eyes searched her face for a moment before he smiled. "Then the impossible has happened. Areenna, I am not unhappy by what was done. It felt right, and you took nothing for which I would have withheld permission."

She closed her eyes and thought back to the moment she'd felt Mikaal's presence. She replayed it within her mind's eye and found the exact moment she thought he'd joined her in the battle. She had reached out to him and he had opened himself to her. It was not so much a matter of her taking from him; rather, it was a gift offered freely.

"I see it now," she nodded. "We must be careful about this."

Mikaal nodded. "Of course we must be careful not to show what is happening."

Areenna shook her head, "No, it is more. We must be careful together. This is a dangerous thing we do. It can become a trap for us—a dependence that weakens us."

"That would not be possible. You are too strong."

Areenna held back a startled laugh. "Too strong? I am an eighteen year old novice—nothing more. We must be careful!"

"As you wish," he said. He placed his hands on her shoulders. "But Areenna, what happened between us, twice now, I sense it is right. And your age has no meaning for what you do or who you are."

She stared at him, his hands were firm and warm even through the material of her robe. "We must give ourselves time," she said, turning from beneath his hands. "Will I see you at the morning meal?"

Mikaal smiled at her. "You may count on it." With that he departed the garden, leaving Areenna alone once again. She sank to a carved stone bench and again gazed deeply at the fountain's freely falling water.

What else have I gained from today's battles?

The southern coast of Nevaeh was warm this morning, the waves crashing against the high palisades echoed throughout the coast. Three thousand years after the fall of the nuclear bombs in Europe and South America, the Southern and Southeastern coastlines resembled nothing of their origins. There were no expanses of beach, rather the shifting of the earth's plates from the massive explosions caused earthquakes thousands of miles from the explosions and had brought enormous changes to the coastlines, which now resembled the high palisades of the Northeastern coast.

And within the haze of the forbidden areas, which led to the palisades, were the wastelands where those who chose life without a dominion or who turned from the rule of Nevaeh and its domains came for shelter. They neither felt nor sensed the darkness that was part of this neglected land, nor did they feel the dark presence infiltrate their minds. If they had, they would have thrown themselves from the highest cliffs, for the creature dwelling there controlled all.

But now this evil entity, the body of which used to be a woman of power, was recovering from the battle *she* had fought in distant Tolemac. While *she* mentally licked the wounds inflicted by the two *she* had battled outside and then inside of Tolemac, *her* misshapen limbs—one of which was but a remnant of an arm—trembled with rage while *she* stood above the body of the King *she* had taken and replaced with the clone delivered by *her* masters.

She placed a twisted hand upon her breast as *she* continued to glare at Olrac's body. *She* had spent years studying the King named Olrac, learning his mannerisms—the way he talked; the way he thought; and, when *she* was ready, *she* had awakened the duplicate and trained it perfectly.

Every bone in Olrac's body was broken, shattered by the thing's insane rage, for *she* knew *her* masters across the ocean would extract a terrible penalty for *her* failure. But until such an event happened, *she* was determined to succeed, no matter the cost. *She* had no choice, for *she* had been created with only one purpose in mind, to conquer and subjugate every living soul coming before her.

She turned from the dead king's body to look north, toward Tolemac and the hated Roth. And then one of the last living remnants of the Circle's dark powers in Nevaeh turned and went into the cave.

The council ended at midafternoon when the Kings reaffirmed their treaties with each other and the rulers of the dominions prepared to leave. Only the delegation from Freemorn remained. After the other processions had departed Tolemac, Areenna, and Queen Enaid left the balcony and descended to the courtyard.

From there, they mounted their waiting kraals and departed the keep through the North gate, and rode toward a secluded place within the surrounding woodlands. Three quarters of an hour after passing through the gates of Tolemac, Enaid turned off the main roadway and onto a seldom used path. Areenna was taken by the beauty of the area.

A hundred yards further along the path their way was blocked by a solid and impenetrable wall of trees and vines so thickly interlaced, no light shone through. It was as if the vegetation had been painted upon a canvass.

Enaid halted her kraal and dismounted. Irii, her white gorlon came next to her. Taking the kraal's reins, she tied it to the bole of a young pine and motioned for Areenna to do the same.

With their mounts secured, Enaid led Areenna to a spot a dozen feet away. She stepped forward and disappeared into the solid wall of vines and trees with Irii, at her side. Areenna stared at the living wall, drew in a breath, and followed, unsure of exactly what she was doing. The wall of vines stopped her.

"See yourself walking through the vines," instructed Enaid in a gentle voice from the other side.

Closing her eyes and following her mentor's instructions, she built a picture of herself walking through the vines and then followed her mind's picture. One deep breath later she stepped through the barricade and opened her eyes.

And gasped. She stood in a field of grass and flowers, surrounded by a circle of trees, their branches and vines as thickly interwoven within as they had been on the other side. To her right was an oval pond, perhaps thirty yards across, its water sparkled iridescently in the midday sun. Gaalrie flew above the meadow.

"Wonderful isn't it?" Enaid asked with a hint of a smile.

Arms outstretched, Areenna spun in a circle. For the first time since arriving in Tolemac, her mind and body were calm and relaxed. Both the evil she had fought and the haunting story of Roth's origins were gone from her thoughts. Completing the circle, she faced Enaid and whispered, "Magnificent."

"This used to be part of Brumwall, my father's realm. When the ten agreed to be governed by a High King, I made sure Roth annexed this part of Brumwall into Tolemac's region." Enaid paused for a breath.

"When I was barely seventeen, my mother taught me how to create a haven. At first I didn't understand why I would need such a place, but as time progressed and I found myself in deep battle at my mate's side, I learned the true purpose of my haven.

Enaid reached out and stroked the younger woman's cheek. She graced Areenna with a warm and maternal smile. "Its sole purpose is to renew oneself after battle, or when you are tired and weary of things weighing upon you from day to day life. It is the one place no man or woman can enter without permission, and not even a woman of power can enter here unbidden."

"You will teach me?" Areenna asked.

"When we have the time, but for now I fear we will be much too busy. In the meantime, I have set my haven to respond to you should you need it."

Areenna was overwhelmed by the gift. "I…"

"Hush, disrobe and join me in the pond," Enaid said and stepped out of her clothing and walked to the edge of the pond where she dove into the waiting waters and disappeared. She surfaced in the center of the pond and treaded water while she watched Areenna follow her, observing her carefully.

The young woman was tall, her body muscular yet feminine with full breasts and gently flaring hips. Her thighs and calves were perfectly formed, the long muscles beneath her skin shifted smoothly with each step. Softly nut shaded skin gleamed in the sunlight, a stark contrast to her long pale blonde hair.

Is she ready? Enaid knew the answer, but wished it were not so. Areenna would be ready when the time came, not because of any training, but because there would be no choice. Without her, not just Tolemac, but all of Nevaeh would fall. *Without her and Mikaal,* Enaid amended, understanding the bond created between them yesterday, and she was afraid.

The instant she entered the cool water of the pond, Areenna felt a tingle race through her. When she broke the surface, she gasped for the second time in five minutes. The water affected her as much as the entrance into Enaid's haven.

"I… This is the same water as the fountain in Tolemac," she said, remembering her mind trip through the underground river to the mountain top in the north.

Enaid's brow furrowed. "How could you know?"

"I could feel it. How did you call it here?"

"With a formula my mother taught me. It is called a divining. In times past when there was drought, this formula was used to find water and draw it to the surface." Enaid paused to stare openly at Areenna. "I knew not where this underground stream came from, only that it was there."

"It comes from north and west. I was there today."

"I knew I was right," Enaid whispered aloud without realizing it.

"About what?"

"I will explain, but not today. Come, we have much to talk about," she ordered and swam to the edge of the pond, her toes digging into the smooth silt bottom. Turning to Areenna, she leaned her back against the moss on the side of the pond and said, "In the coming months much will be asked of you. I sense the evil from across the seas is readying to attack. Yesterday was a test of our strengths and weaknesses."

"A test? If it was only a test, what more can we expect?"

Enaid's eyes narrowed. "Everything! Anything! If you try to 'expect' something specific, you will not be prepared to face the reality. Rather than expect, be prepared. Be ready for anything at any moment of the day or night. Be ready awake or asleep. Allow your senses to become aware at all times. Roth once told me of an old soldier's expression from where he came. 'Expect the unexpected and be always prepared'."

"I don't understand. How can I be prepared when I sleep?"

"Have you never been awakened by a sense of something not right?" Enaid asked as she sat up.

Areenna nodded.

"Then you must remember the feeling and use it." Enaid placed her forefinger on the very center of Areenna's forehead. "Use your powers. Concentrate on my finger and remember the feeling of being awakened."

Doing as Enaid asked, she thought back to a night a few weeks earlier and drew upon the feeling that had awakened her. *Yes*, Enaid whispered within her mind. *Now hold onto that and build it thusly*, she instructed, whispering a formula she used to set this sensory guard.

"Good," Enaid said aloud. "And now we must speak of Mikaal."

"Mikaal," Areenna echoed, making a puzzled face, a slight shade of red deepening her tanned mocha skin.

Enaid laughed so suddenly her gorlon rose and growled at the trees before it. "Easy," she whispered to it. The gorlon mewed gently.

"Why do you laugh?" Areenna asked.

"My apologies. I..." Enaid could not contain herself and started to laugh again. When she finished, and had taken several deep breaths. "You do not know, do you?"

"I don't understand."

Enaid drew Areenna to her. "I know you don't, sweet one, but you will. We must train Mikaal," she said as she released the younger woman, saying only part of what she knew would one day occur.

Caught off guard by Enaid's statement, Areenna said, "Train him? How?"

A frown wrinkled Enaid's brow. "I'm not sure. There has never been a man with abilities. You have seen into him. You will have to decide how."

"That's not possible. I'm not fully trained myself."

"Ah, dear Areenna, now you know the true secret of us women. None of us is ever fully trained. We learn as we age. We find our abilities and our boundaries—as you will one day. After a certain point only you can train yourself."

Areenna held her mentor's gaze for several seconds before lowering her eyes and saying, "You need to know I can not only sense his powers." She raised her eyes to Enaid. "But when we combine, it…it is unlike anything I have ever experienced. I have merged with Mikaal twice and each time my power…"

Enaid waited for perhaps a dozen heartbeats, but when Areenna did not finish, and with no little trepidation, she asked, "What happened to your power?"

"It became stronger. Not just during the fight, but it has stayed so."

Enaid stared at the young woman, whose hair rippled in shining waves across her shoulders and young breasts before it dipped into the water. Enaid's heart began to pound as her mother's words came back to her. *'One day there will be child who will be so powerful nothing will be able to stand in her way. But before this can be, there must be another child, a complement to the first.'*

Enaid had struggled for years with this, wondering and questioning who the complement would be. She had known at the moment of Areenna's birth that she was the child her mother had spoken of, but she had never expected the complement to be Mikaal. *How could I have been so blind?* Yet, from deep within her subconscious came the awareness of what she had always known.

"Your power grew as it should," Enaid whispered. Then she shook off of her thoughts and smiled. "Come."

When they climbed out of the water, Enaid led them to an area of thickly carpeted grass, where she lay down and motioned Areenna to do the same. With the sun drying them, Enaid closed her eyes and told Areenna to do the same.

"You have done much these past few days," Enaid said. "How feel you about what happened?"

Areenna's breath slid from her on a long sigh. "Yes, a lot has happened. I feel…good about what was accomplished. But for those *things*, the clone, the first wraith and that…that flying monstrosity, I feel only disgust."

"It is natural, but it is also one of their defenses—to make you not want to touch their minds. Yet you must delve deeply into the feelings you had when you fought these things because within them are the keys to defeating those who will follow."

"What worse could there be?" Areenna asked. A second later she was answered by a mind picture of a twisted, ugly shape in horrendous and sickly proportions. The revulsion and disgust she'd felt in her earlier battles returned, only worse this time.

"No," she whispered fiercely, shaking her head and fighting to cast the vision from her mind.

"Yes!" Enaid half shouted. "This is part of what you will be facing—a small part! Stop fighting and see the pictures in your mind or you will be ill prepared to do battle with this black hearted she-snuck, this…this slithering poison fanged bitch!"

Areenna stopped fighting and let Enaid's mind settle within hers. *'Feel it, smell her rotting flesh, listen to her insane thoughts and learn who this enemy is—watch!'* Enaid commanded.

Areenna was sucked into the scene Enaid created. She began to experience strange and dreamlike sensations. Instinctively, Areenna knew she was seeing something from the past. Then, all thought faded and the picture formed into a smooth flow of Enaid's memories.

"Yes, child," came Enaid's far away whisper.

Lost in the memory, Areenna watched Roth stand at the head of his army, splendid in his unusual armor and holding his sword in a two handed grip, fighting as many of the enemy as he could reach while his troops engaged the dark army. The fighting was intense and the darkness was pushing the Nevaens back. She watched the dark army move in a pincer-like attack in an effort to cut Roth off from the main body of his army.

Then she saw Enaid, who had been standing off to the side, walk calmly through the fighting mass, her hands weaving patterns in the air, sending formulas outward and closing in toward her king. Areenna saw silver streams of light emanate from Enaid's palms, pulsing bands flowing in ever changing patterns, and watched the dark army part before her even as their soldiers surrounded Roth.

Enaid reached him and together they fought the black horde. Piles of the black dead grew about them, rivers of blood flowed. Roth's sword never slowed as it met armor, slicing through it as if into flesh and bone. Enaid's streaming light was no different than Roth's sword, cutting through the enemy troops, three and four at a time until the fighting ceased.

The atmosphere around Roth and Enaid turned cold. Above them rumbling black clouds gathered. Cold air flowed from the clouds and red lightening danced madly until the clouds themselves speared downward. Seconds later a huge, black and misshapen form grew from the swirling blackness and stood twenty feet in front of Roth and Enaid.

Twice the height of the King with broad, misshapen legs and long, dangling arms, it roared rage down at them. It took a moment for Areenna to realize exactly what she was seeing. The form, horrendous and deformed as it was, had once been a woman, evidenced by small sagging breasts and female genitalia.

She gagged, but could not stop the vision even if she wanted to. Slowly, the scene unfolded. The distorted woman stepped forward, red, glaring eyes fixed on the two small figures before her, one long arm upraised with the palm of a seven fingered hand directed at Roth. Enaid moved sideways just as the apparition sent a shower of reddish lightening toward him.

Raising both arms, palms forward, Enaid drew up a cone of white light and sent it directly at the red lightning. The light shimmered and then exploded when it met the red bolts.

The creature screamed in anger as she put even more force into her next volley. Her rage-fed attack began to push Enaid's barrier back. On the right, Areenna saw her father and mother pushing toward Roth and Enaid. They stopped within yards of the future high king where Areenna's mother knelt, raised her own palms toward Enaid and sent shafts of pale blue light at her cousin to reinforce and strengthen Enaid's power.

At that moment, Roth spun from behind Enaid, raced forward and, with his sword raised high, jumped into the air and sliced into the black witch's arm, severing it close to the elbow.

Releasing an unearthly howl, the misshapen creature turned to him.

When she did, Enaid sent a bolt of silver lightning at her head. In less than a heartbeat, the wounded creature dissolved into the mist it had come from and disappeared, leaving its army unprotected.

Two hours later, the dark army was defeated, its legions decimated with barely a few hundred left alive. The remnants of the dark army fled as fast as they could, returning to wherever they'd come from.

As swiftly as Enaid had entered Areenna's mind, she was gone. Areenna gasped, then opened her eyes and sat up. She hugged herself, feeling strangely cold beneath the warm sun. "I never imaged...the stories never—"

"Nor could they. Those who fought and lived on that day could never express the horror of what they'd fought. Your mother was the power that helped me to stave off that witch. But now you know what will come next and, Areenna, it grieves me deeply to tell you she is not the worst, not by your most wild imagining."

Areenna thought about the powers she had seen coming from both Enaid and her mother. Tears rose at the thought of her mother, but she forced them away. "The lightning? You used it both as a shield and as a weapon. How did you do so? I can build a wall of defense, but that..."

"By willpower. Stand," she said. When Areenna was on her feet Enaid pointed to a tall tree high above the tree barrier around them. "When you fought those things, you created a weapon. Do so now."

Areenna closed her eyes and called up her power. The familiar burning within her belly began and a moment later she held a glowing ball of white energy. Lifting her palm she sent it toward the treetop, where it exploded sending sparks and pieces of wood outward.

"Excellent, now feel yourself...thus," Enaid whispered and gently touched the same spot in her mind. "Now, instead of sending this against a single enemy, first expand it like a mushroom."

Areenna closed her eyes again, built the power and pictured a huge mushroom floating above them. Slowly, she set the mushroom down, surrounding her and Enaid within its stem.

"Perfect, now hold and draw more of your power into a weapon within the shield and release it, but do not release the shield."

Areenna followed her mentor's instruction and created another shimmering ball on her palms. She sent that ball into the shield and, with her eyes locked on the treetop, launched it without dropping the shield.

"Yes," Enaid whispered as more of the treetop exploded.

Areenna released the powers the instant Enaid spoke and sank slowly to the ground. She was exhausted, her entire body covered by a thin sheet of sweat. "Oh," was all she could whisper.

"Rest for a few minutes, we will do it over and over until it becomes easier."

Areenna looked at the Queen. "Will it?"

Enaid smiled. "It will come faster, and be easier to control, but it will never be easy."

"I will work more on this when I return to Freemorn," she said.

Enaid started to speak, but stopped as a familiar prickling tweaked in her mind. Her gaze turned intense upon Areenna. "Have you... Have you been having strange dreams? Dreams of a place hidden within mists and felt a call to enter the mists?"

"How could you know?" she whispered.

"When did this happen? What color was the mist?" Enaid asked, already knowing the answer, wishing more than anything that Areenna's mother still lived, for it was a mother's job to speak of what she must.

"Reddish, strange. I—it started two weeks ago."

Enaid raised her hand to Areenna's cheek. "Child," she whispered in a sad and low voice. "You are not to return to Freemorn. You are to go east. You must be tested and trained for what will soon be here."

"East," Areenna gasped. "I..."

"There is no choice child, not any longer. You are being called. It is your time."

CHAPTER 9

THE RETURN TO the keep was made in silence. Both Enaid and Areenna had much to think on. For Enaid it was simple, she had to prepare Areenna for what she would face. For Areenna, it was more difficult: she needed to steel her mind to what would happen next, although she was unsure she could do so.

Areenna was aware of how the East contained frightening visions for most of the people of Nevaeh. It had been from the East, according to the legends, where the horror that had encompassed their land began. It was also the area of greatest power for women.

She had heard the stories of how, for untold centuries, women who were born with abilities went to the East. Many of them returned, others did not. Areenna knew there was something there, which either made one stronger or took one to its bosom, but no one ever knew what happened to those who did not return, for it was always a solitary journey when women went east.

Areenna's thoughts weighed heavily, bringing back a long forgotten conversation with her mother. It was shortly after she'd found Gaalrie and had been nursing the treygone into the beautiful adult it would one day be. Her mother had come to her at bedtime and explained that since she had found her aoutem, they would move to the next level of training. In the same talk, her mother had also told her how one day she would make a journey to the East, for such a journey would be an important part of her future.

Four years later, riding alongside the high queen of Nevaeh, she recalled the conversation and was filled with melancholy at how her mother had been able to see the future so clearly, yet not see the terrible end that would befall her two years later.

"What is it child?" Enaid asked, breaking their silence just before reaching Tolemac. "I sense much sadness coming from you."

Areenna forced a smile. "A memory of my mother. And Enaid, I am no longer a child."

Enaid laughed. "No, *child*," she said in emphasis, "but you will always be a child to me—you and my son. It is the right of a parent, and as far as I am concerned, you are as much a daughter to me, as your mother was far more a sister than cousin."

Areenna bowed her head in response.

Enaid smiled. "Tell me, Areenna, what memory of your mother brought on this sadness."

The use of her name rather than the endearment did not escape her. "It was a few days after I had found Gaalrie. My mother told me how, one day, I would go to the East. That is all."

Enaid stared at her; the silver motes within her green eyes cast off a low glow in the late afternoon sun. "There's more. You're angry as well because she left you."

"Yes, how could she know what would happen to me years after she died, yet not see her own death coming so soon?"

Enaid gazed at Areenna in silence and, after a few moments said, "I had never given it much thought. We...I never look to see such things for myself. It is unwise to look in that direction, but your mother was a powerful sorceress and she had an uncanny ability to foresee true—her ability was much stronger than my own. Yet," Enaid said with a shake of her head, "I think she would not want to know about her own death, as I would not either. It would shadow everything she would do from that point onward. Do you understand?"

Areenna nodded. "It was just a memory." Then she looked into the distance as another memory surfaced. When she grasped its entirety, she looked at Enaid. "My mother must have had some idea of what was coming. Why else would she have begun my training when I was only nine?"

"Of that, I cannot say, other than she had much reason. But, Areenna, I am certain you will handle the East with the same strength that you have handled everything since you came of age."

Areenna did not reply; she was not so certain.

◇◇◇

"Father, we need to speak."

Nosaj who had watched his daughter dismount her kraal in the courtyard below turned from the window. He enjoyed the familiar rush of warmth and love her entry always brought. She was so much like her mother there were times his eyes tricked him into thinking she was the only woman he had ever loved—it was not that he did not love his daughter fiercely, just differently.

"The princess returns," he joked.

"She does," Areenna replied and Nosaj was instantly aware of something wrong.

"What happened?"

Areenna spent the next twenty minutes telling him about the afternoon and her training before saying, "Enaid shared a vision with me. It was of the final battle of the war, when you and mother went to Roth and Enaid's aid and helped to defeat that terrible creature."

When she paused, Nosaj experienced something he'd never before felt. The low edge of her anger directed toward him.

"Why have you never told me about the final battle you and Mother fought?"

"Why would we? Your mother and I made a decision we believed correct. What need was there of telling you about something no longer important? The war was over, the enemy defeated."

Areenna closed her eyes for a second before pinning her father with a glare. "No Father, you and mother were wrong. Not only did you deny me the knowledge of what you did, of the strength and of the deeds of the parents to whom I have been born, but you left me unprepared for what I have to face. You need to know the enemy was not defeated. Who do you think we battled in the forest when we went to protect Duke

Yermon? No Father, the war is not over and it seems I have been chosen to play some part in this."

"What do you mean?" A sensation of dread built within him.

"Enaid says I must go to the East, I have to go there to be trained further."

It took Nosaj a moment to recover. He knew of women who, unlike his wife, had gone to the East and never returned. "Then Enaid will be going with you?"

"No. Enaid must remain here. Mikaal will be going with me."

"Mikaal?" Startled displeasure was strong in his voice.

"Mikaal. He too must be trained."

The time following the evening meal was filled with preparations and meetings—between Nosaj and Roth, between Enaid and Areenna, then Mikaal, Areenna, and Enaid, then Roth and Mikaal. The first of these meetings began an hour after the evening meal. Nosaj had climbed the inner stairwell to the upper parapets hoping to be alone for a few minutes in an effort to digest everything that had happened since he'd left Freemorn.

It was not easy, for he was having strong doubts about himself and his high king. The strange unveiling of who Roth was had been hard to accept, but learning of Mikaal's powers had been more difficult. On top of those things, knowing the King's son and his daughter—his only child and all that remained of his wife—were about to leave for the East tugged harshly on his thoughts. He could not stop himself from wondering how such unexpected happenings came about.

"Nosaj," called Roth, tearing Nosaj from his reverie.

"My, Lord," Nosaj responded with a bow.

"Come, walk with me my friend." Linking arms with Nosaj, he started forward.

Roth was very aware of how on edge Nosaj had been since the women returned to the keep. The tension had grown even thicker during the evening meal when Enaid had explained more of what was needed. Mikaal had stayed wisely and unusually silent, even distant from the arguments that had followed.

"While we seem to have no choice as to what our children must do, we do have a choice in what we shall be doing. Nosaj, war is coming again to devastate our lands. We must be prepared for what Enaid believes will happen. She has foreseen this war coming and the parts our children must play. But, old friend, it is up to us to prepare ourselves and the dominions for the coming war."

"Do you believe the others will join us?"

"They will join us or fall, but we won't be able to tell them what is about to happen until Areenna and Mikaal return from the East. Those who choose not to join with us...who fall because of their short sightedness, they... Let us hope there will be but few."

"With luck," Nosaj half whispered.

Roth shook his head. "Luck will not play a factor. It will be they who determine their future. My friend," Roth said, putting his hand on Nosaj's shoulder and squeezing gently, "I can tell you this with a clear and open heart—your daughter was born to this. Your wife knew it even if she did not tell you of it, or perhaps she could not because of her premature passing."

"But the dangers of the East to them both..."

"No," Roth said, still holding the King of Freemorn's shoulder. "I have been told Areenna's powers are second to none, and with Mikaal, her power has somehow increased. If anyone in our world can go to the East and return, it will be your daughter. Your wife knew this, for she told Areenna so years ago. Enaid, too, explained all to me when she returned this afternoon. She also told me we have perhaps, a year at the most before the vileness comes at us. The Circle of the Afzal will attack within a year."

"The Circle of...what is that?" a puzzled Nosaj asked.

"I am sorry my friend, I've forgotten myself. You call them the dark circle, but when *they* first started to attack the world, in my time, they were known as terrorists—people who destroyed what others had built and they had as many names as they did factions. But by the twenty-second century they had found a leader who brought them together. From that merging they began to call themselves the Unified Circle of the Middle East. Over the next few years, as their power and reign of terror grew, their name changed to the Circle of Afzal, named after their leader Afzal Mahmud Tarek. But to those of us who remained opposed to them and their horrors, we named them the Circle of Evil, and our name proved to be correct, for they were abominable and evil as they rained death upon the world. Now you call them the dark circle. But whatever name is put upon them, they remain the embodiment of evil.

"What they unleashed changed everything. It changed who we are and who our women have become and it changed them, too. It turned them into physical and mental horrors. Their dark powers are so potent..." He stopped and reined in his emotions before going on. "They have only one driving need—to conquer the world and make us into their images. Stopping them is what I will die for rather than allow such depravity to overtake Nevaeh. I have not travelled through three-millennia to allow them to destroy our world!"

"My Lord, I understand what you're saying, but there are not enough of them in Nevaeh to make war upon us," Nosaj said confidently.

Roth gave his friend's shoulder another gentle squeeze. "In one of Enaid's visions, she saw a great fleet of ships being built. They will bring tens of thousands of their warriors across the sea."

Startled, Nosaj stared with disbelief at Roth. "But this is impossible. The waters are too treacherous."

"Believe me, this will happen. It matters not to them how many ships or men might be lost, all they care about is conquering Nevaeh, for we represent everything they stand against. They will be here, and if we do not prepare, we will fall." Roth paused, deep in thought before he said, "They are vastly different from us. Their mutations are horrible, caused by the radiation they unleashed. Their men and women are more like wild, misbegotten animals. Yet, at the highest level, the leaders of these repulsive people have mutated as well, both physically and mentally. Like our women, their powers are very strong, but only as long as they can draw life energy from others."

"Here, in Nevaeh, before the radiation could affect everyone, the scientists of my time created a defense to help fight off the worst of its effects, and the mutations in Nevaeh are vastly different. Instead of becoming misshapen, the men grew stronger and our women gained wonderful abilities. And these special abilities, this magic as you call it, is what has and will protect Nevaeh from *them*."

Roth paused to breathe. "But this time it will be Areenna and

Mikaal who will have to find the way to lead us."

"But we have defeated the Circle. They are weak."

Roth raised his eyebrows. "When I first began to gather armies to fight them, they were overconfident. In the years we fought them, I used that weakness against them. What allowed us to win was their belief Nevaeh could not be united. In their arrogance, they refused to consider it possible for us to defeat their sorceresses and the armies they had built from both our exiles and those of Nevaeh who had physical mutations."

"They know fully their mistake. They erred because they believed Nevaeh too weak to stand against them. They did not know about me until it was too late. Enaid and I, you and Inaria were the forces that stopped them once we had all the kingdoms behind us. As far as we know, all but one of their dark sorceresses was destroyed. But they have had fourteen years to prepare, and this time the mutated masters of Dark Powers and their black sorceresses and their hordes of misshapen beasts will come themselves. If we are not ready for them, we will be defeated and the last of humanity will be wiped from Nevaeh."

Nosaj remained silent for a long time, grateful for Roth's accompanying silence. When he at last took a deep breath he said, "Then there is no choice but to allow Areenna to go on this...journey."

Roth laughed. The sound was loud and crisp. "Allow? Accept would be a better word. Do you truly believe we have ever had a choice? Know you not the powers of our women?" Roth laughed again, and then shook his head. "While you think of Areenna as your daughter, you must begin to think of her as the most powerful woman in Nevaeh."

Nosaj's eyes widened. His mouth dropped open for an instant before he said, "Most powerful. No, Enaid—"

"—Enaid has already foreseen. The fate of Nevaeh rests on Areenna's shoulders."

Nosaj closed his eyes and struggled against the revived feeling for the loss of his wife, and fearing the same for Areenna. When he opened his eyes, a single tear rolled onto his cheek. "Never before have I wished not to be a king, but today is that day."

Roth exhaled slowly. "I understand old friend, for my son, too, must travel this frightful path."

◇◇◇

Walking quietly through the stables, Mikaal went to the far corner stall where his kraal was eating a mix of dried grass and grain. He stood silently watching the large animal, admiring the sheen emanating from the deep blue-black fur.

"Charka," he called in a low voice, "we go on an adventure tomorrow."

The kraal lifted his large triangular head to stare at Mikaal. He snorted loudly, stepped close to Mikaal, and pressed the flat of his head against Mikaal's chest for a moment before returning to his food.

Mikaal laughed, turned and started away. He had found the young but fully grown kraal caught up in deep bramble bushes. When he'd first seen the trapped animal, it was not its predicament, but its size and beauty and determination to free itself that had called to him.

A wild kraal was a dangerous animal to be close to especially when trapped, but when this one had seen Mikaal walking toward it, it had stopped its mad battle to tear free from the thorny bushes and waited, carefully watching the man's approach.

The closer Mikaal had come, the more blood he saw leaching from the kraal's wounds. When he'd finally stepped next to the animal, the kraal had lowered its head and snorted once, softly. Mikaal had drawn his short sword in his right hand and his knife with his left and begun to cut away the brambles.

It had taken a half hour to free the animal, and when he had, the kraal stood in the same spot, its flanks quivering, but it had not run off. "Go, boy, go," Mikaal whispered.

The kraal did not move; instead it stared directly into Mikaal's eyes. He sensed it wanted something, but had no idea of what. Then he began to inspect the powerful animal and saw that the bleeding was not stopping even with the thorns removed. He reached out slowly and very carefully stroked the kraal's forehead.

The kraal had pushed against his hand and in that moment Mikaal felt something happen within his mind. While he hadn't been sure of what, he had known the kraal needed more help and he had placed his hand on the kraal's neck and urged him to walk with him. That had been three years ago.

"We leave tomorrow," he told the kraal. He shook away the memory and started back to the keep. He made it ten steps before a guardsman appeared.

"The queen asks for your presence, My Prince." So saying, he went off in the direction of the keep. Mikaal followed at a more leisurely pace.

Upon reaching his mother's quarters, he knocked once and entered. He found both Enaid and Areenna sitting on a large cushioned divan, deep in conversation. "Mother, Areenna," he said with a smile.

"Come." Enaid patted the cushion next to her, moving over far enough to accommodate him. When he was seated, Enaid leaned over and kissed his cheek before saying, "We have much to plan and discuss. You are packed?"

Mikaal glanced from his mother to Areenna before saying, "I am."

"Good. Tomorrow, after the morning meal, you and Areenna will leave. You will ride to the far eastern coast. There is a place of great power, a place more potent than any other in Nevaeh. There you must finish your training. It will not be easy, but it must be done—and *they* will do their best to stop you."

Mikaal nodded thoughtfully. He looked at Areenna and gave her a confident smile before turning to his mother. "How many soldiers shall we take?"

Enaid took Mikaal's hand in both of hers and brought it to her cheek. Their eyes locked and she released his hand. "You take only yourselves. No soldier can accompany you."

"Because of my abilities?"

"Yes," Enaid whispered. "But it makes no difference. None other than those seeking their final training can go. It has always been thus."

"I understand."

"Do you?" Her eyes searched his face, seeking any tell-tale signs. "Good," she said a moment later. "Areenna, Mikaal's training is upon your shoulders. It will not be easy."

When Areenna nodded, Enaid went on. "The place you seek is an island set off the mainland. It is where the ocean becomes a bay. The bay itself is fed both by the ocean and by a river flowing from far away mountains of Northcrom into the bay. The Island is surrounded by both water and land. The southwestern tip of the island is the place of power.

It is where, thousands of years ago, the war between Nevaeh and the…the others began.

"Have you been there?" Areenna asked.

Enaid stared at her with haunted eyes. "I have. I was there with your mother, twenty-three years ago."

Her voice was warning enough not to ask further questions and Areenna did not.

"You will first go westward, through King Reltaw's dominion of Morvene. From there you go north to Northcrom, King Maslo's domain. After Northcrom you go southeast through Aldimor. These three kingdoms and their kings are fiercely loyal to us. And more importantly the three queens are necessary for the completion of your journey. While the route is longer than going directly, you must follow this course. It offers safety, knowledge, and a degree of protection from *them*."

"It will be a two, maybe three day trip to Morvene. I know several inns on the road where we can stay comfortably," Mikaal offered.

"No," said Enaid, her voice sharp with warning, "you cannot stay at any inns. You must keep your journey quiet. The son of Roth and daughter of Nosaj will create a stir wherever you go. You travel incognito. You do not make your presence known to anyone other than the Queens of the dominions you visit. As to the Kings…only if there is no other choice. Do you understand the importance of this?"

Mikaal glanced at Areenna and saw her eyes were already on his. Their green depths and golden motes asked if he truly understood. When he nodded, she turned to Enaid. "We do."

"When you are near the borders of each dominion, you, Areenna, must send your aoutem to the Queen with a message of your pending arrival and of the secrecy necessary. I will do my best to alert them as well." She paused, looked at each of them and said, "There is one more thing. Before you reach the Island, you will cross a wasteland, and travel through ancient ruins, the worst in the northeast. There will be considerable dangers from mutated animals and men and women who are…not like us. But once you pass through the wastelands, you will find safety at the Landing from which you travel to the Island. There are two Landings: one on this side of the Island and one at the Island. These Landings are special. They are ancient and protected from anything dark by something so powerful it cannot be described."

Enaid turned to Mikaal. "It will not be easy, the training. A man has never before been trained. Not only must you be strong, you must learn how to be open in your mind. It is not in the way of men, while it is of most women, but you must find a way. Without opening your mind, you cannot learn and cannot be trained."

"I will find a way," Mikaal said easily.

Enaid slowly shook her head. "You will, but not in the way you think. Now, go, rest."

Mikaal and Areenna left together. Mikaal walked her to her quarters. "She makes it seem as if it will be difficult for you to train me."

"Because a man has never been trained, and the training is different from anything you have ever done. It was hard for me in the beginning and I cannot imagine how much harder it will be for you."

He stopped and turned her to face him. He studied her face for several seconds and said, "I have withstood the training of a warrior, what makes you think I cannot handle what you will teach me?"

Areenna smiled, it was a soft and gentle smile. She reached up, much as Enaid had done, and touched his cheek with her fingertips. "Because it is not a warrior's training, it has nothing to do with physical strength, my Prince, it is..." She paused, seeking the right words before realizing there were no words to describe the inner journey that was so necessary for him to learn.

"It is what?" Mikaal asked, his eyes questing as deeply as his words.

Areenna blinked, twice. "Hard," was the only word she could manage.

Alone in her bedchamber, the servants gone for the night, Areenna lay in the bed, staring up at the ceiling and wondering what would happen tomorrow. She closed her eyes in yet another effort to sleep, but opened them a minute later. From a distance came the familiar sensation of Gaalrie capturing her evening meal. She allowed herself to feel the rush of Gaalrie's pleasure at the kill before closing off her mind from the treygone's.

When the sensation of the treygone faded, she realized her inability to sleep was not about being nervous or afraid of the coming journey, rather, it was the excitement at what was about to happen. She'd never expected an adventure of this type, and while she was not prepared for it, she accepted its importance. She reluctantly accepted the burdens Enaid had placed upon her. It was not a matter of going to the East, but of training Mikaal—something that had never before been attempted. At the same time, Areenna recognized the journey would be not just the most important part of her life, but of the lives of everyone she knew and loved.

After leaving Areenna at her quarters, Mikaal went up to the top of the eastern rampart to be alone under the night stars. Looking out over Tolemac, he wondered what would happen when he learned more about the powers he has been hiding for so long. But as hard as he tried, he could not guess. The only indication he'd gotten from Areenna was how hard it would be. And that admission from her had seemed difficult. *Why?*

He wondered about the beautiful princess. He had known her in school, but had paid her scant attention other than sensing she was, even at that early age and without possession of any powers, an unusually intense girl.

Exhaling sharply, he turned and stiffened with surprise when he found his father not a foot away. Roth's smile was open and warm. "I saw you from across the parapet," he said.

"You could have given me a warning rather than scaring me half to death."

"Where's the fun in that," Roth replied with a wide grin. "Yet I sense you want some solitude, and I am being selfish by wanting to spend some time with you before you leave."

When Mikaal nodded, Roth started to turn but Mikaal stopped him. "Stay and talk with me."

Roth smiled. "When you were young, three or so, we would come here and I would—"

"—hoist me on your shoulders and walk the entire parapet."

"You remember?"

Mikaal nodded. "For some reason, I remember everything about my childhood."

"That can be good; it can also be a curse."

"Yes, Especially the spanking! I can still feel your slap on my ass when you caught me taking your broadsword from the sheath."

"A father's duty...and what did I tell you?"

"'This will be yours one day. Until then, your hands stay clear of its pommel.'"

Roth looked at his son. "And?"

"And then, with my ass still burning from your hand, you took me to the smith and had him create a sword I could hold and handle."

"And all without a tear. You did well for a six year old."

Mikaal smiled. "I did, didn't I?"

Stopping, Roth turned to his son and gazed deeply into his eyes. "You leave tomorrow, for how long we know not. When you return, and you damned well better, you will be different. We all make important journeys in our life, some sooner than others. The one you embark on tomorrow, while no different in one sense, is extremely different. It will change you and help you to understand why we must fight and protect not just ourselves, but everyone in Nevaeh."

Roth grasped Mikaal's hand. "Do not once think this journey unimportant, for it may very well be the most significant journey of your life and of everyone else's."

Mikaal swallowed under the intensity of his father's eyes and slowly nodded as Roth's words sank in.

Releasing him, Roth said, "Good, then let's go downstairs, for I would raise a farewell glass with my son, and present him with a gift."

A few minutes later they entered his private quarters, the walls filled with scrolls and books. The books, like the scrolls, were all hand-written. True to his promise onboard the starship, Solomon Roth steadfastly refused to use any technology from the past. If a printing press were to be discovered, then it would be created without his interference.

There was a pitcher and two glasses on the table in the center of the room. The pitcher was filled with deep red wine and Roth poured himself and his son a glass. Holding his glass high, Roth said, "To you and to Areenna, may your journey be swift and clear."

They touched glasses and drank. Then Roth went to his desk, picked up a long cloth covered item, and carried it to Mikaal. "A gift for your journey."

Unwrapping the gift, Mikaal's jaw dropped at the sight of the gleaming longsword. He tore his eyes from the sword to stare at his father. "I…"

Roth smiled broadly. "You are welcome," he said as Mikaal looked back to the longsword, its shaft gleaming in the torchlight.

"While one of my broadswords might work for you, this one was made for you of the same metal as mine. With your size and strength, the longsword suits you better and is more fitting for you than my broadsword, do you not agree?

At a loss for words, Mikaal grasped the metal laced, leather wrapped pommel with both hands and tested the heft of the sword. "It is wonderful, and light," he finally said.

"This metal is from my time. It is light, strong and will not dull, ever. Now put the sword down and finish drinking with me."

"Yes, Father," Mikaal said with a broadening smile. He lifted his glass and said, "To tomorrow."

Roth shook his head and whispered, "No Mikaal, to your safe return and to Areenna's."

CHAPTER 10

THE SUN HAD not yet risen when Areenna woke to the first deep purple streaks of dawn edging onto the eastern horizon. While hard to explain, ever since the battle in the forest and the joining of Mikaal's hidden power, she had become sensitive to everything around her: Gaalrie floating above; Enaid's gorlon, Irii, walking the hallway with Enaid; the troubled depth of her father's sleep; Mikaal's first stirring of wakefulness.

Leaving the bed, she used the toilet and then went to her wardrobe. Just as she opened the ornately carved wardrobe doors, a knock sounded on the chamber door. Areenna smiled when Enaid entered. "How slept you?"

"Fitfully."

"As we all did. Good choice," Enaid said when Areenna pulled a short tunic and pants from the wardrobe. "What weapons have you?"

"What use for weapons should I have?" Areenna asked, puzzled.

"Areenna, your powers are strong, but there are times when they will need the aid of a weapon."

Areenna accepted the gentle rebuke and said, "I have my bow for hunting and my short sword should it be needed."

"Good. Work with Mikaal on the sword. He is his father's equal with the blade. It will also be good to do, for you will be able to train him while you are trained."

"How…oh," she whispered, remembering all too clearly how her mother would work with her as they hunted, forcing her to use her mind even as she used her hands with the bow and arrows.

"It will be a safe way to start his training. It will make it easier for him to understand what you are doing. Remember, we are used to our abilities because our mothers prepared us when we were very young. Did you forget how your mother would tell you the stories of the women who came before you? It is in this way we women begin the training of our daughters long before the start of formal training at their fourteenth birthday. I doubt he will be as comfortable with the training as were you."

Areenna took in her mentor's advice. "You are right. I will start slowly."

"Good." She turned her head, listening. "Ah, everyone is up. Come, it is important for us to share this morning's meal with our men."

Areenna held her face immobile as the meaning of Enaid's *our men,* struck her.

A bare thirty minutes later found the five sitting at a table piled with dishes of eggs, sweet rolls, slices of meat, and bowls of fruit. The servants had been dismissed and the chamber door closed.

Next to Enaid, Roth looked at Mikaal and Areenna and paused between bites of food to point at three rolled sheaths sitting on the side table. "Those maps will lead you to the Island that was, thousands of years ago, the commercial center of the entire free world. It was the very first target of those who destroyed our world. It was a terrible thing."

He took a drink before saying in a thoughtful voice, "Follow the maps closely. Try to stay within the routes I have marked. When you leave the dominion of Aldimore and enter the wastelands, tread carefully. It is wild country, left as such because of the destruction. It was the area hit the worst by the radiation that changed men and women into what we are today. But while most fled the area, there were many who did not.

And there are still people there—if you choose to call them such—but they resemble nothing you are familiar with. Their mutations are different from ours. Their changes are physical as well as mental, and like those in the border lands, many of them are the minions of the evil from across the sea. Never forget this, not for one moment!"

Both Mikaal and Areenna nodded at Roth.

"We are asking a lot of you, more than we or anyone has the right to ask."

"No, Sire," Areenna cut in quickly. "You are High King. It is your right to ask anything and it is our duty to do our best to accomplish whatever it is you ask of us." From the corner of her eyes, she saw her father nod. The proud look on his face helped mask the deep worry she saw in his eyes.

"And while your words find a home within my heart, it saddens me to have had to ask this of you two. I would prefer it be I who goes to the East, but there is no choice and I tremble for what awaits you."

"Rest easier," Mikaal said, reaching cross the table to cover his father's hand with his own. "We will do what we must and return when it is time."

Before Roth could respond, Enaid said in a sharp tone, "Cockiness will not work well where you go."

Mikaal gazed into his mother's eyes, his own eyes wide. "You misunderstand, Mother, it is far from cockiness. I cannot explain exactly what it is, but when we work together, Areenna and I become…something else."

Enaid did not respond, instead she used a silver fork to lift a berry slowly from her plate to her mouth.

"There is one more thing," Roth said. He looked at his wife and then at Mikaal and Areenna. "No one must learn of your powers, at least not yet. No man has ever had the powers you possess. When the people learn of this, there will be great danger. You will represent something fearful. And Mikaal, who you are…it will change our world. No one must know," he repeated.

As if his warning was a signal, all five fell silent. They finished their meal, each lost in thought about what would happen when Mikaal and Areenna left Tolemac.

◇◇◇

"There's a comfortable inn a few miles away," Mikaal said only half in jest.

Areenna shook her head. "You know better. Besides, what would be the point of wearing these capes and hoods? The moment we enter the inn you would be recognized."

"True, but after seven hours upon these monsters," he said, slapping the side of his kraal's neck affectionately, "a bed would be more welcome than the ground."

She looked over her shoulder at the retiring sun, sat higher in the saddle and closed her eyes. A moment later she smiled and said, "Gaalrie has found us a nice spot to camp. This way," she said and, guiding her kraal from the road, entered the edge of the forest. Soon, they were a quarter mile into the woods.

Areenna brought them to where the trees gave way to a small and pleasant clearing. A narrow stream bisected its edges, which were covered with soft, mossy grass. Although the trees surrounding the clearing were not thick, they would prevent anyone further than twenty or so yards from spotting the fire for their evening meal.

"This will do nicely," Mikaal said, dismounting and kneeling on the soft grasses. "And it will be comfortable."

Areenna laughed. "Only two days and we will be in Morvene. You can have a bed then."

"True. But for now we should set up camp."

Agreeing, they unsaddled their kraals. Using three panels of the woven silks rolled on the backs of their saddles, they created a lean-to with several large branches Mikaal had separated from the trees. After the set-up, Mikaal said, "I will hunt for dinner."

Areenna smiled. "What would the prince like for dinner? A dar? A rabt?"

Mikaal's eyebrows lifted. "Ah, the conjurer. Well even as hungry as I am, a dar is too much food. Perhaps a plump rabt will do."

Areenna laughed gently. "As you wish." She closed her eyes and said, "Your training starts now." She reached out and took his hand. "Join me."

With a deep breath, she drew him into her mind and at the same time, sent a thought to Gaalrie, creating a mind picture of the animal for Gaalrie to find. The vision of the rabt grew strong; its white and red fur glowed from the tips of its long ears to the long furry tail and powerful hind legs and thick front legs.

Find—Bring, was her direction to Gaalrie.

With Mikaal firmly anchored in her mind, she watched the treygone hunt for a rabt through the aoutem's eyes. Five minutes after starting her search, the giant bird's sharp eyes spotted one climbing out of its warren. Ten seconds later the rabt was being lifted from the ground, its neck broken.

During Gaalrie's return, Areenna and Mikaal started gathering firewood. "That was strange," Mikaal ventured, "seeing things through the eyes of a treygone, I never imagined…"

"It takes some getting used to, but it is important. You did not have the opportunity to have an aoutem. The time passed and you were unaware."

"Had I been aware, how could I do so? It would be too obvious."

"But if you had told your mother, she would have—"

"—smothered me, hidden me, and not allowed me to become myself."

Areenna laughed openly. "So you think."

"So I know, little princess. My mother has always been overprotective. My father and I had to sneak away in order to do things she did not approve of."

"Things?"

"Training—physical training, sword, arrow, spear."

"Why would she feel that way? It is the way life has always been. Men always train physically."

"When I was not yet seven?"

"Oh…" Areenna said. Male training, like female training, started at the end of school. Before school, all children were educated in letters and groomed to be fit and athletic, but weaponry training did not begin until the fourteenth year—hunting, yes; fighting, no. It had become a tradition centuries before, when the people recognized how immature bodies were not equipped with the reflexes needed for self-protection during weapons training. The time needed to build the proper coordination and mental agility was something to be groomed during the pre-adolescent years when young male children were taught games to develop their dexterity.

As a result—and properly so, thought Areenna—the education in letters and in athletics became the earliest part of training. Once the coordination was mature and the mind as well, weapons training began in earnest. Over the centuries, the people had learned that when training was followed properly, boys matured into extraordinarily powerful fighters, soldiers, commanders, and kings.

A call warned her of Gaalrie's approach. The treygone descended from the sky to lay the rabt at Areenna's feet before ascending to a nearby tree branch.

Ten minutes later the rabt was cleaned and spitted above the fire while Areenna and Mikaal sat to one side. "The way you ordered Gaalrie to hunt was…interesting."

Areenna looked into his deep gray eyes, trying to think of the best way to explain what she did. "I never order Gaalrie to do anything. It is not done in such a way. If I command her, she will not necessarily follow it. Did you not feel the asking I did?"

Mikaal shook his head.

"While I built my mind picture, I also sent a little 'push'. It was of an asking rather than an ordering, like so," she said and pushed a mind picture of Mikaal holding a piece of wood he had been about to add to the fire. She 'asked' him to throw the piece behind him, and he nodded and started to do so. "No," she said aloud. "Hold."

Mikaal, his arm halfway back, stopped and stared at it. "You can tell people what to do?"

Areenna moistened her lips with the tip of her tongue. "No. But because you and I now have a connection, I was able to show you. Do you understand what I did?"

"I think I do. You…suggest, not order, but not really ask."

"I suppose suggest is a better word," Areenna agreed.

"But it doesn't matter for me. I have no aoutem."

"Animals and birds can be 'touched' even if it is not your aoutem. But it is not as solid a connection."

Areenna turned the rabt and rose to her feet. "Come, let us take a walk."

"To train?"

She nodded. "Watch, take in what I do, try to open yourself, but speak not."

◇◇◇

Sitting near the fire, two hours after they had finished eating, Areenna gazed into the cloudless night sky. The array of stars was so intense it looked like thousands of tiny jewels sparkling upon a deep blanket.

"That group there," Mikaal said, breaking into her reverie, "is called Orion".

Areenna's brow knitted. "Orion?"

"In my father's time, before he left the earth, they had names for the groupings of stars. He calls them constellations. So the constellation...there," he said, raising his arm and pointing at a grouping of stars, "is called Orion, and is made of several stars." His finger shifted and pointed to the upper stars. "Those two stars are the shoulders, and the three bright ones in the middle are called Orion's belt. The ones below, there and there," he added, pointing to two stars below the belt, "are the feet, if you will."

Areenna followed each movement of his fingers, studying the stars to which he pointed. His words fascinated her for she had never thought about putting names to the pinpoints of light she looked at each night.

"And there," he added, shifting her view toward the north, "that bright star, the brightest in the night—you know it as the Northern Guide—is the beginning of what is called the Little Dipper, those seven stars. Do you see?"

She squinted at the stars Mikaal was describing. It took a few seconds for her eyes to recognize the pattern, but when she did, she saw the curve of a handle and then the cup of a water dipper. "Yes," she said as the sky revealed itself as never before. She saw the little dipper and below it, the same pattern revealed itself in an even larger way. "There is another beneath it."

"Yes," Mikaal exclaimed, "the Big Dipper. Now look a little more to the left. There is another star, almost as bright as the Northern Guide. My father says in another two thousand or so years, the star, Alpha Cephi, will become the Northern Guide. It is in the constellation Cepheus.

Areenna shifted and lay back. She cradled her head in the palms of both hands and stared upward. "You are teaching me even as I teach you."

Mikaal assumed the same position. "Have you thought much about what is ahead?"

"How can I when I have no idea what we seek?"

"How can you not?"

"Perhaps it is because I need to focus my energy on you. We have, at most, two weeks to give you years of training. Is that not reason enough?"

"Not really."

"I… It will have to be," she stated and rolled over and pushed herself up. "Time for sleep."

Mikaal watched her walk into the woods for privacy and then to the stream, where she knelt at the edge and dipped her hands into the running water and rinsed her face before drinking some of the cool liquid.

Returning from the stream, she went to the lean-to, dropped the silk for privacy, and changed out of her traveling clothes and into a lighter coverall. "Are you going to sleep or stare at the sky all night," she asked him.

"Stare for a while. Have a pleasant sleep."

She nodded at him, opened her sleeping silks and slid between their welcoming embrace. Turning on her side, she was asleep a half minute later.

Mikaal watched until he was certain she slept and then gathered more firewood. He set a small amount on the fire and piled the rest for the morning before he, too, used the woods for a toilet and washed his hands and face in the stream.

When he climbed into his sleeping silks, he turned to Areenna. Her face was calm and her breathing even and he thought, not for the first time, how strong she was both in mindset and in body, and how beautiful: her hair was the color of winter wheat and her skin a soft tan. But he knew he had to hide such thoughts from her for it might interfere with the training he so badly needed. Yet, unlike Areenna's seeming nonchalance, he was curious about what would happen when they reached the East. Curious yet at the same time fretful. His apprehension was not about the fighting that might lie ahead; rather it centered more on what was or was not within the grasp of his strange abilities and of what Areenna's part was in bringing about those abilities.

With those thoughts, he fell asleep.

◇◇◇

The moon floated low in the sky: dawn was only a few hours away. The meadow Areenna and Mikaal slept within was quiet. Charka stood twenty feet from the lean-to, half asleep half alert. In the tree above the kraal rested the giant treygone, its long, thin, and tightly feathered tail wrapped around the branch, the bird's sharp talons locked on its thickness, her wings folded neatly on her back. Treygones slept in snatches—a genetic trait for species preservation. No matter how large or fierce a treygone was, it had many enemies. At this moment Gaalrie was awake, her eyes fixed on the lean-to where Areenna slept. Something had disturbed the treygone, but she wasn't yet sure of what.

A chill washed across the meadow; a dark cloud appeared above. Not a second later did the kraal, Charka, lift its head and snort sharply. He shifted and pawed at the ground. Behind him, Areenna's kraal whinnied and backed away even as the larger kraal started toward the lean-to.

Gaalrie spread her wings and released her hold on the branch just as Charka charged the lean-to. Charka stopped three feet from the silks and reared on his back legs. An instant later it slammed its front hooves downward and let go with what could only pass as a groaning scream.

On the ground where the kraal's front hooves had struck the earth was a ten foot long, thick-bodied snuck. Its pointy head and undulating body slithered toward the lean-to. The kraal rose again and slammed his hooves downward, catching the last foot of the snuck beneath a front hoof.

The snuck whirled, its head raising upward, its mouth open and baring four inch long fangs, its body arched. Venom dripped from the fang's tips as it prepared to strike the kraal while Charka rose for another attack.

Before Charka could swing downward, before the snuck could uncoil at the kraal's underbelly, Gaalrie launched herself at the snuck. The powerful beak set within her dragon-like head caught the snuck behind its head and sliced it from the rest of its body just as the kraal's front hooves crushed the center of the body of the poisonous reptile.

◇◇◇

Areenna and Mikaal awakened instantly at the kraals' first warning, throwing off their silks and racing out of the lean-to, Mikaal's long-sword in his hand. Areenna gripped her short sword.

They stopped short when they saw Charka pawing at the snuck and Gaalrie standing on the ground not two feet from the kraal, the head of the snuck lying at her feet.

Recognizing what had happened, Areenna looked at Gaalrie and then at the kraal. She stared at the large kraal for several seconds before walking to it and stroking its long neck. As she did, she became aware of the kraal in a vastly different way and grasped what had really happened.

She turned to say something to Mikaal, but stayed silent as he scooped the snuck's body upward with his sword to look at it. When Mikaal flung the body away, Areenna looked at Gaalrie. The treygone stared back and then Areenna went to her and knelt. She stroked Gaalrie's head with her fingertips.

When she made physical contact, she read the bird's emotions and got a mind picture of the kraal attacking the snuck. When she released Gaalrie, the treygone arched its wings and rose to the branch it had been perching upon.

Areenna looked at the sky and the remnants of the dark cloud breaking apart. She pushed her senses upward, as Enaid had trained her to do when she'd first started Areenna's training, seeking what might be there. Something cold and dark and vile retreated when she touched it.

Her stomach twisted when she recognized the evil. It was the same as she had faced two days before.

"What?" Mikaal asked, breaking into her thoughts.

"They know."

"Who knows?"

She met his questioning eyes and said, "They do, the dark ones—the one we fought."

"How can that be?"

"I have no answer, but be assured, it was controlling the snuck."

"Then we were lucky to have Charka and Gaalrie." With that, he went to the pile of wood and began to rebuild the fire. "I think sleep is over for the night. We should start early."

Areenna looked at the snuck's head near her right foot. "I agree, sleep is done."

◇◇◇

When dawn rose, bringing deep pinkish bands along the eastern horizon, they were dressed and eating the remnants of last night's dinner.

"Was your kraal from the Tolemac herd?" Areenna asked Mikaal.

Mikaal shook his head. "No, Charka was wild. I found him caught within brambles, three years ago."

"And he let you free him?"

"Yes," he said and told Areenna the story of how he'd found and freed the kraal. When he finished, Areenna closed her eyes for a moment.

When she opened them, she smiled. "That was a wonderful story."

"Why did you ask?"

The smile remained on her face as she shrugged. "I was curious. I have never seen a kraal do anything but run from a snuck."

Mikaal's brows knit together for a moment. He glanced at Charka and then said, "Come to think of it, you're right. Do you believe it's important—his attacking the snuck?"

"I don't know. Perhaps," she shrugged, unwilling to say further until she was certain about what she was beginning to sense.

There would be time to confirm, she thought. *Ample time.*

CHAPTER 11

THE MORNING PASSED quickly on the ride toward Troit, Morvene's capital. The day was cloudless, the air warm with just enough breeze to keep it comfortable. Areenna was heavily occupied with thoughts of the morning's snuck attack and on what other surprises would await them.

Sending a questioning thought to Gaalrie, she closed her eyes and waited. A moment later she viewed the way ahead as clearly as if it were she who was flying. All was clear. They had decided not to ride the main highway, but to cut through the countryside using her aoutem as their guide and scout.

The benefit of traveling this way gave them the ability to avoid people and to cut the distance to Troit by almost half. If everything went right, they would be near the capital of Morvene by nightfall, and not spend another day on the road.

When Mikaal turned to her and said, "I don't know about you, but I'm hungry and need to walk and stretch," the low timbre of his voice broke through her reveries.

A glance at the sun told Areenna the morning had fled and it was a little past the midday hour. She smiled. "Good idea." She closed her eyes and made contact with Gaalrie. "There's a stream a few minutes ahead."

Guiding her kraal toward their left, she led them to the bank of a creek. She dismounted Hero and walked with him to the bubbling stream, where the kraal lowered its head and began lapping water. Areenna knelt at his side, and used her hand to drink.

Behind her, Mikaal watched the woman and the kraal. He was still trying to understand his own powers, but found himself admiring Areenna for her ability not to merely adapt to what she was doing, but to become enmeshed within it.

He released Charka's reigns and when the kraal ambled next to Hero and dipped his head into the stream Mikaal went to his side and drank his fill. He wiped his mouth with a slide of his sleeve and turned to Areenna who was unrolling some of the meat they had saved from last night's meal.

They shared the meat, standing because neither wanted to sit after riding for five hours, and Areenna said, "If all goes well, we will be there by dark. I'll need to send Gaalrie to Queen Layra and let her know. Should we do this now, or wait until we are closer?"

"Does she know we are coming?"

"I'm sure your mother sent a message to her, but with what is happening…"

"Then now would be best. It gives her time to make the arrangements. Can you still lead us there this way?"

"Agreed, and yes, I will still see the land as Gaalrie flies." She looked at Hero and a moment later the kraal came to her. She took a small white cloth from her bag and smoothed it onto her opened left hand. She aimed her index finger at the cloth and began to make writing motions. When she was finished, Mikaal saw her read the words that appeared on the cloth and then watched them slowly fade away.

Areenna rolled the cloth into a small, tight scroll, called Gaalrie to her and tied the message to the bird's leg with a strand of thread. With a quick lift, she sent Gaalrie on her way.

"How did you do that?" Mikaal asked, still looking at her hand.

"Write? Hide the words?"

"Both."

Areenna shrugged. "I never thought about it. My mother showed me and I did it."

"Just like that?"

"Not quite. It took practice, as does everything about our science."

He frowned. "Science? I don't understand."

Areenna looked at him for several seconds. His words brought her back to the Hall of the Tale and to Master Thrumweld's question, *what is magic?* "It is hard, I know, for men to understand that what we call magic is but a form of science."

Mikaal's furrowed brow was the response she expected and she smiled gently at him. "Science is more than creating things; it is using the powers of your mind. I don't know why men and women differ so much in this aspect, but it seems men have a hard time understanding how a woman's mind can create what everyone calls magic."

"My father once told me women's magic is called metaphysics, which he said was not well understood where he came from."

Areenna let the word roll around the confines of her mind before saying. "I like the sound of it…metaphysics. It sounds right."

"Okay, teach me how to write."

She laughed, then sighed. "I don't know if I can truly teach you. I can show you, but you have to work it out."

"Show me," he said, defiantly popping the last piece of cold rabt into his mouth.

Areenna walked over to a rock, wiped a few grains of dirt from it, and placed her hand four inches above the stone. "Think of the message and move it from your mind to your fingertip and from your fingertip to the rock like so."

Seconds later, Mikaal's name appeared on the face of the rock.

Mikaal stared at the rock for a full minute before stepping next to Areenna and then, kneeling, placed his forefinger the correct distance away. He thought of a word and began to write. Nothing happened.

Taking a deep breath, he reformed a word and pushed it toward the rock, moving his finger as if it were a writing feather. His face turned red and droplets of sweat popped onto his forehead as he worked his mind as hard as he had ever worked his muscles.

Finally, he exhaled a frustrated held breath and stood up. "Impossible!"

Areenna touched his hand. "Not impossible, just hard. Remember, you have two disadvantages. You are a man and you are years behind in your training. I learned this as a child."

"None of that matters. I still have to learn," he said.

Areenna looked at the sky. Not a half hour had passed since they'd started working. They could afford a little more time. "My turn." Pulling her short sword from its scabbard on the kraal, she said, "Work with me for a while."

Mikaal offered a lopsided smile. "With that little sticker?"

"Little sticker?" With the two words dripping with sarcasm, she raised her short sword and charged him.

Mikaal reacted instantly and reached for his sword, which was not at his side but hanging on Charka's saddle. He went into a crouch and, when Areenna reached him, rolled forward, snapped onto his feet and raced to the kraal, Areenna running behind him.

Charka turned and moved toward him as if the kraal knew what was needed. Reaching Charka, he grabbed his sword, spun and raised it an instant before hers descended on him. The sound of metal on metal was loud in the silent forest. The force of her blow surprised him almost as much as her attack. It was as if the blow had come from a bigger man than he, not a slender girl.

"Little sticker is it?" She whirled and swung again, her blade whistling through the air.

Mikaal parried and, feeling the full force of her blow realized what she was doing. "No magic!"

Areenna paused, the sword half raised. "You're stronger than I am."

"It makes no difference. No magic!"

She nodded, and pushed forward against him in a wild charge. He cleared his mind of all thoughts other than those needed to protect himself and began to fight earnestly. It took only a few seconds to penetrate her weak defense, flick the sword from her hand and rest the tip of his blade at her throat. "Yield."

Trembling with anger for allowing herself to be disarmed so quickly, she whispered through clenched teeth, "I yield."

They lowered their swords and he smiled at her. "I did not expect so much strength," he admitted.

"But you still outfought me, which is why I need to use my powers."

"It was not because you're a woman, you just haven't been trained properly."

"But with my powers I can do what is necessary."

"You are thinking like a...child. Think like a..." He smiled, recalling her words of moments before, "like a man. And think as well of how much more you can do if you're trained properly."

Abashed and surprised by his wisdom, she nodded. "Then do so!"

"As you ask, Princess," he said and raised his sword high. "Lesson one, defense. Lift your blade perpendicular to my sword. When my blade descends, twist your wrist slightly, lowering the far edge of your blade. Watch the effect," he added as he started his downward swing. When their blades met, his slid from hers and dipped almost to the ground.

"Hold!" he shouted. She froze. "Look closely. If you drop your arms when the attacking blade leaves yours, turn to the right and lunge, your foe is defeated."

Areenna pictured each movement he had explained and when she was done, looked at him. "Ready," she said.

They took their positions. At her nod, Mikaal attacked again. Areenna tilted the blade the instant before his sword touched it. The screech of metal scraping along metal echoed sharply, but as his blade left hers, she straightened her wrists, turned to her right and lunged. The rising tip of her blade stopped the instant it touched the fabric over his heart.

"Perfect," he said. "Again!" and, lifting his sword, he charged at her. But this time instead of allowing her to turn and thrust when his sword touched hers, he twisted beneath both blades, kicked out his right foot and hooked her leg. A half a heartbeat later, Mikaal offered her his hand and pulled her to her feet.

"Overconfidence will kill you," he said. "When you are on the field, you fight man after man. When a soldier...a true warrior sees how you defend yourself, he learns and will find another way to defeat you."

"And you have more ways?" Areenna challenged.

"Do you want to find out?" he asked with a half-smile, half-sneer.

Areenna set herself, dug her feet into the ground and said, "Do your best."

He smiled openly now and gripped his longsword with both hands, did a figure eight in the air and smiled openly. "As you command,

Princess—defend yourself"

He charged forward, his sword only half raised. When she blocked him, he spun and lunged and the next thing he knew he was laying on the ground. "What the…"

And then he saw the aura surrounding her like a low hanging mist. Soft shades of violet faded into a silvery hue. The mist not only covered her body, but extended to her sword as well.

"I said no magic."

"That was before. You said defend yourself. I did."

Mikaal stood, dusting himself off. When he spoke, it was with low, slowly paced words that strangely echoed what his father had told him years ago. "When you are fighting for your life, when you have two or three or even four men attacking you, there is no time for thinking, at that point you must fight instinctively or you will die."

"And what makes you think that my powers aren't instinctive?"

"You did. Science you said. You have to concentrate to use your power. But when you are battling those who want your blood you can't afford to think, only react. Your concentration must be on your attacker. Waiver for an instant and you die. So, Areenna, if you are going to use a sword, you had dammed well better be fully trained so you can use it instinctively and free your mind to watch what's happening around you and prepare for the next attack. Listen to me, Princess, you're training me to use the powers I have, please let me train you to use your body to protect you as well."

Worrying her lower lip with her teeth, Areenna nodded slowly. "You're right. No games. I will not use magic."

"Good. Now, let's try that again."

CHAPTER 12

SWEAT DRIPPED FROM Mikaal's brow. Charka's reigns hung limply while he struggled to make his words appear on the small cloth he was using for practice.

It was late afternoon and the sun was more than halfway to the edge of the western horizon when Areenna said, "Gaalrie is back."

When the treygone landed on Areenna's arm, which almost folded under the bird's weight, she removed the tied message from its leg and sent Gaalrie aloft again. She read the message and handed it to Mikaal.

'Areenna, my husband, the King, has been taken by fever. I must tend him and cannot leave today. Make camp where you can tonight. Upon reaching the outskirts of Troit tomorrow, travel northeast along the Covenant Highway. Cloak yourselves to be simple travelers. No one must know who you are. When you reach Handlebridge Lake, turn east and follow the lake road for two miles. There you will see the sign I will leave. Follow the path to the homestead. I will join you as soon as I can. There is a housekeeper, she will expect you.'

Layra

When he finished reading, a map slowly replaced the words written on the cloth. The map showed the lay of the land and the homestead. He handed the cloth to Areenna, the writing gone and the cloth again only a cloth. "So we are delayed."

"It is not so bad. We had planned on two nights."

Mikaal shrugged. "She does this without our giving her any sort of explanation?"

"Why wouldn't she?"

"If I sent a message to a king to meet me outside his castle for something unnamed, he would not come."

"Or he might. But that is not the way of women. Mikaal, the differences between men and women are enormous, which is why it is difficult for you to understand and master your powers. We—women I mean—have learned over the centuries that with our abilities comes certain responsibilities and trusts. No trained woman of power has betrayed another woman since earliest memory."

When Mikaal started to object, Areenna couldn't help smiling. "I'm not talking about love or lust or whatever label you use, I am talking about magic, about our abilities." She paused, her features turning serious. "Every woman with strong abilities knows, should she betray any of us to *them*—man, woman, child—our race will end."

"Isn't that overly dramatic?"

She stared at him, repeating his words silently within her head. "What is it Mikaal? What are you afraid of? Is it so fearful a thing to consider women can trust so openly?"

He shook his head. "It is not what I expected," he admitted.

"It is a fact that I was taught by my mother and by yours as well. And as far as this being a delay…I see no problem, in fact, it will be good for I can work with you on your powers and you can do the same for my sword work."

"Is that what you call it?" he asked with a wink.

◇◇◇

Five miles outside of Troit, a half mile before the forest thinned into sparse woodlands, they found a place to rest for the night. With the sun a half hour above the horizon, Mikaal strung Areenna's bow and, before she could stop him, walked into the deeper woods.

He needed time alone, and hunting was the only way to ensure he would have it. The afternoon's ride troubled him. He'd always known he was different from other men; he'd learned so as a boy and had learned how to hide his differences by overdoing. He was the best at everything he tried his hand at. By pushing himself to do more, he gained the respect of others, not because he was the son of Roth, but because he accomplished whatever he'd set his mind on.

But magic. Somehow, magic did not respond in the same way everything else in his life had. *Why?* He was deeply troubled because he had no control over whatever abilities he possessed. It was something he had never before experienced.

He went into the thicker woods, keeping close attention to everything round him. There was a wealth of wildlife in the forest, yet he would not bring down a large animal for just the two of them.

Ten minutes later, he broke through the trees to a small clearing, froze and went down on one knee. From across the clearing came the low call of a crave. He closed his eyes and concentrated on the sound until he was able to hone directly on it.

Opening his eyes, he spotted the black speckled gray, white, and orange bird sitting on a low hanging branch not thirty feet away. The bird was preening itself, its elongated head reaching around to a short, fat fantail, separating the ginger tipped feathers, wings folded flat against its plump body.

Mikaal slid an arrow from his quiver, slotted it, and drew back on the bow. When he had the crave sighted, he took in a deep breath, exhaled softly, and released the arrow.

The perfectly turned missile spun toward the bird and, a heartbeat before it struck, the crave turned and spotted Mikaal. Then the arrow pierced its chest and the bird dropped to the ground.

Areenna sat cross-legged by the fire while the bird cooked slowly on a spit made of branches. Mikaal was behind her in the lean-to, once again working on the cloth.

She turned the spit a half turn then settled back and thought about queen Layra's message. A troubled feeling had been growing within her since receiving the message from Morvene's Queen. Something about the King's sudden fever bothered her. *Was it too convenient?*

Ever since she and her father had arrived in Tolemac, everything surrounding her had felt as though there was some dark force closing in. *Perhaps my mind is playing tricks.* Not for the first time did she find herself wishing she was older and wiser than her eighteen years.

"Damn it!" The shout tore her from her thought. Opening her eyes even as she stood, she spun in the direction of the shout and found Mikaal holding the cloth in a clenched fist. "This is pointless," he snapped, tossing the cloth to the ground.

She watched him, accurately gauging the anger on his face. "So simple a task, so hard for a weak mind."

He whirled on her, crimson flushing his skin. His anger whipped toward her in waves so powerful she was almost knocked off her feet. She stood her ground, fighting against the mental waves he did not know he was driving at her. She stood fast, waiting for him to back off. Rage flared in his eyes and she saw something behind it—something not Mikaal.

It took but an instant to recognize the malevolent force that had appropriated his anger. She bent forward, her palms facing Mikaal. She did not set herself; rather, she closed her eyes and released her thoughts. Heat surged through her body like a liquid fire, racing through her veins instead of blood, and she drew all of it into her palms. She opened her eyes and released the full force of her power at him.

A wide flash erupted between them, a curtain-like wall created by hundreds of streaks of lightning. The wall held and then, slowly, Areenna forced the shimmering weave toward Mikaal inch by inch. Carefully, slowly, Areenna built her power.

This was new, and she only had instinct to guide her, yet she sensed what was needed and stepped forward. Her mind screamed a warning to stop before she hurt him. But she knew there was no choice.

Taking two more steps, she pushed her palms forward in a sweeping movement. The lightning spread swiftly, following the guidance of her palms, and seconds later it completely surrounded Mikaal.

It took but a few seconds for the strange burning in his eyes to end. When it did, he sank to his knees.

Areenna closed her fingers into fists and the electrical crackle of lightning stopped abruptly. She ran to Mikaal and dropped to the ground before him. Reaching out, she cupped his face in her hands and lifted it. When she looked into his eyes she saw he was again Mikaal.

"Breathe, clear your mind...get rid of *it*."

He blinked several times. His stomach was churning and his mouth tasted of a bitter copper. "How..."

"Your anger. We have not yet had that discussion. Anger dulls your mind and lowers your ability to resist another's will. When that happens, it becomes easy for others to control you. My mother told me it was how they kept defeating our forces, years ago."

He shook his head. He could still feel tendrils of possession within his mind. Never in his life had he been so beyond his own control. *And it will never again happen*, he vowed.

"I am sorry," he said.

Areenna smiled with an understanding decades beyond her youth. "Anyone with power must feel what you felt. If you never feel the loss, you can never protect yourself against it."

"But how did it find us?"

Areenna shrugged. "This dark one is old and powerful. She found us before; she tracked us here. I should have known so when we received Layra's message. The fever was too convenient. It was the dark one's work."

"How do we protect ourselves?"

"I am doing such now," and she explained how she had already begun to set her mind on blocking the area. She would know if any dark powers tried to reach them again. "But I doubt she will try again...tonight."

Mikaal searched her face, wondering how so young a woman could be so strong. "How can I learn to control whatever powers I have?" he asked.

Again, Areenna shrugged. "I don't know. No one has ever tried to train a man."

Mikaal stood and then reached down and drew Areenna to her feet. "Then there is only one obvious choice."

"Obvious? What?"

"Train me as if I were a woman," he said.

Her jaw dropped. Areenna stared at him in disbelief. She started to protest, but stopped as an old memory tweaked the edges of her mind and transported her back in time. She had just turned sixteen. Her mother was sick, but Areenna did not know the extent of her illness. They were at the edge of the Blue Desert and her mother was instructing her on the use of her powers for defense.

"Remember, a man is trained to exert control over his surroundings: a woman is trained to not just accept but adapt to her surroundings. This means one uses strength, the other uses understanding and surrender. Most men believe their strength—their physical strength—gives them power over others. This is a weakness because a man will fight with everything he has to maintain control. When a man begins to lose control, he becomes angry. The anger opens him to loss of control, exactly the opposite of what he believes."

"I don't understand," Areenna had said.

Her mother smiled. "Anger is so strong an emotion that any defense within the mind is gone. At that point, a man becomes vulnerable. A woman's mind works differently. Because we do not have the physical strength, we must rely on our mind's strength. Surrender in the face of anger defeats the anger. Have you never noticed how, when a man and a woman argue, the angrier a man gets, the calmer a woman tends to become?"

When Areenna nodded, her mother said, "Surrender defeats the anger because the anger has nowhere to focus. This doesn't mean women don't get angry and lose control, but a wise woman knows how to not allow her anger to control her, but to find a way to bank the anger and maintain emotional control. When she fails, she puts herself in the path of harm."

Areenna had listened, had digested her mother's words, and reached an understanding. Only when she had done this had her mother begun to teach her how to control her emotions.

"You're right," Areenna told Mikaal as the smell of burning crave reached her nostrils. "The crave," she cried and turned back to the fire. The bottom of the bird was singed black.

◇◇◇

Even burned, the plump and meaty bird satisfied their hunger. Shortly after they finished eating, when the moon had risen enough to light the area with soft, pale rays, Areenna picked up her short sword and Mikaal's long sword and handed him the weapon. "Teach me."

He accepted the sword, drew it from the scabbard and bowed. "Prepare yourself…Princess."

With a lopsided smile, he attacked her. He swung hard and when their blades met, the vibration from the blow raced up her arm with a painful stinging. She back-stepped, whirled away from him, and then planted her feet and prepared for another attack, her arm almost numb from the blow.

"Don't watch my sword, and never watch my feet or my arm, watch my eyes! Remember, an attacker will try to break through your defenses by overpowering you. Because you are a woman, a man knows you're not as strong as he so he will think it easy to break through. You must defend yourself by not allowing me to get close. The eyes will tell you when an attacker is about to strike. Watch the eyes and only the eyes, nothing else!"

He came at her again. Areenna watched his eyes, not his blade. He moved slowly, his blade swinging in figure eight arcs as he closed on her. She backed away, never taking her eyes from his. When his gray eyes flicked toward her sword, she sensed he was about to swing. She spun as he struck, her sword tilted slightly downward to deflect the power of his blow. The instant his blade touched hers, she did a full turn. His blade slid from hers and, as he had shown her yesterday, she came completely around and lodged the tip of her blade at the base of his throat.

"Good," he said, lowering his sword. "The only way to defeat a more powerful opponent is by letting his own strength defeat him."

"Yes, exactly," she said, seizing the opportunity he had just given her. "And like before, you became so angry you lost every defense you had, which allowed *her* to capture your mind. Do you see?"

Mikaal blinked as comprehension dawned. He nodded. "I do."

"Good. The difference between a man and a woman is surrender. Surrender, not control gives you the strength to use your power. Control of your power is different from control over your surroundings. You must accept not only who but what you are, surrender to your power so you may use it. Now," she said in a very low voice, "with what I have said, try to defeat me."

Confused, he said," I don't understand."

"Attack me, I will defend myself in every way I can. Try to defeat me." When he started to speak again, she shook her head and lifted the sword. "Do it!" she ordered and swung at him with all her strength.

He barely got his sword up in time to deflect the blow and was knocked off balance. He back-stepped, in an effort to regain it. She charged at him again. He switched to a two handed grip and deflected her next blow. He started forward and as he did, his feet became mired in mud.

"What...No!" he cried as his momentum caused him to pitch forward while his feet stayed in the same spot. He dropped his sword so he could break his fall.

"No magic!" he shouted as he gained his feet and glared at her.

"If you had listened to me, my power would not have affected you. Surrender, Mikaal, surrender is the only way. When I attacked you, you not only defended yourself but attacked me as well. Why? Because of your need to control the fight. By doing so, you allowed me to use my power because when you sought to control the fight you abandoned your defenses."

"And how do I build my defenses?"

"With your mind, how else? Picture a wall around your head, a solid wall built of the most impenetrable materials. Build it, hold it, and let your body take care of everything else. When your attacker comes after you, surrender to the attack, let him charge forward, let him believe he's overpowering you, and wait for the moment when his weakness is revealed. Even as you are seemingly giving in to his strength, finish him."

Mikaal took in her lesson, thought about it and said, "Attack me."

Without a change of expression, Areenna lunged at him, swinging her short sword as if it were twig. Charging him, she forced him back. She attacked, pushing at his mind, seeking to make his thoughts bow to hers, but this time she came upon a solid block that allowed no penetration. An instant later the tip of his blade rested at her breast.

"Yield."

"Done," she responded and lowered her sword. "Did you feel me?"

"I felt something, but I was concentrating so hard I couldn't tell what it was."

"Perfect. You will learn, but your defense was strong. And you trusted your body to do what it was trained to do."

"And does this help me with other things?"

She smiled. "I'm a woman, not a mind reader. We'll see. But understand, Mikaal, it is a beginning, nothing more."

CHAPTER 13

AREENNA WAS PHYSICALLY worn out. They had spent the hours after eating in sword work. The muscles of her upper arms and chest hurt in ways she had never before experienced. Her calves and thighs pained her no less than her arms. But the results were exceptional. She was learning how to respond instinctively to whatever situation Mikaal presented.

As she lay in the lean-to staring out at the fire, she admitted it was a good exhaustion because it was physical and not mental. She turned to Mikaal, who lay a few feet to her side and was about to speak when she saw he was already asleep.

The two days they had been traveling had been two days of a growing understanding of her abilities. It was different from anything she had learned or done before—teaching Mikaal had opened her mind further than she'd ever imagined.

With every lesson, with every word she had spoken to him, she had gained greater insight into her own powers. It was as if she was teaching herself as well. What was it that Enaid had said in one of their talks? She tried to recall the exact words but could not. It had been something about teaching herself.

As she thought about how to help Mikaal learn, her eyes closed and her thoughts faded.

◇◇◇

Mikaal lay quietly on his silks, his eyes closed, listening to Areenna's even breathing. He was not tired, but had not wanted to talk after the sword work. His was rooted in his disappointment at not gaining control over whatever powers he might have, and made even more frustrated because he had never before found anything he could not do once he had made up his mind.

He lay there for several more minutes until he was certain Areenna was in a deep sleep before quietly leaving the lean-to.

Outside, he pulled on his boots and wandered the campsite. He spotted Gaalrie perched on a branch, her cinnamon feathers aglow from the low light of the fire. The kraals were to his left. Hero's head hung down as the animal slept while standing, as was the way of a kraal. Charka was a little away, and Mikaal saw the kraal was looking at him.

Watching Charka, he remembered Areenna's questions about the way his kraal had behaved. He went to him and stroked his neck. *What does she see?*

Charka gently pushed his snout against him. Mikaal leaned in as the kraal nudged him, smiling at the familiar feel of the large head against his chest. It was something Charka had always done but... Carefully, thinking about when Areenna had explained how she and Gaalrie communicated, he sent a thought to the kraal exactly the way Areenna had shown him—more asking than ordering.

Charka pulled back and raised his head. The kraal stared directly into Mikaal's eyes and a sudden flooding of colors filled his mind and took his breath away. He stumbled back two steps before catching himself.

Charka tossed his head once and then moved toward Mikaal.

Above him, the treygone's wings fluttered and an instant later Gaalrie dropped from her perch and landed on Charka's back. The kraal stood unmoving when the giant bird settled onto his back as if Charka were but another branch.

Transfixed, Mikaal could only stare at the two animals. Then he reached out and stroked Gaalrie's head.

When his fingers touched the silky feathers, his mind was flooded with abstract thoughts he could not understand, but soon realized the bird was trying to communicate with him.

Reminding himself of Areenna's lessons, he closed his eyes and settled his mind, doing his best to wipe any thoughts away. A moment later he saw himself through Gaalrie's eyes while a soothing energy spread through him as Areenna's aoutem showed him something. Images crossed before his mind's eyes of Areenna, Gaalrie, and then Charka.

He wondered what Gaalrie was trying to do and then, somehow, he knew. He grasped Charka's head in his hands and gazed into the kraal's eyes while opening his mind as he had moments before for the treygone.

It took but a fraction of a second and he was joined with Charka. The feeling of warmth and of soothing energy was so overwhelming he broke the connection and dropped to the ground where he knelt in front of the kraal in an effort to accept what had just happened.

Mikaal had no idea of how long he knelt before Charka, but when he stood again, he knew exactly what had happened. He had found his aoutem.

Areenna woke with a start. It had been a dreamless night and she did not remember falling asleep, only that her last thoughts were about Mikaal and how to help him. She turned and saw he was still asleep and slipped from her sleeping silks.

She went to the small pond and washed her face and then went deeper into the surrounding woods. Ten minutes later she found a succulent tree and gathered the deep yellow ripened fruit from its branches.

When she returned to the campsite, she found Mikaal kneeling at the pond and washing his face, the fire at the campsite rebuilt. "Morning meal," Areenna said, holding up one of the golden succulents.

He turned and smiled at her; the water dripping from his face sparkled in the sunlight. "Good, I'm starving!"

She threw one of the fruits to him. He caught it as he walked toward her, and using both hands twisted it until it split in half. When he reached her he handed her half and then took a bite of the half he'd kept.

They walked to the fire he had rebuilt while she was gathering the fruit and sat. Seated near the fire, they ate their fruit silently. When they finished, she turned to him and was about to speak when she felt Gaalrie push at her. Closing her eyes, she opened herself to her aoutem. A moment later her eyes flew opened and she stared at the giant treygone.

Show me, she asked. In seconds, Areenna saw what had happened during the night between Gaalrie, the kraal, and Mikaal.

"You learned," she said, turning to look at Mikaal.

"When were you going to tell me?"

"I wanted to say something, but I was waiting…no, hoping you would discover what Charka was. You needed to learn for yourself. How did it feel?"

"Amazing," he said.

"It is. And now you know why he did not run from you when you freed him from the bramble. He had already chosen you."

Mikaal looked at the kraal before answering. "I guess he did."

Before leaving the campsite—and following Queen Layra's advice—they put on traveling cloaks with hoods to hide their faces from the travelers they would most likely encounter on the road. The hoods proved effective as they passed others, none of whom appeared interested in them.

They reached the turn-off Queen Layra had instructed them to take just before midday. Above, Gaalrie circled effortlessly. When they started on the northwesterly road and Gaalrie showed Areenna the way ahead was clear, she turned to Mikaal. "I want to try something if you're willing."

"What something?"

"Listening."

"How do you try to listen? You either do or you don't."

"Not that type of listening, but a listening within your mind—tuning your mind into everything around you."

"Such as?"

Areenna inhaled slowly. As she did, she opened her thoughts to what was around them. To her left she heard the skittering of a rabt scratching at the base of its warren. To her right was a dar nibbling on the leaves of a low hanging branch, its mate standing behind her watching for any danger.

"The rabt in the woods to our left, and a dar foraging to your right. Join me," she said and opened herself to him. This time she was fully aware of drawing him into her mind. "Listen, feel, see," she whispered.

She heard his sharp intake of his breath and smiled as he pulled back from her.

"I..."

"No, just listen."

Mikaal did as she commanded. This time he was able to control his ranging thoughts. It soon became clear to him how this form of listening had nothing to do with hearing; rather, it was a feeling of whatever living presence was near. It was about knowing what surrounded him without having to see or hear or feel. It was...*magic*.

"I understand," he said at last.

Areenna did not hear him because at the far range of her senses there was another, darker presence. It was only a faint trace, but she knew it well enough. The dark one was searching for them. They had lost *it* when Mikaal had allowed himself to be caught because of his anger. Now she sensed *it* was searching for them toward the east. She drew her thoughts back swiftly, not wanting to be discovered.

"*They* are looking for us," she said.

"Near?"

"No, far, and have not located us yet. But *they* know, somehow *they* know what we are doing and that we will be going east."

Mikaal shook his head. "You keep saying *they*, but it is only the one."

Exhaling slowly, she shook her head. "No, *they* control her. The dark powers use *her* to do their bidding. Everything *she* does is directed by the dark ones. *She* is a vessel for *their* use, nothing more even though *she* believes *she* acts on her own."

"This can be a weakness."

"It can be," Areenna said.

"If you sense *her*, cannot she sense you as well?"

"If I let *her*. But I will not. When you have gained strength with your powers, you will do the same."

"Can you show me how to sense her?"

Areenna thought about how to explain the process. What she had done a few moments before was simple, and it did not require a lot of power, but to have his inexperienced presence in her mind while she searched might present a danger. "It would be a risk," she admitted.

"Then we will wait," Mikaal said and, with a smile, drew his sword. "Protect yourself!"

She ducked under his swing and drew her short sword.

They passed Handlebridge Lake late in the afternoon. Two miles later Areenna found the symbol Layra had marked by the narrow road, which in reality was more of a thick, tree lined path. Before turning onto the dirt packed lane, Areenna sent Gaalrie ahead.

The treygone rose high and flew swiftly, showing Areenna the road ahead was devoid of travelers and their destination was less than a mile distant.

"The way is clear," she said to Mikaal, who nodded. While he had worked with Areenna on her mounted sword defenses, he had also been practicing the listening that she had shown him earlier. But, with her words came the awareness of how tired he was and how glad the day's journey was near its end.

"I am sorry to be pushing you this way."

He smiled at her. "I can handle it, and I will sleep well tonight."

They rode the final distance without speaking and, as darkness descended, they reached the homestead which Queen Layra had directed them. They dismounted and a young stable boy came out to take Hero and Charka away.

Areenna glanced at Mikaal and saw his features tighten when the boy reached for Charka's reins. "Where is the stable?" she asked.

"Behind the house, My Lady."

She looked at Mikaal who nodded. "Thank you," she said. As the boy led the two kraals away, she turned to Mikaal. "No matter where he is, you will have a connection."

Mikaal studied her face. "You are worried for me?"

"Yes. I remember at the beginning, when I discovered Gaalrie was my aoutem, I panicked because I was afraid something would happen to her."

"And nothing did because of your connection."

"Yes."

"I know," he said. "I can feel him now."

When they started toward the house, Queen Layra stepped through the doorway and started toward them. She too was dressed in a riding cloak, the hood thrown back to show her long mane of silver hair framing a face of undeterminable age.

When they met, the Queen embraced Areenna warmly before stepping back to look at her companion. When Mikaal lowered his hood, Queen Layra's eyes widened. She gave the prince a slight bow of royal acknowledgement.

"Come inside and tell me what your presence here means. Queen Enaid sent word you would be coming, but the message wasn't clear."

Once inside and seated at a long dining table, Areenna began the explanation of their mission, but stopped when the housekeeper brought glasses and a pitcher of water, the stable boy following with a platter of fruits.

When they retreated, Areenna said, "There are several purposes to our journey. Foremost, it is my time to go to the East, to further my learning."

Layra held up her hand. She turned from Areenna to Mikaal, her eyes hardening. "Every woman of ability must make the journey," she said, turning back to Areenna, "but neither are you on the solitary journey required, which is a journey made without a companion—or with a woman of power, but especially not with a male companion—nor are you traveling east. For what reason would you travel from Tolemac to here, why would you go northwest to travel east?"

"Truth be told, My Lady," she replied, "these are troubling times and such times force change. Queen Enaid insisted upon my traveling with Mikaal."

"What are you not telling me? This is still the business from Tolemac, is it not? This is about the dark ones?"

"In part it is," Mikaal affirmed, "which is why we traveled here rather than go directly east."

Turning from Areenna to glare at Mikaal, she pointed a solitary finger at him.

Sensing what was about to happen, Mikaal raised a mind shield the way Areenna had taught him.

"Prince or not, who are you to—" Her words died as her eyes widened. Her finger, still pointed at Mikaal's face, trembled. "How…"

"He is mind blocked," Areenna said quickly, speaking truthfully, but withholding the knowledge of who it was doing the blocking.

Layra turned to Areenna. "I knew you needed to travel secretly, but the prince?"

"Yes, Highness. No one must know lest *they* learn of this. I am going to further my training. Mikaal is to guard me from those who would stop me."

"The journey has never been done with a male companion. It is dangerous for him. Why would Enaid risk the life of her only son? There is much I cannot divine of this," Layra said, her voice dropping to barely a whisper. "Too much."

When Areenna did not speak further, the quiet went on for a few moments before Layra spoke again. "They will not learn from me. Why would they want you?" she asked. "For what happened at Tolemac?"

Areenna nodded.

"I had not thought of that." She covered Areenna's hand. "Of course they would want vengeance on the one who exposed them. You are very young for travel to the Isla—east, but you are very strong."

"Not yet," Areenna whispered.

"Do not doubt yourself." She turned to Mikaal. "Leave us for a moment, please, My Prince."

Mikaal looked at Areenna, who nodded. Standing, he offered the women a slight bow and, with a lilting smile, left the room. He knew he would learn all, later. Outside, he looked toward the forest a few hundred yards away.

Closing his eyes, he let his thoughts wander, pushing himself and his mind toward the tall trees deep inside the forest. As he did, he began to feel the life that filled the wood. The treygones and danglores, craves and even some smidges flew among the branches. He sensed a family of tibbars at the edge of forest; deeper in was a large male dar. Mikaal could almost feel the weight of the rack of horns the dar carried so proudly.

Like a door opening wide, he was amazed at what he could sense. And, the one thing he did not sense was anything dark within the forest.

◇◇◇

"You will need to be careful on the Island. There will be many things that mean you harm. You must leave Mikaal at the Landing. He must not enter the Island—it will go badly for him as it would for any male. The block placed upon him will be useless."

"I understand."

Layra's eyes clouded. "And I will emphasize such warnings. Tread carefully. Look not into places that do not feel safe. When you reach the spot you seek, you will know this. Go only there and when you are done—and I hope you will be done quickly—you must leave immediately." She paused in thought before saying, "Your mother was a strong woman and I can sense her power in you. Be careful, Areenna, when you are on the Island. The forces there will strive to subjugate you."

"I will," Areenna agreed, unwilling to explain why she must bring Mikaal to the Island, and of that she was not the only one seeking the training.

"Good." Layra clapped her hands twice, and the young housekeeper came into the room. "Is the food ready?"

"Yes, My Lady."

"Prince Mikaal is without. Please have him join us."

◇◇◇

An hour after Mikaal had been called to the table, and the evening meal finished, Queen Layra announced her guard had returned to accompany her back to Troit and asked Areenna to step outside with her.

In the foreyard, four mounted guards surrounded a small carriage.

And, as Areenna and Layra walked to the carriage, the guards backed away to allow them passage. At the carriage's door, Layra turned to Areenna. "When you are on the Island, every eye there will be upon you. Never falter, not once." She lifted her right hand and placed it on Areenna's forehead, her palm cupping the skin. "Go with safety, go with strength, feel the power within you, and feel the energy of those who ride at your side."

There was a sudden flash within Areenna's head, and as it stopped and Layra's hand left her skin, Morvene's queen asked, "How many stops are you to make?"

Puzzled by the question, she said, "Three. Here, Northcrom and Aldimor."

"That is good. Enaid has selected three different powers. It will help."

"What will help?"

Layra smiled. "The custom of the blessing—of the gifting. With each blessing comes a different strength."

"I know of no such tradition."

"Nor are you meant to. It is the last lesson we women teach our daughters before they go. It is usually done a few weeks before travel to the Island, but I am certain Enaid has her reasons for doing it this way. Now, return to the house. Rest well tonight and may tomorrow's journey be swift," she said in the traditional parting.

Areenna watched Layra and her guards ride off and, when they were out of sight, she went into the house, wondering what the gift was that Layra had blessed her with. The housekeeper and her son had already gone to their quarters, as instructed by the Queen, leaving Areenna and Mikaal alone in the house.

Sitting in chairs and enjoying the comfort they had not had for two days, Areenna smiled at Mikaal. "She was very concerned about you," she said before launching into the details of what she and Layra discussed. "She has no idea of your ability, or that you are anything other than my protector. What I did pick up from her...what I sensed, was how she thinks your mother sent you because she wants us to—" Areenna cut her words off even as a deep scarlet rose from her neck to her hairline.

"Of course she would think that," Mikaal said quickly. He smiled at her. "Do not be embarrassed, it would seem to be an obvious thought to someone who does not know the real reason."

"Yes," Areenna replied, wondering at the same time if Layra had somehow seen something she herself had not seen....

CHAPTER 14

LIKE A DARK tornado spinning within even darker skies, the seething anger boiling within her mind grew hotter. *Sh*e walked circles inside the large dusky cavern, mutters and curses keeping pace with the uneven steps of her misshapen legs.

One arm was much shorter than the other. Where a hand used to be was nothing but memory, yet using the unseen hand, *she* cast spell after spell, sending her mind ranging, seeking the trail of the two who had escaped her trap. Ever since the snuck had been killed, there had been a block set over them, protecting their thoughts from *her* detection.

She screamed. The sound boiling from her open mouth was like the screech of a banshee. It grew louder and louder until it morphed into a high pitched howl setting the rocks above her head crumbling.

Cutting off the scream as dust from the rock ceiling rained down, *she* went to the center of the cavern and squatted. Her malformed continence blended into the rocks of the floor and walls. *She* slowly worked her mind into the state of fugue needed to enter a full, seeking trance and, as the trance began to strengthen, *she* sent her thoughts on the wings of the newly hatched wraith she had created yesterday.

She made contact with the wraith, which carried the partially transferred mind of its creator, and pushed it to search for the mind patterns its mistress had fought outside the walls of Tolemac.

When the wraith reached the spot where the snuck had failed, it landed. Slowly, waddling on its two clawed feet, it began to scent out the physical traces of their presence. With every step taken by the specter of evil, the grass beneath its clawed feet turned brown.

Less than a minute after arriving, the wraith picked up the trail and launched itself after them. The moon, a crescent sliver hanging askance in the sky, cast enough illumination for the creatures of the forests to see its dark form gliding a hairsbreadth above the treetops. For the wraith to fly higher would mean a loss of scent.

Just before daybreak, the wraith settled onto a high branch a mile distant from the homestead where Areenna and Mikaal slept.

She came out of her trance and a crooked smile broke open a toothless mouth. *She* had them now.

Areenna awoke instantly, the spot in the middle of her forehead burning like a hot-tipped poker. A powerful sense of anxiety gripped her. She fought to settle her thoughts and discover what had broken into her sleep. She closed her eyes and concentrated on the lingering sensation.

Using the feeling of anxiety, she traced it back, seeking its cause. She started slowly by pushing her senses within the homestead, seeking whatever disturbed her within the walls. She found nothing and began to widen her range. The housekeeper was in the kitchen, preparing food; the stable boy was outside doing his chores. She pushed to the stables, where the kraals ate the feed left by the stable boy. She touched Hero's and Charka's minds and found nothing bothering them.

She ranged further, while at the same time feeling Gaalrie join her. She urged the treygone to stay where it perched. She would not risk her aoutem until she knew what they faced. Then she sent her thoughts into the surrounding trees.

It took only a few minutes more for her to discover the blank space within the forest—it was as if there was nothing there, no trees, no life, only a black hole in the middle of the forest.

She approached carefully, testing its edges, pushing a little here and a little there, but it refused to yield its secret. A cold dark feeling seeped into her mind as she tested the boundaries surrounding the emptiness.

She cut off her seeking the instant the coldness pushed back. *We've been found!*

Rising, she dressed quickly and went to wake Mikaal, who she discovered was already up and staring out the window. He was dressed in breeches, his shirt in his hand, the muscles of his broad back cleanly defined.

"There's something out there," she said.

"I know," he responded, still staring out the window.

"You sense it?"

Mikaal shook his head and turned to her. "Not it, you. I felt your disturbance."

"*They* have found us," she whispered.

"How? Are our thoughts no longer protected?"

"I am not sure. I feel no lessening of the blocks. It is something else..."

"Then we need to learn what it is before we leave."

"Morning meal is being prepared," she said. "We'll talk while we eat. We should leave soon."

Mikaal noticed the lines of worry creasing her forehead. "Yes," he agreed.

When the food was set before them at the same table they'd eaten at last night, they began to eat and to discuss options.

"Would Layra have betrayed us?" Mikaal asked. His eyes were on his food rather than on Areenna.

"No. We've talked about this."

Mikaal shook his head. "You are so certain, but many things could happen to change this."

"No." Areenna reached across and grasped his hand in hers. Her hand tingled when her skin wrapped around his. A sensation of closeness enveloped her. "Feel me," she whispered, "join me."

Small shock-like explosions were set off where her skin touched his. "Close your eyes, concentrate."

He followed her lead and a soft comfort grew within his mind —an opening of her thoughts and a welcoming of him to her. "Do you feel me?" she whispered.

Yes, he responded, not with words or even conscious thought, but with a returning of the warmth she had welcomed him with.

"This is how I know Layra did not betray us. When we embraced, we were open to each other." She released his hand and said, "This feeling of openness allows no deceit. It is our most basic protection against them. Should a woman be subverted—and remember no such thing has happened in anyone's memory—we would know instantly."

"Then we must find a way to destroy it, or evade it."

"If we destroy it, *she* will send more. No, we must evade it and in doing so let her think we know nothing of the... It must be another wraith."

"Then we should leave soon, but I think we should start with misdirection and not head directly to Northcrom."

They finished their meal in silence, and then gathered their belongings. The housekeeper gave them a package of food, wrapped within linen cloths and wished them a safe journey.

They started out from the homestead, heading not toward their destination of Northcrom, but away from it. When they reached the small road ringing Handlebridge Lake, Areenna sent Gaalrie upward, not to scout the way ahead, but with a clear warning for the aoutem to hold back and watch the trail behind them.

A half hour into their journey, Mikaal stopped. Dismounting, he withdrew one of the scrolls. The map his father had given them was intricately marked. It showed Morvene, and its capital, Troit, and all the charted roads.

He pointed to Handlebridge Lake and to their approximate position. "We are headed west, Northcrom is north. There is another road a few miles from here that turns northward," he said, pointing to the thin line and following it with his finger. "From here, we can intersect the closest border of Northcrom." He paused. "Perhaps, when we reach Northcrom's borders, instead of going to Syrak, we turn east and go directly to Aldimor."

"We cannot," Areenna said, thinking back to last night's conversation with Layra. "We must go to Syrak and speak with Queen Ilsraeth. It is important."

"Why?"

Areenna shook her head. "My instructions are firm. Your mother has sent us this way for a purpose. You need to trust her."

His eyes narrowed as he stared at her. "You are hiding something."

"I am telling you what we are required to do to make this journey. It is important I speak with each queen before we go to the east. You must trust your mother and trust me as well."

"I trust both of you implicitly. But you are still hiding something."

"Mikaal, there are things you do not need to know, not yet. It has nothing to do with you, only me."

He continued to stare at her, wondering what it was until, finally, he shrugged. "As you say, Princess."

By midday they reached the road that had been marked on the map and Mikaal said, "We take this north, if you still insist on going to Northcrom."

Areenna glanced around and urged Hero to the side of the road where several trees had been downed by a past storm. She dismounted, stretched and untied the linen package attached to her saddle. "A little food before we continue," she said and sat on one of the downed trees.

He dropped Charka's reigns so the kraal could forage along with Hero and joined her on the tree to share the meal.

As they ate, Areenna sent out a questing thought for Gaalrie. It took a moment but when the reply came, it shook her. She closed her eyes and concentrated on what the treygone was seeing.

"That is how," she whispered.

Mikaal was instantly alert. "What is how?"

She opened her eyes and looked at him. Then she grasped both his hands and stared deeply into his eyes. "We are being followed by scent. Gaalrie has seen the wraith again, and it is following us. We need to hide our scent." She opened her thoughts to him to let him see what she had seen. From high above, Gaalrie had watched the wraith drop to the ground outside the homestead and lower its head. He watched as it rose no more than a foot above the ground and flew slowly in the direction they had taken.

"You have no magic to hide our scent? No spell?"

"The first wraith I ever saw was at Tolemac. How can I know how my powers will affect it?"

Mikaal unrolled the map and began to scan it. He traced every road between where they stood and Syrak, looking for a way to hide their trail. When he found what he believed would work, he said, "According to the map, there is a large lake an hour distance from here. There are markings on the map showing a ferry crossing. The lake is wide and if I am right and the ferry is there, it will completely stop our scent. But it will take us a half day out of the way."

"A half day is nothing of concern. We have a destination not a schedule," Areenna said.

"Then our only concern is if the ferry is on this side of the lake," Mikaal offered.

Puzzled, she looked at him for a moment. "Where else would it be?"

"The other side.... How can we be certain? But even if it made a morning trip, it would be back by the time we reach the lake."

"If the ferry is not there, the wraith will find us."

"I see no other choice."

"No, you are right, there is none," Areenna agreed.

"You could send Gaalrie to check on the ferry."

Areenna shook her head. "She tracks the wraith. We must know what *it* is doing."

Mikaal slid the map into the case on Charka's flank. "We should leave now."

"Not yet. Join me here," she said, kneeling in the middle of the road. When he was next to her, she raised her arms, her palms facing the road. "Pay attention," she said. "Create a picture in your mind of a slungk. Close your eyes and picture its pure white fur, see the wide black streak running from the tip of its nose to the very end of its tail. Picture its eyes so small and pale blue. Look at its paws of white fur and black nails. See it raising its tail, the tail widening, bulging. Watch it squeeze itself from its shoulders to its tail and send its spray outward and downward onto the road. See it, create it...do it!" she whispered into his ear as she created her own slungk.

The air turned nauseous, the scent of slungk erupted everywhere. "Come," she commanded him, "we ride. Do not let the image go. Hold it strong."

"How did you—"

"—no, you did that as well. Be quiet and concentrate. Keep expelling the scent."

He did what she asked, and for the next quarter mile held the vision of the slungk. When Areenna told him to stop, he did so gratefully. "I don't understand," he said, weary of the amount of times he'd had to say those words.

"What did you not grasp?"

"How could a slungk be created by thinking of it? What of the formula?"

"Mikaal, you must stop thinking like a man who has heard too many stories of how women create magic. It comes from the mind, not from words. The formula is one of your mind's making."

He shook his head. "I—"

"—Stop talking. Would you have believed me if I said all I have to do is create a picture in my head of what I need to happen and it will?"

He gazed at her for a very long minute. "Before we left Tolemac, no. Now, yes."

"Finally," she whispered, more to herself than to him. "There is no secret among women that the creation within one's mind is the formula—not the words men so badly need to believe are spoken—to create magic."

"So there are no formulas?"

She smiled again. "I didn't say that, and of course there are formulas, but for the most part the formula is...the construction of what needs to be done—a notation, if you will, to remember how it was created. Mikaal, it is the power of the mind, not of the words."

"It is complicated," he admitted.

She edged Hero next to him and reached across to take his hand. His skin was warm and comfortable. She squeezed firmly. "No. You're making it complicated. It's simple. When you want your powers to be there, clear your mind and think only on what needs to be accomplished. It is not a matter of attempting to do something but the act of doing it. Accept it as accomplished and it will be."

Mikaal looked down at the small hand covering his before looking at her. "I shall do my best, Princess."

◇◇◇

Roth and Enaid were walking in the courtyard when a silver and blue winged traimore flew low over them. Reaching up, Enaid presented the small falcon-like bird her wrist. The traimore fluttered above it for a moment before settling gently on her soft skin.

Roth smiled at the bird, remembering its pre-mutated ancestor, which was known as a Peregrine falcon. It was about a quarter bigger than its predecessor, with a longer beak, but identical in all other aspects.

"It is from Morvene, from Layra," she said and untied the small cloth on its clawed limb. She read the inscription and turned to Roth, her eyes troubled. "They have been discovered. Layra says it is the same as was at Tolemac. She tried to put a block behind them, but it did not hold, the dark magic was too strong."

Roth stared at the traimore balanced so lightly on Enaid's wrist. "What choices are there now?"

"None except to trust that together they are strong enough to outmaneuver *her*."

"They are children."

"Oh how I so wish they were," she whispered before exhaling sharply. "Together they are stronger than any who come against them, stronger even than you and I."

"How can you be so certain?"

She smiled lovingly at him. "Solomon, it is time to let go. Mikaal is no longer a boy. He is a man, a special man. And Areenna…"

When she paused, he stepped closer to her. "And Areenna?" he prompted.

"She is the one you have been awaiting. And Mikaal is her complement."

"Areenna…is the woman of your foreseeing?"

"She is, My Lord. Mikaal as well."

He took a step back, his eyes locking on hers. "You are certain of this? When did you know?"

"I think it was at the very moment she was born."

The words should have struck him hard, but they did not. He smiled. "Why did you withhold this from me? Because of Mikaal?"

She shook her head slowly without taking her eyes from his. "I wish I had known. But if I had, you would have treated him differently. Perhaps that is why I was blind to his powers."

"Do you really think so?" he asked.

"Absolutely."

He laughed despite the way his stomach had tightened. "I'm sure you're right. But knowing this you still sent them to the Island?"

She drew a faltering breath. When she settled her mind, she said, "It is where they both must find the abilities that truly lay within them. If they do not, we...all of Nevaeh, are all lost."

CHAPTER 15

"THE FERRY IS there," Areenna said. It was mid-afternoon as they approached the ferry landing. The wraith had been thrown off their scent for a little while, but had picked it up again and was barely an hour behind.

Once she'd known the wraith had recovered their real scent, she had called Gaalrie back. The aoutem was now flying above, watching all areas.

"Then we will be on the water and away from that thing," Mikaal declared.

"Do not be overly confident. It will be only a matter of time, but if all goes well, it will be enough time."

They crested a small hill just as she finished speaking and saw below them the lake and the ferry at the end of a short dock. The ferry looked especially small. Areenna hoped it would be large enough to accommodate the kraals.

Drawing closer, she saw the ferry was bigger than she'd first thought. It was long and flat, with short sides and two sets of oars on each side. There was a long pole at each end for guidance. In the center was a mast with ropes attached to a furled sail.

A few hundred yards north of the dock stood a small stone cabin. A plume of smoke wafted from its chimney. Two small children played in front of the cabin while a woman watched over them.

At the dock, a stocky man watched them approach, arms akimbo, his fisted hands on his hips. Behind him, two younger men worked on the ferry. Areenna turned to Mikaal. "Your ring, take it off," she said.

Mikaal looked down at his right hand. His ring bore the crest of the high king and would identify him as a member of the high king's family. He slipped the ring from his index finger and put it into the small pouch at his belt.

They rode slowly toward the ferry. Areenna watched the ferryman observe their approach. A strange sensation traveled through her mind, and as she studied the ferryman, she was able to sense he was a simple man who worked hard and was forthright and honest. It was the first time she had ever sensed another in this manner and was grateful for the blessing Queen Layra gifted to her—the ability to know the truth of another by looking at them.

Five minutes later they reached the footing of the dock and dismounted. The ferryman approached them. "You seek passage?" he asked and, with a practiced eye, judged their worth by their clothing.

"We do," Mikaal replied.

"It is late in the day," the man said, "and it—"

"—is understood the fare will reflect the hour," Mikaal finished for him.

"You can afford such for two so young?" He stared openly at them.

Areenna, sensing Mikaal's anger at the question, stepped forward. "Please, ferry master, we need to cross. My brother and I must get to Syrak as soon as possible. Our parents await us. My father is King Maslo's record keeper and we carry documents for the King." She pointed to the rolls of maps attached to Charka's saddle.

"King's mission or not, the ferry will still cost you passage."

"Which is only fair," Areenna said. She turned to Mikaal. "Brother, please pay the man."

Mikaal gave her a lopsided smile. "Of course, Sister." Pulling two coins from his pouch, he tossed them to the ferryman. "Is that sufficient?"

Mollified by both coin and Areenna's words, the ferryman put the coins in his pocket without a glance. "Walk the kraals to the ferry. Tie them securely. Kraals do not like the ferry."

"Take them both, Brother, I need to…I need privacy before we cross," Areenna said, giving Mikaal a sharp look.

Mikaal led the kraals to the ferry while Areenna walked toward the ferryman's small house. She waved at the man's wife and walked up to her. Before she could say anything, the woman directed her to the rear of the house.

When she reached the small outbuilding, she did not use it, but she knelt and melded with Gaalrie, who followed her command and swooped down to chase a rabt toward her. When the white and gray spotted rabt saw Areenna, it froze, its tall ears rotating back and forth between Gaalrie who had landed behind it and Areenna. While a dozen feet from it, Areenna created another scent pattern, this time covering the rabt with her scent.

Then she stood and, with a sharp asking, had Gaalrie chase the rabt in a westerly direction. The rabt would run for at least an hour, spreading Areenna's scent in every direction it darted. Hopefully it would confuse the wraith, giving them enough distance from the shore not to be seen should the wraith find their scent by the ferry dock.

It was long after dark when they reached a clearing deep within the forests of Northcrom. They were ten miles from the lake and had been moving in the northeasterly direction to where Syrak was situated. According to the map, Syrak was a least two days further, perhaps three.

The crossing had been uneventful, and once on the far side of the wide lake, they wasted no time in putting distance between themselves and the water, their scent cut off from detection. After leaving the ferry, the ride had been easy and, with the aid of Gaalrie's sharp night vision, they had located the spot where they now made camp.

While Mikaal finished gathering firewood, Areenna set up the lean-to. When she was done, Mikaal lit the fire. "We have been fortunate not to not meet other travelers."

"That will not be the case tomorrow. Northcrom is more populated than Morvene."

"Then we shall have to be careful. We must wear our cloaks."

Nodding, Mikaal went to their belongings and spread out the food the housekeeper had given them. He selected the smoked dar meat and a few slices of bread and brought them over to where Areenna sat.

As the flames of the fire settled into a low glow, they ate their cold meal in silence. After, Mikaal opened one of the map scrolls and laid it out. The firelight was just strong enough to make the writing on the map visible.

"We have three choices," he said, his finger going to the lines on the map showing the routes to Syrak. "These two are the major roads. They will be well traveled." Then he pointed to a line set off from the others. "This one is a rarely traveled route. It will also hide us from that thing, should it pick up our scent on this side of the lake. If my father's notes are right," he said, pointing to the hand written lettering across the line, "and it is what I believe it to be, this road will not carry our scent."

Areenna's brow furrowed. "How is such possible?"

Mikaal smiled. "Not with magic. You must see it to understand," was all he would say.

"I look forward to it." She fell silent then, studying him. She had watched him during the ferry ride. He had been unusually quiet and she was concerned he had begun doubting himself and his powers. "And now, perhaps after a day of riding might I impose on you for a lesson with the sword?"

Mikaal tilted his head and gazed at her. There was something he was picking up from her, but was unsure of what. "If you would like," he said.

"I would." She stood and went to where her sword lay. Sliding it out of the scabbard, she turned to him. "Whenever you are ready."

He hefted his sword. "Defense?" he asked.

"You are the teacher. You decide."

Without further prompting, Mikaal started forward. He struck almost before she was set, slashing at her with a vicious cut that seemed to come from nowhere. She deflected his blade just in time, but the force of the strike knocked her back. She spun, putting a yard between them and grasped her short sword in two hands. He came at her again, this time with an overhead swing, which she blocked, twisted beneath and came around.

Her reaction was instinctive. She did not think, only reacted and came close to catching him, but he blocked her thrust and side-stepped away. Then he spun and, with his sword perpendicular to the ground, came at her.

This time she was prepared and before his sword came within a foot of her, she drew on herself and with her left hand open, sent a flood of power at him. He was lifted from the ground and thrown down hard.

Seeing him sitting on the ground, staring up at her in bewilderment, Areenna began to laugh. She was laughing so hard she could not stop and ended up bent double, leaning on the sword with one hand, the other holding her belly.

"Very funny," Mikaal growled. "I told you no magic."

Areenna gasped for breath and finally gained enough control to stop laughing. She straightened and offered Mikaal a hand. He looked from her face to her hand and slowly extended his hand to her and, with a smile growing on his face, let her help him to his feet.

As he stood, his hand tightened on hers and before she had a chance to react, spun her half around while he grabbed the sword from her other hand. Slamming her against him, he pulled the sword free, raised it, and laid the edge of the blade against her throat.

"Never," he growled into her ear, "no matter what the reason, ever let your guard down. A friendly face can mask a hidden purpose."

When he released her, she spun about, her face a mask of anger at what he had done. But when she saw him smiling, her anger fled. "A lesson well learned, my Prince."

"Good. Now show me how to do what you did."

"It is not yet time. You have other things to master first. Using your power as a weapon takes mastery of other forms first."

"Do we have the time for those things?"

Areenna reached out and took his hand. She squeezed it gently. "We must," she said, but even as she spoke, knew they might not. "But, there is something we can begin with, if you are willing."

"I am."

"Come and sit by the fire." She walked them over and sat a comfortable distance from it.

They sat cross-legged, facing each other. "Close your eyes," she said. "Listen to the night."

Mikaal closed his eyes. He settled his mind, clearing it of all thoughts, and concentrated on the sounds around him. There was the snapping of the fire, and from behind he heard a skittering on a tree. *A skerl*, he sensed. From above came the low clicking of a small night hunter, one of the several varieties of birds that flew by sound not sight. He regulated his breathing the way she had shown him the other day.

"Good," she said. The word was more a feeling than a sound. "Center in yourself—feel your heart pumping. Feel the blood flowing through your veins. Breathe deeply. Feel the power within yourself. Find the place where your power lives. Search carefully for it."

He was at a loss. He wondered how he could search for something he could not recognize. "I…" he began.

"No!" Areenna snapped. "Find it!"

His hands closed into fists. The muscles and tendons of his neck began to bulge. Anger flared so strongly he thought his stomach would twist upon itself and then a sensation of warmth settled over him and he felt Areenna's touch within his mind—felt her as surely as if she was gripping both his hands. And then, with her guidance, he traced the warmth and it filtered through him and settled in a spot just above his groin.

"There," he heard the whisper. "Feel it now."

And he did. The warmth turned hot and a burning began so deep inside he thought he would burst into flames. Yet, there was no pain, just a sensation of a deep burning. The tension in his neck eased. He unfurled his hands and as he did, a flash of light escaped both palms.

There was a sudden cry from Charka. It washed over them, ringing in their ears. Behind them, both kraals stomped their hooves.

Mikaal opened his eyes and he saw Areenna aglow, a bright light surrounding her. He felt Charka's soothing presence build in his mind. Startled, he looked down and saw the glow was coming from the palms of his hands, not from Areenna.

An instant later the light died and all that was left was the flickering of the fire. He was drenched in sweat, his breathing labored, yet he was refreshed at the same time. "That was…incredible."

Areenna stared at him, unable to speak for several more seconds. "That was good," she whispered, "very good." She was stunned by what he had done. He should have only begun to feel the inner seat of his power, not access it as he had. But then, no man had ever had this power before and there was no telling how the power would affect him as he grew in his knowledge and perfected his abilities.

"But you showed me."

"Showed you? What do you mean?"

"I felt you join with me. I felt you guide me."

Areenna shook her head. "I did not join you. I was with you, yes, but we were not joined."

"Oh, you did. I know your touch little princess. It was like at Tolemac when we fought *her* and you drew me into your mind."

Areenna closed her eyes and went into herself. She searched for what he had spoken of and as she retraced her memory of the past minutes, saw exactly what occurred. Only this time it was he who had drawn her to him, not the opposite.

Her eyes flew open and as she started to speak, he said, "I saw. We must learn more of this ability we share."

A wave of exhaustion washed over him. "I... I am so hot," he whispered.

Areenna knew exactly what was happening. It had happened to her often in the early days of her training. She stood quickly, reached out, and drew Mikaal to his feet. Half stumbling, half dragging, she got him to the lean-to and onto his sleeping silks. By the time she released him, he was asleep, the heat pouring from his body like a living thing.

Next, she went to where the kraals stood. Reaching Charka who was trembling from what had happened, Areenna leaned into him, resting her cheek on his long snout and gently stroked the side of his face. "He will be fine, he will be fine," she repeated, knowing how deeply this first touch of Mikaal's power had burrowed into the aoutem.

Only after the kraal was calm did she return to the campfire and sit. She looked up and sent a thought to Gaalrie, who had finished hunting and eating. The giant treygone rose into the air and began reconnoitering for any possible enemy.

Areenna stared at the fire and soon became lost within the flickering of its flames.

◇◇◇

Enaid's eyes snapped open. The burning in her abdomen was intolerable. She glanced at Roth who was sleeping soundly and carefully slid from the bed. Bent in half, Enaid left the bedroom and went into the sitting room where she collapsed. Lying in a fetal position, her arms wrapped around her waist, hugging herself tightly, she held back the moans trying their best to escape.

Hold, she commanded herself, *hold*! Waves of grinding cramps the likes of which she had never before known, ripped through her. She drew the top of her nightdress into her mouth and bit down on it in an effort to stop from screaming.

She lay there for long agonizing minutes before the pain finally eased. Breathing deeply, Enaid made herself sit up while she racked her brain, seeking a reason for what had happened. Finally, comprehension came. It was what she had been denied as the mother of a son. She had seen this happen to her mother when they had started her lessons and she had found the root of her power for the first time.

While she had felt the burning of her power, it had been painless, but her mother had writhed on the floor in agony. Now Enaid understood what her mother had gone through. Mikaal had found his source. And it was more powerful than she'd imagined. So powerful, it was beyond even her understanding.

CHAPTER 16

BY NOON THEY were well into Northcrom, on the main road to Syrak and had just skirted a small town. They had seen only a few travelers, but knew the closer they came to Syrak, the busier the road would be.

Mikaal called a halt. They dismounted and he unrolled one of the maps. As he studied the map, his finger tracing several routes, he said, "Both of the main roads will be well traveled. It's time to find the route we discussed last night."

Areenna followed his finger as it traced the direction they needed to take. "Once we're in the forest, our scent will be strong again."

"We will need to move fast, yes?"

"Yes." Unwrapping a loaf of meat bread, she broke it in half. They mounted their kraals, and began to eat as they entered the woods.

An hour later they were deep into a forest the likes of which neither had seen before. The trees and bushes were so thick and overgrown in places, they wasted precious time seeking ways around the growths.

At one point, with frustration almost overpowering her thoughts, Areenna asked, "How can there be a road here? This is impassable. Every time we find a path, we come up against another blockage. I feel like I am inside a giant maze."

"If the road is on my father's map, it's here," Mikaal stated. "Is Gaalrie still watching our trail?"

"She is."

"Call her back, have her scout ahead. It may be a risk, but we need her help to find a way through this mess."

Closing her eyes, she sent out a call to her aoutem. While they waited for the treygone to return, they dismounted and let the kraals graze. Sitting on the soft grasses between the walls of trees, Areenna stayed connected to Gaalrie while Mikaal sat silently on the grass, lost in his thoughts.

Five minutes later, Areenna opened her eyes and turned to Mikaal. "The road is a few miles ahead, but the way is longer. This forest is a maze—the way the trees have grown is too perfect."

Areenna reached out to Gaalrie. Through the treygone's eyes she examined the pattern of the forest passages. The maze could have only have been created by a woman of great power.

"The way the maze has been set is curious," she told Mikaal, explaining how with every passage through an area, the next led toward the road on the map, but only if you turned in the correct direction, which always felt wrong.

Finally, after another hour of somewhat faster progress, they reached a clearing that opened onto the road. When they did, Areenna was stunned. The road was lined so thickly with trees it was impenetrable by any means other than the way they had reached it. The trees were enormous, rising hundreds of feet into the air, their branches so interwoven they turned the sky above them into a dome of green, which allowed only a few slanted rays of the sun to light the way.

Somehow, there was more than enough light filtering through the trees to illuminate the path, even though not a speck of the cloudless blue sky was visible. Yet, it was not the trees lining and covering the road, but the road itself that held Areenna in thrall: it was a road the likes of which she had never before seen. Its pitted black surface was at least a hundred feet wide and clean and clear of any debris—no leaves, no branches, not even a pebble marred its surface. It was as if the road itself was being constantly swept clean.

She turned to Mikaal and started to speak, but could not find the right words. Mikaal leaned to her and clasped her hand. "Amazing is it not?" he said, understanding her feelings even as they hit her. "A long time ago, when we were exploring another area, my father told me this type of road was once called an 'Interstate highway'. Its solid surface goes down at least three feet, and these highways used to crisscross the entire country and go for hundreds, sometimes thousands of miles.

"They were built, my father said, to carry tens of thousands of people who rode in mechanical carriages across the face of Nevaeh, from one coast to another, but only a few of these 'highways' remain. Most," he added after giving Areenna a chance to absorb some of what he'd told her, "Most are covered by century upon century of dirt and leaves and death... Yet, this one is different. The surface is clean, the pits and holes barely breach the surface."

"It is protected," Areenna said.

"Protected? How?"

"A very powerful woman has cast protection over this road. The maze prevents anyone from finding it in the same way the surface of the road is clean so that our scent will not be found upon it... This is not natural. This is the work of a great sorceress."

"Let us hope it is not one of the Dark Ones."

Areenna stared openly at him. "It is not."

"How can you be so sure?"

"Do you not feel it? The sense of what was done here? Look into yourself, Mikaal. Go to that place of power within you. Feel it."

Mikaal closed his eyes and concentrated on what he had discovered so short a time ago. He made himself turn inward and flow down to where the fire had been unleashed within him. And as soon as he did, rather than heat and fire, a sense of peace welled within him.

"Yes, good...you are understanding more. It would not feel like this if it was the work of the dark ones' magic. You know what such feels like."

"Yes," he agreed.

"And the casting of protection here is old, very old," she added. "Whoever protected this road did so hundreds of years ago."

Falling silent, and with Gaalrie riding Hero's saddle bar, they moved forward along the road, intuitively certain that the dark forces following them could not find them beneath the intricately woven dome of trees. Their sense of time was suspended, but when the very air around them darkened, Areenna knew night was almost upon them and they needed to find a place to camp. She said so to Mikaal.

Within minutes of speaking, a clearing came into view to the side of the road. "We but need to think and what we think of will appear?" Mikaal asked.

Areenna shook her head. "Not exactly."

Mikaal's eyes narrowed. "I was being...sarcastic."

"You still have so much to learn, so much to understand about what magic is. This was here, there are probably many such places along the road, but they are masked by this spell of protection. Speaking of what is needed brings about an understanding within the protection and allows the seeker to find what is sought." She paused when Mikaal's brows furrowed.

"When I was at the school, Master Thrumweld once asked the class what magic was. I knew the answer, but could not speak it because the class, not Master Thrumweld, would not understand. As I've tried to explain to you, magic is science—not the science that men use for building and for weaponry—but the science of spells."

When she paused, he waited silently.

"Consider what is done. When you build a block, like the one you used with Queen Layra, how did you accomplish this? Within your mind, you constructed a...a globe or a box to surround you. You built it block by block and set it to stop anyone from sensing your power."

Before Mikaal could speak, Areenna held up her hand. "Even if you don't recognize how you did this, and believe me few do, save perhaps your mother and some of the more powerful women, it does work this way. We have already spoken of creating formulas but sometimes it happens so fast you don't realize all of what went into its creation. But every spell, every piece of magic is naught but a formula created by your mind to react in a specific way."

Mikaal took in everything she said and, while not fully comprehending it, accepted it as truth. "Can we create a formula to feed us?" he asked as his stomach gave accent to his words with a low gurgling sound.

Areenna laughed. "No," she said with a wide smile. "But we have Gaalrie and Charka and we have my bow."

Ten minutes later a rabt was resting over a fire and Areenna and Mikaal sat near it while the kraals grazed peacefully a few yards behind them.

◇◇◇

Where are they?   How could they disappear so quickly?   What has happened? The deformed sorceress questioned as *she* paced around the fire burning in the center of the cavern. Her liquid reflection cast upon the walls of the cavern made her look even more deformed.

Her seeker had lost their scent hours earlier and the anger boiling from her was like the fire *she* walked near. *It was intolerable! Inexcusable! She* stopped pacing and turned to the fire. *She* reached her hand into the burning coals beneath the flaming wood and withdrew a handful of glowing ashes.

Throwing them into the air, *she* constructed a spell to create another Wraith. Within seconds the dark-winged form grew within the cavern. Its glowing coal-red eyes burned down upon its creator.

"Find them!" the disfigured sorceress commanded.

◇◇◇

"I must send Gaalrie to Queen Ilsraeth," Areenna said after they finished their meal.

"Yes, we should be there tomorrow," Mikaal agreed and then rolled up the map they had been looking at by the light of the fire.

Acknowledging the timetable, Areenna wrote a message to Queen Ilsraeth of Northcrom and sent Gaalrie off. With that done, she turned to Mikaal, who was putting the map back in the bag. "Your stomach is content?" Areenna asked.

He looked at her, puzzled. "Yes."

"Your mind is content about our safety?"

Mikaal wondered what game she was playing at. "Yes."

"Good, then you will be able to concentrate, yes?"

"I am always able to concentrate," he responded.

"So you say." Before he could retort, she said, "In that case, it's time to begin learning exactly what your abilities are. We can start with

159

you shielding yourself."

Facing him, her legs crossed and drawn almost beneath her, her hands resting lightly on her knees, Areenna took a deep breath and exhaled slowly. "As I said before, when creating a spell, you start with a formula. Most women with power never fully grasp the reason for this, because they simply accept their power and use it instinctively, as you have been doing."

She paused to let her words filter into his mind before continuing. "But now is the time for you to create formulas to turn into 'spells'. Think about blocks of stone carved to form walls to repel whatever tries to break through. Picture the stone blocks in your mind and then build a shield that circles you completely, a globe if you want, or four walls, a roof and a floor, all made of the same blocks."

She waited a few seconds. "Have you built your shield in your mind?"

Listening to her, Mikaal had built a perfect globe. He nodded.

"Good. Now, project the shield outward from your mind. Picture the shield surrounding you, with you afloat in its absolute center."

When he had done as she asked, he nodded. "Brace yourself," she commanded and then constructed a glowing ball within her mind and, reaching down into her seat of power, released the ball at him.

The fiery ball struck his shield with an explosive thud. The next thing Mikaal was aware of was lying on the ground, ten feet from where he'd been sitting.

"What?"

Areenna motioned him to come closer. "You need to make it stronger. Mikaal, you have physical strength, great strength, but it's time to build a new muscle—your mind."

He stared hard at her. "So now my mind is a muscle. And just how do I build this mind muscle?"

She smiled widely. "It's rather simple—use your mind instead of relying on the bulk hanging below your neck. And for pity sake, stop thinking about how and just let it happen."

"It's that easy is it?"

"Well, yes," she said thoughtfully. "You need to use your mind to construct the framework of the spell, and then have the internal strength to know it will protect you." Without warning, she sent another fiery ball toward him, holding nothing back.

Mikaal, taken off guard, instinctively raised both hands as the fiery globe streaked toward his face. This time it struck his shield and exploded harmlessly. "How...?"

"You stopped thinking! It was perfect!" Areenna exclaimed. "How did it feel this time?"

Rather than answer quickly, Mikaal allowed himself to search within his mind and body. "I don't know. It happened so fast."

"Yes," Areenna said with a large smile. "It always happens fast. Do you understand more now?"

"Understand what...how I somehow stopped you from roasting my head? No, I don't."

Areenna was surprised. What he had accomplished was amazing. When she'd been in school, she'd watched many girls try to master such spells and it had taken them dozens of attempts before accomplishing it. Mikaal had done so on the second attempt. She wondered what other surprises had he in store.

"How can you not understand? It's simple. It is your natural ability!"

"I don't know what my 'natural' ability is. What I know is when I feel the pommel of a sword in my hand I have the power to protect myself. I don't understand how I have even more power without the sword."

"Damn it, Mikaal. Just look inside yourself. Feel your power—no, *accept* your power. Only in that way can it be done."

"How can I accept what I cannot control?" he half shouted, his irritation at his inability to comprehend making his voice tremble. "I have been trying since I was a child, but nothing I do helps. We have spent days with you attempting to teach me, and I have spent almost every minute of every day since we started on this journey trying to figure it out, but I do not!"

"Because you're too stubborn to let go!"

"Let go of what?"

"The control you believe you need to have over yourself. You don't need it. You already have it!" she shouted, her words echoing from the boles of the surrounding trees.

Before either of them could say another word, the air turned electric.

The hairs on their arms stood out like blades of grass stretching toward the sun. The sensation of something mystical and ancient filled every square inch around them. And then a voice commanded them to stop and come to the road.

Both turned and saw, twenty feet away, a swirling and shimmering mist of pale blues and silvers building in the center of the road. A heartbeat later, the mist solidified into a woman. Areenna gasped when she saw her mother's face grow on the shifting image. Her heart began to pound. Her breathing became forced and labored and the need to run to her mother grew out of control. Unable to stop herself, she moved toward the woman, her heart and mind captured by the visage. Her only desire was to go to her, to hold and be held by her.

She took three steps before Mikaal grabbed her about the waist, refusing to allow her to go. "It is not she... It is not your mother. Look at her!"

The harshness in his voice broke through the trance. She closed her eyes, cleared her mind and looked at the woman again. The shimmering grew stronger until it coalesced into someone else.

As Areenna and Mikaal stared at the apparition, the shimmering turned into a beautiful tall and lithe woman with long and deeply golden hair. Her skin was the color of newly fallen snow. Her face was smooth, unwrinkled and ageless, casting a beauty that held them both in thrall. She was surrounded by a light aura which hid nothing of her.

"Who are you?" Mikaal asked.

The woman smiled at them. "I was known as Bekar when I walked freely, but that was a long time ago."

Areenna stared at the image of the woman, knowing full well she was not a living being. "Why should I accept that?"

"Why should you not. Think you I mean you harm? If I did you would already be destroyed."

Areenna sent a probing thought. A moment later shock raced through her mind, followed by a feeling of warmth so deep it brought tears spilling onto her cheeks.

The woman smiled. "Now do you have belief?"

Without speaking, Areenna took Mikaal's hand in hers and walked toward the woman. At the same time, she built her power, drawing up a ring of protection around them both despite the intense feelings her mind was flooded with.

"It is unnecessary," Bekar said, "You already know I am here for you and him alone. Areenna, I have been waiting a long time for this day."

Areenna felt the truth of her words deep within her.

"Who are you?" Mikaal asked again.

"Reach down, boy," she said, staring at him. "Reach down into that pit of raw power you released within yourself last night. Listen to the words of this woman and stop trying to control yourself and everything around you. Stop trying to be a man—become one! There is no more time left! Both of you must reach into your power and find yourselves!" She lifted her arms, keeping her palms parallel to the ground with all ten fingers pointing at them.

Areenna gasped, grabbing at her abdomen as her insides exploded and burned like never before. Mikaal caught her even as her legs began to buckle beneath her. Despite the agony of the burning within her she felt heat pouring out from the center of Mikaal's body.

As he had moments ago, when Areenna released her attack, Mikaal reached deep inside himself, to the place he had discovered last night and created a shield that flared around them both.

His effort lasted barely a second before the woman made a sweeping motion with one hand and the shield fell apart. "Do not play with me boy. You cannot master what you do not accept."

An instant later the burning stopped and Areenna sank to the ground while Mikaal stood protectively above her. Within them the burning had turned into a soft, calm warmth.

"Look at me girl. Look closely. Think of your lessons. Think of the stories…"

Areenna rose to her feet to face the woman and slowly traced her memories until one rose, slowly at first and then with such great clarity she knew the misty woman had joined her mind and pushed the memory to the surface. "My mother told me of the old stories, but Bekar of the Woods is a legend."

"Were that true, you would not be standing in this spot, nor would I be here, yet there the two of you stand and here stand I. How do you explain such, if it is not reality?"

"I have no explanation other than the bedtime stories of my

childhood. Bekar of the woods…" Her words faded while the woman's smile grew.

"Bedtime stories, am I? What think you of those stories now?"

"How is it possible?"

The shimmering woman smiled. "Ask not how; rather, you should ask why."

Mikaal looked at Areenna. "Who is she?"

"Stop," Bekar said. "She will give you the answers you seek when we are finished."

"Finished with what?" Mikaal asked, ignoring the woman's command to stop.

"Your training…child."

"Boy, child, what other names have you got for me?"

"Enough of them to last an eternity," she snapped. "Listen carefully. There is not much time. The dark ones will find you again, and find you soon. You must build your energies by working together. Alone you are each strong, together you are more powerful than any who come against you."

She flipped her hand at him. A flash of light arrowed toward them. Without thinking, Mikaal blocked her attack as easily as he had Areenna's a few moments before.

"Good. Perhaps you have gained some degree of power after all."

"I am not playing this game," Mikaal said.

"I wish it were a game, boy, because then I could finally rest, but no game is this and it is time you so learned." She flicked her wrist again and the next thing Mikaal was aware of was floating ten feet above the road.

Areenna rose and threw her power toward the woman in an effort to stop her, but Bekar pointed a single finger at her and tossed Areenna to the ground, pinning her there as if tied and staked. "Hear me both of you. You will learn, you will grow strong and you will defeat the dark ones. There is no choice! If you fail, everyone and everything you love will be destroyed, forever. Now, will you listen to me or will I leave you to become their slaves?"

"We will never be slaves. Not to you, not to them," Areenna shouted. Standing, she raised her hands, her palms forward. In the same instant, Mikaal opened his mind and joined her. Together, they released a flare of energy at the woman and the world exploded in a white hot blaze.

CHAPTER 17

"IT IS BEAUTIFUL," Enaid said, gazing at the rising moon. "Yet, at the same time so fragile tonight," she added.

Roth turned to her, drew her to him, and smiled down at her. "Not as beautiful as you, my queen."

She raised a hand toward his cheek, but a bolt of pain ripped through her. She stiffened, her muscles twisted, arching her backwards as if she were a bow being strung. Roth barely caught her before she fell to the ground.

Holding her tightly, he lifted her into his arms and raced inside and up to their chamber, two housekeepers rushing behind them. He had seen this happen once before. It had been a long time ago, and he knew something psychic was taking place—something important. The last time it had happened was almost twenty years before, when her brother, Darb, had been kidnapped by rogue free-blades. He was sure it had to be connected to Mikaal.

He reached their rooms, dismissed the women who followed, and carried Enaid to their bed and sat next to her. He grasped one of her hands tightly while the other went to her face and moved back a shock of hair covering her eyes and, sat silently with her while she worked through whatever was happening.

During it all, Enaid was aware of everything. Although she could not speak or move any part of her body, she drew strength and comfort from Roth's touch and opened herself to whatever was happening while ignoring the paralysis holding her captive.

Slowly, understanding came. A channel had been opened within her mind and, while she lay in her bed, she also floated in the night sky, where she glimpsed a vision of Mikaal, Areenna, and recognized instinctively, the spirit of Bekar of the woods. Welcoming the boiling lava within her, she eased her breathing and accepted the pain of a woman's power.

Teach them, Bekar, teach them I beg of you. Do not forsake them, she pleaded, pushing her petition toward the spirit.

The instant the explosive bolt of power Areenna and Mikaal created sped at Bekar, the misty woman grew larger and spread her arms wide. The fiery explosion hit her and, as Mikaal and Areenna watched, the fire and heat folded upon itself, disappearing as if it had never existed.

"Do not tempt me to put an end to this. You cannot yet overpower me, woman child, even with the gifts of your complement. And you," she said, pointing at Mikaal. "Even now your mother begs for your life as well as hers." She pointed at Areenna. "Shall I accept her plea?"

Areenna and Mikaal looked at each other. A thought flowed between them and acting as one person they turned and released every bit of their power. The night erupted into daytime as they discharged everything they could to overcome the spirit woman. Their muscles screamed, while their minds locked within the battle until, moments later they heard Bekar's command. "Enough!"

The night returned as rapidly as it had left and the three stood staring at each other. Bekar's body had become more solid. "Enough of this," Bekar repeated. "Come, sit with me, the time for teaching is at hand. And you, woman-child, look within yourself to know why your powers have no effect on me."

Areenna closed her eyes and dug within herself. When she did, recognition came. Bekar was not a single entity, not a living woman, but a melding of the spirits of many of the most powerful women who had ever lived. Bekar was the vessel of the power they had left behind—the container that held their collective memories and powers. Her eyes snapped open, allowing her to see the true vision of Bekar, who was now smiling at her. "How is this possible?" she whispered aloud.

"All things are possible when belief is absolute. I am the very belief of the women who helped create all of this," Bekar said, her arms expanding to take in everything around them. "Will you now sit with me?"

Hesitantly, Areenna and Mikaal met her halfway and then lowered themselves to the ground. Bekar did the same and, as they looked at each other, the woman of the woods stared deeply into Areenna's eyes. "The road ahead will be difficult, but it is one the two of you must travel. When you reach the Island and the City of Power, all will turn upon you because of him." She inclined her head to Mikaal. "You may not see it happening, because there will be tricksters, but if you are not true all will turn against you. For centuries, women have been in control of the power. With him, this changes and people do not like change. But our foreseeing has shown us clearly why such a change is necessary—it is the last chance for us, and you must comprehend the absolute importance of this. You must accept and believe because, if you fail, everything and everyone everywhere will fall to the dark powers. The hundreds of generations that have fought to survive, to grow, and to rebuild this destroyed world will have done so for naught.

"Your father's life," Bekar said, turning to glare at Mikaal, "will have been wasted, and with it, all that those who sent him had accomplished will be for nothing."

The enormity of her words was like an unbearable weight within Areenna's head, its oppressiveness making it impossible to breathe. *Why is this happening?* she asked herself. She was barely old enough to think herself a woman, much less the person who must save her world. "How can just the two of us stop them?"

Bekar shook her head. "You do not yet see the truth of it. It is not just the two of you who will do this, it is every living, sentient being of Nevaeh. That is why you must go to the Island. You, Areenna, must finish your training. You, Mikaal, must discover everything about yourself you should have learned years ago. But more importantly, you must find a way to survive the Island. Now, close your eyes. What must be done will be done. I...we have been waiting here for seven centuries. Our sole responsibility is to keep this road protected for you. After tonight, we can all be free."

Areenna stared at her. "I don't understand."

Bekar favored her with a soft gaze. "Do not worry over this. In the coming days and weeks you will understand all too well. Close your eyes!" she commanded.

Raising her right hand, she swept it before both their faces. Areenna and Mikaal fell gently to the ground, as if succumbing to a natural sleep, yet it was far from such. And then, the spirit woman of the forest dissolved within a mist that flowed over and around and into the two sleeping forms to begin their most important lesson.

The rays of the rising sun wove softly through the window to waken Enaid. She opened her eyes to find Roth sitting next to her, her hand gripped within his. She remembered being carried into their rooms and of him sitting next to her while she was in the trance. "You did not sleep?"

Exhaling loudly, he smiled down at her. "I preferred watching over you."

"They're safe for now."

Areenna opened her eyes. She was lying on the ground exactly where she'd been when she sat across from Bekar. She sat up and took several breaths before turning to look at Mikaal, who was beginning to stir.

She watched him and thought about last night. She knew, without knowing how, Bekar was gone, perhaps forever. Yet within her was an awareness of new strength.

Closing her eyes, she dug deep into her mind to learn what had happened after Bekar had placed them in the trance. Finding memories that were not hers, she became witness to battles that had raged centuries before her birth—to the unending fight between the people of Nevaeh and the pawns of the dark ones. She was now a first-hand witness to centuries of death and of survival.

"It is so...so..." she heard Mikaal say as if from a great distance.

Opening her eyes, she stared at him. His eyes were different. A new maturity had settled within their gray depths. The gravity within set them aglow. "Yes," she replied.

Unable to break the stare, she grew conscious of a closeness between her and Mikaal—an intimacy she had never felt with her mother, her father, or even her aoutem. It was so strong, it took her breath away. Her brows drew together with the confusing emotions and she said, "We have changed. I am not sure in how many ways, but we have changed."

"And we will learn how." He paused, his eyes widening. "I see the truth of it...Layra...that was what she gave you, truth seeing. I feel it, too."

Areenna stared at him. Suddenly she was within his mind. She saw he, too, now had the gift. "What do you remember?"

"Nothing after she raised her hand...yet there are so many things I cannot put them in an order...I remember them, I see them, and I can feel them, but I cannot grasp them."

"It is the same with me. We need time." Sensing Gaalrie's approach, she looked up just as the treygone landed on the ground next to her. She took the message from his leg and opened it. They stared at the neat handwriting. It was directions to meet Ilsraeth, the Queen of Northcrom.

Mikaal looked at the dome of branches and gauged the sun's height by the slant of rays filtering through. "We'll have to ride fast," he said as he stood and helped Areenna to her feet. Little shocks passed between them at the touch. They went to where their kraals were grazing at the roadside. Sitting on the edge of the road a few yards from the kraals was a basket of breads.

Mikaal went to it, but rather than take anything from it, he looked at the dirt by the road. There were small footprints leading up to and then away from the road. He glanced at Areenna. "Someone brought the basket. A child?"

Areenna went to him. She knelt near the footprints and carefully touched one of the impressions. When her fingers grazed the earth, there was a sense of warmth. "No, not a child, it was a woman, young, but not with strong magic—not yet anyway. Bekar must have summoned her. Feel it."

Mikaal did as Areenna asked and when he touched the earth, he too felt the warmth rise. He closed his eyes and concentrated on the sensations and, without trying, sensed the footprint had been left by a young woman whose magic was not strong. For just an instant, he saw a vision of her placing the basket by the road. She was young, with deep bronze skin and raven black hair.

"I feel it, too," he said. He looked at the bread just as Areenna picked up a small loaf and broke it in half.

She sniffed drawing in the bread's delicate fragrance. She handed Mikaal the other half, took a bite and then, smiling, said, "It's wonderful, eat!"

Ten minutes later they were on their kraals, following Queen Ilsraeth's directions. Each was silent, searching inside themselves to discover what Bekar had done.

Later in the afternoon—hours after the ancient road had ended and opened into a wide meadow—they turned in a northwesterly direction. Gaalrie flew above them, sharp and watchful eyes sending Areenna visions of the area ahead and guiding them to where Northcrom's queen had directed.

A short time later, they crested the top of a hill and Areenna saw the place Ilsraeth had brought them to. A small cottage built of split trees and surrounded by rolling grassy hills sat near the edge of a long oval, finger-shaped lake, perhaps thirty miles long and a mile across at its widest point. Smoke rose from the cottage's chimney. There was no stable, but three kraals roamed within a fenced hold.

Mikaal, who was studying his father's maps as they rode, said, "The lake is called George."

"Look left," she said.

He did and saw the cottage. "Yes, it seems right. The lake is called George," he repeated absently.

"George? What a strange name."

"My father marked the map clearly."

"What do you suppose it means, George?"

Mikaal shrugged. "It's a name. The old ones had strange names.

My father's names…Solomon and Roth…. Had you ever heard of them before?" he asked.

Areenna shook her head. *But then, there has not been anyone like your father before, has there?*

"No, that's true," he said.

Areenna jerked Hero's reins and stopped the kraal. "What did you say?"

Mikaal stopped Charka. "What? That's true?"

"Yes. What's true?"

Puzzled he stared at her. "You just said there has never been anyone like my father."

"No I didn't," she said.

"I heard you as clear as day."

Catching her lower lip between her teeth, she worried it for a moment before saying, "Mikaal, I never spoke those words, I only thought them…"

Mikaal looked at her. Her coppery skin glowed with the lowering sun. Her eyes were alive, and her full lips were pulled into a frown as she continued to worry her lower lip between white teeth.

"How is this possible? It is not like before…not like the feel of thought. I heard words."

Bekar did this, she directed the thought toward him.

Yes, Mikaal agreed.

"Tell me what I am thinking," she said aloud, and concentrated on a thought of her father, Nosaj.

Mikaal's brows furrowed in concentration, but a moment later all he could do was to shake his head. "Nothing," he whispered.

Areenna sighed. "Good," relief filling her exhalation. *We can communicate better but that is all—for now.*

"For now?" Mikaal questioned aloud.

Areenna shrugged. "Yes. Whatever gifts were given to us, were done for a purpose. It will be up to us to discover the purpose."

"To defeat them," Mikaal said.

"Yes, but I sense there is more. No one can know about this."

"Of course," Mikaal said, dryly.

Areenna glanced at him, his tone making her smile. "Frustration is it?"

"More like irritation. These little bits and pieces... What's the point? Why not just tell us and be done with it?"

"The point, my impatient...what did she say last night? You are my complement?"

When Mikaal nodded she said, "Then, my impatient complement, self-discovery is the lesson for today. A woman's powers are found through self-discovery. We each look inside ourselves to find what it is that lives and grows within us. If we are told, how do we really know? How do we draw this power out? Only through our own recognition can we learn not just what our powers are, but how to use them. Can you not see this, even if you are a...man?"

Mikaal leaned back on Charka. "So, because I am a man, you wonder if I will be able to do this."

Areenna shook her head, the smile tugging at the corners of her mouth fled. "No, Mikaal, it's your impatience, your frustrations, not your sex that concerns me."

"Then it is upon you to teach me patience, is it not?" he asked with a lopsided smile.

She started to give him a sharp retort but stopped herself as the weight of his lightly spoken words struck her. Taking a deep breath, she nodded. *Yes, Mikaal, it is upon me.*

"Areenna—"

She cut him off with a wave of her hand. "It is all right, Mikaal. It took me a little while, but I understand more now." And she did. She realized Bekar had left her with many things, and understanding her role was one of them. She knew what had to be done and, more importantly, how to do it.

In that very moment, the door to the cottage opened and the Queen of Northcrom stepped outside. Next to her was a black rantor, among the fiercest of the animals of Nevaeh. Ilsraeth, with one hand resting on the rantor's head, looked toward the hillside to where Areenna and Mikaal rode and waved.

"Come," Mikaal said, "we are seen."

CHAPTER 18

THEY DISMOUNTED A few feet from where Ilsraeth stood and, as a young boy raced out to them to take the kraals to the small corral, Mikaal said, "Water and feed them." The boy bowed, took the reins, and led the kraals off.

Mikaal and Areenna turned to Northcrom's queen and bowed slightly. Ilsraeth returned the courtesy before saying, "Welcome to Northcrom my Prince, Princess. Please join me inside. I have a meal prepared.

Her aoutem, a large pure black rantor, almost half again the size of a gorlon, walked with them. Its cat-like head moved side to side, looking from its mistress to Areenna and Mikaal. The rantor's muscles flexing beneath its clinging black fur rippled in the remnants of sunlight.

The rantor stopped at the doorway and remained outside when they followed Ilsraeth into the cottage's main room. A long table was set with three places and several trays of food in its center, all illuminated by the soft glow of luminescent night-moss. There were two other doors in the cottage that led to sleeping rooms. The kitchen was at the far end of the main room. The walls were covered with woven silks and the windows were closed off to the remaining daylight.

When they were seated, Ilsraeth poured each of them a glass of wine. Before lifting her glass, she said, "I know why you are here, and I am very afraid."

"Why?" Mikaal asked.

"Because of what you and Areenna, represent…the legends. Your presence here makes them real."

"I don't understand," Mikaal said while Areenna maintained her silence.

"Let us eat and then talk." She lifted her glass toward them. "To Nevaeh," she whispered before taking a sip.

Areenna and Mikaal had not eaten since the bread that morning and ate in the silence Ilsraeth had called for. When they had eaten their fill, and pushed their plates away, a woman came and cleared the table. A few minutes later, she left the cottage by the back door and the three were alone again.

Ilsraeth looked from one to the other. "Areenna, I have known you since you suckled at your mother's breast. I have watched you grow and I have been waiting for this day. But at the same time, it frightens me more than I can express.

"You have been chosen to do what no mortal woman has ever done before. The days ahead will be terribly hard and," she continued, turning to Mikaal, "for you, Mikaal, I can only imagine how hard the days will be in your attempt to accompany Areenna. I know you must, for last night I had a foreseeing. Although it was not clear, I foresaw you somehow play a part in what is about to happen." She stared openly at him, her expression one of deep confusion. "You are a puzzle. There is something about you…what is your purpose here?"

She paused, the pale skin of her forehead grooving deeply in concentration. "Why do you travel with Areenna? Has your mother a death wish for her only child to send you into hell's maw? What is it about you, young man? Who are you to be?"

In that instant, Areenna pushed her senses toward Mikaal to make certain his block was set. Finding it so, she exhaled slowly. "Why so puzzled, My Lady? Enaid sent him to help protect me."

Ilsraeth glared at Areenna and then shook her head. "Protect you? I think not. There is more to it." She fell silent, her eyes flicking from one to the other. Her brows knit as she sent a probe at both of them. She took in a sharp breath and looked at Mikaal. "Who are you?" she whispered. "How can you block me?"

She turned to Areenna. "You are protecting him."

Areenna shook her head. "Not I, My Lady, it is Enaid. She had laid a spell of protection on Mikaal."

Ilsraeth's deep brown eyes bored heavily into Areenna's. Her tongue moistened her lips, but no words followed until, moments later, she said, "It is a huge risk, taking him to the Island. He may die, as might you."

"We understand the risks."

"Do you?" Turning to Mikaal, she said, "Leave us, young heir, we must talk the talk of women."

Mikaal rose silently and went outside. He stopped a few feet from the cottage and looked around. He sensed Charka behind him while he gazed upon the blue waters of the lake but he didn't see them as he concentrated on Areenna. An instant later he joined her mind.

"Why is he with you?" Ilsraeth asked when he left.

"Enaid has sent him with me for protection. The dark ones..."

"Areenna, do not treat me as an imbecile. It is you who will have to protect him...."

Areenna shook her head. "It is...complicated, Highness. Enaid had a vision and Mikaal was important in that vision. She believes I need him in order to be successful with the last of my training."

Without any visible warning, Ilsraeth directed a powerful probe at Areenna, which Areenna deflected easily. Ilsraeth's eyes widened, her brows knitted together. "You are holding back. I see that, but...you have grown very strong."

Areenna reached across the table and took Ilsraeth's hands and clasped them tightly. "My Lady, I have no desire to deceive you. I cannot speak further. You must trust the Lady Enaid, and you must trust me as well. Can you do that?"

The queen looked down at their clasped hands and opened her mind. Slowly she nodded. "Reluctantly and sadly for I sense much in what you carry within you. Note this, child—I see choices will have to be made, hard choices governing life and death for many. Weighty choices will be given to you and you must be careful in how you make them."

Ilsraeth paused. Just as she was about to speak, she stiffened and her eyes went distant. A few moments later, she blinked. "The darkness from Tolemac…it is still around. It is tracking you here is it not?

Areenna nodded.

"I understand more now. Listen carefully, for I have not much time and must return. When you leave, go back the way you came for a day's travel. Then you must head directly southeast. By the end of the second day you will reach the outer border of Aldimor. Turn and go directly east for two days to Dees. When you are outside of the capital, send for Lady Atir. She will tell you where to meet her."

"We cannot. The wraith is tracking us by scent. It will find us if we go that way."

Ilsraeth closed her eyes for a moment. When she opened them she smiled. "Yes, I see it." She exhaled loudly. "Very well, there is another way. Though it may take longer, it will be safer. When you leave here, go directly east. A half day's travel will find you at a river. The river is…" She closed her eyes and grasped Areenna's hand. "Here," she said, and drew a mind picture of the exact spot she was directing Areenna to. "From there, you will need to take a boat for another half day. You will find a road at the small town of Keepsie. Take that road to the borders of Aldimor. From there proceed east to Dees."

"The boat? How—"

"—when you reach the river there is a house, well hidden—here," she said, weaving her forefinger over the table to draw a picture for Areenna. "There is a man, Timon is his name. He is…dangerous if he does not know you. You will tell him I have sent you, and you will show him this," she added, slipping a ring from her finger and handing it to Areenna. "When you show him the ring, he will do whatever is necessary to help you."

"How can you be so certain?"

Ilsraeth looked deeply into her eyes. "He is…a friend."

Areenna felt, more than heard the word. Her eyes widened slightly and then she nodded her understanding.

"Yes, it was…before I became queen. He is a good man, humble yet strong."

"I understand," Areenna whispered. While no words had been spoken, the knowledge of who this man was came easily to her. How difficult it must have been for Ilsraeth to decide to marry another. But such was the lot of a woman of great power, and Ilsraeth had more than just her heart to be responsible to.

"I know you do. But, young Areenna, your reason to be here is for this," Ilsraeth said. She leaned across the table and placed her hand over Areenna's heart.

At the instant of contact, Areenna felt a lightning bolt enter her chest. First there was an explosion of heat, then a rush of cold that sent chills racing through her body. Three heartbeats later, it was as if nothing had happened. But Ilsraeth did not release her until she fed Areenna the knowledge of how to work the gift.

Areenna opened her eyes and looked at Ilsraeth. "Thank you," she whispered.

Ilsraeth stood as did Areenna. "You must be careful with the gift. It is not easily used and a heavy price is paid for that use." Northcrom's queen walked around the table and took Areenna into her arms. "Be careful, child, your path is a hard one. Take all precautions. Sleep here this night, leave in the morning. I sense no evil nearby. Once upon the river, you will be safe."

"Thank you, Ilsraeth," Areenna said when the Queen released her.

The fire burned a sickly green-yellow, the flames reaching toward the cave's ceiling. *She* threw another mixture of chopped bark, flesh and herbs into the flames. The fire mushroomed against the roof of the cave.

She stepped back, nodded, and bent. When *she* straightened to its full height, *she* held a bowl filled with the rotting flesh of a baby. *She* stepped toward the fire and held the bowl into the flames and stood there for a full minute. When *she* withdrew its arm from the flames, not a single piece of flesh was burned, but the bowl was bubbling and smoking.

She set the bowl on the floor and began to speak the unintelligible words of the formula *she* was casting. *She* called upon all the powers her masters had bestowed upon her, which had added to her natural powers.

A moment later a small whirlwind of black mist rose from the bowl and grew until its visage almost filled the cavern itself. This was her third wraith since the two had begun their journey. The wraith *she* had sent out to track by scent had lost the two. This could not be allowed.

She turned and looked up at the burning eyes of the beast and sent a malevolent thought at it. Seconds later the beast screamed and flew out of the cavern, went high, and headed east.

She began to laugh. *She* knew they would not escape this one!

Areenna awoke to the first bands of light breaking across the horizon. She dressed and went into the main room, where she found Mikaal already sipping hot tea. "Have you been up long?" she asked, going to the table and sitting across from him.

There was a bowl of fruit and a plate with bread in the center. A steaming pot was there too, with an empty cup next to it. Mikaal smiled at her and shook his head. "Not long. I've been trying to understand what Ilsraeth did to you last night."

"The gift... You have been trying to use it?"

He nodded. "Trying seems to be all I can do."

Areenna closed her eyes and explored within herself. Slowly, carefully, she studied the internal change created by Ilsraeth's gift of power. A moment later she opened her eyes. "Watch me carefully," she said and thought the words of the new formula. Within her, there was no rising of the heat signaling her power; rather, a chill raced through her. And then everything shimmered before her. She saw Mikaal's eyes go wide and a startled expression transfix his features.

She released the formula and the world returned to focus. "You saw what?"

"You...you disappeared. You vanished before my eyes," Mikaal said, his voice slightly shaken.

"Such a gift," Areenna said. A band of weariness descended on her. She exhaled sharply, realizing how much strength she had used in so short a time. "It can last only a short time and there is a price. It drained me. I need a few minutes to regain my strength. We must practice this new gift, build our strength to use it when we need it."

Mikaal poured her a cup of hot tea. "Drink," he said, pushing the cup toward her.

"It is a truly powerful gift, but one which must be used sparingly—

and it's dangerous if not used wisely." *Here is how it is done*, she said within his mind, and explained every step necessary. "But do not use this unless absolutely necessary. The longer you hold the formula, the weaker you become. For short periods it will be safe," she finished and drank the tea. A few moments later, her strength returned.

"We will have to work on it."

They left the cottage fifteen minutes later and, with Gaalrie scouting the way ahead, began the trip to the river. Five hours later they crested a steep hill and saw the river below. From his maps, Mikaal knew they were near the headwaters of the river, which flowed for several hundred miles, and grew wider the further east it went.

To their right was a small village built on the bank of the narrow river: to their left they saw the mostly hidden house Queen Ilsraeth had described. The house was not visible unless you knew exactly where to look. When they drew their kraals to a halt thirty feet from the house, a tall man emerged from the doorway.

Areenna took in his visage, which emanated strength. He was slightly taller than most, perhaps an inch taller than Mikaal, with long dark hair reaching to his shoulders. His almond shaped eyes were deep blue and made almost luminescent by the sun burnished hue of his skin. A longsword was strapped to his waist and as he looked at the two mounted riders, his right hand gripped the pommel.

His aura was that of a deep internal power and it resonated within Areenna.

He drew his sword, but held it lightly, pointed earthward. "What do you here, travelers?"

"We seek you, Master Timon," Areenna said. The man's eyebrows rose in question as Areenna dismounted Hero and walked toward him.

"No one seeks me other than those I know," he stated, his eyes narrowing. "What business do you have with me?"

Areenna took another step toward him. In warning, the man lifted his sword a few inches. Mikaal dismounted at the gesture, took a step, and gripped the pommel of his own sword.

Easy, Areenna cautioned.

Timon gripped his sword in both hands and lifted it in warning. "Come no further," he ordered Mikaal.

Mikaal froze at Areenna's silent command, not the man's. She held out her hand to the man, palm up showing him Ilsraeth's ring. "The queen has sent us to you."

Timon looked at her hand and took a step closer. He lifted the ring from her palm and stared at it. A moment later he sheathed his sword and nodded to them. "What is it you seek?"

"Transport down river."

"The kraals as well?"

"Yes," Mikaal said.

"What is your destination?"

"We go to Aldimor, to Dees," Mikaal said.

Timon studied them, his features clearly showing he was working it though until, finally, he said, "There is an old road, just north of Keepsie. About seven hours downriver. This road cuts due west, and reaches the closest border with Northcrom. There, the road turns southwest and then south, where it descends into Aldimor and follows the mountains until Dees. Will that do?"

"Well traveled, is it?" Mikaal asked

Timon stared at him. "It's old. People use it," he replied dryly, looking from Mikaal to Areenna. "But not overly so. There are more…direct ways to Dees, of which I am sure you are aware."

"I am sure there are," Areenna said.

Timon looked at the sky. "It is mid-afternoon. I have no desire to travel the river at night. It is shallow and narrow here, and only broadens fifty miles downriver. We leave in the morning."

Areenna glanced at Mikaal. *We cannot stay overnight. We must be on the water.*

Yes, Mikaal replied in silent conversation.

"Master Timon, it is important we travel now, and especially by water. I can make certain this trip and your return will be smooth and your boat safe."

"Can you now?" he responded, a glint dancing in his eyes. "You are that powerful?"

Areenna met his challenging stare. "I am."

Timon gazed at her thoughtfully, his eyes boring into her in an unusually intense way. A moment later he nodded. "Your power remains to be seen, but if My Lady Ilsraeth sent you, she trusts you. I can do no less."

"We are indebted," Mikaal said.

Timon smiled. "No, it is I who is indebted...my Prince. Your father gave us stability and the freedom to live safely when there was none. There is no debt upon you."

"You know me," Mikaal whispered.

"You are your father's image and I spent three years in his camp. You have your mother's eyes. And you My Lady?"

Areenna bowed her head to him. "I am Areenna, daughter of Nosaj of Freemorn."

Timon smiled. "A good man is Nosaj, a noble fighter as well. I had thought of moving dominion to Freemorn, but there is no river large enough and I could not live happily without the waters." He paused momentarily. "There is stew on the fire. Eat while I ready the boat." He led them into his house. After they began to eat, Timon left to prepare the boat.

When the door closed, Mikaal said, "He seems a good man. A bit, ah, touchy though."

"With good reason. He has chosen a lonely life. He and Ilsraeth were...lovers before she became queen. He has never looked to another woman."

"Because he still loves her?"

Areenna sighed. "Because they still love each other—but they have not been lovers since she became queen."

Mikaal took a long breath as her words rolled across his mind. "I envy him not," he said, his eyes locked on Areenna. He broke the stare quickly and unrolled one of the map scrolls. Once laid out on the table, he traced the route Timon spoke of with his forefinger. "It looks easy enough. With luck, the wraiths will not find us after we go down river."

"They won't. They'll be watching the east. They will be waiting for us by the Island."

"We will figure out something," Mikaal assured her.

"We have to," she added.

◇◇◇

Having woken to a dark and deep sense of danger, Enaid had gone to her haven within the circle of trees. Closed-eyed and naked, sitting cross-legged a few feet from the crystal waters of the pond with her aoutem lying next to her, she sent out a thoughtful probe in an effort to feel Areenna and Mikaal.

She cast her thought outward, something she had learned long ago, and searched carefully for them. The sensation of danger was growing stronger and she knew she had to find a way to warn them. As she pushed her senses toward the north, she encountered a terrible, dark visage so vile it turned her stomach.

She held back, testing the areas carefully before expanding her thoughts to discover what this thing was. A moment later her eyes snapped open, her body strangely chilled to the bone.

A wraith—huge and dangerous. It was one such as she'd never before encountered.

She shivered. *Such danger....*

CHAPTER 19

LESS THAN AN hour after arriving, with perhaps two hours of sunlight left, Mikaal brought Hero and Charka to the rear center of the main deck, where there was a pen large enough to hold livestock for shipment down river.

The boat itself was a handsome craft, a full thirty feet long. Its hull gleamed with rubbed oil, and its single mast, three times a man's height, stood proudly. The tall mast was set slightly forward of center and the carved wooden wheel Timon used to steer the ship was on a small raised platform before the mast. There was an opening in the deck just before the elevated wheel platform. Below the main deck was a large area divided in two. The rear for storage and supplies, the front held a bed, a table and four stools. A small kitchen was off to the side, with several cabinets, in which Timon had stored food for the trip, including the remains of the stew they'd eaten earlier along with several loaves of bread. A brazier style stove rested on a counter extended out from the hull.

After Mikaal urged both Hero and Charka into the pen and closed the low gate, Timon stepped next to him. "A fine mount, prince, but you should tie him and the other to the post," he advised, gesturing toward one of the posts in the center of the pen. "It would be ill for them to be hurt by a sudden shift."

As if the kraal knew Timon was speaking about him, Charka moved forward until he could nuzzle Mikaal. Mikaal stroked his head, but made no move to follow the river man's advice. "They are better off untied. On this you will need to trust me."

The river man's raised eyebrows were answer enough. A wise man, Timon knew better than to argue with a prince over advice not accepted. Either the kraals would do well, or one or both would be hurt. It was no longer his responsibility. "Very well, Prince Mikaal."

"Mikaal," he corrected, looking directly at the river man.

Timon held the prince's gaze for several seconds before saying, "As you wish...Mikaal. Be so kind as to untie the stern line." Turning, Timon went to the bow of the boat and untied the line while Mikaal did the same for the stern line.

From her vantage point near the kraals, Areenna watched Mikaal and Timon free the boat. She understood Timon's acceptance when Mikaal would not tie the kraals and liked the fact the river man did not argue. He was, she saw, secure in his own skin and had no need to show his importance—and he knew he was of vital importance to them.

Once the boat was released from its moorings, Areenna went to the kraals and silently called them to her. She stroked each of their heads, and as she did, sent calming energy to them.

Timon allowed the boat to drift outward, using the tiller to direct it. When they were a dozen yards from the shore, he went to the center mast and unfurled the sail. The heavy cloth rippled momentarily and then fell straight. While Mikaal and Areenna watched, the material undulated again and caught the low breeze coming off the water. Although the sail did not fill, it trapped enough of the breeze to coax the vessel forward.

Timon grasped the wheel and, without looking at them, said, "When the sun sets, the evening breezes will get stronger. Until then, feel free to acquaint yourselves with my boat. Your eyes will be needed when dusk comes. The river is dangerous, the rocks the least of it."

"Thieves?" Areenna asked.

Timon smiled broadly. "No thief will bother this boat. It is the life upon the road we travel. Water snucks are particularly nasty and very large and if they are hungry—and there are trigetores as well."

"Trigetores attack us? We are too large," Mikaal said.

"So I once thought. But it depends on how well their hunting has been, and this season has not been good for these nighttime predators. Too little rain has caused their normal prey to move inland. It happened a few years ago, and when a trigetore is hungry, it cares not where its food comes from. They are the dumbest of birds and their blindness is not in our best interests." On the last word, Timon held up his left arm, the material from his shirt dropped to reveal a ragged ugly scar running from wrist to elbow. "This happened eight years ago."

"We will keep a sharp eye. Thank you, Master Timon," Areenna said. With a slight motion to Mikaal, she went to the bow. Mikaal followed.

Areenna went to the left and Mikaal to the right. "This is more comfortable than riding a kraal," Mikaal said lightly.

"Yes, and for us, safer."

"The river is clear?" Mikaal asked.

Areenna closed her eyes and joined with Gaalrie who flew above. Through her aoutem's eyes she saw no other boats on the narrow river and the way ahead was clear.

"Yes," she said.

"There has been no training today," Mikaal reminded her.

"There has been no chance. And now it is impossible."

"Why?"

Areenna looked over her shoulder. "Timon, all is clear."

At Timon's nod, she lost herself in thought. A moment later she sent him a thought rather than speak aloud. *We are to be on watch for rocks, branches, and animals. There are other ways besides your eyes. You learned well the lessons about sensing what living things are around us. Now try to do the same, but sense what is in the water whether living or not. Concentrate on what is below the water.*

Mikaal gazed at Areenna, judging the seriousness of what she asked. *To see something not alive would seem impossible.*

What is not alive?

Rocks.

Areenna smiled broadly. "A rock is neither dead nor alive, it is but a rock. In the water, life is everywhere. Why would life not be upon a rock or under a rock or within crevices of a rock?" *Seek the blank spaces between what lives in the water. You know what a tree feels like within your mind. What of the plant life growing on the large rocks that fall*

186

from the hillsides and mountainsides into the river? she asked silently.

She pointed to the tall, tree-filled mountainsides that angled steeply down to the river.

Mikaal followed her pointing finger, thinking—and far from the first time—of how smart and how wise was this woman who was years older than the barely eighteen she had lived.

I understand.

He closed his eyes and allowed his mind to expand. Pushing his senses down and outward, he began to work on finding what lay below the surface of the river. While he did that, Areenna joined with Gaalrie again, and kept watch on the river ahead.

Two hours later, beneath a setting sun, the river widened and the waters became rougher. Areenna went to the stern, called the kraals to her and gently pushed a thought for them to lie on the deck.

Behind her, Timon watched in surprise. It was a rare event to see a kraal on the ground for they slept standing and only lay down when badly sick. He had never seen one voluntarily lie down. Now he knew why Mikaal had not tied them.

Areenna turned to find Timon watching her and smiled.

"Well done My Lady," he said.

"They do only what is asked," she replied. A moment later the sail filled and the boat lurched forward.

"As promised, My Lady, the evening breezes have begun. Now is the time for vigilance."

Areenna went forward, but paused when she reached Timon. Even in the descending darkness, with the last bands of daylight a bare glimmer of the day just passed, she saw the pain in his eyes. Carefully taking his hand, she whispered, "She loves you still. Do not forget that."

"She told you," he asked, his tone one of disbelief.

She shook her head. "I could not help but sense it." She released him and went to the bow, where she saw Mikaal in deep concentration. Closing her eyes, she opened herself to him and was joined, sensing what he did, beneath the water.

◇◇◇

"What bothers you?" Stepping behind Enaid and wrapping his arms about her, Roth put his hands across her abdomen and pulled her to him. The length of her body fitted tightly against him.

She leaned her head back, resting it at the joining of his shoulder and neck. "I fear for them. I cannot stop the worry filling my dreams. I spend the days thinking about what they are facing, and I am frightened."

"Yet there is nothing you or I can do."

Enaid sighed, covered his hands with her own, and pressed them tighter to her. She took comfort in the warmth emanating from him and drew the security into herself. "There must be something we can do."

"There is," he said. "Keep faith with the visions you have had. To believe we will rise to whatever occasions are demanded of us and to have confidence Mikaal and Areenna will grow into what they must for Nevaeh to survive."

"Ah, only that is it?"

"That," Roth said, his voice lowering, "and thoughts of riding east tomorrow."

Turning within his arms and looking up at him, she searched his face until her heart beat faster. "You know me so well, Solomon Roth. And for that I am forever grateful."

◇◇◇

The hours on the river passed smoothly after the initial roughness. Consistent breezes pushed the boat forward. The travelers stood in the center of the boat, Timon at the helm, Mikaal and Areenna on each side of him. As she had since darkness, Gaalrie flew low in front of the boat, showing them the river ahead, her eyes the sharpest of all.

There had been no flying water snucks, nor had there been any signs of trigetores. The ride down river had been smooth and uneventful.

"We will be there soon. Are you certain you do not want to go all the way down river?" Timon asked.

Areenna shook her head once. "Thank you, Timon, but we must go to Dees. It is of great importance for me to speak with Queen Atir."

"As you wish," he said.

Less than a half hour passed when he said, "We are close."

Areenna sent Gaalrie farther ahead and, a moment later she saw the village and several boats tied to docks. Through Gaalrie's keen eyes, she saw no one walking near the boats or in the village and told the others so.

"There is an inn a half mile along the road. Mostly fishermen stay there when they are caught on the water at night," Timon said as he steered the boat into the curve of the river. He edged the craft toward the right bank and five minutes later said, "There," pointing to several small fishing boats. "There are only a few here now. There should be room enough. The inn is small, its keeper honest."

Areenna glanced at Mikaal who shook his head in agreement with her thoughts.

"I think not, Master Timon. We will find a site to camp," he said.

"At this hour? Not a good idea."

"We cannot take the chance of being recognized."

"That much danger seeks you?"

"No one must know about us, it—" Mikaal began.

"—it is best not to go there," Areenna finished.

Timon stared at them. "Ilsraeth trusts me enough to send you to me. Be honest with me so I can help you as she would want."

Areenna studied him, letting her senses free to discover. She knew the truth of the man, thanks to the gift from Layra, but she needed more.

"You are right, Master Timon, but much of it cannot be told. What I can impart is that the dark powers are regaining strength, and they are preparing for something terrible. I have been charged to go east, to the...the Island, to seek certain things. Prince Mikaal is accompanying me as protector. What we go to do is of great importance to everyone of Nevaeh. More, I cannot say."

Timon remained silent for several long seconds, "Thank you for the trust. We will stay here, on the river, tonight."

"I do not want to keep you from your work," Areenna said.

"You keep me from nothing," he stated. "I will heat some food. It has been a long time since the last meal. Then you should sleep."

Pausing, he turned to Mikaal. "You walk into much danger, Mikaal. No man has ever returned from the Island."

"We will have to change that, won't we?" Mikaal whispered.

A short while later, Mikaal and Areenna were alone on the deck while Timon went below to prepare the cabin. "This is fortunate. It will be better to travel by the sun."

"Yes."

Areenna sent Gaalrie for a final flight around the area. When she saw and sensed all was good and there were no sensations of the darkness pursuing them, she called Gaalrie back. The giant treygone settled onto the railing of the animal pen, near where Areenna stood.

Leaning forward, Areenna stroked her aoutem's back. *Thank you my sister.*

◇◇◇

There was not a single cloud above, and the moon hung low. Stars spanned the sky with such brightness shadows were cast from the trees. Insects chirped their rhythmic nighttime calls. The air was crisp and scents of pine and cedar were strong as Enaid stood on the east tower of Tolemac's keep and gazed outward.

Shortly after Roth's surprising words, he'd asked her to send for her brother, Darb, to sit in their absence, which she'd done immediately. While Darb would not rule as high king, the day to day life of Tolemac had to be overseen, and Darb was well suited to the task. The heir to Brumwall's throne and brother to Enaid was more than capable.

She had spent the last hour working her senses, seeking Mikaal and Areenna, trying to locate them, but her powers were not strong enough to find them. Until the two had gone east, Enaid had never tried to push her seeking ability past its limits, but now, with so much danger ahead, she kept trying.

She suppressed the impulse to stamp her foot in frustration, knowing it was as fruitless as trying to push her seeking, but failure was not something she was used to. *How do I find them?*

She laughed and shook her head. She would not give in to defeat. As her father had often said, 'there is always another way to accomplish a task—always!'

And for now, she would accomplish what she needed by another means. Turning, Enaid walked along the parapet until reaching the south tower and the aviary. When she opened the cage door, she sent a push to the small gray traimore on the center roost. The bird left the roost and settled gently on Enaid's forearm.

Outside again, Enaid transferred the traimore to the ledge while she wrote a note on a piece of fabric she carried in her pocket for just such a purpose. When she finished, she placed the rolled fabric into the leg

190

holder attached to the bird and sent it aloft. It circled once before flying into the darkness, speeding through the night to Aldimor and Queen Atir.

CHAPTER 20

AREENNA AWAKENED WITH the first hint of the new day. It took a moment to remember where she was. While she did, her eyes adjusted to the low light in the cabin.

Sitting, she looked around. Across the cabin, Mikaal's shadowy form lay within sleeping silks on the cabin floor. But when Areenna rose, he stirred and sat.

"Morning," she called.

"Exactly what I was afraid of." His voice was husky with sleep.

"We need to move." She walked over to where he lay.

"No," he said, looking up at her. "We need to take a few breaths before facing the day. Sit and talk with me."

Areenna stared down at him then sat next to him on folded legs. "What?"

Mikaal started to speak, but before he could form the word, an excruciating pain ripped through him. His body arched, spasms ripped through his legs. His body went numb.

He saw Areenna's eyes widen with fright. He tried to speak, but could not.

"Don't move. Not a hair's breadth. Don't speak," she ordered and bent close to look at the dark, snuck-like thing that had slipped from beneath his shirt and wrapped around his neck.

Seconds later, Mikaal was unaware of anything other than the blinding, all-consuming pain tearing him apart. He fought this unknown thing and a moment later felt Charka join him and become trapped in what was happening. Somehow, within a hidden compartment of his mind, Mikaal knew if he did not fight with every inch of his strength, he would die.

"Master Timon," Areenna shouted even as she heard Charka cry out in pain and saw the kraal lying on the deck through Gaalrie's eyes, its body arched like Mikaal's.

Seconds later Timon was standing above her, bending over to look at Mikaal's neck. "Damn, a river craget…it lives on blood. Very bad," he said almost to himself.

Pulling his knife from the sheath inside his boot, he turned to Areenna. "It has to be taken off. Much longer and he will die. This thing has hundreds of legs. Each one punctures the skin of its victim and injects poison. If we do not pull it completely free, it will keep poisoning him and death is but a short time away." He placed the tip of the knife next to the craget's head in preparation for sliding it between Mikaal's skin and the creature. As he did, the craget pulsed and a band of iridescence flowed from head to tail.

"Stop," Areenna commanded. She placed her hand on his forearm. "Let me."

Timon withdrew the knife.

"Be ready. If I am able, you will know when."

"Hurry," he whispered.

Areenna did just the opposite. Taking a deep breath, she sat back, re-crossed her legs and leaned forward. She took Mikaal's fisted hand into both of hers, closed her eyes and sent out her thoughts. When she touched his mind, he opened and drew her in. As they joined, Areenna's back arched and burning lances of pain shot through her. Carefully, she damped off the pain and forced her muscles to relax until she was free of the paralyzing effects. She tried to communicate with Mikaal, but he could do nothing except fight the intense pain attacking every inch of his body, inside and out.

Carefully, slowly, she blended with Mikaal, letting her senses meld into his skin and then deeper into his veins and arteries until she was traveling through him searching for the entry point where the craget's

193

head was burrowed into his carotid artery.

After too many long seconds, she found its mouth and the hair-like tendrils extending into the artery, sucking out Mikaal's blood while its legs secreted the poison to keep him paralyzed. Areenna took all of this in while she studied the thing, looking for its weaknesses, her sense of urgency growing with each heartbeat.

Slowing her breathing as much as possible, she surrounded the tendrils with her senses and let herself be drawn into the craget. Instantly, emotions of pleasure and greed overwhelmed her. The taste of Mikaal's blood and the pleasure of its richness started to consume her. The blood made her body vibrate and flush with warmth. Overwhelming pleasure flowed through every inch of her mind and body, holding her prisoner until she realized she was caught within the craget's blood lust.

She started to withdraw, stopped and, without thinking, sent a harsh cold wave of emotion into the craget, attacking it as fiercely as she had the wraith at Tolemac.

Leaning over her, Timon watched this silent battle, his knife a quarter inch away from the craget, waiting, his attention totally focused on the point where the craget's head dug into Mikaal's neck. The instant the craget's iridescent color went flat, he slid the knife under it and pulled it from Mikaal's neck. He carried it out of the cabin, to the deck and flicked it over the side.

When he returned below deck, he found Mikaal sitting up, the bloody pinpricks of the craget's hundreds of legs a red enflamed band around his neck. "How are you?" he asked the prince.

Mikaal cleared his throat. "Woozy."

"It will take a while for the poison to filter out," Timon said.

Areenna remained cross-legged next to Mikaal, holding his hand. "We need water...a lot of water."

When Timon left to get fresh water, Areenna released Mikaal's hand, rose on slightly unsteady legs and went to her travel bag. She dumped its contents on the floor and searched until she found the vial she was seeking. Opening it, she sniffed its contents and nodded to herself. She would use the herbs in the vial to make a tea that would help ease the pain and reduce the swelling on his neck as well. Thankfully the bite had closed the instant the craget was pulled free. The herb infused water would flush the remaining poisons from his body.

Three hours later Mikaal was able to move freely. The pain had eased to a bare reminder of what it had been and the three sat around the table, eating the bread Timon had brought with them.

"You need to rest here today. Leave tomorrow," Timon suggested.

Both Areenna and Mikaal shook their heads. "We have not the time to spare, Master Timon. We are already behind time because of the route we have been forced to take."

"Riding a kraal after what has happened..." Timon shook his head with the thought.

"I will be fine," Mikaal said. "Charka is an easy ride." Trying to explain why would be impossible, he knew, so he said no more.

"You know the animal far better than I," Timon said. "I still believe your strength more important than the need to regain the time lost this day."

Mikaal reached across the table and gripped the river man's forearm. "I will be fine. There is more at work than can be explained, but I will be fine, of that have no doubt."

Timon stared into Mikaal's eyes. "As you say," the river man nodded. "Then we had best be moving, the sun is well up and the boats have left to fish."

They rose and, as Areenna put their belongings together, Mikaal and Timon went topside where Mikaal's first action was to go to the pen where Charka was already waiting for him. When he reached his aoutem, Charka nuzzled his chest. Mikaal's arms went around the kraal's neck and they stood like that for several minutes while Charka's emanations soothed Mikaal's pain-stiffened muscles.

Less than an hour later, with the sun almost at its zenith and their belongings packed on the kraals, Areenna and Mikaal led them off the boat. On the dock, Areenna turned to Timon. "We cannot thank you enough for your help, Master Timon. Without you..."

"There is no need for thanks," Timon said, looking first at Mikaal and then at her. "But you must take care on your journey. If what you fear is happening, there will be those... I am afraid there will be much danger ahead."

"We are aware," Areenna replied softly as she looked up at the river man and saw his eyes turn distant in sudden thought.

"Until we meet again," Mikaal said, nodding formally and clasping

Timon's forearm with his hand.

Timon looked at the prince's hand and gripped Mikaal's forearm with his own hand. "May your feet be swift, your sword true and your way safe," he said in the warrior's farewell to one who goes into danger.

Mid-morning in Tolemac was hectic as Enaid prepared to leave. A short message from her mother assured her Darb was on the road.

Roth left written instructions for Darb for those things that needed immediate attention, and then went to the stables to prepare their kraals and make certain their supplies were set properly. That done, he walked to the barracks, where he spoke to a small contingent of his special guards before returning to find Enaid just arrived.

While he wore no armor, his longsword hung at his side. Behind their kraals was a kralet—a pack animal smaller and broader than a kraal, used by farmers, merchants, and armies to carry supplies and goods. They had opted for the kralet because both he and Enaid had agreed to avoid towns and inns, just as she had advised Mikaal and Areenna. This kralet was loaded with food, water, sleeping silks, his armor and their personal belongings.

"We are ready?" Enaid asked when he entered the stable.

Roth smiled at his wife. She was dressed as he was, in a tunic and pants tucked into high boots. Her hair was pulled tightly back; a smile curved her mouth, denying the tension lying just beneath the surface. "Yes, My lady."

Turning, he signaled the two guards who stood to one side. "Take the kralet to the Aldimor road. We will be there shortly."

Without a word, the two guards took the reins of the animal and led it out of the stable.

"Have you received word from Atir?" Roth asked his wife.

"Not yet. The traimore will find me on the road."

"We have one stop to make before we leave."

Enaid raised her eyebrows. "For?"

"You'll see," he replied as he mounted his kraal. Enaid stared at his back for several seconds before mounting her kraal.

Roth led them along the main avenue, to the small shop belonging

196

to Tolemac's master arms maker. He dismounted and motioned her to do the same. When they entered the shop, the shopkeeper turned and, seeing who his visitors were, gave them a formal head bow before saying, "Welcome, Solomon, Lady Enaid."

"It is good to see you, old friend," Enaid said, grasping his forearm. The man returned the greeting then turned to his bench and lifted a short bow.

The weapon was carved from the wood of an ebony gazebow tree, and gleamed in the low light of the shop. Its double curved shape was highlighted by the dark wood, and had the look of a powerful weapon. "For you, My Lady, finished this day."

Enaid took the bow from him and held it up. It was lighter than she expected. Turning it in her hands, she felt the strength of the wood and knew it was a magnificent creation. She looked at Roth in question.

"It was to be a present, for your birthing day, next week. But given the circumstances..."

"It is...wondrous," she whispered. Her long, slim fingers gripped the leather wrapped center and she drew back the thin string of gut. She felt a vibration within the wood and sensed the bow's full power.

"My wife has blessed the bow, My Lady," the shopkeeper said. "She is an artist with weapons."

"Yes," Enaid said, feeling the power. "Please thank her for me."

"I shall. Enjoy the bow; there will no other like it. It is the last of the wood from a tree I cut twenty years ago. The wood has been dry aged since then. I knew not why I had kept that piece until Roth came to me."

"There are not words," Enaid began, placing her hand on his shoulder, "to express my feelings."

"Nor is there a need, I see it in your eyes."

"Thank you, Master Halan," Roth said. "Your work, as always, is of great value."

"Thank you, My Lord. Enjoy the remains of the day."

Carrying her new bow and the quiver of arrows, Enaid smiled broadly at her husband. "You do have a way of warming a woman's heart."

They both laughed as the door closed behind them. "Would you have expected something frilly for a gift?" he asked. "Perhaps a flowered basket of fruit? Or perhaps you wanted sparkling jewels?"

"The fruit perhaps, but what use have I for the jewels?"

He smiled and offered her a hand to mount her kraal, which she rarely accepted but did so then. "No, I learned my lesson about jewels a long time ago and have no need to be reminded of it again."

"Good," she said as he mounted his kraal. "Are we ready now?" she asked, a single eyebrow arching skyward.

"We are, My Lady," he replied with a smile that did not betray his writhing emotions. For days a premonition of impending dangers had been building. The need to go east, to be ready, to be available to help his son and Areenna, had become overwhelming. His only hope was to be in time.

◇◇◇

Sitting before the fire Areenna stared into the flames. It was dark; the moon was a quarter into the sky. Mikaal slept in the lean-to behind her, getting the rest his overworked body so badly needed.

It had been close to sunset when he had called a halt to their riding. They'd crossed the border of Northcrom into Aldimor and a short while later had reached the point on the old road where it turned southeast. During their ride, they had passed only a few lone travelers, none of whom had shown interest in them.

Flying above, Gaalrie had found a safe place to camp for the night off the road within a stand of trees. "How are you feeling?" Areenna had asked when they'd reached it.

"Very tired, but I am better. The poison is gone."

"A full night's sleep will fix the rest," she had said, "along with another cup of tea."

They'd entered the open area within the trees and looked around with the help of the few rays of remaining sunlight. Areenna had cast her senses about to make certain there had been no one nearby. "It's safe here," she'd declared.

When Mikaal lowered himself from Charka, she'd watched him grasp the saddle to steady himself and had seen just how weak he still was. She'd looked up at her aoutem and sent a thought. Gaalrie had wheeled in the air and voiced a sharp cry.

"Let's get ourselves settled and a fire started," she ordered, knowing he would fight her if she'd asked him to sit and rest while she set up camp.

By the time they had everything ready, Gaalrie had returned with a rabt for dinner. After they'd eaten, Areenna had forced Mikaal to the lean-to and into the sleeping silks. He'd protested, but barely as the exhaustion from the poison and the ride had taken control and led him into a deep, recovering sleep.

Areenna blinked herself back to the present and looked away from the fire and at the sky. Threads of wisp-like clouds so thin the stars shone through them floated above. She wondered how the evil could threaten them all and gain strength within the beauty of Nevaeh. *Why?* She asked herself, not for the first time.

Then she reached outward with her senses, seeking any touch of the vileness they were trying to evade. For as far as she could reach, she found nothing, and in the finding, was able to relax enough to attempt to learn and study Ilsraeth's gift.

She breathed in smooth, long inhalations, cleared her mind of random thoughts and concentrated on the center of her powers to allow the place within her to open. And then she touched the very spot where Ilsraeth's gift lay.

Bringing it forth, Areenna called up the formula surrounding the power. The gift expanded, filling her with vibrations that pulsed from her toes to the top of her head. Everything turned misty around her. She could see clearly, yet everything appeared as though she was looking through the sheerest of fabrics.

Without a mirror to show her, she did not know if the gift worked. Standing, she went to Hero and stood before him. The kraal did not seem to notice her, yet she knew he scented her as he looked about. She reached out and touched him. Startled, the kraal jerked its head backward.

Areenna withdrew the gift and returned it to where it resided. An instant later, Hero gave a short snort and turned its head to look at her. As the kraal recognized her, a wave of exhaustion washed over her.

She staggered and went as quickly as she could to the lean-to where she collapsed onto her own sleeping silks. *So much energy,* she thought before another wave of tiredness stole her consciousness.

CHAPTER 21

"IT IS FOUR days to Dees, and six to the Island," Enaid said when they finished their meal.

"What do you see?" Roth asked, looking from his wife to the fire.

"Nothing. Something is stopping me from sensing them."

"How is this possible? The Dark Ones?"

Enaid shook her head. "It has no dark feel and it puzzles me greatly." She closed her eyes and concentrated. No matter how hard she tried, she could not break through. That it was the first time since Mikaal's birth she was unable to sense her son was not just puzzling, it was alarming.

Mikaal sat by the low glow of dying embers. He was rested and surprisingly refreshed after yesterday's enormous drain on his body. Behind him, Areenna slept so deeply she had not stirred when he'd awakened and left the lean-to.

He picked up several large twigs and tossed them on the embers. When they were burning sufficiently, he added heavier branches atop the kindling. It took only a few minutes for the dried bark to catch fire and lighten the darkness.

To his left, Charka and Hero grazed, ignoring him and the fire. He sensed Gaalrie's presence on a high branch above and knew the treygone was fixed solely on Areenna. Closing his eyes, he let his thoughts range outward until he touched Gaalrie. He'd never before attempted to join with the treygone other than through Areenna.

Rather than push at the treygone, he sent a thought and asked. A moment later he was seeing himself sitting before the fire through Gaalrie's eyes. It was a strange feeling, yet not uncomfortable. Remembering what Areenna had told him, he gently suggested the treygone go aloft and fly over the area, assuring her that he would watch over Areenna.

Gaalrie let out a soft call, and released herself from the branch. She swooped low above his head before her wings caught an updraft and she lifted into the dark sky. He breathed deeply as he flew with her; the sensation of freedom was exhilarating.

For the next quarter hour he watched through Gaalrie's sharp eyes. The lands were still—there were no travelers moving at this hour. As she ranged outward in ever widening circles, he caught glimpses of animals and other birds, but none of people.

When Gaalrie returned to the perch she'd occupied earlier, Mikaal broke the connection between them. *Thank you.* There was a returning push of warmth into his mind.

The fire had settled into low flames. He unwrapped the remains of last night's dinner and placed the spitted rabt on the two branches erected for cooking. In the east, bands of pale purple light began to rise.

They were high in the mountains, two days from Dees and the closer they would get, the more populous it would become. There would be no bodies of water to protect them from the scent-following wraith. Mikaal hoped Areenna was right, and the wraiths would be waiting for them in the east, which meant they had time to work out the best way to avoid the dark creatures and get to the Island.

He considered waking her so they could get an early start, but decided to give her a little more sleeping time. He was sure that yesterday had been every bit as hard on her as it was on him. He would wake her when the sky lightened completely.

Strange misshapen shadows flickered on the cave wall as *she* rocked from side to side, the deformed body bending in ways no true flesh and blood person could. Strange words poured from her mouth as her hands waved in the air calling forth old formulas to add strength to her already powerful emanations.

She froze when her mind connected with the creatures *she* had created. *She* saw as much as sensed that they had reached their destination. They had found a hidden place deep in the rocky walls of the high palisades across from the Island. It was the perfect place to wait until the two came.

And then, *she* knew, when they arrived, they would die.

Enaid was boiling water and herbs for morning tea when the small gray traimore settled onto the branch above her. She raised her eyes and smiled. She called the traimore to her and it landed gently on her raised forearm. With her free hand, she relieved the bird of its message and gave it a gentle push to stay and follow them. She would take no chance of losing a method of communication.

"Finally," Roth said as she opened the cloth to read the message.

"They have not yet reached Dees," she said. "But Atir received word from Ilsraeth. They have been forced to take a longer route to Aldimor. She writes of placing a blocking spell over Aldimor and that Mikaal and Areenna should arrive tomorrow or the next day."

Enaid folded the cloth and slipped it into a pocket while the tension and worry over Areenna and Mikaal eased. "That explains why I could not find them."

"I knew she had power, but to block her entire dominion? I didn't think such was possible."

Enaid smiled at Roth. "Many things are possible. Atir is strong. She, Ilsraeth, Layra, and I are among the strongest, which is why I sent Areenna to them before the Island."

"For the gifts," Roth said in agreement. He was one of the few men who knew about this tradition.

"Yes. For now they are safe. But we will miss them at Dees. They should be there tomorrow."

Roth took in her words and nodded. "We should go straight to the Landing then."

"Yes," Enaid agreed. "That cuts a day from the journey as well." She turned to Irii, and looked at her aoutem. "Do you agree?" she asked with a smile.

When the gorlon gave a low growl, Enaid laughed and sent Irii off to hunt for her breakfast before taking the tea from the fire and pouring the pale green liquid into the two cups she had ready.

Roth took a loaf of bread from their bag of supplies and broke it in half. They ate silently and, when they finished the tea, Enaid said, "I'm going to try a seeking."

"I'll break camp," Roth said, standing.

Enaid moved to the base of a large tree and sat with her back against it. She crossed her legs, and then placed both hands on the ground and dug her fingers deep into the soft earth. She closed her eyes and cleared her mind of anything other than the picture of the Landing across from the Island.

Slowly and with great care, Enaid built the seeking, tunneling deep within herself and then pushing outward to the north and east. She sent her senses to float along the currents, always moving toward their destination.

When she reached it, her stomach roiled and her throat closed; an overwhelming disgust gripped her. She pulled back instantly, fighting at the same time to draw breath. When she finally opened her eyes, she was lightheaded and her heart pounded heavily.

Forcing herself to take slow, even breaths, she willed her muscles to relax and her heart to slow. When she finally was able to open her eyes, she found Irii staring at her, one paw on her thigh while Roth stood above her, his face carved in concern.

"I'm fine," she told them both. The gorlon pressed against her, a low grumbling coming from its throat while Roth dropped to one knee and reached out to cup her cheek.

"What was it?"

"They are waiting," she whispered.

"They?"

"The dark sorceress, the wraiths that black...snuck created. They wait for Areenna and Mikaal in the palisades above the Landing."

"And there is no way to warn them?"

She thought about the traimore she had released and shook her head. "No, we must go to Dees. We will not reach them in time, but we will need Atir, and possibly others. We will need great power. I have never felt the likes of this before. *It...she* has created something far worse than I ever thought possible."

"What?"

Enaid shook her head. "I...I cannot fully describe it, but the wraith we faced in Tolemac was but a...child in comparison to this new thing."

"Then to Dees."

Areenna woke with a start. The spot on her forehead Enaid had set to warn her of danger burned harshly. She lay still with her eyes closed, trying to sense what was happening. There was nothing. *What then?* she asked herself.

She pushed outward to Gaalrie and caught her aoutem's calmness. The warning was not from the treygone. She pushed toward Hero and Charka, and still there was nothing. If it had been Mikaal, she would have known instantly.

And then the only possibility of what it could be settled into her consciousness. It was a foreseeing. She settled her breathing as her mother had taught her and began seeking what had disturbed her. It took time to sift through wavering, barely understandable visions, but when it came, it was with the force of a blow.

Her breath exploded outward. Her hands clenched into fists. Flashes of light were followed by faint impressions of black beings, large winged creatures whose hunger was for her blood. There were three, and one was filled with the vilest emanations of evil she had ever encountered.

She pulled herself from the vision, threw off the thin silk cover and rose to her feet. When she stepped out of the lean-to, she found a bright, sunny day and saw Mikaal crouched by the fire. She went quickly to him, calling his name as she did.

Mikaal rose and, turning, saw her face. He met her halfway and caught her by her shoulders. "What?"

Feeling the strength of his hands, the heat from his palms unblocked by the light fabric brought her back to reality. "They are there, waiting for us."

"Who is where?"

"The wraiths. They wait by the Island."

He was puzzled by the panic in her eyes. "We knew they would be. We talked of it."

She shook her head hard, her pale hair fanning outward in emphasis. "No, there was one, it was...horrible. It is like nothing I have seen or heard about before. Powerful and evil..."

"We will find a way," he promised her.

"What way? This is not like those things we fought in Tolemac. It is different."

Mikaal's hands tightened on her shoulders. Not since the day she rode into Tolemac had he seen her confidence shaken. Whatever this was had affected her badly and he knew he needed to do something quickly. "Areenna, *it* can't stop us. You must believe that. You are powerful and you are helping me to become the same. We will do whatever is necessary, we can do this together!"

She stared into his gray eyes, and at the silvery green motes floating within them and slowly reached out to touch his face. "The vision..."

"Talk to me Areenna, tell me."

She shook her head thoughtfully. "There is no more to tell. I saw— no, I felt them. The evil awaiting us is overwhelming."

"There will be a way."

"Will there?" She stepped back from under his hands. She looked at Hero and Charka and thought about last night and an idea birthed.

She brought this newborn thought upward, tasting it and, realizing its potential, turned back to Mikaal. "There may be a way."

"There's always a way," he said gently.

She looked at the rabt, and at the water heating on the fire. "First we eat. Then we ride. While we ride, we will begin working on Ilsraeth's gift. We must make ourselves able to disappear when we need to."

She saw Mikaal's face fill with comprehension. "Yes," he said.

"But we must be careful. We cannot exhaust ourselves. We must be able to stay strong."

"That is why you slept so deeply is it not? You tried last night."

"Yes." And then she disappeared.

He felt her hand on his even though he could not see her. And then felt her lips peck his cheek. An instant later she was back. "Like that," she announced and grasped his arm for support.

Aldimor was the most populous dominion in Nevaeh and Dees was its capital. It was late in the afternoon of the second day since her vision when they finally reached the outskirts of the city. An hour before, Areenna had sent Gaalrie with a message to Queen Atir.

They had spent their traveling time working and practicing the second gift and while they rode and rested in between sessions, their concentration on learning this ability remained unflagging. They had discovered, after using the gift and being drained of strength, that it took only a few minutes of physically touching their aoutems to regain their strength. It was hard work, but with it came the understanding that the gift could only be used sparingly, for if they held it too long, they would be weakened beyond the ability to defend themselves. They had been able to hold for a full ten minutes on their last try without succumbing to exhaustion—and had made the kraals disappear as well.

Gaalrie comes, she informed Mikaal silently.

When Gaalrie descended onto Areenna's saddle, the giant treygone held a rolled message in its beak. Areenna opened it. As she read, the words disappeared. "Laira will meet us at the eastern gate of Dees and take us to the Queen. There will be no subterfuge here. We are to go directly to the main keep."

They wore riding cloaks with the hoods pulled forward to hide their faces so that only a person directly in front of them could see them—a difficult task while they were mounted.

The closer they came to Dees, the busier the road became and, even though it was past midafternoon, there were a lot of people heading into the city. Houses made of wood and stone lined the road. Most were small and modest but closer to the main entrance, the houses were larger.

A short time later they passed through the Eastern Gate, an ornamental archway of stone a dozen feet thick, twenty feet wide and almost as high. There they dismounted and walked the kraals toward the meeting point.

Within minutes, Areenna sensed the presence of Queen Atir's daughter, Laira. Mikaal sensed the young girl as well. Turning into a street sparsely populated by homes, they found the young woman waiting, dressed the same as they, in a hooded cloak.

"Welcome," Laira said, giving Mikaal a slight bow. For Areenna she gave a warm smile and a welcoming embrace. "It has been a long time, Areenna."

"It has," Areenna agreed after releasing Laira, with whom she had shared a room at the school, five years before.

"Come, Mother wants to see you right away," Laira said.

"All is well?"

Laira gazed at Areenna. "It seems so on the surface, but I sense something not right."

"In Dees?"

She shook her head and looked from Areenna to Mikaal and back. "Everywhere. I cannot explain it."

Areenna remembered a time when she was fifteen and she and her mother had visited Laira and Atir in Dees. She had learned during the visit that among Laira's growing powers was a leaning toward foretelling.

She reached out, took her hand, and felt the warmth of her skin and something else...something undefined, but very bad.

CHAPTER 22

THE AFTERNOON SKY was dark and threatening, the sun well hidden behind massing storm clouds. By the edge of a cliff overlooking the blue-black waves hurtling against the rocks of the high palisades wall stood the black sorceress. Casting *her* senses toward the east, *she* moved slowly, taking no chance of missing anything. *She* used the eyes of animals, birds, even insects to look and scent for them. But when her far reaching senses tried to enter Aldimor, *she* was stopped by a powerful blocking. *She* knew they were there. "Damn you, Atir, you will pay dearly for this," *she* shouted to the east.

Angrily, *she* called a dangelore. The large black carrion eater responded to its mistress and left the upper branches of a tall tree. The bird dropped to a low hanging branch of long dead tree, under which *she* now stood. The sorceress lifted onto the balls of *her* feet and stared into the depthless red eyes of the dangelore. Then *she* reached up and took the bird down as if its 30 pound bulk weighed no more than a twig. *She* held the dangelore's head to *her* mouth and began to whisper into the bird's ear. When *she* finished the formula and the instructions, *she* held the bird away and stared into the dangelore's eyes once more. "To Aldimor and Dees," *she* told the bird and released it with a powerful upward throw. The image of her servant within the keep at Dees was impressed upon the dangelore's small brain.

The dangelore rose into the stormy sky, where it circled above her head. Then *she* cast another formula and with her hand wove a pattern into the air. Only then did *she* send the dangelore on its way. The bird rose higher than it was ever meant to fly, becoming a mere spec. The dangelore caught the powerful easterly currents, which sped it and its deadly instructions faster than a bird could fly.

With the sun's final descent, Areenna and Mikaal entered Dees' main keep through a side entrance. Laira wasted no time in bringing them directly to the Queen's private quarters where a meal was set upon a round table. After greeting them formally, Atir warmly embraced Areenna.

"Sit," Atir said when she released Areenna. "And tell me how your journey has been."

They ate, Areenna and Mikaal answering Atir's questions until the Queen fell silent. Then, looking at her two guests, she said, "Ever since the council, I have carried a sense of discord—of an evil not yet made clear to me. Five days ago this feeling became more intense and I set a block upon Aldimor. The sorceress hunts you even now does *she* not?"

"*She* does," Areenna replied. "*She* has set wraiths on our trail, which is why we took the river route and came the long way here."

"The water hides your scent, well done. The block will remain until you are in the outlands, near the Landing for the Island."

"But the strength it takes to maintain such a block…"

"Is nothing. When you understand your powers, you will know its strengths and weaknesses as well as your own. It takes little energy to maintain the block when nothing attacks it."

Atir lifted a forkful of food but halted it a few inches before her mouth. "And you, young heir, how has this journey affected you?" she asked, before daintily sliding the fork into her mouth. Her probing eyes were locked on his.

Mikaal met her gaze. "It is an adventure," he replied noncommittally.

"A dangerous one."

"Yes, My Lady, it appears such is the case," he broke eye contact and lifted a glass of wine. "But an adventure none-the-less."

Atir frowned momentarily, then smiled. "Beware your attitude, Prince Mikaal, it could very well bring about your death."

And then her probe struck, quick and clean. He blocked it easily, without as much as a blink of an eyelid.

She watched him for several long seconds before saying, "I have heard from Enaid. Your mother has been worried and because she could not find a sense of you anywhere she sent a message to learn if you had arrived."

They fell silent for the rest of the meal. When the plates were taken away, Atir turned to Mikaal. "I need time alone with Areenna— women's talk, you understand?"

Mikaal gave a low laugh, having expected exactly this to happen. "I do. Thank you for the meal; it was exceptional. I'll bid you ladies a good night." He ignored Atir's questioning eyebrows as he stood. *Be careful*, he said silently to Areenna.

"Leave us now, attend to the duties I cannot," Atir ordered her daughter.

Laira rose and bowed her head to her mother and Areenna. "Allow me to show you to your quarters, Mikaal."

When the door closed behind them, Atir focused her full attention on Areenna. "Would you care tell me the reason Enaid sent her son with you? Besides the fact such is not done, and she is risking his life."

"I know," Areenna replied, her voice soft, Mikaal's warning rife in her thoughts. "And yes, such a thing is not done when a woman goes for the final training, but in this she was adamant. She saw something—a foretelling she believes requires Mikaal to be with me."

"Has anything happened on this journey to prove this?"

So much, she thought. "We were attacked in Morvene. *She* sent a large, poisonous snuck. If it were not for Mikaal..." It was true, she reasoned. Charka would not have been there if Mikaal had not.

Atir nodded. "Make certain he does not go to the Island. He must wait for you on the Landing."

Unable to bring the lie to her lips, she nodded.

"He has a powerful block," Atir stated. "How is Mikaal so protected?"

"It is Enaid—" Areenna began.

"Stop. I will not tolerate a lie. Enaid is powerful. More powerful than I, but this is not of her creation. I know her well, Areenna. We are sisters in heart. We schooled together and trained together often. Her mother and mine were sisters. I know her signature. I know everything about her. This is not her work. Nor, do I think it to be yours. There is no possibility for her protection within Aldimor right now. Not with the blocking I have set about the dominion."

Before she could answer, she felt Mikaal join her. *Be careful.* "My lady, I would rather not speak than lie to you. It is not my way—it is not *our* way. I have promised Enaid I would speak to no one about this."

Atir reached across the table and grasped both of Areenna's hands. She gripped them tightly and stared deeply into the younger woman's eyes. "Know you the danger of what is to come?"

"More than I want," she replied.

"Trust me," Atir whispered.

"Always, My Lady," Areenna replied. "Trust is not the issue. My promise is."

Atir released her hands and nodded. "There is much I do not understand, least of all your traveling companion to the Island. The risks put upon you are considerable."

"I know."

"And you are young to be going, but when the call comes..." She paused to study Areenna once again. "Very well, my trust you have gained. And Enaid is deeply concerned. Her message was itself unusual. I will send word you two are safe."

"My thanks."

"What route will you take to the Island?"

"I am not sure, My Lady. Mikaal has maps. He will choose the route."

"We will go over the route in the morning." Atir took in breath and wiped her hand across her eyes. "It is time, come here and kneel."

Areenna went to the Queen and she knelt before her.

Atir leaned forward and placed a hand on each side of Areenna's head, bending forward until her mouth was a hair's breadth from her skin. "Be strong, woman, hold strong and accept what is given. You must contain the gift, hold it to you and not allow it to escape."

She began a soft chant and on the final word a surge of power drilled into Areenna's head. It settled deep into her brain and then began to travel her body like an eightleg weaving its web.

Areenna's body stiffened with the first jolt of power and, as the force of it drove through every cell in her body, each muscle began to vibrate in turn. "Hold, child, hold strong," whispered Atir in a gentle voice. "Let it roam, let it go freely, fight it not. Contain it you must."

Areenna had no idea of how long it lasted, but when it was over, she collapsed on the floor and lay there for several minutes while, Mikaal's gentle, silent presence and hidden powers helped her to contain the gift.

When her muscles relaxed, she raised her head. "Thank you," she whispered, for the gift was among the most vital a woman could have, and few women were ever fortunate enough to contain it.

"Be wise in how you use this gift. Be not afraid to use it, but do not waste it upon those who are not worthy, and such will be a difficult task," she said as she helped Areenna up.

Standing, Areenna took a deep breath and smiled at Atir. "Thank you."

"How do you feel toward Mikaal?" Atir questioned.

Puzzled, Areenna shrugged. "In what way?"

"In all ways. What think you of him?"

Before answering, Areenna pushed Mikaal from her, cutting the connection she had allowed during the gifting. She saw Atir react to something, but ignored it. "I'm not sure what you mean. He is a good companion. He is smart and strong and has already protected me from harm."

Atir's response was slow as she studied Areenna. "There is nothing else?"

"What else could there be?" she asked, puzzled.

Atir shook her head. "I'm not sure, but he is with you for more than simple protection. Why would Enaid and Roth risk the heir's life by having him accompany you on a woman's mission?"

"The only risks are on the road and he is well trained and strong. There are not many who could best him."

"Not many men perhaps, but a woman…a sorceress of power? That is another story." She stood and paced the chamber for a moment before turning back to Areenna. "He is also headstrong. You must make certain he does not go to the Island, he cannot follow you there or all will be lost."

"I understand."

"And when you step foot in that place, be thoughtful and watchful. Mind everything, hear what may be said, and seek through the words to the meaning. Remember, it is not the words spoken, but the meaning behind them. This was your final gift. The first, who was it from?"

"Layra."

"Ah...Truth was it?" At Areenna's nod Atir said, "Use it well, keep it to the front with every person and thing on the Island."

Person and thing. The words echoed in Areenna's mind.

"And Ilsraeth, she gifted you as well, did she not?"

"The hiding, it is difficult."

Atir seemed not to hear her. Her eyes went vacant for several seconds until she refocused on Areenna. In that instant her eyes widened. "Truth, the hiding and..." She looked Areenna up and down and then said, "How strong are you, child? How powerful have you become?"

Areenna shook her head. "I don't know."

"Then you'd best learn because I... I was with you several nights ago. You were on the hidden road were you not?" She weaved her hands before Areenna and a glowing misty vision of the old road, 'the highway' with its walls of trees and roof of branches above flickered in the air between them.

"I was," Areenna said.

"You saw her."

Areenna held Atir's eyes. "I did."

"You are she," Atir whispered.

"She? I don't understand."

Atir placed a hand on her shoulder. "You will," she whispered, echoing the very words Enaid had spoken to her in Tolemac.

"Is that all anyone can say?" Areenna snapped, pulling out from under Atir's hand and losing the ability to keep calm. "I will what? All I have heard is how I am going to the Island to face something that will either kill me or make me stronger. And then I am told I will be powerful, but no one is willing to tell me what they know."

Atir smiled. Her eyes glowed with humor. "The ways of women are something hard, and sometimes strange."

"Oh, that's even better than 'you will'," Areenna snapped sarcastically. "I don't understand what's going on. I don't understand what I will do on the Island. I do not even understand why I am going there in the first place other than it is what women of power do."

"Afraid? Atir asked. "Are you frightened by what you might find there?"

"How can I be afraid if I know not what to fear? No I am not afraid of the Island, or of the trip there. What I am afraid of is that the next time someone tells me 'you will', I will do something to them to make certain those word are never uttered again." At that, she slammed hands together in emphasis and the large window behind Atir shattered and blew outward.

Both women turned to look at the window then at each other. Peals of laughter rolled from Atir's lips. The queen fought to contain herself in order to catch her breath, but failed. Finally, holding her hands defensively in front of her, she said, "I promise I won't say it again." And then she wrapped her arms around her abdomen and began to laugh again.

Seconds later Mikaal and a dozen palace guards burst into the room to find Atir still laughing and Areenna staring with an even more puzzled look at her hands.

Sitting together in Areenna's chambers, Mikaal had her go over what had happened when she'd shut him off. She explained everything that followed, but after she told him about the hand clap, she said, "I have no idea how it happened."

"You were angry, perhaps it was your anger."

"Do you think this is the first time in my life I've been angry?"

"That level of anger?" Mikaal asked. "It caught me as well. I could feel it through the walls."

"But I set nothing, called no formula, I just clapped my hands and the window shattered."

Mikaal shrugged. "Perhaps the anger was the formula," he said jokingly.

"It's not funny. It could be dangerous. And there is more to it."

"Then you'll have to learn what it is. What else happened?"

"Nothing. She was testing me, and I think she senses something about you. You will have to be wary. I doubt she'll find your abilities favorable."

"I will be careful. We should leave in the morning. Tell me about the gift, for this one is yours alone. I could not assimilate it."

"Because it is completely female in nature. It is for healing, but how to use it remains to be seen. And from what I gathered speaking with Atir, you mother had a plan in sending me for these gifts."

"A plan? In what way?"

Areenna shrugged. "I know not, but I trust her. We will learn why when we are supposed to."

"You are good with that?" he asked, his voice unusually sharp.

She drew slightly back. "Why would I not be *good* with that?"

"You don't feel manipulated?"

A gentle smile filled with understanding grew on her lips. "Manipulated? Oh, Mikaal, no. You must not seek to hold reign over everything. There is a purpose to what your mother is doing—a purpose we will discover when the time is right, or when we need it the most. You must relinquish your need for control. Only then will you gain it."

"It is not control I look for, it is answers."

"Is it? You think answers will clear your understanding and allow you to master what happens. It's the way a man reacts, not so for a woman. Trust is hard to give, especially when you do not know what will result from the giving. But having faith in another is what will make you stronger."

Was it control stopping him from giving blind trust, even to his mother? Or was it something else? Mikaal wondered.

"Let this go. We need rest if we are to be on the move tomorrow," she whispered.

Mikaal stood and went to the door. Pausing, he said, "We will know her plans soon enough."

With the moon in its final descent, and the first light of day not yet showing in the east, the black sorceress's messenger descended on Dees and settled on the balustrade of the stonework. A servant wrapped in a dark cloak waited. The woman reached out and the dangelore hopped from the railing to her arm and stared into the woman's eyes. The bird's red eyes glowed for a moment and then the bird rose into the sky and flew away.

The woman pulled her dark cloak tight about her and left the upper walkway. She quickly descended to the lower quarters and went to her room, where she removed a long, thin bladed knife from a drawer. Slipping the blade into a fold within her cloak, she picked up a basket of clothing and went to the main living quarters. She stopped at Areenna's door, where she silently opened it and slipped inside.

The room was dark, the only sounds those of Mikaal's own breathing. Although he had fallen asleep shortly after leaving Areenna's chamber, he was now wide awake and listened for whatever had disturbed his sleep.

Knowing himself well, he accepted sleep was done for the night. He stared at the ceiling, and decided to practice his sensing. He closed his eyes and let his thoughts free. It happened quicker this time and he began to sense everything around.

He found little movement within the keep as he explored: a few workers were in the kitchen, beginning their work day; he felt Areenna and knew she was in a deep restful sleep. As he withdrew from her, he sensed someone walking down the hall.

Thinking it to be a good exercise, he focused on this woman and sensed she was outside his room. When she bypassed his doorway and stopped before Areenna's, a foul sensation swept through him.

Deep inside, from where he had discovered his power, a burning arose. It flared powerfully, not with pain, but with urgency.

Something is wrong. He knew this burning was a warning as surely as he knew he was alive. Throwing off the covers, he leapt out of bed, grabbed his longsword, and pulled his door open even as he sensed the woman slipping into Areenna's room.

By the low light of night-moss, he saw a basket filled with clothing placed near Areenna's closed door. He walked quietly to the door, opened it, and took two steps into the room.

The darkness, broken by a few streaks of a hallway light, did not reach into the room beyond where he stood. Frozen to the spot, he remained still while willing his eyes to adjust to the dimness. When they did, he looked around, but was unable to see anything other than shadows. Within him, the burning became intense. The urgency was overwhelming. He knew by the foul emanations filling his head, whoever he'd he sensed in the hall was in the room.

He recalled his conversation with Areenna about how he had to learn to give up control in order to better use his powers. He exhaled slowly and did exactly the opposite of the action his screaming muscles demanded—he stood dead still and closed his eyes. The heat in the pit of his abdomen spread fiercely through him. He stopped fighting and allowed it freedom. At the same instant he cleared his mind of all thought and slowly began to 'feel' the room, searching for whatever might be wrong.

The beating of Areenna's heart came clearly to his ears. Its slow and steady rhythm told him she slept; the evenness of her breathing played melody to her heartbeat. He searched on, seeking the other presence he knew was in the room.

He gripped his sword with both hands and concentrated. A moment later he found the second heartbeat. The instant he did, the woman's heart began to race madly with the knowledge she'd been discovered. He located the source and moved toward her. When he did, the woman pushed herself from the dark corner and leapt toward where Areenna lay.

Areenna, he cried in silent warning. She heard him and her eyes opened wide.

Somehow the darkness evaporated and he was able to see her open eyes and the woman in the cloak holding a long thin knife blade aimed at her heart.

Mikaal lunged forward in the very instant the woman launched herself. He thrust the tip of his longsword into her chest even as her knife descended toward Areenna.

At the very instant Mikaal's sword entered the woman's chest, Areenna gave vent to a loud, ear-shattering cry and silver white light exploded from her palms. Caught within the flaring release of power, the woman was lifted into the air and flung across the room, her body slamming against the stone wall, the knife clattering along the floor until it came to a stop at Mikaal's feet.

Mikaal stared for only a second at the woman's sprawled and broken body before turning to Areenna who was on her feet and running toward him. He caught her and held her to him for a moment before she drew back.

"You are unhurt?" she asked quickly, looking at him through the darkness.

"Me? You were the target."

A quarter of a minute later, Queen Atir, Laira and King Nomis rushed into the room, where they stopped short to look at the body of the black sorceress's spy. Behind them the hallway filled with guards.

CHAPTER 23

TWO HOURS AFTER the attack by the dark sorceress' spy, the five were seated around the table in the main eating chamber. King Nomis, no stranger to the dark powers, stared at his plate. His mood was one of deep anger, not at his guests, but that this vileness had been part of the keep's staff.

Nomis was a big man, even by Nevaen standards, with curly red hair and sparkling blue eyes: his skin was the shade of a roasted chestnut and his face was lined with the experience of too many battles. "How did this happen?" he asked his wife, who sat to his right. Laira, whose curly hair was the same fiery red as her father's, sat to his left, with Areenna next to her and Mikaal between Atir and Areenna.

Lifting a cup of steaming tea, Atir sipped and lowered it. It touched the table with a soft click. "I have been going over all my memories. She has been with us for years. She came to our dominion with her mother. Kana was but five at the time."

"From where?" Nomis asked.

"I don't remember," Atir said. "But she has been here since. Her mother died four years ago, a fever my powers could not stop. Kana stepped into her mother's position of housekeeper." Her eyes went distant. When they refocused, she looked at her husband. "And what is even more troubling—no, more frightening—is I had no sense of darkness about her."

"She was well protected, if you could not sense the dark power within her," Areenna said.

"Roth was right at the council, when he said the evil from across the seas is becoming stronger. When do you leave?" Nomis asked Mikaal.

"When this meal is done," Mikaal responded.

"I will assign a dozen of my men to accompany you," the King declared.

Before he could speak, Mikaal caught Areenna's silent warning. "Thank you for your offer, but we must do this without creating attention. Your men would bring many eyes upon us."

Nomis turned to Atir. "Talk sense into them."

"He is right, they must travel quietly and alone. Attention is exactly what need be avoided." She took her husband's hand and squeezed gently. "You can help them, though, with their route. There is no one who knows the ways through Aldimor better than you."

Nomis looked from Atir to the two and nodded. "How planned you to go?"

Mikaal pulled a scroll from the bag at his feet. He moved the dishes aside and spread the map on the table. "My father's map of Aldimor shows several ways."

Nomis stood and went around the table to examine the map. "This is far more detailed than any I have. It is like seeing Aldimore from above…" His voice held an edge of awe at the complexity of the map. "I would travel this route for the first day," he said, his broad fingertip traveling along a line representing a road. "There are only two small villages, and the area is sparsely populated—mostly by farmers."

"From there, you turn northeast, along here. There is no road I know of, but the way is clear: unsettled woodlands, meadows and rolling hills—easy enough for kraals. This route will bring you to the narrowest part of the wastelands and leave you only a day of travel to reach the Landing. The land will flatten at that point. Be wary, outcasts roam freely. Make sure you have water and food. The last miles before the Landing will be the ruins. There are many strange things living there…many. Not even outcasts go into the ruins. The ruins are forsaken and within them are unspeakable dangers, especially without a full complement of men to go with you," he added, eyeing Mikaal carefully.

"Again, I thank you, but we cannot accept the offer. We will manage."

Areenna and Mikaal took leave of their hosts, exiting Dees the same way as they had entered, cloaked with hoods raised to shadow their faces.

They followed Nomis' directions and reached the narrow dirt road leading to the wastelands. As Dees faded behind them, Mikaal asked Areenna about what happened in her bedchamber.

"When I saw the woman coming at me with the knife, and you defending me, I reacted...instinctively. I wasn't even aware of calling on my power, but I did, with more strength than I knew I had." Her voice was low and thoughtful. "But if you hadn't called my name..."

He shook his head. "I didn't call your name. I thought it."

"No matter how, I heard you." She fell silent.

Mikaal gazed at her. Her head was bent slightly and he sensed a deep sadness within her. "She meant to kill you, Areenna. You should feel no guilt about what happened."

Areenna looked at him. Her golden flecked eyes revealed a heaviness he had not seen before. "She was so young."

"But older than you," Mikaal reminded her. "Do not forget it was she who chose to align herself with them."

"You are right," Areenna said.

Roth looked up from his map as Enaid sliced the meat for their morning meal. "We have a choice. We are a day from Dees and at least three days from the Landing, perhaps a half day less if we ride until dark each day. Are you sure about Dees?"

She studied Roth, reading his worry. "Why do you ask? We have decided."

He took her right hand into both of his. "I can't explain, but I think something isn't right. I..." Roth took a deep breath. "I have this feeling that we must go to the Landing, not to Dees."

Enaid studied him carefully. In all the years they had been together, there had only been one time he had had a premonition. It was during the final stages of the war and because of it, they had avoided a terrible ambush.

"Explain," she said.

He spoke for several minutes, trying his best to express his thoughts. When he finished, Enaid leaned toward him and gave him a gentle kiss. "We shall go to the Landing. I will send Atir a message to meet us there."

Roth nodded in relief. "What disturbed you this morning? I heard you waken earlier."

"I am not certain. This block on Aldimor interferes with my ability to sense things at a distance." She shook her head. "It was a feeling of menace—a threat woke me. Something happened."

"To Mikaal?"

"I don't know. But whatever it was has passed. Somehow I know they are all right."

"Then we had best finish here and go on our way. The bird is still here for the message?"

Enaid smiled at him. "Yes...My Lord," she added with a smile she did not feel. She hoped Atir would release the block soon.

By the evening of the second day of travel, Mikaal and Areenna were at the eastern edge of Aldimor. Ahead of them, at the base of long rolling hills, were the wastelands. Although the green carpet of wild grass did not end abruptly, the line of demarcation was boldly visible nonetheless. No trees grew in this wasteland. The grasses there were brown and straggly, and what did grow looked strange. The ground was rocky, more gravel than sand, and there was a low, shadowy haze hanging above the ground.

Their route was not on any road marked upon a map, rather they had followed an old kraal-trodden path paralleling a stream through the higher mountains and then down, into rolling hills. As they came closer to their destination, Mikaal called a halt where the stream became narrower, turning into thin rapids and eventually into a small brook, which dried out short of the wastelands.

They had left the woods a quarter mile behind, and as they entered the wasteland, Mikaal said, "I think it best if we go back to the woods to make camp. There is more protection."

"I sense no danger here, but I think you're right."

They returned to the woods, set in a low hollow between two hills, and made camp near the brook. The woods themselves were sparse, but afforded more shelter than the open hillside.

"Once we enter the wastelands, Atir's protection will be lost," Areenna said. "We will have to be more on guard. This is the last safe place we will have. The wraiths will be waiting."

"Then we stay vigilant." He glanced at the darkening sky. "My muscles are stiff, I need exercise." He hesitated before saying, "And today is the last time I will have to work with you on the sword. Are you able?"

"Why would I not be?" she asked, going to Hero and removing her bags. "Let us set up camp before we practice."

She carried her bags to a level spot between two wide-spread trees. One, a large gazebow offered a multitude of strong branches for Gaalrie's evening perch. Mikaal joined her with his belongings and together they began to set up the camp.

Twenty minutes later, Mikaal stood in an open area, his sword held point down. Areenna stood across from him, her smaller blade held in her right hand. He stared at her, his eyes fixed on hers, his muscles tensing. "No games this time. I need to know how well you can handle yourself."

"You have trained me, you should already know," she retorted. "Do your best."

"No powers," he warned.

She smiled. "No magic," she agreed. Her eyes narrowed intently and she braced herself for his attack.

Mikaal hefted the sword and charged. He came at her with a raised sword and as it descended, she twisted slightly and spun under his blade deflecting it smoothly. With her next breath she whirled and struck at him. He flicked his wrist and their swords met with a loud crash. Each backed away.

"Not bad," Mikaal said an instant before he came at her again. This time his sword wove a figure eight; the low remnants of daylight glinted from the blade. Areenna backed away, watching his eyes, not the blade. When his attack came it was with such blinding speed his sword almost slipped past her defenses. She caught his blade at the last instant and battled back, swinging cross-wise to block his sword.

The fight went on, each blocking the other's attack. Then she sensed a change in him. His aura went deep. She saw the sweat beading on his face and knew he was going to attack with all his strength.

A sudden ripple of fear went through her. *Was he losing control? Was he getting battle fever?* And then he charged. She fought with all her strength, evading his blade where possible, halting it with her own when he got too close.

"Stop!" she cried, her breathing forced, her chest rising and falling with the efforts of the fight. She was filmed with perspiration—even her hands had become sticky with sweat.

Mikaal stopped his swing and placed his sword tip down into the earth. "What?"

"You go too far with this attack."

His eyes narrowed. His breathing was as labored as hers and his voice low and husky when he spoke. "Will your enemies stop because you cry out? Will they show you mercy? Remember the woman in Dees! Keep her in the forefront of your mind. You have much good in you, Areenna. You have what they lack—mercy, but they have none. They will do whatever is necessary to destroy you, to destroy Nevaeh. Now, fight!"

He charged her then, brutally, using every ounce of his strength to defeat her. As she back-stepped to avoid his blade, sparring and deflecting the silvery flashes of metal flying at her, something changed within her. Her fears vanished and the pommel of her sword blended with her skin to become an extension of her hands.

She planted her feet as he took an overhead swing at her. She blocked it, spun and struck at him. He barely caught her blade with his and twisted under it. And as he fought to regain his balance, she attacked.

Everything disappeared from her sight except for Mikaal's eyes and the sword in his hand. The fighting turned frenzied; sparks blazed each time their swords met. Areenna moved forward, her sword a hazy blur of metal and speed, striking at him with every step she took. And then, in one instant of pure clarity, she knew what he would do next and, as he struck at her, she ducked low, lunged forward and pressed the point of her sword into the first layer of the skin on his neck. The tip centered over his carotid artery.

"You have me," Mikaal said, lowering his sword.

Areenna couldn't speak; breathing was the only thing possible. A few moments later, while they stared at each other, she said, "You frightened me."

Mikaal nodded, his face was sober and no smile broke the planes of his lips. "That was my intention. You had to learn you could stand up to me."

"You would have cut me," she stated.

"If you had been one whit less willing to fight, yes."

"A hard lesson," she admitted. "You have done your job, my prince. You have indeed trained me well."

"As you have me."

She stared at him, her insides twisting. "Not yet. I too have one job to complete this eve, for there is yet another step to be taken in your training."

"Can we eat first?" he asked. His stomach emphasized his words with a loud and long growl.

Areenna laughed, the tension broken. "Of course."

They finished the remains of what they had taken from Dees as the full moon rose. The moon's light was strong, illuminating their camp and the sparsely populated woods enough to see clearly.

"It's time for you to find your weapon."

He looked at her, his features puzzled. "Find it? It sits there," he said, pointing to the long sword resting against the bole of the gazebow tree.

She shook her head slowly from side to side in emphasis. "As you know every woman of power has a weapon. You have seen mine...but it has changed. How I know not, but it has. Remember what happened in the bedchamber. That was a part of my weapon. I have always been able to create a power, like a ball made of light is the best way to describe it. When I need to defend myself, I am able to...channel my power through my palms. But what happened in the chamber was more than I have ever experienced."

"And the shattered window? Was that it as well?"

"It must have been. I can tell you my power has increased. How much, I haven't any idea, but in the—has it been two weeks since that day at Tolemac?"

"Almost ten, eleven days."

"But since we first joined there, and then with Bekar...I have changed." She hesitated for a few seconds and then looked into his eyes. "We must find yours tonight. Tomorrow will be too late."

"How do we do this?"

Areenna thought back to the end of her second year of training, when she had returned from school for the mid-summer holiday at Freemorn. Her mother had whisked her away that very day, into the forest at the start of the blue desert and over the next three days Areenna had learned how to access her powers for self-defense. While she was not supposed to learn this until after the end of school, her mother had told her she had reasons for training Areenna early, but no one was to know. Little had Areenna guessed it was because her mother had fallen ill a few months before and had known that the disease would take her life.

The training had been the hardest thing she had done in her not quite thirteen year old life, but when she discovered her ability, it had been exhilarating and freeing.

"We don't have the training time my mother had with me, so it will have to be forced. The way of learning comes from need. When my mother trained me, she put me in dangerous situations. Even while she watched over me and guided me, she pushed me to the very edge of life. Do you believe you can handle such?"

Mikaal studied her intently before he smiled. "You will be hard pressed to push me so far."

"This is not a game, Mikaal. It is the most dangerous part of training. My mother took a great risk when she taught me this, because she was not supposed to do so at my age, but there were circumstances..."

Mikaal's features sobered with understanding. He took her hand. "I will handle whatever you must do. I trust you, fully. When I first saw you at school, you were sitting on the floor in front of old Thrumweld. When you answered his question about the Old Ones, there was something about you, something special. It wasn't until the council at Tolemac when I understood."

"Understood what?"

"How special you are," he whispered. "You're different from other women. Why, I don't know, but you are. And I am different from other men." He smiled. "But at least I know why."

"Then you'll do this?"

"I trust you."

"With your life?"

He stared at her. He could feel his heart speed up and quickly curbed his thoughts. "With all."

Areenna could not respond. It took her several long seconds to nod. "Then we should begin."

"How?

"Look only at my eyes," she told him, turning fully to face him. When his eyes were locked with hers, she clenched her palms and drew on her power. It built faster than ever before and within a breath she was ready. Opening her palms, she released the power at him. The silvery white balls flew the short distance and hit him hard. He flew backwards for a half dozen feet, landing on his back and sliding another two feet. When he stood he saw her eyes were wide, and in them he saw danger.

"Run, Mikaal! Run for your life!"

CHAPTER 24

'RUN FOR YOUR life!' The words beat at his ears as mightily as the streaks of silvery white heading toward him. Mikaal could not believe the change in her from one second to the next. His shoulder was on fire from the strike, his left arm as well. He scrambled back from where he lay and pulled his legs under him.

Even as she'd spoken, lightning leaped from her hand and streaked toward him. He turned, pushed off with his feet and ran. He made it ten yards before he was struck in the back. He hit the ground. His cheek scraped across the hard grass. Without thinking he rolled to his left just as two more white balls hit the ground where he'd been. Gaining his feet, he raced for the protection of the woods. He slid behind the first tree as more of her hellish power struck. He felt the tree shutter and as it did, he raced deeper into the woods. When he was far enough in, and no white streaks flew at him, he stopped to catch his breath.

How do I defend myself against this? His mind sped through all the possibilities, but he already knew the answer lay buried somewhere inside of him. Looking around the bole of the large tree he was using for cover, he searched for her, but did not see her anywhere. *Would she really hurt him?* He knew the answer, because she, like he, would do whatever was necessary to teach him.

Moving carefully, he began to wind through the woods, looking for something to protect himself. Then he stopped dead. *Think!* He ordered himself. *Think!*

Areenna waited until he was deep in the woods. She knew exactly where he was because he had not tried to erect any sort of block. He had not yet reached that point of desperation. She had been careful not to injure him, but it had been difficult because whatever had happened to her over the past days had increased her powers beyond her comprehension. She was certain this new found strength had come from Bekar—a gift bestowed while she had been in that strange half sleep-half daze cast upon them on the old highway. But it made her aware she must exert very tight control over herself.

She cast outward, seeking him, and a moment later found him hiding behind a large tree. She sensed he was trying to work out what was happening and what he needed to do. And then he was gone. "Good," she whispered to herself. "Good." He was learning.

She walked into the woods, moving toward what was now a blank space within the trees. When she was close enough, she stopped and waited for his next move. Above her, Gaalrie flew silently. In an instant she was looking through her aoutem's eyes and found Mikaal exactly where she knew he would be.

Carefully, she built her power, this time making it stronger before releasing it.

Think! he told himself after creating the block he hoped would stop her from finding him. Then he pushed his senses outward, looking for her. It took only a few seconds before he found her close to where he hid.

Before he could move, light exploded around him. The power had not hit him, but its force knocked him to the ground. His anger burst outward and he screamed defiantly before running on an angle toward the nearby brook.

As he ran, he concentrated on finding the power hidden deep within him. And he did. It erupted, spewing rivulets of heat through him. Strength flowed through his muscles as he ran. His breathing smoothed into a rhythmic pattern and his mind raced. He sensed she was running after him, speeding along on an angle to cut him off. His longsword kept hitting his knee and he drew it and held it tightly.

When he reached the edge of the creek, he saw her emerge from the woods and stop to stare at him. Time altered, everything slowed. He saw her brace herself, her legs spread slightly, her feet planted. She was in a high crouch, her palms turned toward him. Silvery white light grew within their centers.

He grasped the sword in two hands and faced her. When the light flashed and shot toward him, he did the only thing possible, he raised his sword. The first streak hit the sword blade and flared out. The second hit his shoulder and spun him around.

His shoulder burned, but he retained his footing and faced her again. Her face was taut, her eyes narrowed. He knew she was getting ready for another attack and knew, too, this was no game. It had never been.

She started forward, this Areenna he had never seen before. That she was a warrior was unquestioned, that she had enough power to destroy him was absolute. As he watched, he knew something within her had changed—it was something requiring him to change as well, because if he could not, the journey would end and he would have failed. And that was out of the question.

He gripped the sword tighter, working out how to stop her and how to find his own weapon. The instant she drew on her power, he sensed it and raised the sword. She sent a single bolt at him, and he knew exactly where it would go. The white fiery ball sped at him faster than anything he had seen before. He turned sideways and swung the flat of his blade at the very instant the power reached him. The light exploded and disappeared.

Areenna continued toward him. Both palms began to glow. *Your sword will not help you this time,* she said in his head.

Mikaal knew truth when he heard it. Dropping his sword, he closed his eyes and sank to his knees. In an instinctive movement, he dug his hands into the earth as he had seen his mother do many times during his younger years. *Help me,* he asked the very earth his hands had penetrated.

An answering tremble ran through his fingers and continued upward into his arms and then branched off. It went into his head and then downward, flowing through his body until his entire being trembled. The trembling stopped, but before he could take a breath, a wave of heat spread through him, burning hotter than any flame he had ever been near, consuming him with a fire that flowed through his veins. The fire poured into his heart and then stopped.

He heard Charka cry loudly in the night, and above him, Gaalrie screeched. Areenna, not a dozen feet distant, froze.

Pulling his hands from the earth he rose to his full height even as Areenna rekindled the power and let fly two massive bolts of white light. He raised his hands, the fingers of one pointed at her, and released every bit of the forces racing through him. He held his other hand palm outward. A sheet of flame erupted, not from his hand, but from the ground, encircling Areenna, exploding in every direction and rising to the branches in the trees above. The twin orbs of white power struck his upheld palm and vanished.

The instant he saw what had happened, he called his power back and the flames died as quickly as they had come. Areenna stood unharmed within a circle of burning grass, her eyes wide.

His body was icy cold now, and he began to shiver, but his fear of having hurt Areenna made him ignore the cold and race to where she stood. "Are you hurt?" he asked, turning her in a circle and tracing every inch of her body.

She shook her head. Her breathing was forced. "I…I have never seen… I…"

"Don't speak, breathe."

She shook her head. "I am…fine. I never expected it to happen so fast. I was startled."

"I could have hurt you."

She reached out and touched his cheek. "But you did not. You're very cold. We have to get you back."

"I'm fine."

"You are not fine. You're white, your shoulder and leg are injured. I used too much force. Do not argue with me."

He nodded. "My sword."

"Stay here," she commanded and retrieved the weapon. Once it was in its scabbard, they started to camp. At one point he stumbled. Areenna caught him and helped him the rest of the way. At their camp, she brought him to the lean-to and laid him on his sleeping silks. She removed his shirt, leaned over and said, "Close your eyes and I will attempt to use Ilsraeth's gift." He tried to speak, but she put her finger to his lips. "Hush."

She lowered herself to his side, leaned forward and placed her hands over the burns. She closed her eyes and dug inside herself to release the gift. It took her several minutes and while she built the power of her new gift, Mikaal drifted off to sleep.

Areenna worked slowly, learning the gift as she used it. She drew upon it, allowed it to flow within her and take her over completely. A few moments later, everything went dark except for the light around her hands and the glowing areas of his injuries. She slowly moved her hands over his shoulder, where the burn was the worst, and minutes later, his flesh was unmarked. Then she gently ran her hand along his chest, slowly and carefully tracing every muscle in his abdomen. Moving lower, Areenna paused to remove his pants. Still she could not see him, only feel the flesh over the glowing places of his injuries.

She traced down to his thighs, to the spot where she had hit, and worked the muscles for several minutes. Then she turned him over and healed his back, releasing the tight muscles and drawing out the pain.

When she finished, she turned him onto his back, covered him with his sleeping silks and rose above him. As she did, her sight returned and she went outside and sat by the fire, knowing that when he awoke in the morning he would be as he was before the training.

"Thank you Atir, for this blessing."

She stared into the fire, her mind churning with the evening's events. She thought about the sword fight, replayed every bit of it in her mind, and recognized she had reached the point of not being afraid and of understanding how good she was with a sword. Much better, she decided, than she had imagined.

His power of fire was something she had not seen before—she knew of no woman with such an ability. It was a fearsome thing, one to be reckoned with. But did they have enough time for him to learn its use? She could only hope.

While her thoughts revolved around Mikaal and the power he had unleashed, her eyes closed and she fell asleep before the fire. Her body leaned sideways and, as if someone was helping her, descended slowly to the ground. Above her, Gaalrie rested on a branch, watching. Then Areenna's aoutem floated to the ground, stepped next to her and sat alertly looking around. The treygone turned its head to Charka. A moment later the large kraal came over and lay down next to Areenna. His body heat was more than ample to keep her warm through the quickly cooling night.

◇◇◇

"We are being followed," Enaid stated. Turning to Roth, she studied him. "But I sense no danger."

"It is probably nothing," he replied without looking at her.

"Nothing?" Closing her eyes, she cast about.

"Enaid," Roth called, breaking her concentration.

She looked at him and knew. "Your men are following us—your Sixes. Why?"

"They are there to protect us."

"Against what? They would not stand a chance against *her*."

"They will against those *she* may have sent."

"Against men, yes. Against her creatures…Solomon, it is doubtful." She exhaled slowly. During the wars, he had trained groups of six men at a time in ways no men of Nevaeh had been trained before. They were the deadliest fighters in Nevaeh, and fiercely loyal to Roth.

When he had first thought of training men for this he had explained to Enaid about the past, about the armies of his country. For over two hundred years, the warriors of his time had several specialized branches. One, he told her, was called the Seals, another was the Rangers, and yet another was Special Forces. They were highly strained soldiers and the deadliest fighting men and women of his time. Years before he was born, all the special branches were united into one, and were called Seals.

He had explained how they were bonded together, and worked with absolute trust in each other. They went on only the most dangerous of missions, and to any part of the world. These men and women could go anywhere, survive in the most hostile areas of their world: they could fight with any weapon, or with only their hands.

A year before he was sent into space, Roth and two others of the crew and three of the 'colonists' were sent for Seal training as part of the overall training for landing on a strange world. Roth excelled in this, and had taken the knowledge of this specialized training into space.

And now, one of the Seal groups—who he had renamed 'Sixes', as seals were unheard of in Nevaeh—was shadowing them. It should have made Enaid feel more secure, but it only added more concern to her already heavy burdens. She knew she'd had to send her son with Areenna, but the worry for him and the guilt she carried at putting him into so much danger was hard to bear.

"If what I fear comes to be, their lives will be in danger."

"They were not ordered to do this. They volunteered," Roth explained.

Enaid drew her kraal to a stop, lifted in her stirrups and turned to face him. "There is not a man among your Sixes who would not volunteer his life for yours as you well know."

"Or for you," he said in a low voice.

"You should have talked to me about this first. If what I have foreseen comes about, there will be no hiding Mikaal's power. Would you have your men see this?"

"It is a chance I take. I will not lose my son."

She reached across and took his hand. "Then keep faith he will be strong enough to gain what is needed on the Island, and to leave it and live."

"And Areenna?" he asked. "Does the same hold true for her?"

She looked deeply into his eyes before saying, "Even more so. For Areenna's life is dependent on Mikaal. Without him she has no chance...and Solomon, without her, neither shall you."

CHAPTER 25

THE MORNING SKY was cluttered with low hanging clouds of white gray puffs so thickly massed only a little daylight filtered through. Mikaal awoke slowly and refreshed. There was no pain or stiffness from last night's battles.

Throwing off the sleeping silks he started to rise, but stopped when he found he was naked. "How?"

He looked to Areenna's sleeping silks, but they had not been used. He searched for his clothing, dressed quickly and left the shelter. What greeted him was perhaps the strangest sight of their journey.

Areenna was sound asleep before the cold ashes of the fire. Charka lay on the ground against her back, Gaalrie was snuggled into her abdomen and chest, her head resting on Areenna's side. Both animals lifted their heads at his approach, but did not move.

He went to Areenna and crouched by her head. Stroking her hair, he called her name softly. Areenna opened her eyes and Gaalrie and Charka moved. The giant bird lifted onto her legs while Charka clumsily gained his feet.

"Wha…" Areenna started when the animals stood, then she saw Mikaal's smiling face floating before her.

"You slept well I presume?"

Memory flooded her as last night's events raced across her mind's eye. "How are you? Is there still pain?"

Mikaal shook his head sharply. "I feel like I've slept for a week. There is no soreness, no pain. I feel...strong."

"Good, then the healing worked." Areenna glanced around, her features puzzled. "I don't remember falling sleep. I was sitting here by the fire," she said, sitting up, "and then you were above me." She wrinkled her nose. "I smell like kraal."

"That's what happens when you sleep with one," he joked.

"I need to bathe."

"Ah, shall I prepare hot water for you, Princess?"

"Very funny. What you can do is find some real food. I think we're going to need it today. We need to save the dry food for the Landing. I don't think there will be much there or on the Island."

"Not around here. We haven't seen so much as a skerl, and I wouldn't want to eat one of those. We're too close to the wasteland. We'll need Gaalrie. Perhaps she can find a plump crave or, with some luck, a chillen."

Turning to where Gaalrie still watched them, Areenna extended her arm and the treygone hopped onto it. She lifted the heavy bird so their eyes were level and sent an easy push. Gaalrie flew upward with Areenna's arm thrust, circled above them and then flew west.

Areenna started toward the lean-to and her bags. "Perhaps a fire is in order," she threw back at Mikaal.

"Of course, My Lady." A wide smile grew on his face as he watched her gather her clean clothing. A minute later she was headed to the creek and he turned toward the woods to gather more fallen branches.

Areenna returned fifteen minutes later, just as the fire licked skyward. "My turn," Mikaal said. He pulled a fresh shirt and pants from his bag and headed to the creek.

When he disappeared over the ridge, Areenna gathered their things and began to pack. She had slept deeply and had wakened renewed. But as she thought about the day ahead, darkness settled over her. Today would be the last before reaching the Island; she was worried about the night ahead. She had no desire to gain the Island when it was dark. They would have to camp at the Landing, which she sensed would be dangerous, even though Enaid had assured them the Landing was a safe place.

And the wraiths? They would be close by. Once they crossed the border of Aldimor and entered the wasteland, Atir's protection would be gone and they would be visible to any who could sense or see them.

She knew there was no choice. The miles of wasteland had to be crossed and there was no way around it. She shrugged and went back to packing.

They entered the wastelands an hour after eating. The sky remained overcast and filled with low hanging gray and white clouds, which seemed to hover but inches above their heads. It wasn't the clouds but the land that gave this illusion. The flat brown wasteland had little vegetation and stretched as far as the eye could see, disappearing into a mist that blended into the clouds hunkering along the horizon.

Even the air had changed. On the western side of the Aldimor border it had been comfortable, but here every breeze held a damp chill even though the temperature remained steady. Areenna wrapped her traveling cloak tighter. Mikaal had already done so moments before.

"Tell me how you accessed your power, your weapon. Truthfully I have never seen the like before."

He shook his head. "I'm not sure. I asked for help."

She nodded. She had gone through the same experience as had all women of power. Her brows knit together as she worked on a way for him to discover what he had done. "When my mother trained me to find my weapon, it was much like I did with you," she began slowly and thoughtfully. "We were in the deep forests ringing the blue desert. She was chasing me and I was running. Her power was very strong. Her weapon was her ability to move things. She could make a rock the size of your head fly a hundred yards so fast you could barely track it, and she always hit whatever she aimed at. There seemed no limit to what she could move."

A dozen memories flicked through her mind. "She used the weapon to help as well as fight. One day we had been traveling past a farm where we saw a kraagen pulling a tiller. They were skirting the edge of a pond because the farmer wanted to plant as much seed as possible. As they worked, they'd hit a buried boulder. The lead leather bindings on the tiller snapped, and the kraagen lunged forward, lost its footing and went into the pond."

She paused for a breath. "The bottom was quickmud. The kraagen was stuck and by the time we got there, it had only its mouth and horns above the water. My mother knelt beside the pond and closed her eyes. A moment later the water around the kraagen bubbled and then the kraagen began to rise. She lifted it from the water and set it gently on solid ground twenty feet from the pond. That too was her weapon."

Areenna's face brightened with the memory. "When I asked her how it was she could use her weapon to help, she simply smiled at me. 'There are always two. Nothing is simply one thing.' When I said I didn't understand, she explained how, with understanding everything becomes clearer and what can be done is there to be learned."

"All good and well, but how does that help me?"

"Your weapon can be used to protect you, to fight an enemy, but it can also be used to help."

"If you know how to use it," Mikaal said, his voice rough edged.

"When she trained me, she chased me, hurling rocks and sticks at me. At one point it was raining hard sharp pebbles and small rocks. They struck me everywhere. The pain was bad and I couldn't find a way to stop it or her. I was desperate. I ran, trying to get out of the rock storm when one hit me harder than the others, right in the center of my back. I fell, badly scraping my shoulder and arm, and I got angry. I rolled over, jumped to my feet and screamed at her. 'No more!' I shouted. My fists were balled tight and the power came alive in my belly. The next thing I knew I was holding two glowing orbs in my hands. They were hot, and when I looked at them, I knew what they were and flung them at my mother."

She paused within her memory. "She evaded them easily, for her abilities were great, but I was too stunned to even think."

"And you knew how to do this after that."

"No, it took me a few days to understand. Once I did, my weapon was always ready."

"How?"

"That's the problem. You have to replay it over and over until you find the exact instant it happened. Remember the feeling, see it and recreate it."

He looked at her and then at the horizon. "A simple enough task. We have plenty of time for me to figure it out—all the way until tomorrow morning," he added sarcastically.

"Sometimes, Mikaal, you are an idiot."

She spoke so calmly he could only stare at her. "Really, why so?"

"You should ask why that isn't so." She gave Hero a slight kick with her heels and the kraal moved forward past Mikaal.

Behind her stiff back, Mikaal smiled. He sobered a moment later. He had only been half-joking about the time they had left. Taking a deep breath, he concentrated on the previous night, and did the best he could to relive what had happened.

He remembered the way his lower belly had flared when his power came to life. He remembered the burning in his veins, the heat and the pain, and tried to replicate it. He called up his power, which had become increasingly easier with each day's practice, but when he tried to raise the weapon, nothing happened.

What did I do? he asked himself for the twentieth time.

He spent the next three hours working on the problem, going back over it time and again, but no matter how hard he tried, nothing seemed to work.

They stopped at what they estimated was midday and ate what was left of their morning meal. He watched Areenna clean a small bone with her teeth, and a flash of memory from last night slid across his mind. He had dug his hands into the earth and had called for help. *Was that it?*

Kneeling on the rocky ground, he tunneled his fingers past the small rocks covering the dirt below. There was coolness on his skin, and something else. He closed his eyes and drew up his power. Then he concentrated on the fiery growth he had felt last night. It came explosively, and fire erupted everywhere.

"Stop!" he shouted, jerking his hands from the ground. The words barely crossed his lips and the fires went out.

Areenna stared at him, the clean-picked bone held in one hand. "It's a start."

Later, as the horizon grew close, Areenna turned to him. "It is not that you need what is in the ground. It's the earth itself…it gives you the power. This is true for all women."

It took him a moment to realize she was continuing their earlier conversation. "How can the ground give power?" he asked, although he knew it was what had allowed him to create the fires.

"Women have always believed all life was created from what lay beneath our feet. We call it sister, for our world is built from and upon it. Existence is held by it and we but accept its gifts."

"Even if it is so, how can I use my gift if I must stop and sink my hands into the ground each time?"

"I tried to tell you before, when I spoke of my training. It's not what enabled you to first use the weapon. It's what is in you that allowed it to awaken…to come alive."

Mikaal exhaled sharply, but said nothing. Instead, he thought about what had happened when his fingers entered the earth. He recreated the sensation, but nothing happened.

"What about a formula? What formula do you use, perhaps something—"

"Stop! There are no damned formulas! There never have been, not in the way you perceive such. Men always want to know how we do our magic. The truth is it's our minds. Everything we do comes from our minds. If we are fortunate enough—or perhaps unfortunate—to have received a gift of strong power, we have to learn how to control what we do by controlling our minds, not our power."

"But you use formulas to bring forth the magic."

"Have you learned so little these past days?" she bit off her words tersely, her voice barely above a hoarse whisper. Within it was a depth of sadness he had never heard from her.

Her tone and inflection shook him so badly he closed his eyes to stop from showing the emotion. But when her hand touched his cheek, he opened his eyes to find her face inches away.

"Listen to me, Mikaal, no formula can possibly 'control' our gifts. What we do is to join with the power and use our minds—our thoughts— to make use of the powers we have been gifted. It is what I have been hoping you would learn when you discovered your power."

He stared into the ovals of her eyes, the warmth of her hand still on his cheek. Her breath washed across his face and he began to hear what she had been saying these last days. It took barely a heartbeat for him to see. *I understand.*

241

Smiling, she lowered her hand. "It's about time."

"Why is this secret? Why hide your abilities with talk of formulas?"

"It can be confusing because there are what you think of as formulas as I have tried to explain more than once. But they're more like...notations. I construct one for everything I can create with my power. The notation allows me to visualize the process. The formula does not create. The formula allows me to practice until I need nothing to remind me of how to accomplish the task. It is nothing more."

"Tell me."

"Better if I show you, yes? I can create fire, too, but not as a weapon." She dismounted Hero and went over to a lone patch of brownish weed where she crouched and spread her hands to both sides of it. *Move the air, swirl it fast, spin like a storm. Close together heat will grow, spin air, spin faster and faster and faster. Heat grows strong and flame will burn now."*

The dried out weed burst into flame and Areenna stood and turned to him. "I made that up when my mother taught me to build fire. She explained how, when the air moves very fast, faster than you can imagine, little particles we can't see are in the air and the speed of the air heats them until they ignite. It is science, is it not?"

"What I know of science is what I learned from my father. He told me many stories about science, and about how science destroyed his world. But it is—no was—nothing like this."

"So now you know our secret."

"No, Areenna, now I have learned our secret. We need to go," he said. "It's best if we reach the Landing before dark."

"Create a formula for your weapon while we ride. We will practice at the Landing."

◇◇◇

The instant they crossed the border into the wasteland the air changed. Roth stopped the kraal and withdrew a map. It was a hand drawn copy of the computer generated map he'd made almost two and a half decades earlier. The map was well detailed for he'd had a lot of downtime in the year he'd orbited the earth.

"We will not make it to the Landing today," he told Enaid after he spotted a landmark allowing him to gauge distance, "unless we ride through the night."

Enaid began to mind search for Mikaal, hoping now that they had crossed from Aldimor's protection she could find him. She pushed herself, ranging her senses as far and as fast as possible. A few minutes later she found Mikaal's familiar emanations. It was a sensation she had known since he'd been growing within her womb. She withdrew. "They are safe and in the wasteland. We may be able to reach them before they cross to the Island."

"You are still certain we will be able to stop the attack?"

"Do you still feel your premonition?" When he nodded she said, "Then we must try. What *she* has created is far too dangerous for them to handle alone."

"Are you certain it is not just your—our—need to protect him?"

Enaid's eyes blazed angrily, her body stiffened. Then her features softened and her muscles unwound. "Do you think this is for him...for them? Solomon, you are the smartest man I know, but you are still only a man. How could you consider I would risk everything, risk Nevaeh itself by doing this? They will never know we are there. They cannot. Our purpose is to protect them. To hold back the horror *she* has released on them. They must reach the Island. My—our—responsibility is to give them a chance to gain the knowledge they seek, or we are lost. What happens to them on the Island, whether they succeed or fail is something we cannot interfere with—the duty is theirs. But the danger is enormous. Even you feel it is so."

He sat silently on the back of his kraal, listening and reading her face and body language and, when she finished, said, "I needed to hear that. You, above all else, are his mother. There are times when a mother's love causes irrationality, and it could be that I feel."

"In this matter, I cannot allow such—" Enaid stiffened; at her kraal's feet, her gorlon released a high pitched howl.

"What?" Roth asked, moving closer.

Enaid's eyes had rolled back, her hands were balled into fists; fear crawled coldly along his spine. "Enaid," he shouted reaching out and shaking her.

Her eyes returned to normal, but her skin was pale and damp. *"She* has found us…and them."

CHAPTER 26

IT WAS LATE afternoon when Areenna and Mikaal halted their kraals near to the edge of ruins far older than either had seen before. Contrary to the warnings, they'd crossed the most desolate part of the wasteland without seeing a single outcast or for that matter, anything alive.

The ruins before them were the remnants of ages of deterioration. Piles of rubble stretched like small hills as far as the eye could see. Interspersed within the millennia old ruins were what appeared to be the skeletons of large structures reduced to shambles of fallen stone, glass, and twisted strands of metal.

All his life, Mikaal had heard stories of the strange ruins of 'before', but had never seen them himself and had only half believed they existed. What they rode through now, what surrounded them, could be nothing other than the evidence of those legends.

He stopped Charka by one large ruin and went over to a long deformed piece of metal, perhaps a foot thick. It looked as if two giant hands had grasped it and twisted it in opposite directions. Rust flaked from it in dust-like puffs that broke apart at his lightest touch. "I cannot imagine how old this is. The metal is held together only by rust."

Astride Hero, Areenna looked around. "I do not like this place. Mikaal, we need to go."

In echo to her words, Mikaal heard a scuttling a few feet away beneath another pile of rubble. What at first glance looked like a misshapen coor stuck its head out. It was smaller than a coor, but with a similar head shape—which was where the resemblance ended. It had a single, large eye. There was no white, only the jet black of the pupil. The eye socket was extended from the head on a thick stalk that moved in all directions. The ears were several holes at each side if its head.

When it spotted Mikaal, its lips drew back, exposing large, pointed teeth. A low growl issued from its throat. As it slunk forward toward him, the rest of its body became visible. Perhaps three feet long, it had triple-jointed forelegs with what appeared to be two knees on each leg. The body was long and muscular, yet emaciated at the same time. The hind legs of the small beast were thicker than the body itself and unlike a coor, there was no tail.

Within the rubble came movement, enough for him to turn and jump on Charka. As he mounted the kraal, a dozen of the mutated coor-like animals appeared. They joined together in a pack and turned their eyes toward him and Areenna.

Saliva dripped from their jaws in thick drools of foam. They inched forward, anticipation of a meal emanating from them.

From a camouflaged opening ten feet behind the one-eyed coors, Mikaal saw two sets of amber yellow eyes peering out. A moment later a misshapen hairless head, followed by a deformed hairless torso astride three stubby legs stepped from the darkened opening. It stood perhaps four feet tall. Another like it followed. Their arms were almost as long as their entire bodies and they held spears in large hands that scraped the ground.

Areenna looked at Mikaal. *Those were once people.*

Mikaal looked around. Ahead of them, toward their destination, were more ruins. To the left, the ruins went as far as he could see. Straight, or to the right appeared to be the only clear paths. *Follow me to the right.*

Above them, Gaalrie circled. Through her eyes Areenna saw what lay ahead in all directions. To their left and to their right, more of the mutated animals and men were coming from beneath the rubble. *No, straight*, she corrected and pushed Hero forward.

Mikaal had no choice but to follow.

Urging their kraals into a gallop, they moved through the ruins' twists and turns, always staying on the narrow dirt road and avoiding the blockages ahead with Gaalrie's help. Behind them the pack of deformed coors and what once might have been men followed. Racing along the edges of the ruins, they jumped from one pile of rubble to the next in their mad effort to catch the riders, but they were no match for the kraals.

Minutes later, Areenna and Mikaal reached the edge of the ruins and burst onto a road that reminded them of Bekar's 'highway'. Ten feet ahead, the road dipped. Reining in their kraals, they inched the large animals forward before stopping to look around. Behind them, the mutations were no longer on the chase, but stood together at the very edge of the ruins, howling with rage.

Ahead and far below, barely visible in the far off mist, was their first sight of 'the Island', a distantly discernable, dark shape floating in water, its entirety veiled in a reddish mist. The Island extended to the left for as far as they could see, but to the right it went on for only a short distance. There were strangely shaped silhouettes standing on the Island, many reaching upwards into the high mists; all seemed to be twisted and broken. What they were or even how large they were was uncertain, for the distance made judgment difficult. To their left, at what appeared to be miles distant, was a wavering outline of a high bridge. It arched upward from the Island and reached westward. But a quarter way between the Island and the land across from it, the bridge stopped and hung in midair.

Mikaal studied the landscape. They were on a palisade high above the water and the road they were following was carved into the palisade. The road ahead twisted and turned on itself all the way down—the entire area was bleak and desolate; he was certain nothing lived there, yet there was something about it that did not fit.

"The Landing," Areenna said, rising in her stirrups for a better view.

Mikaal looked at the eastern horizon. Purple-black bands heralding the night were rising upward. "We need to get down there and set up camp before nightfall."

Areenna's eyes darted everywhere. She shivered. "There is an evil here, a darkness far worse than the night. We must be alert. The Landing will be safe, Enaid has told me so, but between here and there I sense....something."

Mikaal released the tension tightening his muscles and breathed deeply. A strange sensation piqued the edge of his mind. He pushed it and received a gripping chill. "I feel it."

He drew his longsword and grasped it in two hands before pressing his knees to Charka's flanks. A rush of strength flowed to him from the kraal. He gave his aoutem a gentle push to start them down the road to the Landing.

She paced frenetically within the entrance of the cavern. Deep in the confines a fire roared, producing shapes upon the walls no human eye had ever seen and lived after. An hour before *she* had received a message from her masters across the sea. Roth must die and the ones who had defied her at Tolemac must be destroyed. Their message was clear. And with it came the news of her masters' impending voyage.

Her bitter laugh, echoing loudly in the air, reached no other ears. *Destroy them I will do my masters. It will be as you command. She* turned and started into the cavernous mouth of the home *she* had chosen fifty years before, as a young outcast woman. While her body had changed over the years, age had had no effect on her. Her masters had blessed her when *she* had come to them, a broken woman cast out by her family because of the powerful abilities which *she* used for *her* own desires, refusing the training so often offered. Although her face and skin had aged, giving her the appearance of an old woman, her body was stronger than when *she* had arrived here at the age of twenty and found Mother Tashra, the masters' chief priestess—the woman who took her in and gave her the most powerful gifts imaginable.

Inside, *she* went to the fire, bent before it and stared into the flames. *She* sent *her* mind outward, questing everywhere. Then her breath lodged in her throat when the image of the hated Roth crossed her eyes. *She* stared hard at the visage of this unholy person, this usurper of her kingdom. *He was in the wasteland. She was there too, the witch who protected him.* How such good fortune came to her *she* cared not: what was important was the opportunity to do her Masters' bidding had fallen into her hands.

Then *she* sought to look for the two who had defied her. Seconds later *she* had them as well. They were a half day ahead of the most hated ones.

She laughed again, a low choked off visceral sound that could shrivel skin. Standing before the flames, *she* removed *her* robes and sat naked on the cold rock of the floor. *She* closed her eyes and began to sway, her upper torso revolving on deformed hips as *she* called up the formula *she* had created to control her wraiths, building it within *her* mind and making it stronger with each breath she took.

She would send a wraith after Roth and his woman. Tonight would be their last. And for the two who were attempting to reach the Island, *she* would stop them before they could reach the safety of the Landing place.

◇◇◇

"Your men have crossed into the wasteland." Enaid looked around. The sensations of danger she'd glimpsed earlier had stayed with her, neither growing nor lessening, yet she was certain the feeling of peril would grow stronger the closer they came to the Island.

"They are further back than I thought."

"They must not follow us. I am certain of this. It has nothing to do with Mikaal. It is for them. I fear they will die if they continue on."

Knowing Enaid well, Roth studied his wife. From the day he had met her, he had discovered her intuition was absolute. He had never ignored her warnings and had survived battles and dangers that would have killed anyone else because he did so. As he studied her, the inner sense that had guided him soundly all his life, told him she was speaking truthfully and he must listen.

"How can we stop them? How can we tell them to return to Tolemac?"

Enaid shook her head. "There is no way."

Roth wasn't so sure. "They are following our trail. They will come to this exact spot."

"Yes," she said hesitantly. "How does that help?"

He drew out a thin sheet of writing material and wrote instructions and handed them to her. After reading it, she returned it to him. "How do we send it?"

"An arrow, my love, if you please," he asked with a smile.

She cocked her head to one side. "I hardly think an arrow will travel such distance."

Laughing, he extended his hand. She drew an arrow and handed it to him. He pierced the top and bottom of the sheet with the shaft and slid it up to the quills then, dismounting, went to the middle of their tracks and jammed the arrow into the ground. "They will see it and obey my instructions."

"Will they?" she asked. "Remember, husband, you chose men who are much like you, headstrong and stubborn."

He smiled. "They will obey my command as it is written."

"As you say, My Lord. I hope such happens, for their sake and for yours."

The weight of her words was not a light burden. "Yes, let's hope so."

Night smothered the remnants of the day as Areenna and Mikaal descended to the Landing. Built of switchbacks hidden by the mists rising from the water below, what had looked to be only a few twists and turns was more illusion than reality.

The night grew dark, and unease wrapped the pair tighter than their riding cloaks. The air turned cool and the high chirps of blind night hunting trigetores was the music that accompanied them.

The mist-veiled Island seen from above was hidden by the night. "Keep a sharp watch," Areenna said to Mikaal, and silently asked Gaalrie to do the same.

Charka added his own warning with a low sounding call and Mikaal sensed his aoutem's unease both in his head and from the kraal's body itself. Using the technique Areenna had taught him, he sent out a sensing. A moment later a shudder ran through him when he touched something cold and dark.

"It's waiting," he called to Areenna.

Having already tasted the vileness that lay in wait, the heart of her power flared. *Be ready*, she told Mikaal silently.

Mikaal had no need to call his power; it had burst forth seconds before and was filling him. He had spent the hours of travel following their midday meal working on the means to call forth his abilities and had reached the point where he could almost bring up the fire at will. He'd created his formula—his method of visualizing the building of his power, by utilizing a simple phrase: *Cold to hot, hot to fire, from the sister beneath to the air above.* It was childish, he thought, but it was for him and no one else to know and it had worked more often than failed.

His only hope now was for it to work quickly when called.

She watched the two who were descending to the Landing through the eyes of her wonderful creation, the third wraith. *She* saw them clearly: the daughter of the dead one and the son of the hated Enaid. *She* laughed, though the sound did not travel past her lips as her mind was filled with anticipation.

She stiffened when a bare whisper of a mind-touch caught her. It was Enaid. *She* concentrated on the touch, which had pulled back as quickly as it had come, caught it and followed it to where it originated.

"No!" *She* screamed aloud, the sound vibrating from the cavern's stone walls like a wail. *She* squatted down, her mind spinning. They were racing to help the other two, and had gotten closer than *she'd* anticipated. It could not be permitted. *She* started to send the two smaller wraiths after Roth and Enaid, but stopped.

There were other choices, *she* thought. A smile grew wide. *Of course... They must cross the water to reach the Island. It would be perfect. The woman child and the boy must cross the water to reach the Island. They would be helpless on the water while the hated one...*

She sat on her haunches and began to sway, mentally building the fugue that would allow her to put her changed plan into motion. When it was done, *she* knew her enemies would no longer draw breath. *But first,* she knew, *they must think they have defeated her. There was one way.... There would be sacrifice, but the sacrifice would serve a greater purpose.*

"Yes," *she* whispered happily.

"Strange," Areenna said, stroking Gaalrie who rode the saddle horn.

Areenna had not wanted to take any chances on the ride downward. Three wraiths were too potent an enemy to risk Gaalrie.

"What is strange?"

"We are halfway down and yet I feel nothing from the wraiths. Why?"

"Perhaps they wait for us near the bottom."

"Perhaps, but there is something… Be prepared."

"I have not stopped being so," Mikaal assured her, truthfully. He had been casting about his senses, looking and waiting for the feel of the vileness he had tasted so clearly in Tolemac.

Areenna halted Hero and waited for Mikaal to come next to her. "Give me your hand," she commanded.

When he opened his hand to her, she gripped it tightly. *Let me join with* you. He nodded, and an instant later they were together in thought. *We should be able to see more now*, she said.

"They are somewhere on these palisades, hidden within crevices," she whispered aloud as she pushed outward. She became aware of a heaviness growing about them. As if the air itself was pushing down on them. Her ears blocked for a moment before they popped clear.

"Do you feel that?" Mikaal asked. "The air has become oppressive."

They are near.

Charka cried out, and Mikaal felt the kraal's muscles go tighter beneath his thighs. He reined his aoutem, but did not release Areenna's hand. *Be ready.*

Gaalrie spread her wings and gave vent to a piercing screech. A moment later, a shadow darkened the moon as a wraith flew above them. It dipped and then reversed itself and sped upward into the night, blending with the darkness until it disappeared.

"What…"

"It is coming," Areenna said and released his hand. *Your weapon.*

◇◇◇

The white gorlon that had spent the last five hours running slightly ahead of Enaid and Roth stopped unexpectedly. Irii's head rose, her nostrils quivering as she scented the air. She let out a wail, spun and returned to Enaid's aide.

"It comes," Enaid warned Roth.

"Which?"

Enaid spread her senses, seeking for what was near and hunting them. When she caught its emanations she exhaled slowly. "Not the beast—not the abomination."

Roth drew his sword, Enaid her bow. "I don't know if these will have any affect, but we shall try." She closed her eyes and concentrated on building a shield to protect them in the same way she had shown Areenna at Tolemac.

An instant later, the dark-winged wraith appeared out of the black sky and slammed against the barrier, ripping at it with huge, sharp claws and its beak, which was more of a wide swath of dagger-like teeth slashing against the unseen force.

Almost unsaddled by the power it directed at her, Enaid concentrated solely on holding the barrier against it. Irii screamed her battle cry and Roth sat on his kraal unable to do anything. But this was far from the first time he battled alongside his wife.

Dismounting as she fought the creature, he raced to her kraal, rose on his toes and grabbed her around the waist. He knew she needed to be on the ground, to draw strength from contact with the earth. He lifted her roughly, not caring about anything except getting her to where she could fight.

Enaid was aware of but one thing—the power of the beast above. It took all her strength, all her vast energy to hold the flying atrocity at bay. She was unaware of Roth's arms pulling her from the kraal and dropping her to the ground. But when her knees touched the earth, her mind cleared. Slowly and carefully, she raised her eyes to the creature and, as she'd explained to Areenna, maintained the protection around them while she drew more deeply on her powers. She released a bolt of fiery, blue light at it that hit something and flared out before it struck the Wraith.

"It is shielded," she said. She pushed her senses at it and found it was protection against only her special abilities.

Behind her was a large rock half buried beneath the surface of the earth. She called it up and, using the blue light still hovering on her palms, sent the rock flying at the winged malignancy. It was a weapon Areenna's mother, Inaria, had gifted and taught her how to work.

The shield did not work on the rock, for it was a physical thing, and it slammed against the side of the wraith's head, knocking it back. It fought for balance, flapping its wings madly to stay aloft. As it did, Enaid drew up another stone, larger this time and, dropping the barrier, raised the stone and flung it at the thing.

The wraith screamed its fury when the rock hit the joining of wing and body.

Batting one wing in a furious fight to stay aloft, the wraith's misty shape spun toward the ground. The sound of its rotting flesh smashing into the scorched earth reverberated loudly. Irii leaped toward it, a battle scream issuing from her mouth, but Enaid called her back sharply, knowing the wraith was not badly injured and had the power to kill the gorlon.

Irii stopped at Enaid's command, as did Roth who had started forward with his broadsword. "Wait," Enaid called to him. "It is not time. It is not badly hurt."

The wraith gained its long, twisted legs and turned to them. From the center of its wide, misshapen head, two angry, fire-red eyes burned at them. A heartbeat later it rose into the air and Enaid built the shield once again.

The wraith did not attack, nor did it leave; it hovered above them, watching and waiting for an opening.

"What now?" Roth asked as he tracked the wraith.

"It waits for me to falter."

"Can you hold?"

"Is there a choice? It stays far enough away so I would have to drop our protection to fight it."

"What can I do?"

Enaid shook her head. "Let nothing disturb my concentration. I will hold until daylight. Its strength will diminish then."

"Till daylight?" he echoed. "We will be too late to help them."

She looked around and then at him. "Try my bow. Perhaps..."

Roth pulled her bow from the carrying case on the kraal, strung it, and readied a shaft. He took careful aim and released the arrow. It flew straight at the thing's chest. At the very last instant, the wraith flexed a wing and deflected the arrow.

"Damn," Roth muttered.

"Sit next to me, my love, lend me your strength."

Roth moved, not next to her but behind her, where he knelt and wrapped his arms about her, pressing his chest to her back. "Take it," he whispered.

CHAPTER 27

"WHERE IS IT?" Mikaal asked, searching the starless sky.

"It plays a game," Areenna said. "It's there, up high. Waiting for an opening."

Mikaal worked out the options. If it attacked, they would use their weapons against it, but it would be better to move forward. *Ride slow, but ride*, Mikaal instructed. *We must get to the Landing.*

Areenna caught his thought. *Yes.*

They pushed onward, their legs and minds guiding the kraals while their eyes and senses remained glued to the sky. They made a quarter mile before the wraith's dark shape grew large above them.

"It comes," Areenna said aloud.

The wraith spread its wings wide and dove at them, its glowing eyes haunting specks in the blackness.

Areenna raised her hands, using her power not as a weapon, but for protection. Mikaal recited his formula and the heat within him surged quickly. The wraith struck the outer edge of the barrier with explosive force, its claws and teeth slashing at the invisible wall surrounding them. At the very instant the wraith hit, Mikaal released the fires from within.

Shafts of fire spewed skyward to blanket the winged malignancy. The wraith's shriek of pain and anger was bone-chilling in the silence of the night. A moment later, it lifted upward and disappeared in the blackness.

Areenna stared at Mikaal, her eyes dancing within a myriad of colors in the aftermath of the bright flames. When she was able to focus, she exhaled softly. "Well done, Mikaal."

Mikaal shook his head. "Not well enough. It is unharmed."

"Not so," Areenna whispered, looking skywards, seeking the putrid creature. "Your fire stopped it."

"But I sense it is unhurt."

"Still, it knows it can't reach us. We need to keep moving," she reminded him.

They started forward again, but when they did, Hero began to tremble. A minute later, the large kraal refused to move. Areenna could do nothing to calm or move the frightened animal.

Mikaal edged Charka next to Hero, grabbed the reins and said, "Dismount."

Areenna stepped down from the shaking kraal and Mikaal dismounted Charka. He took Hero's reigns and hooked them to his saddle. Reaching out, he touched Charka's head and gave the kraal a push, asking him to hold Hero calm.

"We walk from here," he said and, sword in hand, led them down the road as Areenna held the cone of protection around them.

They walked for ten minutes before the next attack came. This one was swift and from behind. The wraith hit the barrier a second after Mikaal sensed it coming. Areenna's power flared brightly around them. Mikaal spun and released fire at the creature, which was already veering out of its path.

The fire struck empty air and faded harmlessly into the sky. Refusing to give up, Mikaal tracked the deformed thing as it flipped in midair and dove back at them. Hatred, dark and putrescent, struck them with the force of a falling wall. Yet they stood firm against this dark power, rejecting the efforts of its grasping tendrils to take them.

When I tell you, release your protection and join with me, he commanded. A half second later the wraith, its wings spread a full twenty feet wide, hit the edge of Areenna's shield. The instant it did, Mikaal shouted "Now!" She dropped the protective shield and the wraith, expecting to hit it, plummeted through.

Areenna joined Mikaal's mind in the instant before he released his fire: the stream of flames shot upward and enveloped the falling creature. Screams of rage and pain blasted their ears as the monster struggled to stop its fall even as its wings began to burn. It twisted and screeched and tried to fly away.

"Again," Mikaal shouted and released another wave of hellfire.

Caught within the sudden blast, the black apparition spun, not ten feet above the ground. Trailing sparks of burning feathers, the wraith flew upward and, as they watched, dove toward the waters below. Just as it hit the surface, it exploded in fiery shards.

"Ride!" Mikaal shouted.

Jumping onto their kraals and urging the big animals into a gallop, they raced toward the Landing. Their only means of guidance on the pitch black road was Gaalrie's sharp night vision—their only hope was that the other two wraiths would not attack before they reached the safety of the Landing.

While Areenna and Mikaal raced for safety, Roth held Enaid close. Her back pressed securely to his chest, his arms around her, his hands clasped together over her abdomen. Irii, the white gorlon lay next to them, her warm fur against Enaid's legs.

It had been over an hour since the last attack, and the muscles of Roth's thighs and calves were cramping from holding the same position for so long. But he had called on his earlier training to ignore the pain. As long as the black monstrosity hovered above them, he would do everything necessary to help his wife.

Enaid, sensing Roth's pain, lowered one hand while maintaining the shield around them and pressed the heated skin of her palm to his clasped hands, giving him whatever energy she could spare to help soothe his strained legs.

"It does its job well," Roth said when the cramps eased. "We are trapped." The ground, in every direction within a hundred yards of where they knelt, was pock-mocked with small craters, evidence of Enaid having drawn rock after rock from the ground in preparation for the beast's next attack.

"Yes," Enaid agreed. "There is no way to reach them before morning."

Anger bubbled within Roth. "Are you certain? If we could defeat it now, we could reach the Landing before they go."

"We would not survive crossing the ruins at night. If we die there, then there truly will be no help for them."

"So close." His anger rose as her words filtered through his mind with a heaviness that took away his strength. Darkness followed, and despair spread through him. His eyes went distant and his body stiffened.

Enaid felt the change in him and recognized the danger immediately. Her protection, the shield she used to protect them, was physical to prevent the beast from reaching them, but, it did not hold back the dark emanations the black sorceress sent through its flying creation.

She twisted from his arms and faced him. Leaning forward, she grasped Roth's face between her hands and stared deeply into his eyes. A moment later he blinked and focused on her face. "What?"

"Your anger left you vulnerable," she whispered.

He took a breath and steeled himself. "Stupid," he whispered.

"Frustrated perhaps but you are not stupid." She touched her forehead to his. She released her hold on his face and wrapped her arms around him. "Hold strong, husband, we will do what is needed."

Roth's mind raced. There had to be a way to defeat it, but *how*? "How is your strength?"

"Good. What are you thinking?"

He explained his idea to her. She listened, thought it carefully through, and said, "It is a risk."

"No more so than anything we have done before. Do you have enough strength?"

"Yes."

He released her and stood. His legs were shaky, but he held still until the circulation returned. When the stabs of needles and pins faded, he exhaled a sibilant breath.

"I have been thinking about what's happening now, and what comes when we get to the Landing." She paused to look up at the still hovering creature and met its red eyes in challenge. "I believe that thing has but two purposes. The one is to stall us, to hold us back until it is too late for us to reach Areenna and Mikaal. The other is more basic. To kill us if it can."

Roth's teeth were clench together. "It may have accomplished the first, it will never succeed with the last."

"Then let us be at it," Enaid declared.

Above them, as if in answer to their words, the flying caricature of evil released a deafening scream and charged downward, its black form a nearly invisible streak heading directly at them.

A half-breath before the crazed wraith struck Enaid's barrier, everything around them glowed a pale blue. From behind them roared the ear-shattering scream of a rantor.

"They are here," Enaid whispered.

"Who?"

"Atir, Ilsraeth, and Laira."

Above them, as she spoke the names, the wraith gave shrieking cry, spun in midair, and disappeared into the night.

Turning, Roth watched the three women appear out of nowhere and gallop toward them on kraals. When the three reached them and dismounted, Roth and Enaid greeted them warmly.

"How—" he began.

"Ilsraeth had a vision—a foretelling of this," Atir said, sweeping her hand around them. "She came to Aldimor the day Areenna and Mikaal left for the Island."

"We had hoped to make it here before it attacked... In that we failed."

"Perhaps not," Roth said as he looked at the four women, among the most powerful of Nevaeh. "With your abilities, can we not get through the ruins safely?"

Enaid's brows furrowed. She looked at each of the others. "It has never been tried after dark—four women of power together—perhaps. What think you?" she asked them.

The bonds between the women were deep, a melding of hundreds of years of bloodlines; an even stronger blending of abilities created a unique kinship. As one, the women nodded.

"Many women have died crossing the ruins in the night, died before they could reach the Landing, but the four of us...and with Ilsraeth's powers cloaking us, yes," Atir said.

Above them, Atir's treygone, black streaks highlighting its white feathers, swooped low to settle on the saddle of her kraal, while Laira's aoutem, a silver and brown furred ret peeked a pointy head out from Laira's cloak at the joining of her neck and shoulder.

Roth stared at the small furry animal. He was surprised, for it was unusual to see a ret—which reminded him of a small ferret—as an aoutem. But, he thought wryly, there had rarely been a day when something in Nevaeh did not surprise him.

Ilsraeth's black rantor padded slowly to Irii. The two aoutems, natural enemies in the wild, sniffed at each other and then touched their heads together. They were old friends.

"Then, my ladies, we need to be on the move if we want to reach the West Landing by morning."

The haze floating over the road ended. There was but one twist left between them and the Landing. Mikaal slowed Charka and drew him to a stop. Next to him, Areenna did the same. The Landing spread out below them was clearly visible though shaded in darkness. Perhaps a few hundred yards wide and half that deep, it appeared to be made of wood and rock. There were no structures.

"Finally," Mikaal whispered as he looked at Areenna, whose eyes had grown wide. "What is it?"

She looked to her right, staring off into the distance. *There is something. I feel it, but barely.*

The wraith?

"No. Whatever it is, it is not of the dark. Can you not sense it?"

Mikaal pushed outward searching, seeking, but sensed nothing. He shook his head.

She urged Hero forward in accent to her thought.

Mikaal followed, still trying to find what Areenna had sensed. When they rounded the final switchback and started toward the Landing, they were hit by a blast of dark emanations. Like waves of water rising and falling upon them, the force of the dark power struck, not physically, but lashed out at their minds. Charka cried out and reared and Mikaal was hard pressed to stay on his aoutem's back. Above them, Gaalrie shrieked and faltered in mid-flight.

Go! Areenna cried silently to her aoutem, telling her to fly to the Landing, while Mikaal fought Charka's sudden madness by bending against the kraal's neck and lending him the strength of his mind while at the same time fighting off the dark forces striking into Charka's head. He felt his power grow and a moment later, Charka settled into a run.

Next to him, Areenna pushed Hero into a run alongside Mikaal. The last fifty yards to the Landing was a mad race while above them on a ledge in the high palisades the huge wraith emitted a deafening, rage-filled roar.

"We are safe here," Areenna said after they dismounted in the center of the Landing.

Mikaal felt the difference in his head and in the air around them, which seemed altered from that of the wasteland. There was no scent other than of water—it was pure and clean and, as he filled his lungs, he felt energy flow into him. He stroked Charka, who nuzzled against him, a peaceful sensation rising from the kraal.

He looked eastward, at the hazy dark and misshapen Island and what lay ahead of them. "Until morning."

CHAPTER 28

WHEN THE MORNING came, Areenna and Mikaal arose more rested than they'd thought possible. While they had been unable to see the Landing clearly at night, daylight brought amazement. The wood they had slept on appeared new. The surface was smooth and clean, reminding Mikaal of Bekar's old highway, which had barely a leaf or branch upon its surface.

The only things on the Landing were two large bowls near the ramp connecting the Landing to the land itself. The bowls were filled with rainwater.

The Landing stood on rock pilings, five feet above the water, and was larger than it had seemed from above. There was a ladder on the side of the Landing facing the Island. It led down to a small skiff tied to a piling.

"How is this possible? The Landing...the boat?" He turned to look at the far end of the Landing. "And why is it so long? It makes no sense."

"It's kept this way, but by whom I know not," Areenna said. "There are stories I have heard of certain places in Nevaeh that are protected by the spirits of women past, but those are old legends, yet...." Her voice trailed off as she thought of Bekar and how long her spirit had waited for them.

"Yet we must cross soon. Are you ready?" he asked, searching her face as he spoke.

"It is why we came," she said with a lopsided smile. "This is where our real journey begins."

"Are you afraid?"

"Yes," she admitted, agreeing with the quickened pace of her heart and of the thoughts that had accompanied her waking. "But not for me."

His eyes narrowed. "Of what then?" he asked, already knowing her answer.

"For you. This has never been done before. It is…"

"Stop, Areenna. You have trained me, taught me how to use the powers I somehow have been given. I will not die there."

Her stomach twisted. She longed to touch him—no, to pull him to her and protect him from whatever they would be facing, but knew she could not. "No, you will not," she agreed, promising herself that no matter the cost, she would find a way to safeguard him.

They looked at the Island. The shapes they had seen within the reddish haze were clearer now. They were indeed structures—or had been in some long ago time. Crumbling badly, with ragged strands sticking into the air, some twisted even more than the metal of the wasteland's ruins. From the distance, most appeared only a dozen or so feet tall, but a few, scattered throughout were as tall as trees, and looked like elongated and contorted fingers reaching skyward, seeking something far out of their grasp.

His senses told him these structures were as old as Nevaeh itself. "What is this place?" he asked.

Her eyes glued to the Island, Areenna shrugged. "What else could it have been but the dwelling place of the Old Ones who came before?" She paused, took a breath, and said, "I can only believe it is a place like one from which your father came."

Mikaal looked at the Island again and a shiver swept across him. "Who would have wanted to live like that?"

Areenna did not answer, she could not. Instead, she pushed outward in an attempt to sense what might be on the Island. What happened startled her. She hit a solid wall. It was a block such as she had never encountered before. There was nothing there but an absence of everything. She knew, too, it was not the work of a sorceress, but seemed to be the Island itself.

She exhaled loudly and looked at the skiff bobbing gently in the water. "We cannot take the kraals."

For the first time since bonding with Charka, Mikaal felt real alarm. He looked from Areenna to the kraal and then at the Island. "You're right...even if we could get them into the skiff, it's not somewhere they should be."

"Let us make ready." Going to their things, Areenna picked up her bow and slid the strap of the quiver over her head so the leather case rested on her back and did the same with the bow. She adjusted the leather tunic she wore, setting its thickly padded shoulders firm so the quiver and bow would not be caught on the material.

Mikaal would have preferred using a back scabbard, but the gift his father had given him was too long and he strapped the sword scabbard to his side. He too wore a padded leather, the top cut to mold to his body protectively.

Each added a knife to their equipment. "How long do you think we'll be there?"

"I have no idea."

"The kraals will need to eat."

"Yes." She went to one of the bags that had been attached to the saddle and removed the pouch within. "Your mother told me I would need this. It should be enough for them." She pointed to the two bowls from which they had slaked their morning thirst. "Those will keep them well watered. You will need to have Charka hold Hero here. There is no gate to keep them."

He followed her pointing finger and nodded. He went to Charka and, touching his head, pushed his request. His aoutem's response was gentle and warm. He turned back and looked at the Island. "What of the wraiths? They will attack when we try to cross the water."

"If they do, we fight. Is there another choice?" Areenna asked.

Mikaal's mouth twisted into a semblance of a smile and said, "For us, no." Then he walked to the ladder, one hand on the pommel of his sword.

◇◇◇

She had spent the night staring into the fire, sharing her mind with the wraiths she had created, taking over the tiny spark of their brains and controlling them, seeing through their eyes and manipulating everything exactly the way *she* wanted, the way her masters had decreed.

The sacrifice of one wraith had been necessary and, although *she* had failed to kill the two young ones, *she* had discovered something so impossible *she* knew her masters would heap rewards on her when they learned of it, for such had never happened before.

When the man child had joined the battle and attacked her dark spirit, it had shaken her. Throughout the short battle above the Landing, *she* had found the two impenetrable. The woman child's defenses were too strong for the small wraith. But the final fight, when the man child released the fire, had stunned her. *It was impossible! He was a sorcerer.* Recovering from shock, *she'd* fought back, charging them, diving at them, her hatred boiling outward, raining black despair down upon them as *she* attacked.

The woman child's defense had been very strong. The child had gained much knowledge in the short time since their battles at Tolemac. She was exceptionally powerful, but inexperienced. The black sorceress had laughed; the sound of it seemed to have been sucked directly into the fire, which had flared high before banking back.

Knowing the battle was only a delaying tactic, *she* searched for any weaknesses *she* could use later when she sent *the one* after them. The man child's fire was a weapon as *she'd* never before faced. It was impossible, but it was true.

Screaming in pain, feeling what the wraith felt as *she* occupied its black mind, *she'd* fled the fight and let the wraith be sacrificed. Then, *she'd* joined completely with the second wraith, which flew over the old ruins.

As *it* flew, *she'd* guided the misty specter in a search of the hated ones and found Roth and the witch halfway to the ruins. They were alone; no other women of power accompanied them. *She'd* smiled into the fire on the cave floor and directed the wraith to them.

This battle had lasted a long time. *She* knew well the woman Enaid's defenses. *She* had fought against her in many battles. But in the midst of the wasteland, with no others to aid her, the witch was vulnerable and he was her weakness. *She* had attacked, time after time, only to be stopped by the woman's shield. *She'd* waited, watching and flying above them, diving to test them.

After hours of attacks and feints, *she* had accomplished another of her goals. Roth and Enaid would never reach the Areenna and Mikaal before they took to the water to go to the Island. There, the two young ones would be exposed. There, they would meet their deaths and the hated ones would be unable to stop it from happening.

With one massive effort, this embodiment of evil, pawn of the dark masters, had sent the wraith in a final mad attack. But even as the massive wraith dove at them, *she* felt others join the battle. The woman Enaid's powers were suddenly amplified and as the wraith struck, the shield glowed and turned solid.

Then three other women had appeared out of nowhere. The wraith hit the barrier and the instant it had, *she'd* turned the wraith and fled into the night, her anger burning deeply at this unforeseen failure. But, *she* had gained victory as well for they would never reach the other two in time.

She'd sent the wraith back to the ledge on the palisades to join the other one then slipped into the mind of *her* third creation and through it, had poured every bit of desolation and anger *she'd* been able to bring out at the two who were racing down the switchbacks to the Landing.

When they had managed to reach the Landing, *she'd* stopped pushing at them and had the giant wraith settle back. Everything was going as *she* had envisioned. The morning would bring her final stroke.

At the Landing's edge, preparing to descend to the skiff, Mikaal said, "What do we expect to find there?"

Areenna gazed across to the rubble strewn Island. "I know only that something there awaits us. What it is, we must discover. And other...things await us as well, dark things meant to stop us from reaching our goal."

He shook his head. All his life his father had trained him to plan, to prepare for what lay ahead, and to develop a strategy to gain advantage. Never—he had been told again and again—never walk blindly into the enemy's camp. Today he was doing the exact opposite, going into the unknown.

"Then go blindly we will," he said, offering Areenna his hand and adding, "together."

They descended the short ladder to the skiff, where Areenna went to the bow and Mikaal the stern. They unhooked the ropes holding the skiff to the Landing and Mikaal pushed off. He went to the center and looked around. There were no oars. "How…?"

As he spoke, the skiff began to move. It straightened and slowly started to cross the water under its own mysterious power. "How…?" he repeated.

Stop questioning everything. Accept what happens, came Areenna's sharp thought. *Open, accept, stop seeking control. It can no longer be your way.*

He swept his eyes from the Island to her face and saw the determination in her eyes. He closed his and took a deep breath, exhaled slowly, and let himself free. *Yes,* came Areenna's response and with it a rush of warmth.

They moved steadily, their eyes locked on the Island, each lost in thought, unaware of a larger boat trailing behind them. Midway between the Landing and the Island, a sensation of impending danger grew strong in their minds.

The Island?

Areenna shook her head. She looked at the sky and, tracing the emanations, focused on a ledge. Despite the morning sun illuminating the cliff-side, it remained in shadow. "The wraiths," she whispered.

No sooner had she uttered the words than a massive shape sprang from the ledge. Swirling within a gray fog, the largest creature she had ever seen rose skyward. Its wingspan was gigantic and the emanations coming from it swamped them with foulness.

Areenna raised her shield instantly, blanketing the small skiff. Her hands balled into fists, the skin of her knuckles turned white as she fought the flood of despair overspreading them.

Beneath them, the water churned madly. Waves grew and whipped against the skiff. *Prepare yourself!* Areenna's command hit Mikaal and his power flared within his lower belly. Heat raced through him faster than ever before. He looked up and saw the massive beast flying over them.

Still connected to Areenna, his vision shifted and he was seeing through Gaalrie's eyes above the black-feathered wraith as the treygone arrowed down at the creature.

No! Areenna commanded her aoutem. *Stop!*

Gaalrie pulled out of the dive, twisted in mid-air and flew skyward. "It is too strong for her," she said to Mikaal. "Be ready for its attack."

Mikaal braced his legs against the rowing bench and watched the wraith. The skiff was tossing about madly and he was having trouble holding his balance, but refused to give in. Water rushed over the sides of the skiff in waterfall-like torrents. When he looked down, he saw the water had filled the small boat halfway to the rails.

"We'll sink before we make it across."

"We must get there. Attack now. Chase it."

Mikaal released his power the instant she stopped speaking. Lances of fire streaked skyward, surrounding the beast, but as the flames reached it, the flying evil shifted direction and flew upward, its wings beating the air so powerfully their sound could be heard in the skiff.

While the creature raced upward, the skiff sank lower. Only a few inches separated the water from the rail of the skiff. The small boat was sinking fast. And then there was a shout from nearby.

"Here! Hurry!"

Turning, they were greeted with the most unexpected sight of their journey. Timon was standing at the bow of his boat, the master boatsman's arms outstretched, reaching for them. Mikaal grabbed Areenna about her waist, lifting her as if she weighed naught and raised her to Timon's waiting hand.

He pulled her up quickly and set her on the deck. Then he turned back to Mikaal, who leaped up and grabbed the edge of the deck. Timon caught him under his arms and dragged him in.

"What is that thing?" he asked, staring up at the disappearing speck above them.

"A wraith," Areenna said as she watched the skiff sink beneath the surface. Then she turned to him. "We are grateful, Master Timon, but... Why are you here?"

Timon laughed. "So like a woman. I have no idea why I'm here. I only know, when you left me to go to Dees, I felt something...a premonition you might say, telling me I would be needed here. I seem to

269

have been right, yes?"

"Yes," Mikaal said before Areenna could speak. "But you have put yourself in great danger."

"Life is filled with dangerous things. But today I have seen something never before witnessed, haven't I young prince?" he asked, looking at Mikaal.

"You saw?"

"How could I not? How was that possible, the fire? I have never seen the like before…man creating magic."

"We do not have the time to explain," Areenna cut in quickly. "We must get to the Island. Can you bring us there?"

"And will I get the explanation?"

Areenna looked at Mikaal, who nodded. "Master Timon, if we survive the Island, you will have an…explanation, or as much of one as is possible. It will serve as payment for bringing us back. But," she added, her eyes locked tightly with his, "you may not want it."

Timon smiled. "We'll see. Will that thing return?" he asked, looking skyward.

Mikaal followed his gaze and saw the shadow flying high above. "Count on it."

"Then let us make swift passage." He moved to the wheel and turned the boat toward the Island. It lurched in the choppy waters, the bow slamming hard as it crested the waves.

Where is Gaalrie?

Watching. It follows us and she follows it.

How do we stop it?

Areenna closed her eyes, her mind racing. She opened her eyes, reached out and grasped Mikaal's shoulder. *Ilsraeth's gift. When the wraith attacks, we must use it. Together, we can increase the power. We can hide ourselves and the boat.*

But the drain on us.

Regardless, we must use this gift. "I know what to do, Master Timon, but you must trust me," she said to the boatsman. "No matter what happens next, keep moving toward the Island. The waters will soon grow worse."

Without taking his eyes from the Island, he said, "I'll handle the boat. You keep that thing from us."

Moments later the churning waters grew wild. The waves crashed against the boat; its single sail billowing madly. The bow rode high on a wave and slammed down as it receded, sending water over its sides in pounding rivulets to swamp their feet.

As the boat was lifted on another rushing wave Gaalrie answered Areenna's call and dropped, Landing on Areenna's shoulders, securing her claws to each shoulder of Areenna's leather tunic. The massive black vision of evil dove at them.

Areenna watched carefully, judging its speed and the distance separating them. When it grew large enough to blot the sun, she grasped Mikaal's hand tightly and said, "Now!"

CHAPTER 29

ATOP THE PALISADES, the five riders drew their kraals to a halt in the center of the road leading down to the Landing. Five sets of eyes watched the small skiff carrying Areenna and Mikaal start its journey to the Island.

"We're too late," Roth said, stating the obvious. "She delayed us long enough."

"They are on their way, which was our purpose in coming—to ensure they would reach the Island," Enaid reminded him.

Before her words registered on the others, Laira said, "There's another boat." She pointed to a larger boat that had just come into sight below.

"No," Ilsraeth cried. "It cannot be."

Everyone turned at her cry and saw the larger boat heading toward the skiff. "Who is it?" Enaid asked.

"Timon," Ilsraeth whispered.

Roth stared at the boat while drawing up the memory the name had triggered. He remembered Timon. The master boatsman had been a strong fighter, well skilled and had fought many times at Roth's side. "What would bring him here?"

Ilsraeth and Atir turned to Enaid. "What know you?" Atir asked.

Enaid shook her head. "Nothing," she whispered.

"Do not withhold from us Enaid. Why is Timon here? Why is Mikaal crossing to the Island with Areenna? It is forbidden."

Before she could respond a wave of darkness such as they had never before experienced washed over them. They looked up and saw the giant wraith appear in the sky. Moments later they watched the waters grow storm heavy and start to toss the skiff about like a toy.

Enaid directed her powers at the black infection flying across from them, but it deflected her effort easily. "Help me," she asked the others.

Together, the four women joined powers and attacked the beast. But it was to no avail as the creature appeared unaffected. Moments later they withdrew. "It is too strong, the distance too far," Atir said.

"What has *she* created?" Ilsraeth whispered. "That...thing, it is like nothing else. *She* controls it, but the atrocity is more than what *she* intended. I cannot explain...but I know this."

When the beast dove, they saw fire streak upward at it—fire emanating from Mikaal, not Areenna.

"Impossible," Atir said, her voice trembling as she spoke. "What have you done, Enaid?"

The three women turned to fix Enaid with heated stares. "How has this...this outrageousness happened?"

"Not now!" Enaid snapped, turning back to the battle below. The creature was flying high above boat; the waters below it were rushing madly in every direction and the small skiff was sinking rapidly.

The scene unfolded quickly. Just as the skiff sank below the water, Mikaal and Areenna scrambled onto Timon's boat. Then, on the deck, Areenna and Mikaal came close together and, an instant later, as the giant wraith descended, the boat and the people on it disappeared.

The wraith's scream was ear-shattering, and the five on the crest of the palisades cried out in pain, the women's' aoutems began to wail. The flying abomination, the culmination of the black sorceress's evil, shrieked its outrage and dove to the spot where the skiff had last been. It slammed into the water, the impact of its gigantic body sent water spraying fifty feet into the air. Moments later, the wraith broke out of the water and circled in a frenzied search for its prey.

They watched silently for a quarter hour; tension growing thick around them. The only sound was of their breathing, until, at last, Timon's boat reappeared across the water, docked against the far

Landing. The wraith flew off, howling in earsplitting rage.

Only then did the three women turn to Enaid again. "Tell us, now!" Atir commanded.

Enaid squared her shoulders and drew herself straight. She looked at Roth first and smiled gently. Then she looked at each woman in turn before saying, "It is not what you think. I have not gone to dark magic and even if I had, it would be impossible. Mikaal was born of power."

They stared at her. Their silent command was for Enaid to continue.

"He is the complement to her, and she is the Sister of the old foretelling."

"She is a child," Ilsraeth said, her voice almost inaudible. "Yet the power I sensed in her... She used the gift and not just she, but everything vanished."

Enaid looked over her shoulder but the distance was too great to make out anything other than the boat. When she turned back, she found the others waiting, their faces expectant.

She turned to her mate and put a hand on his arm. "May I explain, My Lord," she asked formally.

Roth held her gaze, but before responding to her question, turned to the three women. "You two," he said to Ilsraeth and Atir, "are the rulers of your dominions, along with your husbands. And you will one day be the same," he added to Laira. "I ask for your word that what passes here not be spoken of until the proper time, if such a time ever comes."

He gazed deeply into their faces and waited.

The wait was short. Ilsraeth spoke first. "You have my pledge, My Lord."

Atir repeated the same response, but when it came to Laira, she seemed to be staring across the water at the Island, but without any focus. "What is it child?" Enaid asked.

Laira's eyes rolled back and she collapsed. The women bent to her. When Atir reached out to touch Laira, her aoutem came squirming out from within her cloak, hissing and snapping at the hand reaching for its mistress.

Atir pulled her fingers back quickly, having known well the ret's sharp teeth in the past. "She is caught within a vision. We can do nothing but wait." The queen of Aldimor sat on the ground next to her daughter. Moving carefully, she took her daughter's hand in her own. The ret hissed, but allowed this action.

Atir looked up at Enaid. "I give you pledge for my daughter. Speak."

◇◇◇

The three in the boat watched the dark creature's feverish hunt for them as they crossed the water unseen. The power of the gift slowly drained Areenna's strength as it did Mikaal's. She reached her free hand to her shoulder and grasped Gaalrie, drawing on whatever energy her aoutem could provide.

A surge of strength rushed into her and from her to Mikaal. They accepted the treygone's help and renewed their power even as the boat reached the Island. The dock was the twin of the Landing they'd left a short time before and Areenna breathed a sigh of relief. The only difference between this and the one across the water was that this Landing was at boat level, not above it.

The Landing was clear and clean and somehow sparkled in the sunlight. Not the same could be said for the Island, for the red mists had grown heavy and at the very edge of the Landing, visibility was nearly impossible.

"Master Timon," she said as Gaalrie left her shoulder to settle on the boat's railing. "Should you decide to wait for our return, you will be safe here. It is a place of sanctuary from what lies within the Island and without as well."

"And if I choose to leave?" he asked with raised eyebrows.

"Then I wish you good fortune and thank you for our lives, which you have saved."

"And if I wait for your return, do I get the truth of who the two of you truly are?"

"If you are here when Mikaal and I return…if we return, we shall be forever in your debt."

"That is not an answer."

"It is the best I can do, Master Timon, but you already knew so did you not? And if you choose to stay, Gaalrie will keep you good company."

Timon looked uneasily at the reddish haze curtaining the Island. He was a brave man, yet his eyes reflected apprehension. "We'll see what develops while I wait here. That is my only promise."

"Understood," Mikaal said before Areenna could reply. "Whatever happens, we are indebted for your help." Turning, he hopped from the boat to the Landing, and held out his hand for Areenna, who took it and joined him.

When their boots touched the Landing, Areenna sensed its protection and gave a sigh of relief. Her energy was growing again, quickly, as it had when they'd reached the opposite Landing. More importantly, and as she had said, she knew this to be a safe place where Timon could wait for them should he choose.

While Mikaal helped Timon secure the boat with the boat's own ropes, Areenna felt Gaalrie's touch and turned to the treygone, who was staring at her from the boat's railing. She reached up and stroked Gaalrie's head. *You must wait here unless I call. Keep watch.*

The treygone's anxiety wrapped around her and, as her aoutem had done for her since their bonding, Areenna bathed her with a calmness she did not feel. Gaalrie settled easier on the railing, and Areenna gave her a final gentle stroke before turning to Mikaal.

"I'm ready," she said.

Mikaal turned to the steps leading to the Island and nodded. "Then we should go. We have perhaps eight hours of daylight left."

Placing a hand on the pommel of his longsword, he started forward, Areenna a step behind. *We must go slow and be watchful*, she warned silently.

He pushed his senses forward, as she had taught him. He hit a blank wall. *What is it?*

Areenna joined him and fared no better. *Perhaps when we are on the Island itself we cannot use our abilities*, she offered, doing her best to hold back the anxiety created by the blankness ahead.

They climbed the short ladder and stepped through the misty curtain and onto the Island, where they both stood frozen, their eyes searching everywhere. They were on a pathway, a dozen feet across, made of rocks, chunks of debris and earth and littered with a layer of reddish dust. Everywhere they looked were piles of rubble—twisted beams of steel rose from the ruins, covered with deep brown red rust that shed a constant stream of fine particles onto the ground.

"The haze is caused by this," Mikaal said aloud, waving his hand toward the various metal beams. "It is strange, there is only a thin coat of dust on the street, yet it appears to fall constantly."

Areenna looked around while he spoke, taking in everything, yet she sensed no danger. She closed her eyes and pushed again. She was able to feel Mikaal and, pushing harder, focused her energies on this one task. A few seconds later something touched the edge of her senses, but what, she could not determine.

"We must be careful. This place is...different. Our abilities may not work properly. There is something..."

"I feel it," Mikaal said. He drew his sword, more for comfort than need. He reached inward and drew on his power. Areenna did the same.

Forward?

Forward, Areenna agreed.

She moved next to him. Together, they walked deeper into the Island, the presence of the long dead hovering at the edges of their minds.

It was impossible! How could they have disappeared? *She* paced angrily along the edges of the high cliffs of the southern palisades, not hearing the crash of waves below or the whistle of the winds through the rocky crevices above and below her.

Just as *she* had been about to destroy them, a boat had appeared to take them safely from the small skiff. And through the wraith's eyes as *she* joined with it to dive at the boat and finally destroy it and those on it, she watched the boat and the people vanish.

Impossible, *she* thought again. The woman child was too young to possess such a degree of power. How could she have done so?

Stopping her mad pacing, *she* forced herself to think. *She* knelt on the rocky ledge and closed her eyes. *She* rejoined her greatest creation and flew with it, high above the Island and the two ancient and protected Landings. Below, *she* saw the boat tied to the Island Landing.

It was protected now and *she* could not use the wraith to destroy it. *She* guided it across the water to look down at the other Landing, where the four women and the hated one, Roth, stood within the protection of the West Landing. A protection set so strong and created so long ago no one knew from when or how it came to be.

Rage filled her. Black, seething anger grew to a fever pitch. Above the Landing, the wraith's scream echoed the fury of its creator.

◇◇◇

"There's something over there," Areenna said, pointing to a joining of two streets.

Mikaal used his sensing to search ahead. *There is something...but what?* He grasped his sword in both hands as the hot churning in his belly grew strong. Power rushed through him.

To his right was a scuttling in the debris. Areenna turned toward the sound and tracked it. A half minute later the small head of a skerl poked out, but this skerl was different. The head was hairless and fatter than any skerl she had ever seen. When it locked eyes with her, it growled, baring inch-long fangs.

Mikaal raised his sword the instant he spotted it. A shiver of revulsion slid over him.

"Hold," Areenna called to him as she approached the skerl. The animal arched backward, small pieces of rubble falling from its hairless body. She pushed her thoughts to it, and received a shock in return.

Its mind was the opposite of its appearance. There was warmth and gentleness emanating from it, a low purr in her mind. She leaned forward, extending her hand toward it carefully as she tried to probe and learn.

Mikaal moved next to her, his sword held at the ready. Joining Areenna, he too sensed the gentleness coming off the skerl in soft, rolling waves. But then he saw the animal tense. With only inches between Areenna's hand and the skerl, it launched itself at her hand.

Mikaal reacted instinctively. Before the skerl reached her hand, Mikaal's sword severed its head from its body.

Areenna jumped back, her eyes wide, her hand shaking. *'Trust not what you see or feel. Be wary'* came Enaid's voice, reminding her of their talks about the Island. She stepped back to the center of the deteriorated street and took a deep breath.

"I forgot," she said.

"What?"

"Your mother's warnings, and Atir's...they told me not to trust what I see or feel, but to look past and see deeper. The Island is a trickster. This was our first lesson."

"Then we best be careful," he said, his tone wry. "Do you have any idea what we are seeking?"

Areenna shook her head. "There's something about the Island out of tune with...us," she said, her mind tunneling inward, seeking a thought she knew was buried within. "I need to think," she whispered.

Mikaal sensed her struggle and edged closer. He did not try to join, but stood rigidly on guard while she hunted through her memories. The presence he'd felt before seeing the skerl still hung at the edge of his mind. It was ahead of them, not far. He could not tell what it was.

From his left came more scratching within the rubble and he turned slightly to face what was there. Then there was silence. Unease rippled through him. More noise came from behind. Even as he turned to this new disturbance, the noise came again, louder this time, and he knew it was not a lone animal.

Areenna opened her eyes. *The sword. Scabbard it.*

He returned the sword to its scabbard without question and the noises within the rubble stopped. "What?" he asked aloud.

"We must tread carefully. Our actions are...felt by what lives here," she said. "Bekar left messages in me. She... We must not disturb the balance here. Our powers are different from what lives here. She said we must use the energy within us, and not draw on anything else. It is the only way."

"How do we do so?" he asked.

"By not reacting. When that thing attacked, it was because I was drawing from it and it took such as a threat. We cannot use our abilities to read other life here. It is a great danger."

A wave of discord washed across them. "Ahead," Areenna said, shaking off the feeling.

They walked cautiously forward, their powers primed and ready for anything. There was a junction in the street, ten feet ahead. They approached it slowly, searching every crevice, every pile of rubble. A yard short of the junction, a cloaked shape appeared in its center.

Mikaal and Areenna stopped. The cloak was covered in reddish dust, but what was within the hood was visible. Luminescent, pale blue eyes stared out from the deep ebony skin—skin so wrinkled the shape of its face could not be fully made out. A small mouth with pale lips stretched in a taut slash sat beneath a wide, flat nose.

"Seek you death, man?" she asked, her voice a whisper carried on the air, but loud enough to be heard clearly.

Mikaal's hands turned hot, the power within him ready to be unleashed, yet he held it in tight control. "We seek only knowledge."

"A man seeking knowledge," the dark-skinned woman said, her words followed by a gale of cackling laughter. "No knowledge is possible for your sex," she said, again in a soft voice, so different from the laugh. She raised her hand, two ebony fingers pointed at Mikaal, "You are forbidden here," and released an attack of blistering energy.

The moment she raised her arm, Mikaal braced himself. When she released the force at him, he opened his palm and deflected the attack. Flames erupted on the palm of his left hand, but he did not release them.

"Your magic will not affect him, sister," Areenna said, her own weapon glowing within her fists. "Do not force us to use ours."

The woman stared at them for several seconds and drew her arm back into the folds of her cloak. She turned her shinning, blue orbs on Areenna; a purple-black tongue slipped between her lips to moisten them. "This is wrong. It smells wrong. A man... This is wrong," she repeated. "What seek you?" she asked.

"What all women come here to find."

"But not with a man, it is forbidden."

"Not for this man. Can you not tell?" Areenna asked.

The cloaked figure started forward. She moved slowly, as if dragging one leg behind her, and said, "I must be closer."

The flames in Mikaal's hand burned bright. He was prepared to do whatever he must, but the most important thing was to protect Areenna.

"Protect her not, for she needs it not. You are who must be protected," the woman said as she drew within a foot of him. She leaned forward and sniffed the air. "How came you to be? Of whose womb are you the sad fruit?"

"Who are you to ask questions of me?" he snapped in challenge. The flame in his hand rose higher.

Careful, was Areenna's warning.

"Quiet you!" the old crone said without looking at Areenna. "I am the one who watches. I am she whom every woman stepping onto this Island must pass or die." She exhaled loudly. A wash of sour air filled Mikaal's nostrils. "Put out the flame, boy!"

Mikaal met the woman's stare and held it for a dozen heartbeats. He drew back the power, but held it ready.

"Answer my question," she commanded him.

"My mother is Enaid of Brumwall," he said.

"Enaid..." The woman's eyes went dull for a moment before springing back to life. "A powerful child was she—strong, confident, but not powerful enough to create a man child of power. Yet, I sense you lie not."

"What need is there for lies?" Mikaal asked.

The woman laughed again. "What indeed. All men lie. They cannot help but do so. I cannot let you pass without being tested, man of power," she said. "And you as well, girl child. Who was your mother?"

Areenna met the woman's gaze. "Inaria of Lokinhold."

The old crone nodded slowly. "From good blood you sprang, nonetheless you bring this...creature."

Areenna stiffened and her power flared.

"Put away your weapon, it is meaningless to me," the other woman told Areenna, looking at her fists. "Save your energy. You will need it if you are to pass through."

She turned back to Mikaal. "Are you ready, man?"

He glanced at Areenna who stared back at him. When she gave a slight nod, he turned to the cloaked woman. "Yes."

Her arm shot out from her cloak, her hand open, and five gnarled black fingers reached out and slammed against his chest. There was a jolt, like being struck by lightning and he was no longer on the Island. Everything was black—blacker even than the skin of the woman who had sent him there.

CHAPTER 30

"WHAT HAVE YOU done," Areenna cried and lunged at the old woman.

"Quiet Girl!" the crone commanded, raising her free hand palm first at Areenna.

Areenna hit a wall where there was no wall. She slammed against it, her face flushing in pain when it met the invisible barrier. "What have you done with Mikaal?"

"Quiet! You will be his death if you disturb me further. I have held those men stupid enough to come here, thusly. I have held them until each one died—hundreds have tried, none have gained the Island past this point. This man is the first I have ever known who appears to have power. If his abilities are true, if they are not some formula cast by your doing or those of another, he may not die. But know you now, foolish child, there is only one possibility for his survival: he must think right, learn quickly, and free himself."

Her heart pounding, Areenna fought to calm herself and ease her strained muscles so she could find a way to help him. She closed her eyes. Concentrating deeply, she created Mikaal's image down to the very last detail. Then she pushed her thoughts to him, pushed to join with him, and felt a far off response.

Like a rantor on hunt, she followed his faint essence, pushing closer and closer until she gained the very edge of his mind. *Mika—*

She was flung to the ground and before she could move, the hissing growls of fifty skerls surrounded her. When she struggled against the force holding her, the skerls growled louder.

"Stop!" the crone shouted. "Continue and you kill him...and yourself!"

◇◇◇

The blackness was solid. He could see nothing, not even the hand he raised before his eyes. Instinctively, he called up his powers. He wanted light. Nothing happened.

Adrenalin pumped through his veins. His heart was pounding and he knew the odds of this test were weighted heavily against him. His mind worked madly in too many directions, but he forced himself to recall Areenna's lessons. *Calm yourself. Give up control. Open to what is. Find what is needed.* All the words and all her lessons played through his head.

From a distance came the tentative familiar tug of Areenna in his mind. And then it was gone, but it was enough. As he had done once before, and against everything he had known in the years leading up to this journey, he sat down in the blackness and stopped fighting whatever held him prisoner—the old woman or something else, it mattered not. His only desire, his only absolute need, was to be free and to make certain Areenna was unharmed.

He breathed slowly, taking deep even inhalations and exhaling sibilantly. He needed to hear the sound of his breath in the dead silence, and then he concentrated on the sound until the blackness no longer taunted him. As he gave up trying to control what was happening, he sensed something within the darkness other than him. He did not try to discover what; rather, he sat cross-legged, breathing slow and steadily.

"I am ready for you," he said aloud.

Following his words, came the certainty he was no longer alone. An instant later what felt like a hand touched his right cheek. It wasn't a hand he recognized, but he didn't flinch when the fingers traced his face. Another hand joined the first; cool dry fingers moved over his face much in the way a blind man sees another's image. One hand withdrew while the other lingered on his cheek for several seconds before it too withdrew.

Following the departure of the hand, there was a slithering near his crossed legs. *A snuck?* The head of the reptile touched his ankle and slid upward. The weight of its head pressed on the leather of his boot and he knew it was a large snuck, perhaps larger than the one that had attacked them near Morvene.

He held himself immobile while the snuck continued its travels, sliding from calf to thigh and moving to his belly. It slid under his leather tunic. Its dry, cool scales moved against his flesh. He breathed shallowly as the snuck continued the journey, its head reaching a spot exactly over his heart. It stopped there and he knew it was poised to strike.

He held still, his mind open to any who would seek his thoughts.

You do not fear this, said a voice from the very center of his head. *Yet there is fear. Show me.*

The voice was so alien it took him off guard. It was neither male nor female but something else. He sensed evil, but at the same time, good.

"I am not afraid," he said aloud.

You are not afraid, but you fear. What is it you fear for? Look to yourself and find it.

How I can find what I know not? He tried to work out what was being asked. The snuck tensed. The chilling twin points of its fangs touched his chest, but went no further.

His mind was open to whoever was there, but instinct warned him such was not the objective of this…being. He settled his thoughts and cleared his mind of anything not relevant and sought to understand what he must find. In a fraction of a heartbeat, he knew what this other had been sensing.

Within a far corner of his mind, he found the block he himself had placed there without knowing. Carefully, he unlocked it and, when he did, emotion overwhelmed him. It struck in waves, boring into the very core of where his power and abilities lay. He contained it and as he did, allowed it to open.

"Areenna," he said. "I fear for her."

Yes, because you fear in this way, you will never be able to protect her. But that is always the way of man. Man protects what he believes is his by right. You believe Areenna is yours by right.

For the first time since gaining the calmness within the black, his anger rose. *Of course,* came the thought and on its tail, a heaviness so deep it threatened his ability to breathe. *Anger is a man's way of denial.*

Moving quickly, the snuck drew its long body upward and wrapped its length around his chest, its fangs never moving from the spot above his heart.

"You are afraid of me," Mikaal said, the understanding of what was happening clear now.

Naturally, we fear you. This Island is a living memory of what man has done. The ground you sit upon has been defiled, destroyed, and the remains poisoned for eternity, held in place by the memory of every spirit who died here.

"And you think by stopping us you will be doing good?" he challenged. "By stopping her you will stop more death from happening? If that is so, then this is no test, it is an exercise in stupidity. If Areenna does not succeed, there will be nothing left of Nevaeh, and nothing left of our world except the darkness that began this battle. They will never give up. The Circle of Evil will destroy what good remains in Nevaeh. Afzal will win all."

Something changed in the blackness. The snuck constricted further around his chest. If it squeezed tighter, his ribs would crack and his lungs deflate. *How know you of Afzal?*

Why ask questions when my mind is open to you? There are no blocks, there is no deception. If you want answers, seek them yourself or kill me. But she will succeed no matter what you do."

You invite me completely in?

I said the words did I not? Accept the invitation or let your snuck be done with me. I will play your game no longer."

We accept.

Like a waterfall he'd once stood under in the mountains of Brumwall, the entity poured into his mind. Mikaal stiffened when it delved inside, his stomach churning at this violation even though he had permitted it. He did not know how long it lasted, but when it was over, he collapsed, the snuck no longer a part of him.

Rest while we think.

He sank into unconsciousness.

The cloaked black crone turned to Areenna. With a wave of her hand, the skerls scattered and disappeared into the rubble. "Stand woman," she ordered.

Areenna scrambled to her feet and faced the woman. She stared into the luminous blue eyes, glaring with a combination of anger and fear—fear for Mikaal. While she stood there, face to face with the woman, she calmed her anger and concentrated on her abilities.

"Do not try, it will not work. Will you open to me? Will you risk your mind?"

"Just my mind? And to what purpose?" Areenna shot back. Her words, brave as they were, did not appear to have any effect on the other.

"Perhaps to save his life. Perhaps to die."

The words hung dark and heavy before winding through her mind, infiltrating her thoughts until strangely, a new realization was born: Mikaal had become as much a part of her as anything or anyone could be. Why, she knew not, but know it she did, and accepted that she would do whatever was asked of her to save him. She would not allow him to die. Without him, she would be...

Within her core, the abilities making her what she was built stronger, yet at the same time, on the heels of her thoughts, a change came over her. There was a cooling, not within her belly, but her mind. Slowly and carefully she released the locks and gave herself over to the other. *Do what you must,* she told the woman.

Gently, in opposition to what was done with Mikaal, the old woman raised both hands and placed them on either side of her head. There was a slight jolt, barely felt, when her fingers touched Areenna's skin. Seconds later, the touch was gone.

Confused, Areenna could only stare at the other woman. "You did nothing."

The thin pale line of the crone's lips broke into what could barely be described as a smile. "I did only what was necessary. Had the darkness found a hold within you, you would not be standing here now. And your...man," she added, somehow turning the word into a sneer, "will live as well...for now. And for you, young Areenna, the testing is done.

For him, I cannot say. Be wary, much is not what it will appear to be. There is danger ahead. Use your abilities but understand well, his maleness will be an affront to all you encounter."

"He has passed the test?"

"He has passed this test…only this one."

There was a rumbling beneath her feet. From the corner of her eye, she saw Mikaal appear in midair and then fall to the ground. She spun and raced to him, knelt at his side, and found relief in the rise and fall of his chest. She looked over her shoulder at the old woman, but found only emptiness where the cloaked crone had stood.

Putting her hands on his chest, she closed her eyes and called up Atir's gift. She sent a surge of healing energy into him and seconds later his body arched. He opened his eyes and she saw Mikaal alive within them.

"Are you unharmed?" were his first words to her.

She nodded quickly. Seemingly of its own volition, her hand went to his cheek and cupped it. "And you?"

He blinked a few times. "Where is that nasty old she-coor?"

"Gone," Areenna said with a laugh.

"What happened?"

He shrugged and sat up. Then he shook his head. His features were puzzled. "I… I'm not sure. I remember the woman touching my chest and then everything went black. I was somewhere…else." His brow creased as he tried to bring up the memory, but nothing came. "And then I was here."

Areenna gazed at him for several seconds. "Whatever happened, you have survived this test."

"Then can we do what we came here for?"

"You should rest a few minutes."

He smiled, his eyes dancing as he looked at her. "I'm fine."

"Why are you smiling?"

He shrugged. "I have no idea. But something is different."

She was about to ask more, but stopped herself. Whatever happened when he was taken would eventually come forth. Until then, there was other business at hand. "Can you walk?"

"Why couldn't I?" He stood, then took her hand and pulled her to her feet. When she was facing him, he asked, "Where?"

She turned in a circle, and ended up looking in the direction they had been walking before the crone appeared. Staring into the reddish mist, Areenna cleared her mind and searched everywhere. Her eyes flicked to and fro before settling on a distant object. In that instant a sharp jolt snapped within her. "There," she said, pointing straight ahead.

He followed her finger, and in the distance, saw a deteriorated structure, much higher than any they had yet seen. Atop the crumbled stone and twisted metal sat something long and thin. Unlike any other metal around them, it gleamed brightly within the dim reddish haze. "It looks like a giant needle."

Mikaal adjusted his scabbard and straightened his tunic. There was a tinge of soreness around his ribs and he wondered at its cause. "We've wasted enough time. We should go."

Areenna stared at him, speculating on what had happened. Was he not telling her or did he truly not remember? *I would never lie to you, my Princess.* Her cheeks flamed scarlet when she caught his words.

"I only wondered if you were sparing me the details."

"If I knew what happened, you would as well."

She looked into his eyes and saw truth.

"Shall we go or is there more?"

She shook her head. "We go. But Mikaal, the…woman said there would be more tests."

"We'll get through them as we did this one."

"Not we, you. She said you faced more, not I."

"Which still leaves us no choice."

"There is always a choice, Mikaal." *Yours.*

He shook his head and placed both hands on her leather padded shoulders. "I think, for us, there has never been such a thing as choice." *You know this even better than I.*

CHAPTER 31

"IT DOESN'T LOOK too far," Areenna said, staring at the needle.

"Distance is deceptive in this mist."

"I think it's not the distance, but what lies between here and there," Areenna said.

"Why do our abilities fail us here? Do you have any idea?"

Areenna had been wondering the same. Within her, she felt no differences. Her powers were there, the heat within her belly told her so, yet when she tried to access them, she could not.

"I feel whole, yet there is nothing."

"Then we move carefully," Mikaal said. He started forward, but not before he took her hand and gave it a gentle but tight squeeze. A flash of darkness swept across his eyes when he touched her.

"What was that?" Areenna asked.

"You saw it?"

"How could I not? Darkness so deep…" She shuddered.

"It was where they took me."

She searched his face. "They?"

Mikaal shrugged. "It's but a fragment of memory, yet it seems right."

She squeezed his hand. "It will come."

Mikaal was not as sure as she. "We are wasting time. I think we don't want to be here come nightfall."

"No, we do not."

Still holding her hand, Mikaal started forward. The street was strewn with debris, yet it was clear enough for easy movement. They walked for another five minutes until they were stopped by a mound of rubble.

"This looks purposeful." Areenna studied the pile of multi-colored rock and rusted metal. It rose six feet, and the top was the same ragged height across the entire street.

"It is," he said. Releasing her hand, he moved to the side of the street, where he searched for passage. Areenna did the same on the other side. "We must go over."

"What about the junction we just passed?"

He looked back. Twenty feet behind them was another junction of two streets. He looked at Areenna and then at the barricade. His training kicked in, not of magic, but of the hours of lessons in strategy his father had pounded into his head.

He returned to the junction, Areenna two steps behind him, and looked both ways along the crossing street. In one direction, the way was strangely clear of debris. The opposite direction was strewn with piles of rocks making it almost impassable.

"We're being directed—or perhaps herded."

Areenna went to the mouth of the open street and knelt in the dust. She moved her hands back and forth, clearing the tiny red flakes until the ground became visible. She pressed both palms to it and let her senses free. The instant she did, warmth flowed across her skin. "Directed, not herded," she whispered. She stood and clapped her hands free of the dust and dirt. "We must go this way. But be wary. I wish Gaalrie flew above."

Mikaal caught her longing. He nodded understanding then knelt and repeated Areenna's actions. When his palms touched the ground, there was a sharp crack as a jolt arced and skittered across his palms.

Instead of drawing back, he pressed his hands tighter to the ground. Another flash of black crossed his eyes. He felt fingers on his face. And then they were gone.

"What?"

He stood and turned to Areenna. "They are afraid."

"Of you?"

"Of what I represent." He tried to dig deeper, but found nothing. "But you're right—this is the way."

Areenna slipped a water skein from the hook at her side and drank. She offered it to Mikaal, who did the same. When he handed it back, she reattached it to her belt and they started off.

They passed three closed off junctions, but the fourth revealed another clear street. Turning into it, they walked a dozen paces and froze at the sudden appearance of another cloaked figure. This one was tall and straight, and as they watched, the cloak fell, revealing a tall broad woman with a sword as long as Mikaal's held in her hands. Her helmet covered everything but her eyes and mouth.

Long black hair flowed from beneath the helmet, cascading over her shoulders. Her breastplate gleamed in the wavering mist. Her boots reached mid-thigh and both a short sword and a knife hung from her waist. Her exposed skin was the color of a moonless night.

At the same instant, Mikaal and Areenna drew their swords.

That she was a powerful warrior, Mikaal did not doubt and knew this was yet another test. "Stay here," he told Areenna.

We do this together.

No. It is a test meant for me.

Areenna looked from the woman to him. Something was wrong, but what, she was uncertain. It was another test, which she accepted, but how could she not stand at his side?

"Protect my back," Mikaal said. "There may be others." He started forward, sword held securely in a two-handed grasp. He looked only at the dark woman's eyes as he approached; they were twin luminous pale blue orbs, a match to the crone who had sent him into the black chamber.

The closer he came, the more a sense of wrongness surrounded him. It was a heavy cloying sensation pressing on his body. Areenna was right. His muscles tightened into coiled springs ready for whatever would come. His eyes never wavered from hers. She was the tallest woman he had ever seen. Her bare arms were solid muscle, her thighs the same.

"You have no business here, man."

"But I do," he replied in a low voice.

"Only if death is your business and such you will gain."

"I have no fight with you."

"Who you are is reason enough to fight. I give you one chance to live. Return to where you came."

"That I am afraid I can't do."

"Of course you cannot. You are a man." With that the warrior woman swung at him.

Nothing is what it seems, came a sharp warning from Areenna at the same instant.

Mikaal caught her blade on his, the sound explosive in the quiet surrounding them. He turned beneath the blades, slid his free and spun, his sword held over his left shoulder at the ready.

The woman back-stepped and hefted her sword. Seconds later he saw her eyes narrow imperceptibly and, even as she moved, he countered. Their blades met, separated, and met again. Flashes of metal and sparks flew as they fought, neither gaining, neither losing ground.

With a final massive swing, the woman attempted to cut through his defenses. Mikaal raised his blade at the last instant to deflect the blow. Pain raced up his arms when their swords met. The pommel vibrated madly in his hands.

He spun and attacked before she could fully recover from the blow, reigning blow upon blow at her as quickly as his powerful muscles would allow. He beat her back a half dozen feet, as she tried to stop his attack. And then she stumbled over a piece of rubble and fell hard. She hit the ground awkwardly and her sword was knocked from her hands.

Mikaal stood over her, his sword already descending when deep within his head he heard the voice from the black chamber he had been cast into.

This Island is a living memory of what man has done.

He stopped the blade inches from her neck and then lowered the tip to the ground next to her.

The woman warrior stared up at him for a drawn out moment before rising to her feet. She slowly lifted her helmet off and stared at him.

The skin of her face was the palest white he had ever seen, even lighter than that of his father. Her tongue darted out to moisten her lips. "A surprise," she said and vanished as if she had never been there.

"How did you know?" Areenna asked when she came next to him.

"I didn't, not until the last instant. I remembered something from the blackness. Something they said to me."

"You keep saying they. But it was the old woman who took you."

He shook his head. "There are only little bits that come up. While it was a single voice I heard, she always said we, not I."

"What did *they* say?"

"*'This Island is a living memory of what man has done'*. Man, not men and women, but man did all of this," he whispered, waving his arm about at the rubble that stretched on as far as their eyes could see. "That is why no man is permitted here."

"It was another test," Areenna said.

Mikaal nodded. "So it seems." Sheathing his sword, he looked down the street. "Let's find the next one."

Areenna laughed as the tension fled from her nerves.

Once again, they started toward their destination. At the second junction, they turned left, the route obvious by the wide clear street. Halfway to the next intersection, Areenna froze. "There is something...there," she said, turning slightly left and pointing to a mound of rubble with a cave-like opening in the center. They approached it slowly, cautiously, Mikaal's hand again on his sword's pommel.

The opening was dark and permitted no sight within, yet both sensed something within its black recesses. Areenna mentally pushed toward it, but again she encountered a block.

"I cannot sense anything."

"Nor I. Let's leave it and push on."

"Yes," Areenna agreed and started forward. She took a step and stopped when she hit another of those invisible walls. "What's doing this?" she asked, frustration crisping her words.

They are, came Mikaal's silent response.

This time we go together. It wasn't a question.

Her face, set in strong determined lines, brought a smile to his lips. "Yes, Princess."

They turned and, side by side, entered the darkness. The mustiness of things long gone assaulted them. The darkness was complete. They could see nothing. Areenna took a deep breath and then silently began to recite her old formula for power. On the second refrain, an answering response came from within and in a flash of a heartbeat, twin spheres of white light lay in the palms of her hands.

As the sparks and colors bouncing in their eyes disappeared, they found themselves in a tunnel, but one such as they had never imagined. All was glass, but not clear. It was as if the glass had melted and fused together to form the tunnel.

Light bounced from the mirror-like surface, yet within it, behind its blurry, fused facade, things could be seen—horrible and revolting things that should never have been, for they were the misshapen forms of people imprisoned with the glass.

A hand hung within the tunnel's glass ceiling. Near it was part of a face. The walls were filled with parts of bodies: deformed faces stared out, caught in wide-eyed panic at the instant of death.

Melted faces, skeletons, and entire bodies were sealed within the fused glass like animals Mikaal had found trapped within rocks he had broken open under his father's watchful eyes during their excursions into the northwestern wastelands. He was certain there were animals trapped within this glass prison as well, but didn't recognize any of them.

"This... This is terrible," Areenna whispered, an appalling grief filling her. The light in her hand began to flicker and die. She closed her eyes, cutting off the repellent scene to concentrate on keeping the light burning.

"There are hundreds here. What could have done this?" Mikaal asked, pushing the words from within his clogged throat.

"You know, Man, you know!" said a voice from deeper within the tunnel.

Areenna and Mikaal turned toward the direction of the voice. In the distance was a low form. Areenna grasped Mikaal's hand, releasing the light from one palm to hold onto him. His power surged through her, strengthening hers, and together they moved as one toward the voice.

The air turned cold the deeper they descended. While the light from Areenna's hand lit the way for them, it was unable to reveal the form in front of them. They stopped ten feet from the dark shape.

"Frightened you are, woman, by this sight. And you, Man, how feel you?"

"Sad," was his only response.

"Sad at what you have wrought, Man? Such emotion is not a part of you."

"You know nothing of me or my emotions," he replied, his eyes narrowing in the effort to see the woman before him.

Certain are you that you want to see me?

Areenna's hand tightened around his when the unspoken words struck at her mind. Coldness spread through her, a dread of what was to come. *Yes, woman child, you should be afraid for you have brought this abomination to us.*

"Show yourself!" Mikaal said aloud. His words echoed repeatedly in the glass tunnel.

Nothing is what it seems, Areenna said, pushing Enaid's warning to him.

The dark shape rose, the cloak falling to the ground as she did. Around her, light chased away the darkness and both of them gasped. The woman's skin was as black as the old crone's face had been, but by Areenna's light, they saw her skin was not of flesh and blood but scales. From her shoulders downward, iridescent black scales shimmered beneath the light. Areenna trailed her eyes down the woman's body and found where her legs should have been were the coils of a gigantic snuck.

She gasped. Mikaal gripped her hand tighter, steadying her with his hand and his mind. "What are you?"

Eyes, yellow and luminous with vertical slits for pupils, glared at him. "The result of man," she said aloud.

"Man created you?" Areenna asked as her pulse slowly returned to normal.

"Man caused all who live here to be. Man's need to conquer and control created us. And you have brought *him* into our domain. For that you shall pay dearly."

The huge coils swirled, the woman-snuck rose higher, arched the way a snuck prepares to strike. In the moment the woman moved, Areenna released Mikaal's hand and stepped protectively in front of him.

Mikaal started to push past her, but stopped as yet another memory of the black chamber opened within his mind. *...you will never be able to protect her. But that is always the way of man.* Understanding washed across him, not just his mind, but his body as well. His muscles loosened, his unclenched hands fell to his sides and he stood quietly behind Areenna, his mind open and clear.

"No!" Areenna shouted. She lifted her palms even as she stepped before Mikaal. Her powers flared and she willed her abilities to come to life. Her shield rose to form a solid wall of protection.

The black woman-thing's torso moved from side to side, testing Areenna's shielding powers until the coils settled and the woman was no longer threatening them. *Lower your shield*, she commanded.

Areenna held steady until Mikaal's hand pressed her shoulder and he whispered, "Release it."

She did and the snuck-woman's coils relaxed further. *Another surprise, Man. Perhaps you have some little value. Step aside, Woman. Let me see all of him.*

Areenna did as asked and when she was at Mikaal's side, she took back the hand she'd released moments earlier. "Son of Enaid, you are a puzzle. You allowed this woman to protect you against all male instinct. Why?"

"Why would I not? Areenna is no less than I."

"Tell me of your powers. No man has ever had such before. Who did this to you?"

"No one—it is the way I was born."

"You have a block that prevents this memory," she stated. *Let me in.*

"I have no such block." *You have already seen. You were there in the black.*

The snuck-woman laughed. "Something created you."

"What created you? How can only women live here? Are you so old that you were here when this occurred?" Mikaal shot back.

The black half being hissed loudly. "You trespass on our Island and you challenge me with questions?"

"We do," Areenna answered for them. She had been listening while at the same time trying to gain a deeper sense of the thing before them without success.

The hissing grew louder. The woman-snuck's coils tensed and rose as its upper torso arched menacingly. "You have no right!" she screamed and launched herself at them.

CHAPTER 32

LIGHT FLARED IN Areenna's hand, glowing and growing.

No, Mikaal threw the thought at her as the snuck-woman attacked.

Areenna drew back the power and stared unflinching into the woman's eyes as she struck at them. The instant she reached them, she stopped. Her face hung before Areenna's, then swiveled to stare deep into Mikaal's eyes.

"Thrice now you have done what no man has done before. Three times you have done the unexpected. Will you survive more?"

The snuck-woman retreated to where she had been before striking and rested her torso on her coils. "Come closer, sit before me."

Hand in hand, Areenna and Mikaal walked to within a yard of the thing and sat before her. The musky, cloying scent rising from its body was strong but bearable. "We will answer your question of how we came to be. Brace yourselves."

Before either could take a breath, the alien feel of the snuck-woman's thoughts pushed into their minds, spreading within and sucking them into the whirling vortex of its mind.

◇◇◇

297

The next thing Areenna was aware of was standing in the center of a large green field, holding Mikaal's hand. She knew she wasn't there, but was seeing this in her mind.

People walked all around them. Unlike Nevaeh, their skin colors were a rainbow of differences: white, beige, tan, shades of dark brown, some reddish and even tannish yellow. And their hair was vastly different with dozens of shades of colors, many glaringly unnatural to her eyes. Some walked with what looked like coors but were not, others walked with gorlon sized coors on long chains. There were trees, but only one or two looked familiar. She glanced quickly at Mikaal, who was staring at everything.

In the near distance were strange structures reaching into the sky. Made of glass and metal, stone and mortar, the behemoths were everywhere. *This is the world as it once was. More people lived on this island than do now in the whole of Nevaeh. This is before...*

A woman with white skin and red hair screamed and pointed at the sky. Looking up, Areenna saw a silver shape, like a flying lance. It was heading directly at them.

Seconds later there was an explosion unlike anything she had ever witnessed. A massive flame leaped skyward rising hundreds of feet before turning into a gray, cloudlike mushroom. She watched people disintegrate before her eyes. One second they were there and the next they were gone. Others blew outward, carried on the winds of the explosion. She turned to look behind her and saw huge structures blow apart, sending glass and stone and metal spewing outward.

And then they were sucked back into the mental vortex and when it stopped, they were far beneath the earth's surface, in a dark place where anguish struck them with the might of fists. *Here is where the survivors found sanctuary, deep below the ruined surface. Here is where many more died of the poison man had released.*

They watched the scene unfold—men and women lay dying, their skins covered with erupting sores. Even those whose skin had not been burned from the horror were dying...

The animals, too, suffered terribly as the effects of what happened destroyed their bodies as well. Man let loose a force over which he had no control. The results changed everyone, everywhere, not just on the Island. But here, we suffered terribly. In three years, all but a few hundred out of millions survived. But what the dark ones unleashed changed us in many ways.

Of the survivors, there were women carrying fruit within their wombs. These yet to be born children suffered as well and when they came forth, they were changed. Their very essence had become something...else.

They found themselves watching a woman—her skin badly burned and scarred, her body thin, and stomach massively distended—twist and cry out as she gave birth. Unable to do anything but stare, they watched the baby come forth. What they witnessed should never have been. The baby was born with its entire body covered in dark gray scales.

In the moment of birth and delivery, time sped forward, and Areenna and Mikaal watched people die and others be born. All were female, and all were covered with scales except for their faces. Some were so deformed as to take on the appearance of snucks, while others like the snuck-woman guiding them now, were hybrids of snuck and human.

In the next instant they were back in the glass tunnel, facing the snuck-woman. Mikaal took a deep breath, realizing the people and animals in the vision were genetic mutations caused by the men sent by the Dark Ones across the sea.

The woman stiffened. "How know you these words, genetic mutation?"

Mikaal threw a block around his mind as he stared at her, meeting the vertical pupils unflinchingly, refusing to allow her to see the truth about his father. "My mother told me how whatever the Dark Ones did caused people to become different. She called it mutation."

"Yes, that is what we are. Remove your block."

"No," he said. Areenna's hand, still wrapped securely around his, tightened. He returned the pressure.

"You know I could destroy you easily."

"And destroy yourself at the same time?"

"You are overconfident."

Mikaal smiled for the first time since stepping onto the Island. He shook his head slowly. *You know better. You have always known. Would you risk her life?*

You think yourself better than we are. You think you can do what no other has done.

Areenna, watching and listening to both the verbal and the silent conversation, released Mikaal's hand and said, "No, it is you who think yourselves better than we. It is you who are so afraid of man you are willing to let Nevaeh be overrun, letting them destroy everything."

The human part of the body turned to her, its hands clenched as it stared at her. "Your emotions, your feelings for him matter not to us."

"Then we have wasted everything in coming here. I was to learn what was intended. I was to gain something unsaid. But I have found nothing worth the sacrifices we have made to come here. Without him, I am but half a woman."

And then Areenna let her powers loose. White bolts of fury rose from her hands and shot toward the snuck-woman. Instantly, Mikaal followed suit, sending flames at her. Neither expected what happened next.

The snuck-woman disappeared. She was there and she was gone, just as the last two had done.

"She was never here, she was only in our minds," Areenna said a moment later. The light glowing from her hands gave them enough illumination to see.

"What we saw was truth," Mikaal added. "Of that I have no doubt."

Areenna stared at the spot where the woman had been. "Do you think she could have harmed us?"

"Yes, if necessary. And it is They," Mikaal said. "I have this feeling, I don't know what to call it, but somehow I know, she was not one, but more than one."

"How is that possible?"

"How is this possible?" he asked, pointing to the people and animals caught within the glass, perished three thousand years before they had been born. "How is a woman part snuck?"

"A false image?" Areenna asked.

Mikaal shook his head once. "No, it was a true image, we would have known otherwise."

"We should get out of here, go back to the street and find that…needle."

Agreeing, Mikaal turned and started back to the entrance of the tunnel. He made it five feet before he was stopped by another of the invisible barriers. He gave a short barking laugh. "Apparently, they do not want us going that way."

"They herd us still," Areenna whispered.

Perhaps, Mikaal thought back. *But we are now permitted our abilities. Light the way, Areenna.*

Instead of moving forward, Areenna knelt on the smooth yet wavy surface of the glass floor and, with her hands pressed to it as she would have to the ground outside, she let her senses roam.

Nothing blocked her this time and she pushed forward, seeking what might lie ahead. "I feel nothing living within this tunnel."

Rising, she started in the only direction they could go. Behind her, Mikaal drew the sword, gripping it with both hands and taking comfort from its solid feel as they walked past the dead, who stared blindly at them from within their glass prison.

They walked in silence for almost an hour, each wrapped within solitary thoughts, when the first wisp of a breeze reached them. "I smell water," Areenna said.

Only at that moment did Mikaal realize they had been on the slightest of upgrades and had unknowingly been moving toward the ground above. "Give us more light," he said.

Areenna called forth more power and the tunnel brightened. The walls still contained the dead, but they could see further now. A few minutes later, the mouth of the tunnel appeared. "Hold," Mikaal whispered.

With the light from the entrance filtering in, Areenna closed her hands and drew back her energies. They stood still in the grayish light, staring at the tunnel entrance, looking for anything.

There was a sensation of being watched. Mikaal spun, sword at the ready, and stared into the tunnel.

"What?" Areenna asked in a whisper.

Something is behind us.

Light flared in her hand and she threw it into the tunnel. It blazed higher, exposing a half dozen traats, their eyes yellow and glowing in her light. "We never heard them."

As she spoke, more traats came into the light—a lot more.

Their rodent-like bodies, elongated and muscular, were tensed. The one in front lifted its head, its ears rotated forward as it stared at them.

Mikaal looked over his shoulder at the opening a hundred feet ahead. Now that he had control of his abilities, he was about to tell Areenna to run while he stopped them from chasing her, but held back. *Why had they given them their abilities in the tunnel? To defend against the traats?* The lessons from the three times he had met the women of the Island told him that was the wrong answer.

Areenna stepped past him and stood between him and the traats. She looked at them for several seconds. They held still. Then the leader lifted on his haunches and stared directly at her. Their eyes locked and something passed between them, but it was unlike anything she had ever experienced from an animal.

A half breath later the pack of traats turned as if one and disappeared into the tunnel's darkness.

Mikaal grasped Areenna's arm. "What happened?"

"I have no idea. I felt something—not danger. It was as if it were deciding our…worth."

Mikaal nodded. "It was a test."

"For me?"

"For me. All the tests are for me, but you play a part in them as well," he said with a shake of his head.

He slid the sword into its sheath, understanding at last that the metal was the least effective of their weapons. The most potent, he discerned, was their minds. He grasped Areenna's hand again and started toward the opening. "I itch for this to be done," he said as they neared the entrance and whatever awaited them in the red mist outside.

When they stepped onto the street, which was clear of debris, they found themselves facing a mound of metal and glass the height of fifty people. Atop this was the needle-like strand of metal Areenna had pointed out on the start of their trek through the Island's pathways. Sunlight gleamed off it even within the constant swirling of the red dust. When Areenna recovered from the sight, she said, "So large, so high. How powerful our forbearers were to create such a thing."

"And how stupid," Mikaal said. "To have done this to Nevaeh—to have destroyed their world."

Such is the nature of man, came the thought.

Mikaal looked at Areenna. Her green eyes were wide, her mouth partially open in reaction. Her pale blonde hair was covered with red dust. "Not all men," he said to them as well as Areenna.

"So say you."

Mikaal turned to find the old crone with them. This time no hood covered her head and face as she stood at the base of the rubble. "But if man is allowed to rule, it will happen again. It always does."

"It does not have to. But if *they* conquer us, your words will be true."

The old crone's eyes glowed luminous and blue. "You make a good argument, but can you promise man will not rule as he has in the past, that this will not happen again should the Dark Forces be defeated?"

How could he make a promise so far beyond his power to keep? He studied her, looking at the blue eyes and saw something in them that made him look deeper into himself.

It took a few seconds, yet for Mikaal the moment drew on forever; but when answers came, they gave him a deeper knowledge of who he was.

"I can promise but one thing," he said. "Whatever abilities I possess and for whatever reasons I have been given them, I will never allow what has happened to be repeated. But to promise what you ask…I am only capable of speaking for myself."

"And her?" the old crone asked, pointing the gnarled finger at Areenna.

"Have you not taught me the lesson yourself? Have you not shown me in the black place, then with the warrior on the street, and again in the tunnel what I had to learn? I have no claim on Areenna. I cannot speak for her nor tell her what to do. Perhaps together…but only in that way."

The woman moved forward. She did not walk, but seemed to float toward them. When she was a short distance away, she raised her arms. "Kneel before us." As the words left the pale slash of her mouth, there were suddenly eight cloaked figures circling them, each with their black hands held toward Areenna and Mikaal.

A crackle sounded in the air. Bands of blue and orange lightning issued from their hands, going not toward Areenna and Mikaal, but connecting the eight together. The scent of an approaching thunderstorm filled the air. The red mist disappeared from within the circle and the voices of the eight reverberated in their heads.

Woman, they said to Areenna, *you are young to be here, but this day we have seen coming for...a long time. You are strong and powerful beyond your years and even your knowledge, yet there is more you must learn.*

Man, they said, *you have shown us your abilities, and they are powerful to behold and frightening to us. But more so, you have shown us a man can learn, a man can think—not like a man, but as does a woman.*

There is more you need to learn about yourself before you can do battle with those who seek our end. The eight stepped forward, moving as one, drawing the circle closer and closer until their robes touched Mikaal and Areenna.

What follows next is the most dangerous. Over the centuries, more women have died or have lost the abilities they were born with than have survived. It is a choice you each must make now. You are free to leave with the abilities you possess, or you can accept whatever gifts we give. But with these gifts, should you survive the giving itself, will come terrible responsibilities and a future of what...we cannot say, but choose your path now you must.

The last silent words were sent at them with such deadly certainty it caused shivers to race through Mikaal and Areenna, who still tightly clasped each other's hands, each understanding the other's mind. *We agree,* they responded in unison.

Blue-orange lightning exploded around them, spun in a circle over their heads and rose skyward for hundreds of feet. It reversed and, in a jagged bolt, struck downward into them.

CHAPTER 33

ON THE LANDING across from the Island, the four women and Roth continued their watch. "It's late. The day is speeding past. How long does one stay there?" Roth asked.

Four sets of eyes locked on Roth. Enaid moistened her lips. "It is different for each woman. Some take only a few hours, others the entire day."

"Longer? Have any stayed longer?" he asked, his face etched with worry as he looked at the declining sweep of the sun.

"And come back whole? No," Enaid whispered. "But they are not those others. We can only wait," she added, laying a warm hand on Roth's bare arm.

On the tail of her last word, Enaid stiffened. Her gray eyes went wide and she spun to face the Island. Atir, Ilsraeth, and Laira turned at the same instant, staring.

A streak of blue-orange lightning shot skyward **from** the center, near the tip of the Island, moving almost too fast to track. And then, as if time stopped, it hovered in the air, reversed direction and dove back from where it had come.

Behind them, near the edge of the Landing, Charka reared and gave vent to a loud cry. And then the kraal charged across the Landing, toward the water. Without thinking, Roth dove as Charka ran by him, wrapped his arms around the kraal and planted his heels on the wood planks in an effort to stop him.

Behind him, Enaid cried out in distress, but Roth could not release the kraal. When he had Charka under control a mere yard from the edge of the Landing and, as the large animal stood there shuddering and whining, Roth turned to find Enaid had collapsed and the other three women had surrounded her.

He ran to where they huddled over his wife and saw the strain written across their features. Helpless, he watched them minister to Enaid. "What is it?"

Ilsraeth looked up, her eyes haunted. "I don't know. It is something from the Island. Let us work."

He watched as they hovered over Enaid. Atir pulled open Enaid's cloak and slipped her hands beneath the tunic to press them to Enaid. She closed her eyes and bent her head low. But there was no response.

Numb with fear for Enaid, all Roth could do was watch as the women did their best to aid his wife. Finally, Ilsraeth looked up at Roth. "We can do nothing. She is not being harmed. She is caught within something and we can only wait until she frees herself."

"Is it the sorceress?" Roth asked.

Atir shook her head and without looking away from Enaid said, "It is not of the Dark."

Roth took a deep breath and looked at Charka, who stood where Roth had left him. The kraal was immobile, staring across the water to the Island, huge shudders passing through him.

Roth went to the animal and stroked it gently. He lost himself in thought, reflecting on anything other than Enaid or Mikaal and soon time slipped by until he noticed the day was almost gone.

He turned to see what had happened to Enaid and those surrounding her. And then, from across the water, came the echo of an explosion. At the same instant, Enaid's body arched and a sudden flash of sparks discharged from her. The three women were thrown a dozen feet away.

◇◇◇

Timon sat on the deck of his boat, a pot of water and herbs brewing nearby on a small metal brazier set astride three legs. To his right,

Areenna's treygone perched on the railing in the same place it had been since she had left it there. Gaalrie had not moved or looked in any direction but that which Areenna and Mikaal had taken.

He had never seen a bird stay rooted for so long without food or water and he was becoming edgy at the amount of time the pair had been gone. He had, not for the first time, thought about taking the boat and leaving, but the instinct that had brought him so far east held him where he was.

He looked at the pot and saw the water was boiling, the herbs dancing madly within, and turned to pick up the clay cup waiting to be filled. As he did, there was a loud popping, much like a rock exploding within a heated fire. He turned back just as the air above him opened in a brilliant display of sparkling light and two tangled forms crashed onto the deck.

Gaalrie's wings spread wide and the treygone gave a loud shriek.

When the power of the eight struck them, a white explosive light swept Areenna and Mikaal away. Like the twisting winds of a funnel storm, they were drawn within and, even as they grabbed hold of each other, their arms and legs entwined, they were picked up and sent spinning at the speed of the winds.

Stinging bolts struck their heads and bodies with a combination of fire and pain and all they could do was cling to each other as they gyrated in maddening circles. Within their minds myriad visions raced far too fast for either to understand.

The spinning stopped as unexpectedly as it had begun. They crashed to the ground.

Areenna lay still, her heart racing, her body crushed by something. She forced her eyes open and found Mikaal lying atop her, his arms still locked about her, her arms and legs holding him in a tight grip.

He moved then—his eyes opened and a low groan escaped his clenched teeth. He lifted his head and saw Areenna beneath him. He rolled to the side and felt her release him. "What happened?" he croaked.

Areenna shook her head and then sat. She looked around and found

Gaalrie next to her on the deck of Timon's boat. "How...?"

Mikaal rose unsteadily and drew her up. They turned at the same time and found Timon but a foot away.

"Impressive entrance," Timon said, a single eyebrow raised high above a brown eye, the empty cup forgotten in his hand. "A bit overdone, think you not?"

Mikaal stared at Timon and dusted himself off. He looked at Areenna who was doing the same and the two of them burst into laughter. "You have no idea," he said to Timon.

"Ah, but I can't wait to hear the tale."

Without responding, Areenna looked at Gaalrie who, impatient, half hopped and half flew onto her shoulder where she pressed her beak into the curve of Areenna's shoulder and neck. Areenna stroked her aoutem and drew from it the warmth it needed to share. Yet her exhaustion did not ease.

"How soon can we cross?" Mikaal asked, his voice growing stronger, but he, too, felt the heavy strain of the day.

Timon nodded. "As soon as I pour myself some tea and put out the stove. There is enough for three. Care for some?"

Mikaal looked west and saw the sun was almost gone. He turned to Areenna. "It was afternoon when we..."

What seemed seconds was much longer. We will have to look deep to learn what happened to us, she responded silently. She gazed across the water, expanding her senses until she found the faint emanations of the dark thing hidden within the crannies of the palisades. The instant she did, she withdrew. *It still waits.*

"The tea will be appreciated," Areenna replied. "But, Master Timon, I must warn you, the crossing will be treacherous."

"Of course it will. I carry the two of you and it seems many ah...strange things happen around you. What will it be this time?"

Mikaal exhaled loudly. "The same as what attacked us this morning."

Timon shrugged. "Why should it be a problem, you outwitted them before."

Areenna and Mikaal shared a glance before she said, "The day has taken its toll. What I did on the crossing took much strength. We are tired, the day has been...difficult."

"Then we must trust ourselves and my boat. She has never failed me." He stroked the wood of the table he stood beside. "Perhaps, as we drink, you will answer my request from this morning. As you see, curiosity is a strong force within me. Why else would I have waited for you?"

"Why else indeed," Areenna said with a look that told him she appreciated his lie. "But the time is not yet right to answer your questions. One day, I will fulfill my promise to you, Master Timon, but I am afraid today cannot be that day."

Timon shook his head. "Women," he muttered with a smile that showed he expected nothing less and turned to retrieve two more cups. After pouring the tea, and when Mikaal and Areenna were seated, he went below, returning with some smoked meat.

"Eat." They took some of the meat, and Timon, looking up at the fast darkening sky asked, "Just how bad will the crossing be?"

Charka stopped shuddering and Roth raced to where Enaid lay. Her eyes were open and she was struggling to sit. The others were doing the same and when he knelt, she reached up and pulled him to her. "They are out. Mikaal and Areenna have survived," she said and drew him tight.

He held her until the tautness in her body eased. "How long?" she asked.

"The day is almost gone."

She looked for the others and saw they were gaining their feet. "I need to stand." Roth helped her up. The other three came to them and, without speaking, waited for Enaid.

"I was with them," she explained, "but I was not. I saw them kneeling in the center of a closed circle of *cloaked ones*. They...Mikaal and Areenna were covered in such energy as I have never witnessed." She looked at the darkening eastern horizon. "It seemed to have been only seconds. Such power," she whispered. "And there were eight, not one."

"Eight," Atir echoed. "So many gathered in one place and they allowed Mikaal to live... How can such have come to be?"

As one, Ilsraeth, Atir, and Laira turned to Roth. "The time is now to tell us the truth of Mikaal."

Enaid stepped between them and went to Roth's side. "No, it is time to tell you of Solomon Roth."

Three sets of eyes, one set as brown as the earth, another as blue as the sky, and the third a pale brown with specks of reddish colors dotted within the irises turned to her. Their stares were powerful and commanding and Enaid nodded her head before them.

"Let us circle, it will make it easier." With her right hand she grasped Atir's; with her left, Ilsraeth's. Laira took each of their hands in hers. The four women closed their eyes and, thus connected, Enaid showed rather than told her story.

When they separated, they fell silent, each lost within their own thoughts. Atir spoke first. "So much have you gone through, My Lord," she began, but faltered. "And how much you have brought us cannot be measured in words. Nothing of this shall pass our lips. You were right to keep it hidden. It shall accompany me to my grave."

Ilsraeth spoke next. Her eyes were sad, her voice barely a whisper. "There will be much danger from this point on. When the people of Nevaeh learn of Mikaal's powers they will...react badly, especially the women. But it will go deeper than that." She turned to Roth and looked from him to Enaid. "Mikaal and Areenna will change everything in our world. Their children..."

Roth stared at her, comprehension not quite dawning. "You speak as if they are—"

"—mated?" Ilsraeth smiled. "They know it not, but they are already so. Yet it will not happen for a long while."

Before Roth could say anything else, Laira called out. "They leave the far Landing." She hesitated and added, "The wraith will return. It is a terrible abomination. I saw it when the foretelling took me. But it remains unclear. I only know it attacks the boat and..."

At the Landing's edge, Charka gave a long high pitched cry that echoed hauntingly.

"It comes," Enaid said, looking skyward at the rapidly descending night. "It comes to destroy them and with them our hopes."

"We must protect them," Laira said, looking from woman to woman, Roth no longer a part of the picture.

"We failed before."

"We must try again," Enaid said, her eyes locked on the boat bobbing in the water, its sail limply awaiting a breeze.

"Push," Timon commanded when Mikaal released the stern rope.

Bending, he shoved the stern with all his strength and when the boat moved, jumped aboard and made his way to where Areenna and Timon stood. "Now we drift and await a friendly breeze," the master boatsman said.

While they drifted, twilight settled into darkness. Timon stood at the wheel, keeping the boat's bow pointed at the far Landing. After too many minutes of watching the sail hang limp, he said, "Unless you can find a way to raise the winds, we may end up as easy pickings for those things."

"My abilities lie not in that direction," Areenna said, her tone apologetic.

Mikaal, listening to them, paused in thought. With a motion of his head to Areenna, he signaled toward the stern. They went and sat on the rear rail. "When you received your gifts from the three women, you sensed…I don't know how to explain it, but it was like something striking into you. Do you not feel a change in you since we…arrived on the boat?"

Areenna looked down at her hands. "I have been reluctant to look within," she admitted, "I am afraid of what they may have done."

"I understand," he said. "But we have to look. We have to know."

She stared at Timon's broad back. "We should be alone without other eyes."

"We have no choice, Areenna. Do you not sense what comes?"

"I do," she whispered. "I have since I woke on the deck."

"Bring up your power. Show it to me."

She closed her eyes again and delved within. Her power flared instantly, the heat in her belly exploded, its strength taking her by surprise. When she opened her eyes her hands were encased in a blue so pure it bespoke a crystal pool, sparkling beneath the midday sun.

"Mikaal," she whispered.

Hold, ease back.

She did as he asked, containing the shimmering blue light with no small effort, but after a few seconds the strain eased and she became comfortable with the increased power.

Try, she asked him.

Mikaal took in a deep breath and without needing the formula he had created, pulled his own power forth. The flames did not just rise—they appeared instantly. No racing hot blood drew them up. He only started to think about them and they spread a hairsbreadth above the surface of his hands. He lifted his arms, his palms facing each other and the flames leapt across the short distance and combined. He dropped his hands and the fire was extinguished.

Join with me, Areenna said. Before his nod was completed, they were together. It was not as it had been before, it was vastly different. Each saw and felt everything about the other; there was nothing hidden.

When they separated, Areenna's face was covered by a deep red flush. "I didn't know."

"I tried to hide it. I didn't want it to come between us. I never…" *I didn't know how it would affect us.*

She smiled. *Now you know. They knew as well,* she told him.

He thought about the eight snuck-women whose darkness held no taint of evil, of this he was certain. *Yes, they knew.*

No one can know how we feel about each other, not until we are free of the darkness, Areenna told him, and stored away the newly discovered sharing of their emotions just as Timon spoke.

"Princess, we need your magic, now!"

Gaalrie's fierce hunting cry rang at the same instant.

Looking up, Areenna and Mikaal saw the shadow of the giant wraith circling high above, blocking stars from their sight as it moved toward them.

CHAPTER 34

"THERE!" *SHE* SHOUTED, staring outward from the edge of the cliff, seeing not what was before her, but what her two hidden creations saw.

She had waited throughout the day; sitting patiently, awaiting their return. *She* had known the moment the two had left the protection of the Island and appeared on the boat: one second they were not there, in the next they were. *She* saw them, felt them and, the instant *she* had, cast a formula to still the air surrounding the Island. When *she* was certain of their helpless floundering upon the night water's choppy flow, *she* sent her final creation at them.

Jet black and surrounded by a visceral aura of gray-black mist, red-eyed and angry at having been forced to wait, it gave off the putrid stench of death. Its legs, as thick as saplings, hung below a wide heavy body; each of its claws was the size of a coor.

Behind it, the smaller wraith sat on the shelf within the rock wall, awaiting its mistress's command with ragged impatience, its claws scratching harshly on the rocky ledge. *Not yet, she* whispered into its head, *wait*. *She* watched the boat for several minutes. Then, while the extension of her powers circled above the boat, *she* sent the command to attack.

When the giant wraith aimed its body downward, *she* released the smaller one to join the fight.

The crystal blue power erupted in Areenna's hands at the sight of the flying monstrosity and without thinking, she pushed it at the limp sail. When the power met the sail, it billowed outward. The mast groaned with the strain of filled silks and the boat shot forward.

The muscles of the boatsman's arms bulged as he fought the wheel for control of the now hurtling boat. Areenna and Mikaal watched the black sorceress's evil corruption bank into an angled dive.

Held there by Areenna's strong asking, Gaalrie screamed from her perch on the deck, her wings spread wide for balance as she watched the charging wraith.

Together, Mikaal said, the fires of his abilities swelling between facing palms. Next to him, Areenna withdrew one hand from the task of moving the boat. The boat slowed slightly, but continued toward the far bank.

They joined, two entities and two minds with new powers and abilities, and became one. Their powers swirled around them in an aura of light and fire and they released this new weapon at the fast approaching evil.

The sky lit with a bright flaring of blue, yellow, orange, and red against the fast darkening sky. Within the blazing light the monstrous black thing continued diving. The closer it came, the bigger and fiercer grew the ball of fire and light surrounding it, pushing against the shields the black witch had built to protect the wraith and slowing its attack.

Areenna and Mikaal's concentration was so totally fixed on the monster above they were unaware of the second wraith's silent approach from the opposite direction, but Timon was not.

"Another comes from the south," he shouted, fighting the wheel to hold the boat on a steady course.

Take it, Mikaal said.

Areenna drew her hand from the large wraith and turned to the new danger from the south.

With the loss of Areenna's aid, Mikaal drew deeply from within and, breathing heavily, ramped up his power.

Areenna struck at the smaller wraith, sending a stream of the crystal blue low over the water to where the dark beast jetted toward them. Just before the light struck the smaller creature, it dove beneath the water and disappeared.

Areenna searched madly for it in the bouncing waters, but could not find it. She started to turn to Mikaal, to join with him again, when the boat was hit from below.

There was a loud, shuddering crash. The boat lifted into the air, hung there for a moment and then crashed wildly downward. The bow cut beneath the surface of the water; waves rushed over the ship's deck while Timon fought to keep the vessel from floundering as the bow returned to the surface.

Mikaal was knocked from his feet and sent rolling across the deck, his stream of energy cut off while he fought for a grip to stop from being thrown off the boat. Areenna cried out sharply, her feet ripped from beneath her when a second surge of water roared over the side and caught her unprepared. Swept across the deck by the rushing water, she was halfway over the far side railing when a hand caught her arm.

Trapped within the surging water that spun him across the deck, Mikaal slammed into a post of the animal pen and grabbed onto it. Everything around him was a water-blurred vision. When he saw Areenna fall, he pulled himself forward and, as the water whirled her past him, reached out and caught her arm. His was almost torn from its socket, but he held tight, refusing to lose his grip on her.

Beneath him, the boat shuddered and settled. The sail hung limp, the boat lay dead and at the mercy of the currents and the two monsters attacking it.

The five standing on the western Landing watched the display of fiery lights discharging in the sky. Each of them was lost in the awe of the power they were witnessing. They followed every step of the deadly battle and when the smaller wraith dove into the water, and the boat was thrown into the air, Ilsraeth cried out.

When the blue light and the bright flames disappeared, Enaid turned to the three women. "We must try now." Together, gripping each other's hands and closing the circle, they built their own abilities, funneling all of their powers into the strongest of them, Enaid.

Enaid focused first on the boat, which she steadied with an easy push of her bloodline's ability to hold and move objects. Then she raised her eyes to the flying monstrosity about to crush the craft from above and sent a charge of energy at it.

There was a flash and the huge wraith was knocked sideways. Its rage echoed across the water and, as it fought to regain balance, the smaller wraith rose from below the surface. Sheets of water poured from its wings. It circled the boat and then swept downward.

Atir pushed her powerful blocking ability at Enaid, who sent it speeding to shield the boat. The wraith struck the shield, skittered wildly and fell into the water. Seconds later it rose and joined the larger wraith now circling above.

As Enaid and the other women fought to protect the boat and its passengers, there was a flaring of energy twenty yards from the Landing, as if a wall had suddenly formed above the water to stop their energies.

"You won't stop us you black-souled snuck!" Enaid screamed at the wall as a spurt of anger unlike anything she had ever experienced blasted through her.

Closing her eyes, she grasped intuitively at the rage, channeling it, using it to fuel the women's combined powers, and released it at the wall.

Sparking streaks of light erupted and raced across the invisible wall, seeking the chink within its armor. As she threw everything within her at the enemy attempting to destroy her son, the wall shattered and disappeared.

But as she stared at the shadowy outline of the boat, she saw they were too late. The two wraiths were almost upon the boat.

Areenna and Mikaal scrambled to their feet as the smaller wraith descended on them. Just as it was about to strike, it hit something, slid off and twisted back into the air.

"Enaid is at the Landing," Areenna said between gulping breaths.

Mikaal looked up, searching the sky. He spotted the wraiths above the boat, circling. Then he glanced over his shoulder toward the far Landing and saw the bright flaring of power grow across a solid barrier.

"They fight the sorceress."

Mikaal! Up! Areenna shouted, but the sound was only in his head. He craned his neck to stare at the charging wraiths, so close their bodies blocked out the stars.

Darkness shrouded them like a blanket thrown over their heads. Black and evil, it leeched into their minds with a force that held them in thrall. *Fight!* Areenna commanded. *Fight!*

Though he didn't know how, Mikaal found a force within him that gave him the strength to raise his now flaming hands to the sky. He used all the power within him to send the fire upward.

In the space of a heartbeat, the small wraith exploded when the fire hit it. Burned shards of the dead beast rained onto the water, but the larger creature didn't hesitate in its downward dive.

Areenna joined Mikaal and added her ability to his. Gaalrie dropped onto Areenna's shoulders. The fire crackled with blue light, flaring in a wide barrier above their heads. And then, from somewhere, more power joined with them, swelling their abilities.

Areenna knew instantly what it was. Even as she recognized what was happening, Mikaal became aware, too. *Now*, he commanded and, together, they released this new combined power.

Above them, the giant wraith, the creation of incomprehensible evil burst into a ball of fire that lit the night for miles. Nothing was left of it, not a feather, not a piece of its body fell to the water. It had disintegrated in mid-air.

Mikaal and Areenna sank to the deck, their knees hitting the smooth wood at the same instant, their hands still clasped together, their heads bowed and their chests rising and falling from the work done while a vision of the eight Cloaked Ones floated within their minds.

Go now, Man, go now, Woman. Do what is required. Do what you have been created for.

Timon's boat docked at the Western Landing and the three climbed the ladder to its wooden surface where they found Roth, Enaid and the other three women waiting for them. Before they could reach them, Charka charged across the Landing and when he reached Mikaal, he nuzzled against his chest.

Mikaal stroked his aoutem's neck for a few seconds, absorbing the gentle warmth emanating from the kraal before stepping around him to face the others with Areenna on one side of him, Timon on the other.

Gaalrie lifted from Areenna's shoulders and hopped onto Charka's back, much to the surprise of those who watched.

Roth stood to one side, watching the trio. Relief flooded him as he ran his eyes over his son. The first thing he noticed was the way Mikaal held himself. He stood straighter, taller, and his skin had a glow to it. He saw the same glow on Areenna as well.

Enaid crossed the short distance between them and drew Mikaal and Areenna into her arms, flooding them with emotions of love and welcome while the other three women watched.

When she released them, Mikaal went to hug his father. When Roth pulled back without completely releasing his hold, he gazed into his son's eyes and said, "We'll talk later, when we are alone. I look forward to hearing about your adventure."

Mikaal nodded slowly. "It was...I don't have the words yet to describe it."

Releasing his hold on Mikaal, Roth clapped him solidly on both shoulders. "When it is time, you will."

While all the attention was on Mikaal and Areenna, Timon approached Ilsraeth. When he stepped before her, he bowed and said, "My Lady, I am surprised...and pleased to see you here."

"As am I to see you, Master Boatsman, and happy to see you survived the journey across."

They fell silent. There were no further words they could speak, and both understood so. A moment later, Roth called Timon's name.

He turned to find the high king approaching. "Master Timon, I am forever in your debt."

The boatsman bowed his head slightly. "My Lord, there is no debt. I did only what was needed."

"I would like to hear how you came to help them."

Timon smiled. "I have no answer based on fact. When I left them at Northcrom, I was about to return home, but had a feeling something more was needed of me. Why I can't say, but I followed that feeling here, nothing more."

"Nonetheless," Roth said, his voice tight with emotion, "your service to Nevaeh, to my son, and my family are a debt I accept. You have my lasting gratitude."

"And again, I must repeat, there is no debt. Whatever I have done, I have done because I believed I should."

"I understand. If there ever comes a time when you have need of me, I will be there for you." Roth clasped the boatsman's muscular arm; Timon responded in kind.

"My thanks," Timon responded. They turned to the others who now sat on the Landing, encircling Areenna and Mikaal.

"I think we are not a part of what they now do," Roth said.

"No, but I have wine aboard, if it survived the crossing. Shall we?"

With a nod, Roth and Timon went to the boat. When they went past the five women and Mikaal, Roth smiled at Enaid, who returned it before returning her attention to Areenna and Mikaal.

Looking at them, she said, "Atir, Ilsraeth, and Laira know the story of Roth, and of you," she added, looking at Mikaal. "Both of you may speak freely before them." She paused in thought before saying, "While what happened to each of you is meant only for you, is there anything you can tell us about your time there?"

Areenna looked at Mikaal, who silently said, *tell them what you can.*

An hour later, Areenna finished speaking. The women had been transfixed and it took a minute before they responded. Atir spoke first. "Eight cloaked ones gifted you?"

"There were eight cloaked ones," Mikaal began, "they were a single mind."

"Is this possible?" Laira asked, looking from her mother to Ilsraeth and then Enaid. "How can it be?"

"We were shown what happened when the dark circle destroyed the world. We saw it happen on the Island, we saw how the cloaked ones came to be. And it was...terrible," Areenna whispered.

"She—they were old, very old," Mikaal added. "And when they used their powers, they..."

Sensing the difficulty he was having, Enaid cut in, "You're both exhausted. We can talk more in the morning. Now is the time for rest." With nods of agreement, each found a spot on the Landing. A few minutes later Roth returned, leaving Timon to sleep on his boat.

But after spreading her sleeping silks near Mikaal's, Areenna looked over at Enaid and saw her mentor watching her. Standing, she went to Mikaal's mother. "We should talk," she whispered.

"What bothers you?"

Areenna gazed into her mentor's eyes and took a breath. "You knew what would happen when you put Mikaal and I together, did you not?"

Enaid nodded somberly. "Your power would increase, you would become—both of you would become—who you were meant to be."

"No," Areenna said. "You knew what would happen between Mikaal and me...our feelings."

As she stared at the young woman, understanding came. A smile tugged at the corners of Enaid's lips. "That you might find each other as mates? That there might be love? No, child, I only knew that you and he belong together."

"Is that not the same?" she questioned.

"No. What I sensed was only a possibility of what might be. But I knew you needed to be together in this journey and to prepare for what is coming."

Enaid fell silent for a moment, and then reached across and took the young woman's hand. "May I ask a favor?"

Puzzled, Areenna nodded.

"When I watched you battle that creature, the powers you and he raised were...inconceivable. The fire Mikaal used. I have never seen abilities such in a woman. Will you tell me what happened the first time Mikaal found his power?"

Areenna told Enaid of the night he had discovered the root of his power. How she had forced him into a battle, chasing and attacking him without mercy. She spoke of his discovery of power and how it had flared out and encircled her with roaring flames.

When Areenna fell silent, Enaid gently squeezed her hand. "He circled the fire around you, but it did not touch you, did it?"

"It did not."

Enaid smiled. "Were you able to control your first release of power?"

She shook her head. "My mother was prepared and stopped me

from hurting her."

"Yes. The first release is always the most dangerous, and it was my mistake not to prepare you for it. But don't you see, child? Do you not understand what happened that night? Why you were unharmed?"

When she shook her head once again, Enaid leaned closer, her mouth so close her breath washed Areenna's cheek when she said, "He knew, even though he was unaware of it, that the two of you were meant to…no, you were not just meant to be together. Born to magic were you both."

CHAPTER 35

BENEATH THE NEW day's crisp blue, welcoming sky, the sleepers on the Landing awakened. Roth rose and, as he did, saw the others stirring.

"A fitting morning after yesterday's drama," Timon called from the stern of his boat.

"That it is," Roth replied, looking at the sun, floating above the horizon. "A good day to sail, is it not Master Timon?"

"Perfect," Timon agreed then climbed the short ladder to the Landing.

Behind Roth, the others left their silks. Atir went to where the kraals huddled together and separated one bag from the others. She carried it to the center of the Landing and pulled out several loaves of bread while Laira, who had trailed her mother, prepared the small brazier to heat water for morning tea.

While they worked, Enaid went to the boatsman and said, "I did not thank you for your services, Master Timon. Please allow me to do so now."

When Timon began to object, she stopped him quickly. "It is a mother's right."

He smiled at her. "As you wish, My Lady."

She took his hands in hers and smiled warmly at him. As she was about to speak, her vision blurred and went dark. She stiffened against the flood of images. It passed within an instant and she was once again looking at Timon. A sense of sadness lingered from the vision.

"My Lady?" he asked in concern.

"It is all right," she whispered.

"What happened? You saw something."

"It matters not," she said. "What matters most is how you helped my son and Areenna. What matters more is that very soon you will find the peace you have been seeking for so long."

"You saw my death?" he asked in a whisper.

Enaid shook her head emphatically. "Far from it. Stay close to your home for the next few weeks...and ask nothing more of this."

He searched her face, looking for a clue, but found only her expression of warmth. "I will do as you suggest."

She smiled. "Good. Let us have our morning meal." Turning, she started back to the others.

While they ate, conversation was sparse, and when the food was gone, Timon stood. "It is time I return home." He looked at Mikaal, and at Areenna who stood next to the young prince. "I can't say it's been a pleasure, but it has been an adventure." With a nod at the others, he started toward his boat.

"Boatsman," he heard Ilsraeth from behind. He turned.

Ilsraeth stood still, her hands clasped before her. "I...we wish you a safe and speedy journey home. Make certain it is."

Timon did not stop the smile that broke across his face. "I will do my best, my Queen." So saying, he descended the ladder and prepared his boat.

While Timon worked, the group gathered their belongings and readied their kraals for the return to their lands. By the time they were set, Timon's boat was a quarter mile north, its sail billowing proudly in the morning breeze.

Laira strapped the last bag to her kraal, checked the binding and then gazed across the water at the red-misted Island. She wondered how long it would be before it was her turn to be tested. She started to say something to her mother, when she saw movement near the edge of the Landing.

Walking to the ladder, she looked down and gasped. In the instant she saw it she knew its significance and saw the rest of the foretelling she had been given the day before. "Mother…"

Atir, talking with Ilsraeth and Enaid, turned at the strangled sound of her name. Everyone went to the young girl, who was pointing at the water and the small skiff bouncing gently upon it.

When Mikaal looked and saw what appeared to be the same skiff he and Areenna had started their journey on, he shook his head. "How…"

Enaid came up behind him, Areenna at her side. "They sent a new one. There must always be transport for the next woman."

Laira faced her mother. "It is meant for me," she said.

Atir, her features stiff, nodded slowly. "Yes, I feel the truth of that."

Enaid sensed the same and moved close to her friend's daughter. She gave Laira a confident smile and drew her into a gentle hug. "Fear not what you find there. Face it openly…and honestly and with all your strength. You will be welcomed and return even stronger. Of that I have no doubt. Now kneel."

When Lira knelt, Enaid placed her hands to each side of the young woman's head and closed her eyes. An instant later, Laira gasped.

"Hold this tight, use it well."

Ilsraeth replaced Enaid before the kneeling woman and placed her hand on Laira's chest. A spark of energy flared between them. "Draw it deep within you," she whispered before stepping back.

All eyes turned to Atir, who shook her head. "She is my daughter, it is not permitted." She looked at Areenna and nodded.

When Areenna stepped forward, she heard Enaid within her mind. *Gifting is the sharing of abilities. Select the one you feel will aid her best and offer it freely.*

She stared into Laira's umber eyes and within a heartbeat knew what to do. Reaching out, she placed one hand over the young woman's heart and the other atop her head. She closed her eyes and pushed. Light rose quickly to encircle them in a globe of shimmering blue. Seconds later, the light was drawn into Laira.

Areenna stepped back.

"I shall stay and wait," Atir said, breaking the silence.

"And I with you," Ilsraeth added.

Startled, Enaid took in a short breath. "A word," she said to Ilsraeth.

When they were far enough away for privacy, Enaid said, "When I bid Timon farewell, I was caught in a foretelling. You cannot stay here. You must return to Northcrom. Your husband... He has been hurt. You must go now."

A flash of concern sparked in her eyes. "How? What?"

Enaid shook her head. "I saw not what, only that it is bad and you must hurry."

"The black witch...she has—"

"No. Although I was given only a small glimpse, I sensed nothing unnatural."

"I will leave now."

"Leave with us. It is safer through the ruins if we go together. I will tell the others."

Ten minutes later, their goodbyes said, Roth, Mikaal, Areenna, Enaid, and Ilsraeth started their kraals up the winding road leading to the top of the palisade while Laira climbed down to the skiff to begin her trip across the water.

Atir alone remained on the Landing with her treygone and Laira's ret, watching as her daughter began the crossing.

They stopped two hours later, and a half mile away from the ruins, through which they had passed safely. There, Ilsraeth took her leave and, with her black rantor loping along next to her, pushed her kraal into a cantor and headed north across the wasteland toward her home.

"She will be fine," Enaid assured Roth, who watched the woman ride off. "The rantor and her magic are more than enough protection." Then she looked at Areenna and Mikaal. "You two have been withholding something. Speak now."

It is time to tell them, Areenna pushed to Mikaal.

Yes. I leave it to you.

Areenna could not stop the short laugh from getting out. *Coward.*

"What?" Enaid asked anxiously.

Areenna cleared her throat. "Mikaal and I decided to wait until we were alone with you. When we were on the Island, when the cloaked ones gifted us, they also gave us instruction." She paused to look questioningly at Enaid.

"Continue," Enaid said.

Areenna took a slow breath. "They told us we are to go to the far northwestern mountains—to the Frozen Mountains. We have been given an undertaking that must be done before the dark ones cross the seas and reach us here. Without accomplishing this, they said, Nevaeh will fall and we will be overcome."

"The Frozen Mountains," Enaid whispered, her voice a breaking croak. "What are you to seek in that frozen desolation? Nothing lives there."

"Something does. Something that must be awakened," Areenna said, her voice low, but the words resounded loudly in everyone's ears.

"You will have to wait. It's a two month journey to that region, in the best of weather," Roth said. "No man or woman can survive the mountains in winter."

Mikaal nodded in agreement. He took Areenna's hand. "We have preparations to make. We only know a little of what they gifted to us. We know we must learn everything before we leave. And we will leave a month before spring thaw."

"You have a full three months before you leave. It will be enough time to learn and make you ready," Enaid declared. But her words did not reflect the overwhelming sensation of fear tying her thoughts into knots.

She knew whatever they had been charged with, would be fraught with dangers none could imagine.

"Until then," Roth said, cutting into all their thoughts, "we work and train and prepare, not just the two of you, but all of Nevaeh. If war is coming, as you have been told, then such will be met by power of all the peoples of Nevaeh."

EPILOGUE

SHE LAY ON the cavern floor, unmoving, her twisted limbs spread awkwardly as *she* stared at the high ceiling above. *She* had failed, and with failure came fear. Her masters would soon know of this failure, if they did not already have the knowledge.

Trembling on the rock floor, exhausted from the battle fought with the forces *she* had never encountered before, *she* pleaded with her masters even as *she* sent the message of her failure to them.

She was explicit within the message, sparing no detail of what had happened and filled the mist-carried winged messenger with her impression of the powers that had defeated her creations and herself. At the end of the woeful tale, *she* added her plea for mercy, knowing full well it might never be answered.

But there was no choice. There was no one other than her dark masters, the rulers of her world, the ones who had entrusted this part of the world to her with the most important task of all. To destroy Roth, his woman, his child and the woman-child called Areenna, just as *she* had killed the woman child's mother with a lingering painful death.

She dragged herself from the floor and half-walked half-scuttled to the cavern's opening, where the winged mist awaited. *She* drew into herself, all the strength *she* could muster and once her message was complete, and the mist swirled about her impatiently, *she* would either live or die at their whim. Yet, until that day came, *she* would not cease her attempts to finish what her masters had commanded.

"I will destroy them, I will do as you have commanded. Or I will give my life in the attempt."

A rush of confidence filled her when *she* swirled her hands and called up the formula to send the message on its winged way.

She completed the formula and the mist disappeared. *She* looked up into the sky and saw not the cloud-filled heavens above, but the faces of the four *she* had sworn to destroy. From within the black remnants of what once was her soul came a haunting laugh, for she knew what was coming.

<>◇<>

The End

Tales Of Nevaeh, Volume I
Born To Magic

A special preview of book II, **The Dark Masters,** follow these pages.

Author's Notes

Dear Reader,

Thank you for your support! Without you my stories would sit on a bookstore shelf, a warehouse, or in a database somewhere in a 'cloud' waiting for you to find them. I don't write because it's a job, I write because it's my passion. I hope reading and enjoying the worlds created by writers is your passion.

I hope as well, you have enjoyed this first book in the *Tales Of Nevaeh* series, *Born To Magic*, as much as I did writing it, and I would love to hear from you about your reading experience.

If you enjoyed this book, and would like to lend me your support and help spread the word about *Born To Magic*, please tell a friend and share it with the world by writing a review. Nothing fancy, just tell the world what you think—even just a sentence or two would be appreciated.

Reading your reviews, and receiving emails from you, means a tremendous amount to me. And I would like to thank you in advance for your help in spreading the word about Areenna and Mikaal and the people of Nevaeh.

I have included below, some convenient links for you.

Thank you for taking the time to read ***Born To Magic***,

David

Click here to write a review on Amazon.

Click here to write a review on Goodreads.

Email me at david@davidwind.com

ABOUT THE AUTHOR

David Wind

When my first novel was published in 1981, I had no idea where I was headed. Since then, I've published thirty-five novels, thirty-three of them with traditional publishers, but in 2007, I decided I wanted more freedom than the traditional publishers would allow and began a new phase in my life as an Independent Author.

I live and write in a small village about thirty miles upstate of NYC, and share my house with my wife, Bonnie and our dog Alfie, an apricot poodle. Our three children have ventured out into the world on their own (or so they think). Our son Zach works on the CBS show 48 Hours. Our daughter Devon, her husband Russell and my grandson Sawyer live in New Jersey where Devon teaches Special Education. Alana, our youngest daughter, is a Pastry Chef in San Francisco.

In 2008, I published *Angels In Mourning*, my 'homage' to the old time private detective books of the 50's and the 60's. I used to love to sneak them from my parents' night-tables and read them as a young boy. Angels, is a modern day take on the old style hardboiled detective. In April of that year, *Angels In Mourning* won the Amazon.com Book of the Month Reader's Choice Award.

My Fantasy, *Queen Of Knights*, reached #2 on the amazon.com bestseller lists for historical fantasy and medieval fantasy, and my sci-fi of parallel worlds, *The Others*, received wide acclaim.

I am currently working on the third volume of the *Tales of Nevaeh*. Volume II will be out in the late spring.

My novels have been translated into 11 languages and published in 15 countries.

David's Links

David's Links
Twitter: @david_wind
Facebook: http://facebook.com/authordavidwind
Goodreads: http://bit.ly/1v1IE6B

For more information about David Wind, please visit:
http://www.davidwind.com

Available Novels by David Wind
The Dark Masters, Tales Of Nevaeh, Book II
Born To Magic, Tales Of Nevaeh
Queen Of Knights
The Others
The Cured
Angels In Mourning
The Hyte Maneuver
A Conspiracy Of Mirrors
As Peace Lay Dying
Co Op
Shadows
And Down Will Come Baby
Short Stories
The Guardian At The Edge Of The World – Published in André
Norton's **Witch World 2** anthology, TOR Books
Prelude To Nevaeh: Roth's story—A free download of the back
story to the *Tales Of Nevaeh*
Non-Fiction
The Lifeboat, (non-fiction)

A special preview of

**The Tales Of Nevaeh
Volume II**

The Dark Master

CHAPTER 1

AREENNA OF FREEMORN sat stone still: her breathing soundless, her senses ranging, searching. Hidden by the branches of a low hanging gazebow tree, she eased her tense muscles before making her next move.

Challenging her inner strength while willing her body to rest and recover, she could not help but marvel at how much had happened in the few months following their testing on the Island.

She had changed in so many ways there were times when she barely recognized herself. Her strength and her powers had increased more than she'd ever imagined possible—far more than the short eighteen years she'd lived. Her ability to meld her mind with his was as if they were one person. Harder though, was the knowledge that the emotions within her could not be permitted to rise to the barest of thoughts—not yet.

From above, Gaalrie's warning tugged within her mind and she stopped thinking. *He is near.* She stood, let her senses expand, and then shot off into the thicker woods.

Racing through the forest, zigzagging between trees like a mad weaver creating a bewildering drapery, Areenna moved with the swiftness of a rantor on hunt. Above her, silver streaked cinnamon and black-feathered Gaalrie, the foundling treygone she had rescued and bonded with four years before, flew in pace with her running, its six foot wingspread rode the currents above the treetops. The thickness of the forest prevented her from seeing her pursuer through her aoutem's eyes, yet she knew he was close and coming fast; exactly where she wasn't sure for he'd blocked himself well. She paused for a breath.

To her left was another giant gazebow tree, its long and heavy branches curved downward to kiss the ground, offering her a degree of protection. To her right stood a tall pine, hundreds of years old, its trunk almost as wide as the gazebow.

Standing between the two trees, Areenna sought him with her mind. *There!* He was close. She could not read him through the block, but recognized the complete absence of anything as the block he'd raised around himself. She closed her eyes and drew on her inner power, seeking one of the new abilities she had been gifted with on the Island. When the heat roared through her abdomen, she created a mind picture of herself and set it under the gazebow tree, where the barest glimpse of her arm and shoulder could be seen between the leafy branches. She moved behind the bole of the tall pine and drew her short-sword. Gaalrie settled on a branch above her. She slowed her breathing, knowing she could not hold this ability for long.

Thirty seconds later came the faint echoes of dead twigs and old leaves crunching beneath boots. She drew a slow breath and held it.

Emerging from behind a small cluster of trees to her left, tall and broad, black hair hanging to his shoulders and gray eyes searching everywhere, Mikaal of Tolemac stepped between the gazebow and the pine, took three steps and turned. He spotted the mind picture hidden by the branches.

When he moved toward the gazebow, she launched herself from behind the tree. She was on him in three strides, her shortsword swinging in a deadly killing stroke.

Before the blade reached him, he spun and caught her sword on his longsword. The ring of metal upon metal echoed loudly in the quiet forest. A smile broke across his face. *Good!*

Good? "Is that all it was?" she asked aloud, lowering her sword and sheathing it. "Anyone else would not have known I was behind them."

I am not anyone else, Mikaal told her in their wordless way.

True, she replied, returning his smile with her own. "Let's rest for a minute. We've been at this for hours."

Mikaal lowered himself to the mossy grass and Areenna did the same. Sighing pleasantly, she looked at the sky. The sun had crested three hours before and was deep into its western descent. Rays of staggered sunlight, filtered beams of yellow and white, slipped through the tree branches of the forest near the border of Tolemac, at the edge of the Southern Outlands. These shafts of light, like fences separating the trees, marked the boundaries of the training field Areenna and Mikaal had been using for the past months. Here, away from prying eyes, and for days at a time, they worked on their abilities, sharpening them, practicing each until they were available at the merest hint of a thought.

Here, they worked on their physical fighting abilities—sword work, bow work and knife training. Mikaal, halfway through his twentieth year, was the equal of any warrior of Nevaeh; at eighteen, Areenna, under his tutelage was not far behind.

Yet more potent than the training of blade and shaft was the understanding of their special abilities. Areenna's abilities had grown twenty fold since the Island. Still her most powerful weapon was the blue white light she could wield to stop or destroy an opponent. And Mikaal's ability with fire had grown into a weapon both fierce and fearful.

"My father's Sixes will be here shortly," Mikaal said, offering her his gourd to drink from. The 'Six groups' were his father's specially trained guards—trained in the same manner Roth had been trained in the twenty-second century, before boarding the starship that had kept him alive and in stasis for three thousand years.

Our final training, yes? she asked, using thought rather than word as she removed her padded leather tunic to allow her skin to cool in the chilled air. The short sleeved undergarment was damp with sweat. While the weather in Tolemac was never too cold, this winter had been one of the coldest in many years. For them, it was beneficial, as they had spent the past months acclimating themselves to the cold, in preparation for the Frozen Mountains of the northwest.

The only bad part of the winter was that instead of leaving for the northwest when they had planned, their journey was delayed by a month because of heavy blizzards in the northwest and western dominions.

Watching her, Mikaal traced her features, taking in the smooth lines of her cheekbones set beneath sea green eyes and hesitated only monetarily on her full mouth before dropping to her exposed arms. The lean muscles of her upper arms glowed in the afternoon light. "If we are to leave in three days, today will be our last here," Mikaal agreed.

"Are you sure about the Six?"

Mikaal's smile was gentle; his nod emphatic. "They will be a good test. We must know if we can handle fighters of their level, individually and as a team."

"But we already know this."

His smile faded, his voice turned low and serious. "We are, you and I, good against one or two, but there are no fighters in Nevaeh who are their equal. If we can hold our own against six of them, we will know we are ready, physically, to do what we must."

We cannot use our abilities with them. It will not be easy.

True. Then, aloud, he said, "Today isn't about how we combine our powers; it's about how we blend together in physical battle." He sat straighter, the water skein in his hand forgotten. His eyes glazed momentarily. *They come. Put on your leather, they are near.*

Areenna put on her padded leather tunic, closed her eyes and pushed out with her mind. Gaalrie left her roost and flew low through the trees. A moment later she joined with Gaalrie and through her aoutem's eyes, saw the 'Six' moving silently through the woods. She watched their progress while she closed her padded leather tunic, which would be worn beneath the special armor Roth was creating for her as he had for Mikaal.

Join with me, she asked.

Mikaal immediately connected with her. Since their testing on the Island, their joining had become fast and natural. When he was settled in her mind, he too watched through Gaalrie's eyes as the six warriors wove toward them in silent passage.

Charka's warning came as a tweak within his mind when the men passed the kraal and closed in on them. When Mikaal stood, Areenna did the same.

"Leave your sword sheathed until the last second; let them think us unprepared."

Areenna smiled at him. "Your father said he will have my armor ready tomorrow," she said aloud. *They have surrounded us*, she added silently.

"I know," he responded, to both her voice words and the silent ones as well. *Now!*

They spun, drawing their weapons and ending up back to back as the six men charged from behind trees, racing toward Areenna and Mikaal with their swords held high.

Like all Nevaen men, they were tall, broad and powerful. Today they wore full battle armor. Their bodies encased within hammered metal, the joints subtle leather, they broke into two packs of three and charged.

Areenna eyed the three who veered toward her. She set herself, her stance solid just before the first man reached her. Tall and broad-shouldered, the soldier sword glinted in the waning sun, its long blade blurring toward her. She moved fast, ducking low and weaving to the left while reaching out with her sword. She struck him hard across his thighs with the flat of her blade, recovered quickly and blocked the second man's sword when he attacked from behind.

The third man swung. She summersaulted forward beneath his blade, rose to her feet and, in a smooth and swift movement, blocked the descending blade of the second man who had recovered and followed her move.

◇◇◇

Mikaal had taken out the first of his attackers, but was backing away from the other two who struck simultaneously at him. His sword reflected sunlight as he wove a defensible figure eight over and over, deflecting their blades as he moved toward them. While he sensed Areenna's battle behind him, he kept his concentration fixed upon his attackers.

Mikaal watched the two carefully as he parried their thrusts and saw, in a quick exchange, when their eyes met and the one on the left nodded imperceptibly. Something inside him flashed and he saw, to the very last detail, every movement they would make. The man on the right shifted slightly and side stepped. When he did, the one on the left lunged forward in an attempt to push Mikaal toward the other. Instead, Mikaal moved directly to the man on his left, caught his sword with his own blade and spun. The tip of his blade reached the attacker's cross guard and with a flick of his wrist, tore the sword from the man's hand.

While the sword arced in the air, Mikaal followed through and placed the tip of his sword on the man's neck. The instant it touched skin, Mikaal lowered the sword and spun to catch the swing from the third man. Behind him, the clash of metal rang loudly. The light touch of her mind whispered across his senses and he knew she was holding her own while he dodged a killing blow aimed at his head.

Mikaal's eyes were fixed on his attacker's, their blades locked. Just when the man began to withdraw his sword, Mikaal sidestepped, lashed out with his right leg and swept his opponent's feet from under him. The warrior hit the ground hard and the same instant, Mikaal placed his sword at his throat.

The fighter released his word. "Well done My Prince."

Mikaal lowered his sword and turned to watch Areenna, who was holding off the other two. He started forward to aid her, but the man he'd just defeated grabbed his leg. "Hold. Let her deal."

◇◇◇

The two men were separated just far enough so Areenna had to face one while the other edged slowly around her. Sensing what was about to happen, she let instincts take over—there was only one chance and it had to be used right. When the second man edged past her peripheral vision, she turned to face the first. She feinted with a lunge; the man raised his sword defensively. Twisting in the opposite direction, Areenna dove toward the ground and rolled forward. Like flowing water, she rose behind him even as the other fighter swung at the space she'd been standing in a half second earlier.

Gaining her feet before the man could turn; she slammed the flat of her blade against his head and faced the third who was regaining his balance from his swing. In the heartbeat before he could plant his feet, Areenna pulled her knife from its scabbard and lunged. The knife caught the man just above the groin, slipping into the exact spot between the joining of upper and lower armor. The tip of the blade did not break skin.

The man dropped his sword, took off his helmet and looked down at the blade, which was slightly above the joining of his legs. "Good choice, Princess" he said with a smile.

**The Tales Of Nevaeh
Volume II**

The Dark Masters

AVAILABLE ON AMAZON.COM

29895936R00193

Made in the USA
San Bernardino, CA
31 January 2016